The Moghul Hedonist

Farzana Moon

PublishAmerica
Baltimore

© 2005 by Farzana Moon.

All rights reserved. No part of this book may be reproduced, stored in a retrieval system or transmitted in any form or by any means without the prior written permission of the publishers, except by a reviewer who may quote brief passages in a review to be printed in a newspaper, magazine or journal.

First printing

ISBN: 1-417-6406-1
PUBLISHED BY PUBLISHAMERICA, LLLP
www.publishamerica.com
Baltimore

Printed in the United States of America

For Seemi Dearest, my one and only sis-in-law

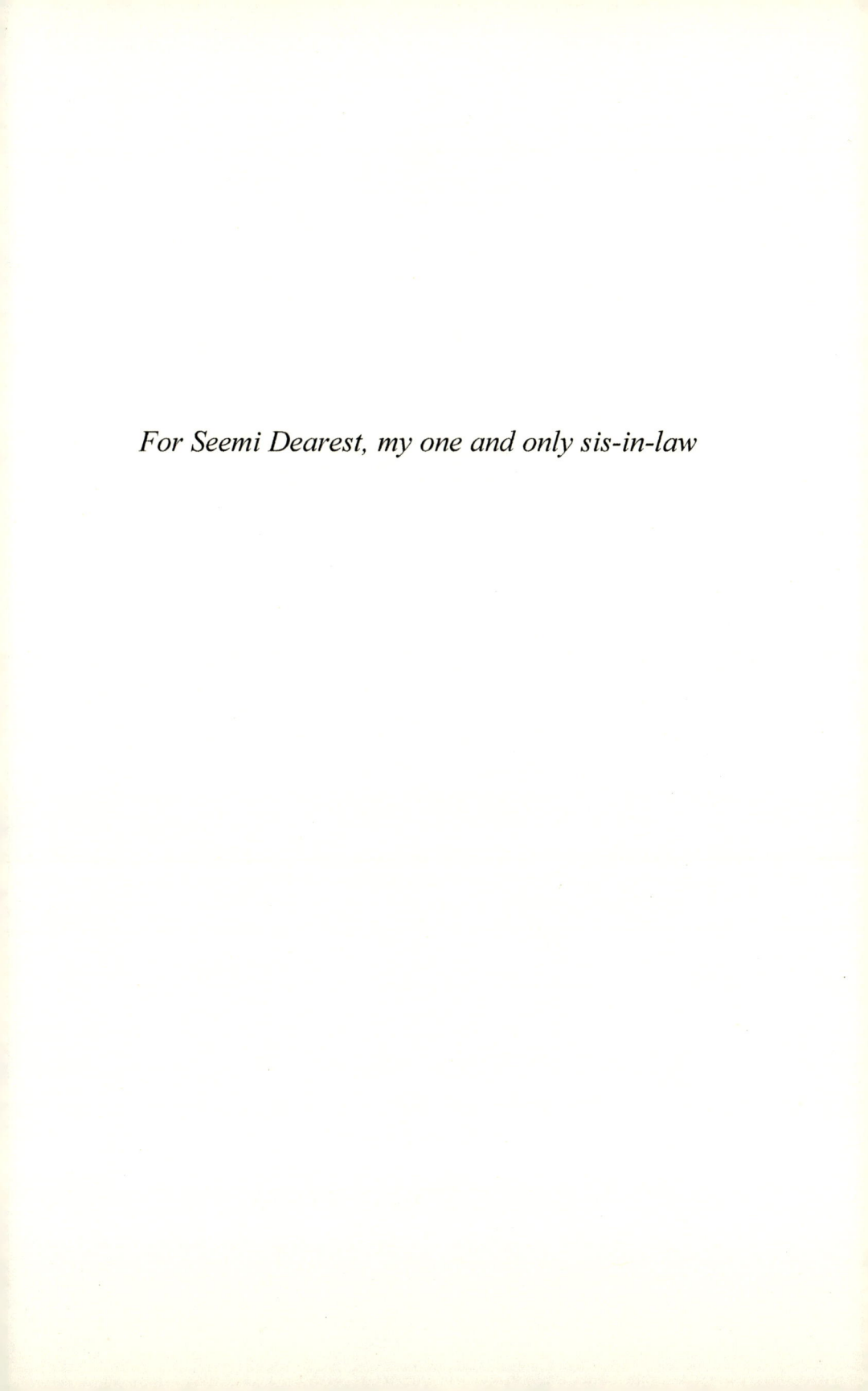

Special thanks to my friend Lemoine Rice for supplying me with photos for my books.

His genius is much appreciated.

Chapter One

Always, everywhere, with everyone, and in every circumstance
Keep the eye of thy heart secretly fixed on the beloved

This couplet was heaving mute sighs inside the head of the Emperor Jahangir as he approached closer to the garden of *Bihishtabad*. Attended by a retinue of viziers and grandees, he was feeling more like a pilgrim than the emperor of Hind. He wished only to kiss the cold marble on his father's tomb and to pray for peace inside the vast ocean of his own heart, wild and turbulent. Peace and serenity, such treasures, were the rare gifts of his happy childhood for him to keep and possess, but he had lost them both during the spring of his youth when he had fallen in love. A beautiful courtesan had stolen his heart, and she had taken it with her under the shadow of the cruel fate to a world Nether, from where no living soul could dare claim it back. He was heartbroken, and incapable of forgetting the unforgettable. Even now, carrying the weight of his long-lost love inside his heart, his fair features were haloed by an aura of sadness. His eyes were sparkling, much like the fire of rubies and diamonds in his turban, his features almost gaunt and translucent. He was wearing a silk robe, the jeweled cummerbund at his waist a profusion of color and sparkle. His long, artistic fingers were decked with gold rings, glinting jewels large and precious.

This bejeweled emperor visiting the tomb of his father in the city of Sikandrah was no other than the eldest son of Great Akbar, Prince Salim himself. After the death of Emperor Akbar in 1605, Prince Salim, now styled Jahangir, had acceded to the throne of Agra as the fourth Moghul Emperor of Hindustan. Even amidst the jubilations of his accession, he had felt forlorn and lonesome, recalling with profound sadness that it had been seven years since he had lost his beloved, his Anarkali. Seven more years were dissolved into a whirlwind of memories, and Anarkali was still reigning inside his heart like the queen of love and life. His heart, this afternoon, was throbbing like the heart of a young lover, though he could not return to that bloom of youth in age and time even if he could slice away half the years of his forty-three summers.

Anarkali, my life and my soul, my very own Anarkali. Angels spoke through her lips when she sang. Thunder and lightning danced in her very eyes when she danced. Oh, how she sailed in the clouds, fair beloved...Jahangir's thoughts were arresting his beloved's youth, not his own.

An alien throb of joy and pain was rippling inside the very emptiness of Jahangir's soul, as he sauntered past the poplars and cypresses toward the tomb of his father. The emperor's heart was on fire, as if it was going to leap out of his body and embrace the whole world in its bosom, vast and throbbing. He was becoming aware of the octagonal towers in the distance, looming high over his father's tomb of all marble, where he lay resting in eternal peace. The four gateways of red granite and the open pavilions, too, were unfolding before his sight in some maze of magic and mystery. A sheet of gold from the very bowl of the sky was gilding the white domes and slender minarets, lending light and warmth to the late emperor, whose entire life was spent striving after the light of truth. Jahangir's senses were exploring the light of beauty in *Bihishtabad* then following the broken trail of his late father's quest for truth. His gaze was arrested to the ripple of colors in roses, the dark, deep-scented Indian rose the most glorious of them all. From the vaulted balcony in the distance, the drums and trumpets were already blaring to announce the arrival of the emperor at his father's royal tomb.

Against these shades of light and color, Jahangir's sight and senses were dissolving into a pool of memories. His thoughts were racing headlong, lurching close to his father's feet in an act of humble obeisance, then rising aloft like the wounded martyrs to crush Anarkali into one eternal embrace. He was caught inside the bubble of time, suspended there in the garden of his own youth as a young prince, Prince Salim. His memory was polished like a mirror, reflections upon reflections shifting in there with a painful urgency. Anarkali was singing in the hall of mirrors at his father's court. He was sitting beside his father rapt and stricken, arresting each pulse of Anarkali's beauty inside his soul with the longing of a lover gone stark mad. He had poured out his longings before his father, wishing to marry Anarkali, to make her the queen of his heart and soul. But the emperor was incensed; the Great Akbar had forbidden this marriage. He, the Moghul prince, an heir to the throne of Hind, could not marry this common courtesan! Prince Salim could not make her the queen of his heart and of this world? The queen, who had usurped the throne inside his heart and had begun to reign there like a king and queen both? He had fallen ill, the pangs of despair and yearnings cutting the very throbs of his sanity into rags of torments. Great Akbar had relented then, arranging for a private nuptial to appease his son's sufferings. But, alas, the joys of the wedding night were turned into the hot coals of agony. Wearing death as her bridal gown, Anarkali had fallen limp into his arms even before he could imprint the first kiss of love upon the lips of his bride. Against that haze of a memory, Prince Salim had no recollection of that tragic night and of the days following that tragedy. He had fallen into a coma, remaining insensible for days, and awakening only to receive the savage blow of fate that Anarkali had died. Anarkali had relinquished her beauty to the cold hands of death, and shock and grief had hurled him once again into the bliss of oblivion. Recovering the second time from his comatose state, he had begun to dream as if Anarkali was with him inside each and every breath of his soul and psyche.

The throne of love in Prince Salim's heart was empty, but he had replaced it with an altar pure where he could weep and lament for his loss in utmost solitude. He had suffered, but he was to suffer more terribly than before under the assault of rumors, wild and strange, concerning Anarkali's sudden and mysterious death. Many a canards had been afloat here and there, reaching his ears with the fury of the tempests, knocking at the gates of his silent agony with the violence of hurricanes. *Anarkali was not dead*, even the courtiers had begun to whisper amongst themselves, *but was entombed alive inside the dark dungeon of a hole by orders of the emperor himself.* Great Akbar was incensed by the defiance of his son and by Anarkali's own defiance in keeping trysts with the prince when she was forbidden to; that's why this punishment was brought upon her by the wrath of the emperor. Another rumor was that Anarkali was granted clemency from the emperor. That Great Akbar had spared her life, permitting her to live in obscurity as long as Prince Salim could be kept ignorant of her prison-paradise. Prison-paradise was the term they had coined, for they believed she was banished to some enchanting palace furnished with all sorts of luxuries, so that she would not be tempted to return to her lover. All those rumors were rendered powerless before the naked facts recorded by the court historians that Anarkali had died on the night of her wedding, that her body was transported to Lahore where she was buried in a simple grave with a tombstone depicting her age and tragedy. Slowly and gradually, not even seeking the balm of healing, Prince Salim had succeeded in discarding all rumors, cherishing within the wound of his own tragedy, and his beloved. Anarkali was with him, inside the purity of his silent love which craved not to witness the tomb of reality. And he had no need to visit her cold grave in Lahore as advised by his friends, who, he knew, wished him to hold on to the hem of reality, and not to live in dreams. But he, Prince Salim, had no wish to abandon his dreams, hoping that Anarkali would materialize some day like one of the Hindu goddesses from the very waters of the Ganges.

That reed of a hope inside Jahangir's heart this particular day had awakened wild and throbbing. It was swollen with the nectar of pain-joy, anticipating some miracle which would transform his whole being into the light of love and serendipity. So intense was this feeling inside him that his gaze seemed to arrest the entire cosmos into one eager embrace, beholding nature in all its eternalness, which could not cease its rhythm of life, and death could never tarnish its profusion of scent and beauty in this world. His thoughts were inward bound, and his gaze admiring the wealth in blooms brimming with the wine of beauty from nature's own treasure chests.

He was approaching close to Akbar's mausoleum, all lofty and exquisite. More than exquisite, it was as if fashioned by the sorcery of the titans and finished by the artistry of the jewelers. Jahangir's gaze was alighting on the fountains in the distance, their ripple and dance gathering gold from sunshine. Awe and bliss were replacing the sadness in his eyes, but his heart was aching with loneliness, embracing Anarkali with all the sweet pain in living and suffering. Anarkali was with him, his loneliness tasting one small whiff of nostalgia and longing.

Jahangir's thoughts were dissolving the scents of longing and nostalgia, sinking deeper to reach the sanctuary of inner peace, but he was not succeeding. Anarkali was gone, leaving behind a vacuum of hope and grief. His heart was clinging to hope, willing it to live with the promise of love, but it was melting in its own pool of silence and vacuity. Even the clumps of roses in bright colors over the trellises appeared dull and lifeless to him, reflecting the inner haze of his own misery and loneliness. And yet he should neither feel lonely nor disconsolate...Jahangir's thoughts were flashing reproof, reminding him of his harem, boasting many wives. *Eleven, thirteen, maybe twenty, and many more concubines;* his thoughts were giddy and exploring. A few faces were surfacing in his memory, slashed by the arrows of joys and sorrows. Man Bai, the first wife of his youth, was one portrait of a tragedy. He had loved her truly, and she was devoted to him with a passion as true as his own. She had blessed him with a lovely daughter, Princess Sultanunissa, and a handsome son, Prince Khusrau. Unfortunately, Jahangir's love alone could not keep Man Bai alive. She had committed suicide after a lengthy estrangement from her brother and from her own son, Prince Khusrau.

Prince Khusrau, an inveterate rebel, even now at the age of twenty-five, was incarcerated in his own palace at Agra. Jahangir's thoughts stumbling on such rugged paths were overwhelming his senses with the weight of fresh sorrow. He was trying to slough off all his past sadness, commanding his thoughts to heed and surrender. His thoughts, against the sheer power of his will, were quick to obey, trampling over the mounds of tragedies and crushing them to invisible lumps, all insignificant.

The emperor was sailing toward his father's tomb, his thoughts humbled, ready to pray for peace, for peace within, and for peace of the whole world.

Baidulat, baidulat, Jahangir's thoughts were murmuring. Baidulat, meaning unfortunate, was the epithet Jahangir had bestowed upon Prince Khusrau after the undisciplined prince could not be restrained from the temptations of rebellions.

The loud music from drums and the trumpets was carving its way down the cloistered thoughts in Jahangir's head, and he was becoming aware of the royal entourage behind him. On each side of the emperor were his viziers, Bir Singh Deo and Mahabat Khan; behind them were Mutamid Khan, the historian, and Abdur Rahim, the chief advisor. The royal guards were keeping their distance; Jahangir was trying to remember their names, but his thoughts were straying down the wounded trails where Prince Khusrau languished unrepentant. Prince Khusrau had raised the banners of rebellion once again not too long ago, and this time he had fallen prey to his own acts of defiance and insurrection. After escaping out of his own prison-palace, Prince Khusrau had acted most blatantly, marching onward to the Punjab and plotting to capture Lahore with the intention of proclaiming himself the sole sovereign of this city. This was an open act of treason, and though the son of an emperor, he was to be hanged by the unanimous verdict of the Moghul jurists. But the emperor's love for his son was greater than his wrath, and keeping the rod of justice in abeyance, he had requested clemency from the judges to spare the life of his first-born son. The emperor's request could not be denied, and Prince Khusrau's life was spared in ransom for his sight. Prince Khusrau was blinded by the orders of the judges, and then incarcerated under strict vigilance.

Blinded! My son, my prince. Another painless murmur was escaping the silence in Jahangir's thoughts. Turning abruptly, his gaze was holding Mahabat Khan captive.

"Mahabat, what's the name of that physician from Persia?" He was resuming his walk toward the square platform of white marble.

"Hakim Sadra, Your Majesty," was Mahabat Khan's quick response.

"He is a skilled surgeon, working wonders beyond belief. Command him, Mahabat, to restore the sight of Prince Khusrau," Jahangir intoned dreamily.

The emperor stood by the wall of marble latticework, his gaze arrested to the glory of the garden down below where the fountains serenaded the flowers. And the fields upon fields of oleander were reaching out to embrace the gleaming terraces, it seemed.

"Yes, Your Majesty." Mahabat Khan's low response remained unacknowledged by the emperor.

The emperor was floating ahead toward the great vault, graceful and dream-like, the royal entourage following at his heels. The music from the balconies above was flooding the vault with notes sad and sweet, something like the hymnals, half pensive, half jubilant. Man Singh had edged closer to Mahabat Khan, more so to gain the emperor's attention than to seek the company of this reticent vizier. Abdur Rahim and Bir Singh Deo were lingering a few paces behind the emperor, mindful of the etiquette in not getting too close to the royal monarch until he himself wished to summon them closer. And the emperor did not, as it was obvious, for Jahangir stood facing the cenotaph, his expression aloof and contemplative. His gaze was sweeping over the gold inscriptions where the ninety-nine names and attributes of God shone pure and bright, but he was not reading them, only fascinated by the artistry of calligraphy. His thoughts were retracing their steps, getting lost into the vast chambers of his own palaces and gardens, and melting inside the surge of faces and names.

Nurunnisa, Khairunnisa, Salihah Banu, Malika Jahan. Jahangir's thoughts were entering the harem of his lovely wives. *Many a youthful brides, twenty of them lawful, the rest concubines*...His very senses were feeling a whiff of ache and memory.

The names of his beautiful wives were some allusive jingle in the emperor's head, a few faces emerging and dissolving, all haze and loveliness with sparkling eyes. A pair of lovely eyes were mocking him, Man Bai's? They were tearing the shroud of death and surcease, flashing accusations at her ever-estranged son, the unfortunate Prince Khusrau. Jahangir's own eyes were gathering arrows of defense and aiming to slay the impudent thoughts ambushed somewhere inside the dark recesses of his mind. The vision of pain was gone. His thoughts were closing shut the tomb of the dead, and gasping for breath to enter the tomb of the living. Prince Khusrau, along with Man Bai, was banished from his mind's sight by the sheer volition of his thoughts, now contrite and humbled.

Another vision was alighting in the emperor's head, pure and bright, that of his wife Sahiba Jamali, the mother of his second son, Prince Perwiz. He could see her lolling against the satiny pillows, perfumed and bejeweled. Jagat Gosaini was there too, the mother of his third son, Prince Khurram. And Karamasi was the proud mother of royal twins and a beautiful princess, the six-year-old Princess Bihar Banu. Her twin brothers, Prince Jahandar and Prince Shahriyar, a year older than her, were much loved and cosseted by the emperor. Even now the remembrance of them was bringing a gleam of love and warmth into the eyes of the emperor.

Prince Shahriyar, the most handsome of all my sons. Jahangir's thoughts were a wistful murmur.

This tenderness was a wild throb, parting its lips and revealing another handsome face, that of his son Prince Khurram, a youth of twenty springs, loved and favored by the emperor with the profoundest of joys and prides. This star-prince with bright eyes and fair features was flooding the emperor's mind and heart with the light of love and sunshine. Prince Perwiz, three years older than Prince Khurram, was knocking at the portals of the emperor's mind, holding a string of candle-lit faces in his very eyes, but the emperor was shutting the gates of his mind. His gaze as well as his feet were leaving the cenotaph, the viziers and grandees following behind him. He was hurling all visions small or great to exile by the sole virtue of his practiced will, and becoming a part of the present with the alacrity of a young tourist.

The royal entourage were emerging on one sun-spangled terrace, to be dissolved into the dusky gloom of a passage which would lead them straight to the tomb of the Great Akbar. Another lofty vault was waiting at the end of this passage, and the emperor was the first one to feel its peace and simplicity. His visit to the tomb of his late father was actually a wistful homage to the emperor who was loved and mourned by the people of Hind as the Great Akbar.

Jahangir was approaching the simple, unadorned tomb of white marble with a reverence akin to humility and worship. The wistful look in his eyes was gathering the warmth of peace and serenity as he stood facing the head of the tomb, his hand caressing the cold marble where the single word *Akbar* was inscribed to identify the royal occupant. Jahangir was kneeling beside the tomb ceremoniously with his head pressed against the smooth marble, with closed eyes, his lips murmuring prayers. Suddenly, his heart was aflutter. Something inside it was stabbing and churning, as if it was being ravished right this moment by the throes of pain and loss. These were the same daggers of pain and loss which he had felt only when Anarkali was no more.

Jahangir's heart was at peace all of a sudden, much like the caprice of the tempests, replacing the stormy gales with the calmness of blue skies, as if no violence had marred the face of nature.

The royal guards had covered the tomb of Akbar with a sheet of fresh roses, offering their own respects to the late emperor before retracing their steps somberly. The royal entourage had already returned to the full glory of the Bihishtabad with all its color and fragrance. And Jahangir was standing under the bower of deep-scented Indian roses, smiling to himself. He was attended only by Bir Singh Deo; the rest of the viziers and grandees had wandered away to absorb and explore the beauty of this garden where magnolia blooms stood gathering sunshine in their own cups of pink and alabaster. Jahangir's gaze was arrested to the wisteria blooms, his thoughts sailing over the palace at Agra where he was to return soon to attend the *Mina Bazaar*.

Mina Bazaar was a kind of shopping mall where the royal ladies displayed their precious wares, luring the royal customers, especially the emperor, the wealthiest of the patrons. Mina Bazaar had become the perennial trade-festival of the royal ladies, commencing with the first day of each new year, called *Nauroz*, and lasting for nineteen days in conformity with the Nauroz celebrations. While Nauroz was celebrated all over the empire, Mina Bazaar was the privilege of the royalty alone, where only the members of the family and the closest of friends could visit by invitation alone. Paradoxically, even the emperor had to be invited, but then he had no dearth of invitations from the ladies of his harem. This was the only time the emperor could shop and squander his wealth, and he was accustomed to doing both, just to enhance the fun of these festivities. Pretending to be cautious, he would go from stall to stall, ranting and haggling, and giving in to his temptations for a few impulsive purchases.

The festivities of Nauroz were lowering their festive colors in Jahangir's thoughts as he stood gazing at the wisteria blooms. Last year, on the very first day of Mina Bazaar he had purchased a ridiculously expensive gold necklace studded with emeralds from his wife Jagat Gosaini. The very next day he had presented to her the same necklace as her birthday gift. Within a week, Jagat Gosaini had put it up for sale again, demanding double the price of what it had fetched before, and Jahangir had left her stall, laughing hysterically. The same laughter was choking his thoughts as he stood there absorbing the haze in memories. Drunk with mirth and sweetness, his thoughts were falling prey to reveries, but were snatched quite abruptly from their abodes by one song of a prayer.

La Illaha illah Allah... The words carried on the strings of the breeze were not from the lips of a muezzin, but from some devoted disciple of the late emperor. They appeared to be slipping down the white minaret with the poignancy of a lone cataract.

Jahangir stood there motionless, listening, his heart filled with awe and dread. This ripple of a cataract in words was followed by the beating of *naqqarah* drums, and Jahangir's own heart had begun to hum a tune, brimming with grief and anguish. Anarkali had stolen close to the very throne of his bruised heart. She was with him in this paradise of a garden, in this abode of the dead and the living. A familiar, long-forgotten ache with all its loneliness was tracing a large rent inside his heart and soul. He could feel one throb of a laceration inside the very silence of his soul and psyche, but it was pulsating with the pain-joy of hope, with the promise of love! With the flowering of a miracle? Some sort of bliss-anticipation was overwhelming his senses; he could inhale the perfume of union. He would be united with his beloved? He was smiling, but alas, the smile in his eyes was replaced by anguish so stark that he could feel the pain and sting straight from the flames of agony inside his soul. His eyes were flashing commands as he turned to Bir Singh Deo abruptly, his heart still lit with hope and agony.

"Bir Singh, you are to search the whole of Hind once again, and bring my Anarkali to Agra. And this is the emperor's farman," Jahangir commanded.

"Your Majesty!" was Bir Singh Deo's abashed exclamation. "You know, Your Majesty, Anarkali died.... Her tomb in Lahore testifies to this fact, the tomb which the emperor never deigns to visit."

"She never died, Bir Singh. No, she never did," Jahangir chided vehemently. "And no tombs or monuments could attest to her death as long as I live. Anarkali is alive, my heart tells me so. My father spared her life. She is living somewhere! I will find her. She is alive, right here, with me, in this garden, even now. Our love is true and holy, and it will bring us together, soon, soon, I can feel that." His gaze was gathering stars as if he was arresting a beautiful vision inside the very profusion of blooms.

"Anarkali never loved you, Your Majesty, if I may be so bold as to say that." Bir Singh Deo whipped up a lie to jolt the emperor out of his reveries. "And you loved a dream, Your Majesty, a dream," he murmured apologetically.

"A dream which is capable of living and throbbing with the pulse of reality! It lives, absolutely and eternally, inside the tiny mirrors of one's own soul, till it becomes a glittering reflection strewn with the light of reality," Jahangir murmured heedlessly. "I might even find my dream-reality inside the shimmering bowl of today, Bir Singh? And then you would be spared the perils of long journeys in search of my long-lost beloved. And if I don't find her soon, my farman stays in affect. You will commence your journey on the third day of Nauroz, wearing knighthood as your armor with the holy quest as your talisman." His eyes were glinting the warmth of hope and promise.

"I will ring the Gold Chain of your justice, Your Majesty." Bir Singh Deo resorted to wit and flattery. "And all its sixty bells will not cease their pleas and clamor till you retract your farman, Your Majesty."

"Ah, my chain of justice, my truant knight, would shackle you to the chains of treason." A gale of mirth escaped Jahangir's lips. "Farman or no farman, the emperor would make you cross Jamna on the sharp edge of a sword, if not order you to fend for your life on the top of *Shah Burj* with all of Agra watching you."

Some sort of hysteria and delirium was escaping the emperor's mirth, as he stood there checking the deluge of his pain and laughter. The daggers of reality were stabbing him; Anarkali had left, her sweet vision replaced by the tragic face of Prince Khusrau. His sightless gaze was searching Anarkali, and before all the demons could break loose the gates of hell inside his head, he was becoming aware of the slow approach of his viziers. Man Singh, followed by Abdur Rahim and Mahabat Khan, though edging closer, seemed flustered by the emperor's mirth, his eyes glinting astonishment.

"Your Majesty, since you are in a jubilant mood, may I ask why you changed your name from Salim to Jahangir?" Man Singh inquired with one flourish of a curtsy.

"Seven long years since my succession, my dull-witted vizier, and you still don't know?" Jahangir's mirth was dwindling, his eyes gathering sunshine in their merry cups. "You mean, none of you have ever probed into this matter of learning the significance of names apart from words, or of Emperor Jahangir apart from that of princely Salim?"

"Our lips were sealed due to the awe and propriety of the occasion, Your Majesty." Mahabat Khan was the first one to confess his ignorance.

"Your accession, Your Majesty, was a feast of joy, breeding no thoughts but the thoughts of gaiety and celebration," Man Singh offered humbly.

"No one could dare violate the sanctity of that feast with inquiries which could be interpreted as rude, Your Majesty, least of all, any of us who are close to you!" was Abdur Rahim's low exclamation.

"Seven heedless years, and no one had the audacity?" Jahangir murmured.

"Not heedless, Your Majesty, but brimming with the eternal springs of rejoicings and celebrations," Bir Singh Deo murmured back with a dint of apology and flattery.

"Ignorance can be rightly named fear, if it hinders one from the path to knowledge and understanding," Jahangir contemplated aloud. "On my accession, it occurred to me that my name Salim resembled that of the emperor of Rum. That was when I wished to change it, and was inspired by a thought that the business of the emperor is in controlling the world. So, I selected the name Jahangir, meaning the *World-Seizer*. With the same inspiration as my talisman, another title dawned upon me. And I added the name Nuruddin, which means the Light of Faith. It coincided with my attaining the throne in conformity with the sun rising and shining with its great light. When I was a prince, one Indian sage told me that after the reign of Jalaluddin Akbar, one named Nuruddin would sit on the throne. Therefore, I changed my name to Nuruddin Jahangir Padishah." His gaze was ruminative, gathering the fire of memories.

"A propitious year that was, Your Majesty, that year of your accession." Bir Singh Deo's font of devotion was doling out more flatteries. "And this one is more propitious than all the rest. Peace and prosperity reign high in the empire of Hind. And the zenith of your justice is gaining continents in friendships and alliances. The letter from the Shah Abbas of Persia alone has marked this year with the stars of fortunes, though our fortunes outnumber that of the monarch of Persia."

"Ah, flatteries, all the way from Persia to the streets paved in dust-gold of Hind." Jahangir laughed. "Shah Abbas! I call him my brother. Is it appropriate for the emperor to call him brother? Perhaps, so, for he in his letter bestowed upon me *the exaltedness of Sikander, with the banner of Darius, he who sits on the throne of the pavilion of glory and greatness*, my brother says. Lending me the dignity of *Jamshed* among the stars of the hosts of heaven..." He paused, his gaze straying over to the monument of Great Akbar, its marble and red sandstone gleaming under sunshine. "But the emperor's heart is yearning for the wine and gaiety of Mina Bazaar. Back to Agra with its riches in beauty and laughter," he announced abruptly.

The viziers and grandees, following the emperor, were feeling giddy, rather drunk with the wine of beauty in Bihishtabad. They were walking jauntily, laughing and whispering amongst themselves as if free from the cares of the world. The royal guards too were possessed by the scent and beauty of this garden, drifting along dreamily, and lagging behind in the mist-haze of their own languor. The songs from the fountains were luring all to stay, but the emperor was pressed by his own will to hasten toward Agra.

"Shah Abbas is in love with the gold and jewels in Hind, Your Majesty, and in love with you, it seems." Abdur Rahim appeared to recite his own thoughts.

"I sit beside thee in thought, and my heart is at ease. For this is a union not followed by separation's pain." He quoted this couplet of Shah Abbas. "I can't forget this sentimental couplet, Your Majesty, though the contents of the letter escape my memory."

"Shah Abbas rightfully named you, Your Majesty, the sovereign of *Gurgani* throne and an heir to the crown of Tamerlane," Mahabat Khan sang proudly.

"Though this Persian monarch was late in sending his felicitation to you on your accession, Your Majesty," Man Singh was quick to voice his skepticism, "he could be excused, I guess, for he was piously involved in conquering Shirnon and Azarbijan." He commented low, feeling slighted that the emperor was not heeding.

The palace garden where Jahangir sat enthroned seemed to encompass the entire city of Agra in its efflorescent bosom. From where he sat, the emperor could see his palace of red sandstone, honed and chiseled, its majestic contours spiraling upward in domes and arches. Its four imposing gates, and two sally-ports, where his sight could not reach at this moment, were etched magnificently on the canvass of his mind. He had reached Agra a few hours ago under some spell of great urgency, as if pressed by the very hands of fate to arrest time in its whimsical flight. His heart and mind were sailing on the clouds, his sense of euphoria some swollen bubble inside him which could neither be contained nor punctured. He had dined alone in his chamber, holding the same whip of urgency over his shoulders which had made him fly back to Agra in utmost haste. He was anxious to join the ladies at the Mina Bazaar, but the amenities of the royal court were to be observed before he could seek the diversions of gaiety and laughter in the bazaar of trade and treasures. Right now, drinking goblets upon goblets of wine, he was being entertained with music and gifts to commemorate Nauroz with all due felicitations. A few cumbersome embassies were splintering the joy of his drinking and merrymaking, but he was forcing his farmans and commands to a disciplined trot where his justice and patience were to remain intact.

The makeshift throne upon which the emperor sat receiving embassies was made of wood and inlaid with mother-of-pearl. The canopies of gold cloth splashed with silk and velvet were erected on all sides for shade as well as protection from heat and wind. The canopies were held in lofty abeyance by four columns strung with pearls and embellished with pure gold in shapes of pears, apples and pomegranates. The silk friezes in shimmering colors were afloat over the trees and balconies, vying with the abundance of colors in robes and turbans. This profusion of color and adornment was more of a ritual to celebrate Nauroz than to display the emperor's riches in this garden of delight, already brimming with natural treasures.

The sun-spangled evening with the banners of early dusk was weaving a few clouds on its horizon, as Jahangir sat mired inside the clouds of his own decisions and embassies. He waved dismissal at Bhanu Chandra, the Jain monk, whom he had just appointed the tutor to Prince Shahriyar. His heart was heavy with the burdens of royal duties, and weariness was alighting in his eyes, dimming their sparkle and intensity. Besides, the gray clouds hovering above the trees were cutting his spirit of fortitude to rags of fatigue. And the wine coursing smoothly in his veins was gathering bouquets of melancholy, his spirit yawning with a familiar sigh of ache and yearning. He was longing to explore the silken comforts of the Mina Bazaar. Before another embassy could squeeze its way into his audience, Jahangir turned his attention to his court poet.

"Talib Amuli, recite a few couplets of yours, before the emperor's heart is buried under the heaps of more embassies," Jahangir commanded.

"Your Majesty, if you honor me with such commands more often, my couplets will be as abundant as the pearls in your royal treasuries." Talib Amuli bowed his head.

"Both first and last, love is eye, music and joy. A pleasant wine both when fresh and when mellow."

"A sublime verse, and more sublime than the lover who may sing it." Jahangir smiled, his eyes lit up with inspiration, an impromptu verse escaping his own lips.

"The cup of wine should be quaffed in the presence of one's beloved. The clouds are thick, it is time to drink deep."

A thunder of applause erupted forth from the sea of viziers and grandees, which was silenced by one imperious wave of the emperor's arm. His other arm was poised in a staccato gesture, signaling his consent to proceed with the embassies.

Suddenly, all the rings on his fingers were aglitter, catching shafts of sunlight from the parted lips of the clouds, as he watched Muqqarab Khan stumbling forward. This nonchalant courtier was trying his best to curtsy, but the bird behind him pulled by a string tied to his wrist had fluttered forward, getting in his way. Muqqarab Khan was attempting another curtsy, and was almost crushed by a sudden volley of mirth from the lips of the emperor.

"Your Majesty, a rare gift this is, causing so much royal mirth!" Muqqarab Khan began hastily. "I fetched this bird from the port of Cambay, for you, Your Majesty. This rude creature comes straight from Goa." He swept the fluttering bird into his arms, and held it tightly against his breast.

"A rarity indeed!" Jahangir exclaimed laughingly. "Hold this impudent beast of a bird a little higher, Muqqarab. Let the emperor have a good look at this untamed clown." His gaze was avid and shining. "A strange mixture of beauty and ugliness. Its face is like a fox, and its eyes are larger than those of a hawk. Its feathers are more like the wool of a sheep. Its color, look! The color of ashes, if I am not mistaken. How it is spreading its feathers, much like a peacock? How the colors change? Is this magic, or are the emperor's eyes catching false hues…coral red under its wings." The naturalist in him was fascinated, his attention shifting to his court painter.

"Bishan Das, get your canvas ready. And hold this chameleon of a wild creature in your captivity, before it wears rainbows under its wings," he commanded. His gaze returned to Muqqarab Khan. "A rare treasure. It would delight us in our royal aviary. Does this bird bear any stamp of a name, or should we bestow one on it?" he asked amusedly.

"It's called turkey, Your Majesty. Its meat is lean and tender. The Portuguese eat it with relish," Muqqarab Khan expounded happily.

"To kill beauty for gluttony is a crime." Jahangir was appalled. "Fetch a mate for this beauty, and they would breed happily for Hind. Not to be devoured, but to be admired." A sudden recollection as to the recent crime of Muqqarab Khan was kindling his eyes to rage. "Don't you stand charged for violating one young girl? The daughter of a widow, and this girl died, didn't she?" His look was probing, mirth gone from his eyes.

"No, Your Majesty, yes, I mean the girl died, but I am not guilty," Muqqarab Khan murmured low. "The judges have proclaimed me innocent…have discovered the truth. The truth, which I have been telling all along…" He was becoming flustered. "The judges are right here, attesting to the facts. My attendant was found guilty of that crime, Your Majesty, and he is sentenced to death. The judges are here to…" He could not continue against the flash of rage in the emperor's gaze.

"And yet you are an accomplice to that crime?" Jahangir flashed him a quick rebuke. "You kept that young girl in your own house, didn't you? Had not that widow, the much-wronged mother of that young girl, sought the chain of justice, the emperor would have been kept ignorant of that heinous crime. Death for your lout of an attendant is not a punishment, but kindness! He would be tortured, feeling the agony of his own corrupt flesh, before his soul could be delivered into the hands of death. The emperor will look into the verdict of the judges later. But as for now, you stand guilty as an accomplice. Yes, Muqqarab Khan, the emperor's justice is quick to bestow a just reward. Your salary would be cut into half, and that part of your income will be allotted to the widow, though nothing can compensate her loss, the irretrievable loss of her daughter. Begone, Muqqarab Khan, begone, before the emperor does injustice to the justice proclaimed by the judges." He raised his arm, his eyes flashing regret and reproof.

"Your Majesty." One mute protest trembled on Muqqarab Khan's lips.

Muqqarab Khan stood hugging his arms, as if clutching something warm and alive to his breast. But if he was hoping to find the feathery bird into his arms, he was sadly mistaken, for his turkey was relinquished into the care of Mukhlis Khan long since, who had departed straight toward the aviary.

"Don't look so stricken, Muqqarab Khan. At least you are not to die on the gallows as the emperor feared," Jahangir intoned rather gently. "The emperor's justice may yet reinstate you to his favor.

"The blood is drained from your very lips. Before your strength returns to hurl you to obedience, inform the emperor if our ship *Rhimi* has entered the port of Cambay." He paused, murmuring, as if to himself, "The emperor is hoping that his mother, Mirayam Uzzmanni, might be able to join him for the Nauroz celebrations. Such a long journey back from Mecca; even to fathom that distance takes time and courage. My spiritual needs suffer neglect against the material ones as I sit burdened by the weight of my royal duties, and no time for a pilgrimage to Mecca. But I remain a pilgrim at heart, taking not the long roads, and savoring the journeys in my head to lands holy and incorruptible." He paused again. "Has your tongue expired, Muqqarab Khan? Speak, lest I cut it and feed it to that rarity of a big bird."

"No, Your Majesty, I didn't hear anything about the ship." Muqqarab Khan attempted one quick response. "Mirayam Uzzmanni is traveling in Rhimi, I have been assured." His look was dazed and pleading.

"Mahabat Khan." Jahangir shot one abrupt command at his vizier, who was appointed to parade the embassies before the emperor. "Summon the next embassy, and make it a short and a happy one. The emperor is wearied of cruelties and tragedies."

A small group of Englishmen stepped forward, curtsying as best as they could, after Mahabat Khan presented them, retracing his steps. Jahangir sat watching the alien faces, while sipping his wine slowly and thoughtfully. His eyes were lighting up with amusement all of a sudden, as he espied Thomas Best amongst the Englishmen, his curtsy most impeccable. Almost a year ago, the emperor was recalling, he had granted permission to Thomas Best for a free trade between India and England.

"Your Majesty." Thomas Best was the first one to step forward. "It's my privilege to present two envoys from England. They are to represent the trade treaties between India and England. Thomas Aldworth and Paul Canning." He indicated the two tall men beside him with a flourish of his arm. Two more younger men were standing behind him, bashful and flustered.

"Treaties don't grow on the trees, Thomas! Even if they did, the emperor has no mind to climb one to explore the intricate patterns of greeds woven inside the very veins of those leaves, exposed to the gluttony of foreign dreams." Jahangir laughed. "Didn't the emperor grant you permission for trade in Gujrat not too long ago?"

"Yes, Your Majesty. Your generosity has not been forgotten. And we hope to achieve more." Thomas Best smiled affably. "Paul Canning here, Your Majesty, has brought two musicians with him to present before you." He nudged Paul Canning, as if urging him to make a signal impression upon the emperor.

"Musicians are always welcome in the Moghul court. Not the traders! And certainly not the traitors!" Jahangir exclaimed mirthfully. "Paul Canning. Such a heavy, swollen name. Reminds me of pears and peaches. Don't ask the emperor why. Well, Paul, introduce your musician friends."

"With all due respect and great delight, Your Majesty." Paul Canning curtsied, requesting the two young men to step forward. "Lancelot Canning, Your Majesty, is my cousin, and he plays the virginals. This young man here is Robert Trully. He plays the coronet." He made the introductions with the profusion of a cavalier.

"Welcome to our court, and you will play for the emperor tomorrow along with our own singers and musicians, who will most certainly vie with you both." Jahangir's gaze was shifting to Man Singh. "Man Singh, summon Hafiz Had Ali to court tomorrow. He is to sing before the emperor. Right now, the emperor is longing for the gaiety of the Mina Bazaar." He was about to rise to his feet when his attention was caught by a rude rider galloping toward the throne most boldly.

This rude rider was no other than the governor of Delhi, Zulfiqar Khan. He had been entrusted with the duties of a sole messenger concerning the ship *Rhimi's* safety and its safe arrival at the Indian ports.

His fiery steed was claimed by the emperor's attendant, Sharif, he himself charging toward the throne as if whipped by the breeze of urgency.

"Your Majesty." Zulfiqar Khan bowed low, gasping for breath. "The Portuguese have captured *Rhimi*. And all seven hundred people on board at Port Goa are their prisoners. Mirayam Uzzmanni refuses to leave the ship until all the prisoners are released." He could speak no further, fear and consternation choking his thoughts.

"How dare they capture the ship of the emperor's mother!" Jahangir thundered, his eyes flashing rage and disbelief. "The emperor's wrath would rain fire on them for this outrage." His gaze was turning to Muqqarab Khan. "Step closer to the emperor, Muqqarab Khan. This outrage of the Portuguese have reinstated you to the emperor's favor. Your fortunes will rise in exchange for the downfall of the Portuguese. And downfall it is, for the Portuguese," he prophesied. Allowing a pause before his vizier could raise himself up from his lengthy curtsy, he said, "A grand army will be entrusted under your command. You are to march to Daman and to reduce this evil city of the Portuguese to ruins. Also, order Iradat Khan to repair to Surat to chastise these wicked intruders."

"Yes, Your Majesty." Muqqarab Khan could barely murmur.

"Abdullah Khan." The smoldering of rage in Jahangir's eyes was falling on his next vizier. "You are in charge of sealing off all the churches of the Portuguese in our empire. Father Xavier too must share the ill rewards wrought by his own countrymen, though the emperor loves him dearly. He is banned from proselytizing until further order." He got to his feet slowly and ponderously, dismissing all with an impatient wave of his arm.

Jahangir's restless gaze was arrested to Madho Singh as he dismounted his throne. Madho Singh, cradling two beautiful pigeons into his arms, was scaling the length of the imperial carpet that was unrolled all the way from the throne to the garden entrance where the Mina Bazaar bustled with teeming festivities. He was edging closer; his eyes, shining with anticipation, were seeking the emperor's attention.

"More rarities from the lands evil and alien, Madho Singh?" Jahangir smiled.

"The rarest of breeds, Your Majesty, all the way from Benares," Madho Singh chirped happily. "May I present these pigeons to you, Your Majesty? They can sing and somersault, and you will be delighted by their tricks."

"The rarest of the treasures, indeed!" Jahangir claimed the pigeons eagerly. "They will delight the royal ladies more than they will the emperor, adding charm and novelty to the opulence of Mina Bazaar." He strolled away, the silken carpet under his feet his guide toward the gate of Mina Bazaar.

"Man Singh and Abdur Rahim, you are welcome to keep the emperor company," he murmured over his shoulders.

Chapter Two

The silken city of Mina Bazaar was unfolding before the emperor's gaze like a dream distant and opulent. It was welcoming him with jewels and perfumes in flowers, but comforting not the ocean of rage and sadness inside his heart. He could feel their surge, much like the stealthy turbulence in waves and tides, carrying the burden of past regrets, and billowing forth with warnings to disfigure the face of the present. The ocean of rage within him was for the Portuguese, exploding forth to annihilate all who had dared seize the imperial ship of the Moghuls. His sadness, apart from this ocean of rage, had a life of its own, hovering over one lone chamber at Agra Palace where Prince Khusrau sat imprisoned. His thoughts swooping down to explore the tides of rage and sadness deep within, were but discovering only ache and yearning for his beloved. *Anarkali,* each throb within his heart was murmuring and pleading. Somewhere, from within and without, an alien ripple of joy was making its presence known. It was curling and uncurling its lips into the promise-bloom of love and union with his beloved. His eyes were gathering the mirror-reflection of the blue, blue lakes.

The colorful stalls of the ladies were boasting all the treasures to be purchased by the emperor and by the family and friends of the royal household. The young princesses, to vie with the emperor's wives and aunts, had decorated their stalls with damasks and tapestries, and with gold and silver friezes. They had not succeeded though, for the stalls of the emperor's wives were the most opulent and attractive, displaying a precious variety, from jewels to vessels in gold and silver, from cloths of silk to velvet and brocade. The larger stalls were housing rosewood furniture of exquisite pattern and craftsmanship. Some of the pieces were carved in semblance of flowers, and the others inlaid with lapis lazuli and mother-of-pearl.

Jahangir was fluttering from stall to stall with the ease of a butterfly, his aesthetic senses draining cups of beauty from the lovely eyes of the ladies as well as from the eyes of the jewels so artistically wrought in silver and gold.

He was attracting more attention than usual due to the docile pigeons, either perched on his arms or luxuriating on the palms of his hands, depending upon his royal whim. These tamed birds appeared to be swooning with pleasure, as if aware of the royal favors bestowed upon them by the sheer indulgence of the emperor. The emperor too seemed happy, no trace of rage or sadness surfacing in his eyes, his wit as well as his gaze sharp and sparkling.

He was getting expert in haggling. The emperor's attendants were claiming the royal loot purchased by the emperor, and carrying them to the emperor's own tent furnished with carpets and paintings. Jahangir was ecstatic, his heart drunk with the wine of joy from the very goblets of coquetry in the lovely eyes of the ladies of his harem. Besides, the real goblets of wine offered to him at each stall were soaring his spirit to a verge of giddiness.

Man Singh and Abdur Rahim were keeping their own purchases to a minimum, and urging the emperor to buy more.

The camellia tree, under which Jahangir stood admiring the large ruby, was boasting its own rosy blooms. The emperor had just purchased this ruby from his wife Khairunnisa, and had relinquished his pigeons into the care of Abdur Rahim. Now, he was standing there, admiring this walnut-size ruby with the intensity of an artist and a jeweler.

One connoisseur standing opposite the emperor was Man Singh. He was devouring this jewel and assessing its worth in his mind, and was unable to tear his gaze away from the glowing gem in the emperor's hands.

Abdur Rahim was simply delighted with the company of the pigeons, not even noticing Man Singh's rapt silence.

Man Singh and the emperor were completely absorbed in the glow and warmth of this fiery gem, its beauty alive and alluring. But Abdur Rahim, not interested in jewels, was left free to let his gaze and thoughts wander. He was becoming aware of the graceful approach of the emperor's wife Sahiba Jamali. She was dressed in an opulent gown of silk, the color of citron. Her round, white face with large almond-shaped eyes seemed to glow with some inner warmth of joy and love. She had a slight figure with a tiny waist and ample bosom. Abdur Rahim could not help noticing a mysterious smile kindling her eyes and lips, as she floated closer to the emperor, nimble and soundless. Her smile was radiant all of a sudden, spilling songs if not protests.

"Your Majesty, you didn't buy anything from my stall today!" was Sahiba Jamali's mirthful complaint.

"Ah, my mistress of beauty, how you spy on the emperor!" Jahangir joined her in her mirth. "Do you have anything more precious than this ruby, my dear? This ruby, the size of a plum!" He looked into her dark eyes adoringly.

"Only large emeralds and diamonds, Your Majesty, if you are to judge the worth of these pebbles by size." Sahiba Jamali's eyes were shining with mirth and raillery.

"The diamonds in your eyes, my sweet, are cutting the emperor's heart to pieces," Jahangir retorted mirthfully.

The mirth of the royal couple was ebbing and surging. They appeared to be riding in tides upon tides of light-hearted gaiety. Jahangir was the first one to notice the slow approach of Prince Perwiz. He was holding a goblet of wine in one hand and a jeweled scimitar in the other. On the verge of twenty-three springs, he was tall and handsome. Some sort of drunken mirth was shining in his eyes as he approached the emperor.

"I bought this from the stall of Nurunnisa Begum, Your Majesty." Prince Perwiz held out his scimitar proudly. "This is an exquisite piece of art, Your Majesty, won't you agree?" He drained his cup thirstily.

Laughter faded from Jahangir's eyes as he stood watching his son intensely.

"And you neglect to visit the stall of your own mother!" Sahiba Jamali chided. "Your mother, whose love and jewels you receive with ingratitude." Her very gaze was teasing. "Loosen your purse, my gallant prince, and buy some trinkets for your wives, from your mother's stall I suggest."

"My wives, Mamma, have enough trinkets to open up one continent of a bazaar," Prince Perwiz chanted with good humor, though his heart was constricting by the mute intensity in the emperor's eyes. "Besides, you are forgetting, I bought a jeweled hookah from your stall just yesterday!"

"That too an exquisite piece of art, a jeweler's dream, you said." Sahiba Jamali's mirth was dwindling, as if slashed by the brooding expression of her husband. "The jewels on that hookah are worthless, my prince. I must tell you now that you have bought it. A jeweler's nightmare, I should say," she confessed.

"You need to part with your gold cup, my gallant prince. Its color is rubbing on your cheeks." Jahangir broke his silence, his eyes spilling reproof.

"I don't drink much, Your Majesty, only when there is an occasion to celebrate." Prince Perwiz sighed, a quick protest shining in his eyes. "And Nauroz is a festive occasion to be royally celebrated with wine and music, and with…" His thoughts were left unuttered as the twin brothers, Prince Jahandar and Prince Shahriyar, stormed into view with the swiftness of a hurricane.

"Mamma told me you bought a scimitar for me." Prince Shahriyar was the first one to plead his case by tugging at the arm of Prince Perwiz.

"Mamma didn't say that. She said Shahzada Perwiz would hold a contest for us and whoever wins, gets the scimitar." Prince Jahandar spirited his brother away from the arm of Prince Perwiz.

Before the six-year-old twins could gain any sober attention from their laughing big brother, their older sister Bihar Banu bounced into the circle to claim the prize for herself.

"I am taking lessons in archery, Shahzada Perwiz, and fencing. Mamma said I can have this scimitar." Bihar Banu was smiling most adorably.

A volley of laughter escaped Jahangir's lips, watching this scene of royal scuffle and intrigue. Sahiba Jamali was smiling too, her eyes brimming with love and adoration. She could not help admiring the handsome twins and this beautiful daughter of Karamasi Begum, her gaze embracing them all as if they were her own royal children. Princess Bihar Banu was bobbing her curls up and down, the flaxen tinge in them bright and silken. She was dressed in crimson silks, broidered with silver stars, looking more like a life-sized doll than a young princess. Karamasi, the mother of twins and of this doll-princess, was not far behind, sailing toward her royal brood with the air of an avenging goddess. The emperor was smiling, as if admiring his brave warriors with little scimitars of their own hung loose from their jeweled belts. Karamasi was quick to snatch them away from their belts, her gaze alone flashing reprimands at Princess Bihar Banu.

"Such rude behavior! It doesn't become the royal princes...and my heedless princess. You have fed your manners to the winds?" Karamasi Begum's voice was choking with royal indignation. "Your indulgence, Your Majesty, makes our children neglect their royal manners. They should be curtsying and standing in awe of the emperor. How you spoil and cosset her, Your Majesty, makes her utterly forget her manners!" she exclaimed, her eyes flashing.

"They are royally spoiled, the emperor admits." Jahangir's look was warm and ardent. He swept the defiant princess into his arms and planted two kisses on her rosy cheeks, before returning his gaze to his wife with a flash of mock accusation. "And yet, didn't you mislead them all?" His gaze was arrested to the emerald décolletage on her robe of silk, all green and shimmering. "Didn't you raise their hopes, individually, I am sure, that they would receive from Prince Perwiz the gift of this scimitar?"

"Your Majesty!" Karamasi Begum protested sweetly. "I only mentioned to Prince Jahandar that Prince Perwiz might make him a gift of this scimitar which he purchased!" Her light-brown eyes were glinting disbelief.

"And yet, Nauroz gives license to our princes to behave like the street urchins." Jahangir's gaze was turning to Prince Perwiz. "Do you intend this scimitar to be a gift, my generous prince? And if so, who is going to be the fortunate claimant?"

"I bought it for Prince Jahandar, Your Majesty, if you kindly approve my decision," was Prince Perwiz's laconic response.

"In all justice, then, bestow your gift upon Prince Jahandar," Jahangir commanded.

Prince Perwiz was relieved to get rid of this controversial gift. Prince Jahandar was in a stupor of ecstasy, hugging this scimitar and bowing before the emperor, before sprinting away to flaunt his prize. Prince Shahriyar was standing there pale and sullen, simmering with rage. His expression was one of defiance and mute challenge.

"I want a scimitar…that scimitar," Bihar Banu was whimpering, and burying her face into the folds of Jahangir's robe.

"The emperor would give you his own, my sweet princess," Jahangir murmured confidentially.

"I want that scimitar!" Prince Shahriyar protested in a loud, blatant tone. A mysterious challenge was shining in his eyes as he stood there raging inwardly.

"For your impudence alone, my prince, you will weep for mercy from the emperor," Jahangir chided with a sudden impatience.

The shining challenge in Prince Shahriyar's eyes was meeting the emperor's gaze without remorse or contrition. A sudden flush was creeping over his cheeks, and under the sheer weight of his bitterness, he was unable to speak.

"You will, you mannerless colt, if you keep standing there defiant like some raging lord." Jahangir's eyes were shooting daggers if not commands.

Prince Shahriyar had turned to a statue of fire and ice. His fair cheeks were burning with rage, and the gold-brown in his eyes kindling to one enigmatic blaze of a challenge which he dared not voice. The emperor's silence itself was breathing a threat of rage which could explode without warning. The air itself was charged with silence, leaving everyone in abeyance, with the exception of Prince Perwiz, who was slipping away cautiously, his flight even unnoticed by the begums.

"Come hither, the fairest of my princes, and let the emperor humble your childish pride." A whimsical challenge splintered through Jahangir's lips.

Prince Shahriyar obeyed slowly and reluctantly. Hauteur and bitterness were his weapons of defense, his eyes bright and burning. With his head high, he stood there unintimidated, his gaze bold and defiant.

"No tears of guilt or apology in your eyes, my prince, but the flames of defiance and rudeness! Bend down, my royal rebel. The emperor must toast your royal bottom, to pour the warmth of discipline into your royal veins." Jahangir whipped his bottom harshly, even before the prince could obey the emperor.

The royal ladies were in utter shock, unable to speak or protest. Their eyes were widening in disbelief at the sudden rage of the emperor. Princess Bihar Banu was the next one to flee, more so to chase Prince Jahandar, than to escape this unhappy scene. But Prince Jahandar was returning with a sense of childish intuitiveness. Sensing the charged silence, he was edging closer, quiet and contemplative. Upon seeing his brother, Princess Bihar Banu had halted momentarily, pressed by an urge to stop him, but then had fled as if pursued by fever and excitement.

"Stand straight, my young prince." Jahangir flashed another loud command. "No tears in your impudent eyes yet! Let me test your pride." He slapped him on his right cheek. "You will not weep?" He landed another blow on his left cheek.

Prince Shahriyar's eyes remained dry, and shining with some inner challenge he dared not voice. The ladies were startled out of their shock and silence, and were protesting. Prince Jahandar was offering the scimitar to Prince Shahriyar, but he was molded into a statue of pride and immobility. Standing there erect, his expression was taut and unflinching. Only his red cheeks smarting against the impressions of the emperor's fingerprints were revealing the traces of his pain and chagrin.

"Your Majesty, what are we witnessing here, rage and impropriety? As far as I know you have not ever struck anyone before, let alone a child. And your own child, too?" Sahiba Jamali's voice was trembling under the weight of shock and outrage.

"Impudence and discourtesy from my own royal brood are not to be tolerated by the emperor," Jahangir murmured under his breath without meeting the gaze of his wife.

"Your Majesty! How could your love turn to such violence?" Karamasi Begum's bold protest was barely audible. Her arms were locked around the twins protectively and possessively. She was kissing their hair with a profusion of love and tenderness.

"My sweet, he is the best loved of all my sons," Jahangir murmured with a dint of remorse. "As you yourself admit, the prince is royally spoiled. And the emperor's love knows no violence when striking with the rod of discipline. Take him away, dear Karamasi," he intoned, half imploringly, half soothingly. "Yes, take him away, before the emperor sends him to the tower, where Prince Khusrau languishes alone..." he breathed hoarsely, noticing the hurried approach of Jagat Gosaini.

Jagat Gosaini, the white rose of the harem, as Jahangir called her, was best loved by him. She was, on this auspicious day of Nauroz, dressed in pale silks stitched with rubies and diamonds. Her eyes, the color of agates, were liquid-bright and sparkling. She was sailing closer like the goddess of wind and fire, and even the emperor was feeling humbled and remorseful.

"Your Majesty, what do I hear? How could you grant your rage such freedom on this auspicious day of Nauroz?" Jagat Gosaini's eyes were flashing accusations.

While the emperor's sad gaze was fixed to Jagat Gosaini, Sahiba Jamali was slipping away quietly. So was Karamasi Begum, her arms still cradling the twins into a comforting embrace. The emperor was aware only of the white rose before him, his sight and senses swooning with that familiar ache which he could never dissolve when she was near. He was rather awed by the marble purity of her features, haloed by the glitter of rubies in her ears and around her throat.

"My love! The daggers of accusations in your eyes are cutting the emperor's very soul to islands of wounds." Jahangir smiled.

"Your Majesty!" exclaimed Jagat Gosaini. Before she could voice her protest, Prince Khurram emerged forth from behind the bower of roses like a silvery knight.

"Mamma, Your Majesty." Prince Khurram bowed with the ease and grace of a charming knight. "A horde of patrons, dear Mamma, rich and impatient, are laying siege over your stall. And no prudent owner there to benefit from their gold and riches?" His sharp features were attaining the warmth of ivory and sunshine. "I followed you right after you left, Mamma, but you vanish like a cloud, you always do! I was distracted on the way, though." He laughed.

"How handsomely you lie, my handsome Khurram!" Jagat Gosaini's eyes were holding her son captive. "Lies don't sit graciously on your face, sweet prince, so young and innocent-looking," she murmured.

"Would I lie to you, Mamma, if I were to benefit from your gold?" Prince Khurram smoothed his silver coat stitched with pearls and diamonds, as if feeling its warmth and opulence.

"No!" A ripple of mirth escaped Jagat Gosaini's seductive lips. "Cheer the emperor with your keen wit, while I earn gold to satisfy the greed of my prince." She flitted away. "And warn the emperor about the forthcoming inquisition by his wives commencing this very evening, which he won't be able to postpone." She shot this edict over her shoulders before fleeing.

"The emperor doesn't need cheering, my beloved prince, but obedience and discipline from his sons," Jahangir reminded Prince Khurram, laughing. "And you are the pillar of discipline, my ascetic prince. How old are you? Twenty odd springs, and still practicing abstinence! How many times the emperor has urged you to taste wine, tell me? Still resisting. When would you learn to appreciate this soma of the gods?"

"Never, Your Majesty, I hope," was Prince Khurram's suave response. "The pure and fresh juices from the bounty of God's good fruits are more delicious to me than any wines smooth and tempting. Why do the gold flagons and jeweled cups brimming with such sweet nectar fail to tempt me? I can't tell."

"Do you ever feel the stab of any temptation, my heedless prince?" Jahangir asked capriciously.

"Jewels of the earth tempt me, Your Majesty. The gems most precious in nature and in your royal treasuries! Beauty in all its form and color is the greatest of temptations to me, to explore its mystery, to know and befriend this art."

"Ah, the poetry in youth." Jahangir smiled profoundly. "Are you besieged by the longings of your heart, yet? What does your heart seek or long for?" His eyes were gathering agog and mischief.

"My heart is always longing to get lost in the beauty of the gardens, Your Majesty. Longing for the sight of the hills and the valleys. My heart, yes, Your Majesty, goading me to wed the bride of architecture where the monuments, grand and ancient, celebrate the art in living. And archery is my love, not longing, if you care to know more about my heart, Your Majesty," Prince Khurram chanted dreamily and poetically.

"What poverty in love, where maidens most beautiful stay unloved and neglected by my heartless prince," Jahangir chided merrily.

"Do you love birds?" He turned abruptly to retrieve his pigeons from Abdur Rahim.

"Only a few, Your Majesty, if they are songbirds, or blessed with colorful plumage," Prince Khurram sang merrily.

Jahangir had not even heard his son's response, completely absorbed by the sea of mirth in his viziers' eyes and on their lips. Both Man Singh and

Abdur Rahim were startled to awareness after becoming the subjects of the emperor's abrupt attention fixed upon them. But Jahangir, after reclaiming his pigeons, turned swiftly to face his son.

"Have you ever seen such a breed, such strange and lovely pair of pigeons? The emperor wishes not to part from them for all the jewels on this earth." Jahangir held out the tame pair to his son. "You are not afraid, my valorous prince, are you?"

"Forgive me, Your Majesty, I am loathe to touch anything with feathers, dead or alive. They..." Prince Khurram could not continue, his fear itself trembling against the thunder of mirth on the emperor's lips.

"Ah, my craven prince!" Jahangir was foundering into the ocean of his own mirth and incredulity. "Get thee gone, my handsome prince. Get thee gone, before the emperor makes your silver coat the home of this lovely pair." He stood laughing, while Prince Khurram fled, with not as much as a glance at the tame birds.

Jahangir's laughing eyes were turning to his viziers, then following his son's swift flight. This time, neither Man Singh nor Abdur Rahim were startled by the emperor's surge of attention and indulgence; they joined him in his mirth. They too were watching the fleeing prince with a keen interest. Prince Khurram's flight was truncated all of a sudden close to the stall of Salihah Banu, as if he was confronted by another feathery foe. From where the emperor stood, he could see his son caught under some daze of chill and inertia, but he returned his attention to his viziers.

"In my love and indulgence, I have neglected to perceive the craven, and at times, the impudent nature of my sons," Jahangir murmured to his pigeons, rather to his viziers. "Let us fill our coffers with worthless treasures from the bounties of Mina Bazaar." He bestowed a generous smile upon his viziers. "If the emperor is fortunate, his perception might lead him to discover the weaknesses of his wives." His feet themselves were leading him toward the inviting stalls of the Mina Bazaar.

Man Singh and Abdur Rahim were following the emperor a few paces behind, quietly and respectfully. Jahangir's leisurely stroll was coming to an abrupt halt a few paces away from Prince Khurram, from where he had not stirred an inch as if planted there in some stupor of dream-haze. A ponderous spell was upon the emperor too as he followed his son's gaze. Prince Khurram, oblivious to all, was standing there rapt and smitten. His gaze was devouring the young princess behind the stall, who was spilling jewels on a velvet cloth from a gold casket.

"Who is that beautiful flower? She has smitten my son with her charms," Jahangir asked of no one in particular.

"Don't you remember, Your Majesty?" Man Singh began thoughtfully. "That princess is Arjumand Banu, the daughter of Asaf Khan. It has been a long time since you celebrated her betrothal to Prince Khurram with a great feasting and rejoicing."

Jahangir appeared not to hear Man Singh's slow, thoughtful comment. He was lost into the mists of his own intensity and oblivion. His gaze was fixed to his son under some spell profound, the ripples of music and gaiety all around him grazing not the slumbers in his awareness.

"You yourself put the ring on the finger of Princess Arjumand Banu, Your Majesty, not too long ago." Abdur Rahim sought the emperor's attention. "More than five years though. Too long a time for the emperor to remember?" He fell to ruminating, as stark silence was the emperor's only response. "A year after Prince Khurram's betrothal to Princess Arjumand Banu, you made the prince wed the daughter of the Persian monarch, that may refresh your memory, Your Majesty. Mirza Muzaffar Husain Safavi, a long, long name for Prince Khurram's father-in-law, and a long, long wait for Princess Arjumand Banu. This betrothal has lasted the longest time, in my opinion, Your Majesty." He succeeded in catching the emperor's attention.

"A young man in love, my own son!" Jahangir smiled. "Such purity of love is tragic for a youth of his age," he murmured inaudibly. "My prince must be wedded, soon."

He resumed his stroll.

Jahangir did not disturb his son's immobility as he strolled past him, his gaze now admiring the fresh beauty of Princess Arjumand Banu behind the stall, though she herself was unaware that she was being admired by her betrothed and by the emperor. The emperor's own heart had begun to ache with love and longings. It was awakening to the pulse of time where Anarkali was buried alive, or living in obscurity inside the vacuums of her own unmarked grave or palace. There was a sudden violence in Jahangir's heart, a thunder and an explosions, embracing the promise of some precious boon it could neither see or fathom. He was drifting in a dream-haze, neither stopping at the colorful stalls nor seeing the dancers and the jugglers eager to be noticed by the emperor. The sparks of elation were now alighting in his eyes, leaving behind the world of illusions, and welcoming the facade of joy and laughter. His inner sadness too was wearing the mask of festivity, and the violence in his heart was breaking into mists to cover the altar of his beloved in a shroud of holy longings. The beloved, his unforgotten and unforgettable Anarkali, was breathing anguish into the pools of his elation, sending chills down his spine and beckoning him to the raptures in union. His fingers were tightening over the feathery gifts in his hands, though he himself seemed not aware that he was about to choke the innocent pigeons. Against the drums of violence inside his own heart, he could hear the hearts of the birds heaving a million sighs. *Dreaming about freedom, yearning for flight!* One abrupt thought was claiming the emperor's attention.

Jahangir's dreamy thoughts were turning to the silent rebels in his hands, but his gaze was straying toward the field of poppies in a blaze of orange. His gaze as well as his thoughts were chasing the delirious poppies, their half-parted lips gleaming under the sun like the gold goblets. Suddenly, the field of poppies was disappearing before the emperor's gaze, his attention shifting to the glittering stalls huddled together with brocaded canopies overhead. The first colorful stall which caught his attention was brighter than the poppies, and dreamier than the dream-haze in nature. He was drifting toward one stall in particular, fresh poppies in a jade bowl on the velvet-lined counter, attractive and alluring. He almost stumbled to a slow halt as if struck by a bolt of lightning, his gaze arrested to the lady behind the stall who was absorbed in arranging gold vases on a shelf already crowded with precious bric-a-brac.

The living, pulsating incarnation of his beloved! Anarkali! Jahangir's heart had missed several beats, and was now thundering inside his breast with the violence of a hurricane. Which dream was true? The one he was having right now, or the one he was wont to conjure up in the insane asylum of his thoughts? The emperor's mind was caught into a whirlwind of chaos and shock.

The dear, dear face with the warmth of ivory and marble! The small mouth with lips the color of red, red poppies. The fair, smooth forehead haloed by the gold in flaxen hair. The large, dream-boat eyes fringed with silken eyelashes. This sweet, youthful face was his beloved's which he had stolen from the colors of reality and had etched it into his dreams. Anarkali had returned from the valley of death to the abode of the living, in Agra, and the emperor didn't even know? The light of joy and anguish was alighting in Jahangir's eyes, brimming with the fire of worship and adoration. His mind and soul were frozen inside the caskets of time, only the pain inside his heart alive and stabbing. This sudden violence inside him was demanding action, bubbling forth to dissolve this enchantment, and to crush his beloved into his arms in one eternal embrace.

An eternity was suspended inside this one cosmic bubble of silence. The lady behind the stall was stepping back to view her crowded treasures. Suddenly, she turned her head, as if she had felt the intensity of a burning gaze which was reaching out to devour her. Her eyes met the emperor's, and a lovely smile curled upon her lips.

The enchantment was broken!

Jahangir's heart fluttered like a wounded bird, and lay sprawled in his breast, with one last cry of agony before dying, his very thoughts confessing. The large, blue eyes were not the eyes of Anarkali, and he could not mistake his beloved for another. The unforgettable eyes of his beloved were still kindled in his soul like the candles of holiness with a liquid softness absorbing the night-blue skies in their very depths. This dream-vision before him had the eyes of a temptress, his wounded heart was murmuring in throes of longings. He could not take his gaze away from the bright, sparkling cups in the eyes of this lady whose youth and beauty were cutting his sanity into splinters of desire and madness. Her eyes were light, holding colors of the seasons in their seductive pools, where love for life could be seen stark and shimmering.

Anarkali, and yet not Anarkali? She is the goddess of torment and vengeance. Jahangir's thoughts were a thunder of fury and outrage.

The emperor's gaze was holding this lady captive, but she had escaped into her own world of silks and brocades, which she had begun to hang and observe with utmost attention. Blind to his own devouring intensity, Jahangir's gaze was slipping from the top of her head to her toes, caressive, lingering. His gaze was embracing her tiny waist, singing hymns of adoration to some divine sculptor who had fashioned each contour of her body with love for perfection. Jahangir's gaze was weaving a spell over the smooth, round pearls around her throat, and in return becoming entangled inside the coronet of pearls in her hair, but his fair prisoner was not aware of his mute intensity. After that one brief smile, she had resumed her work as if oblivious to the whole world all around her.

Man Singh and Abdur Rahim, standing a few paces away from the emperor, had watched the emperor's expression change from one of shock and disbelief to that of a stark naked agony of the spirit tormented and tormenting. Their eyes, following the emperor's, had discovered the object of the emperor's torment and longings, both exchanging a quick glance of alarm and caution. Both Man Singh and Abdur Rahim were well acquainted with the lady, and their hearts were sinking in unison at the mere thought of the emperor falling in love. And the emperor was smitten with love, it was obvious. His expression was that of a man struck by a cupid's arrow, as if he was about to fall at his beloved's feet and profess eternal slavery to his passion wild and terrible.

"Who is that lady in that stall in possession of fresh poppies from our imperial fields?" Jahangir addressed his query to the winds, without tearing his gaze away from the object of his pain and desire.

"She is Mihrunnisa Begum, Your Majesty, the daughter of Mirza Ghiyas Beg," Man Singh murmured.

"Mirza Ghiyas Beg," Jahangir murmured back. "The same one who was the pillar of government in my father's time? After my accession, didn't I bestow upon him the title of Itmadudaula Khan?" he ruminated aloud.

"Yes, Your Majesty." Abdur Rahim offered to refresh the emperor's memory. "He is also the father of Asaf Khan, whose daughter Arjumand Banu is betrothed to Prince Khurram."

"The sister of Asaf Khan, then! Is she married?" Jahangir turned his eyes upon Abdur Rahim, his look wild and commanding.

"A widow, Your Majesty, the widow of Sher Afghan," Abdur Rahim responded quickly, discomfited by the look of anguish and wildness in the emperor's eyes.

"Ah, Sher Afghan!" Jahangir's eyes were now gathering memories sad and painful. "You mean Ali Quli, who won the battle at Mewar. For this act of his courage, the emperor bestowed upon him the title of Sher Afghan, and you know what this title means, the Tiger Slayer! But then this Tiger Slayer turned into a faithless viper. Girding his loins to join in revolt with Prince Khusrau. Was that a couple of years after my accession or more?" he ruminated aloud, a downpour of memories escaping his lips. "Didn't he murder my vizier? Oh, that vile murderer, he slit open the belly of Qutbuddin Khan. Tried to escape, didn't he, but was cut to pieces by the avenging men of Qutbuddin Khan." His very thoughts were breathing rage, his lost beloved exiled into the dark recesses of his soul. "How grieved was I then, for my vizier, for gentle Qutbuddin. My gentle vizier, he was to me like a dear son, a kind brother and a congenial friend. And the same year, Qutbuddin's mother, she died of utter grief. That black-faced scoundrel! The Tiger Slayer!" He paused, fighting the urge to look at the treasure of his newly discovered pain and love. "And this widow, was she not brought to Agra the same year?" His eyes were seeking confirmations.

"Yes, Your Majesty, she was brought here as a lady-in-waiting for Ruqqaya Begum," Man Singh intoned obediently.

"Ruqqaya Begum, the beloved widow of my father! Her own palace is next to the palace of Itmadudaula; the emperor has been there several times. Strange, passing strange that the emperor never saw this lady. Mihrunnisa," he murmured, his feet carrying him toward that stall where fates stood mocking his passion and madness.

This stall was no ordinary stall, but an artistic gallery with homespun silks and exquisite embroideries. More jade bowls with a swath of orange poppies were coming into view as the emperor drifted closer to the stall. Mihrunnisa, assisted by another lady, was becoming aware of the emperor's approach, though displaying no signs of courtesy or recognition. Her eyes were lowered and her heart fluttering. Before wending his way closer to the stall, Jahangir's lips and eyes were shooting another command.

"Who is that lady standing right next to Mihrunnisa?" Jahangir's eyes were gathering rills of memories. "The emperor has seen her before, when, he can't recall." He was being lured closer to Mihrunnisa like a moth to one burning flame.

"Asmat Begum, Your Majesty. She is the mother of Mihrunnisa Begum." Abdur Rahim was quick to satisfy the emperor's curiosity.

Jahangir was not heeding. His heart and soul were on fire, kindling a volcano of passions so scalding that he could feel his whole being suffering the tortures of the damned. So excruciating was the inner torment of his burning self, that his thoughts had forged dead Anarkali into the living mold of Mihrunnisa. The blue light in her eyes was the color of the sky, enveloping his senses into some bliss supreme, where pain could transform itself into pearls of longings. She was standing there like a wraith of light and purity, and he could neither speak nor tear his gaze away from her laughing eyes. *A white flame*, he was thinking, feeling the scent of her body and nearness. His own body was melting and dissolving into some whirlwind of the noblest of passions in love and self-surrender. Like a man possessed, he was drinking the nectar of life from her eyes and lips. Mihrunnisa's sing-song voice was reaching his dazed awareness with the murmur and sweetness of a distant cataract.

"Your Majesty, would you care to purchase this gold flagon studded with jewels? The rare treasures from Arabia and Tartary?" Mihrunnisa held out the gleaming treasure, enjoying the emperor's smitten look with implicit pleasure.

"Dear lady, the emperor wishes to purchase the most precious of treasures, not this worthless flagon," Jahangir murmured to himself.

"I have many a priceless treasures, Your Majesty. And the emperor's riches are countless, making him a benevolent patron to purchase all, I hope." Mihrunnisa's eyes were shining with the glow of mockery.

"Many a priceless treasures, which even the emperors can't afford!" Jahangir murmured, his heart unwilling to escape the spell of this dream-haze.

"Choose one, Your Majesty, and I would suite the price to match your desire," Mihrunnisa challenged with a radiant smile.

"Your heart, my dear lady." Jahangir's gaze was gathering dreams and poetry. But his thoughts were rising in stealthy rebellion, protesting against the mockery of this Venus on Earth.

"Your Majesty! I do not give my heart to strangers, until the course of action is known." A slight tremor escaped Mihrunnisa's bold response.

Both the emperor and Mihrunnisa were stung to silence, both gazing into each other's eyes mutely and ineffably. To rectify her blunder, Mirhrunnisa's hands were reaching out to caress the pigeons in the emperor's arms. But this act of friendliness on her part had stirred the pigeons to sedition and challenge. Immediately, she had shrunk back as if whipped by the hands of fate.

"Your beauty and mockery, my lady, have made the emperor bereft of his own wit!" Jahangir declared. One inception of a ghazal was trembling upon his lips, more of a memorial to his love lost than his serenade to this idol of perfection.

"What shall I do, for the arrow of loss of thee has pierced my heart. So that the evil eye not reaching may again reach another. Thou movest as if frenzied, and the world is frenzied for thee. I burn rue lest thy eye should reach me."

"Your Majesty, Your Majesty," both Mihrunnisa and her mother exclaimed, more in protest of the emperor's naked torment, than in praise of his dark couplets.

The emperor had fallen prey to his own mute reveries and to agonies of the spirit suffered and suffering. The unvoiced rills of applause throbbing upon the lips of the viziers were left unuttered against the breezy approach of Princess Bihar Banu. She had bounced upon the scene like a gale of wind, demanding attention from the emperor.

"Your Majesty, you must come. There, by Malika Jahan Begum's stall are roses and roses, big and heavy. One rose, Your Majesty, I want to show you. It's as big as the moon, she says. Let me show you, Your Majesty, please," Bihar Banu pleaded.

Jahangir was half listening, his gaze still arrested to the idol of his pain and passion. He flashed a brief glance at his daughter, indicating that she had the emperor's attention, then returned his gaze to Mihrunnisa.

"Here, dear lady, lend them the comfort of your sweet arms until the emperor returns." Jahangir held out the pigeons to Mihrunnisa, who claimed them happily. "The emperor must comfort his heart with the heart of a rose, before he returns to beg the heart of beauty. And to claim his pigeons, of course." He turned to his daughter.

The emperor was being led by the young princess toward the bower of roses, beside which Malika Jahan had installed her stall. Man Singh and Abdur Rahim were the silent escorts of the emperor. Their spirits were deflated by this sudden meeting of the emperor with Mihrunnisa. In their estimation, the emperor was becoming a victim to the beauty and witchcraft of Mihrunnisa. The emperor, though talking and laughing with his daughter, was accosting dreams and reveries. His heart was foundering inside the white realms of pain and reality. A wild cry from the bottomless depths of his soul was reaching his awareness. A lament most disconsolate, Anarkali pouring tears of grief? The cry and pain were leaving him; he was transported into the scented abode of the roses where his little princess was leading him. Princess Bihar Banu's ripples of excitement were making him indulge and participate in her joy and elation. He could inhale the scent of love, drinking the wine of beauty, beholding and cherishing only one rose, the white flame of a rose. Anarkali, Mihrunnisa? The entire nature was painted in the color of the sky. In this cosmic revelation was the bluest blue stolen from the eyes of his beloved *lost*, and from the lovely eyes of his beloved yet to be wooed.

"Your Majesty, look, that moon-rose." Bihar Banu was drawing his attention to that red rose which had possessed her little heart to possess it.

That red rose with petals the size of butterflies, was flaming before Jahangir's sight, but his reverie was accosting the white flame within his soul. His heart was yearning for the nearness of that white flame of a face which had shackled him into the chains of slavery and worship.

"The emperor likes that white one. The one over there, with the color of a diamond in its heart, my sweet. The emperor wants that one." Jahangir's gaze was turning to Man Singh. "Man Singh, get that white rose for the emperor, the one almost kissing the cheek of the yellow one."

"I want that red one, Your Majesty, may I?" Princess Bihar Banu was chanting impatiently. "That moon-faced one, Your Majesty, may I?"

"Yes, my rude princess, yes." Jahangir smiled, commanding Abdur Rahim to pluck that disk of a rose for the princess.

Princess Bihar Banu was clapping her hands and singing gleefully. She was lifting her small, white face to the emperor, her eyes shining with adoration. Jahangir hugged her daughter wistfully, searching her face as if he had seen her for the first time.

"The beauty of this rose must never die, my sweet." Jahangir laughed indulgently. "Take it to Bishan Das. He will capture its beauty on a cloth of silk. And the emperor will order a gilded frame for it." His eyes were gathering warmth, as he watched her claim the rose from Abdur Rahim greedily.

Bihar Banu was prancing away, leaving behind the pools of glee, as if sailing on the wings of mirth and pride. The emperor had claimed his own rose absently, his gaze following the happy princess as if she carried a world into her little hands. His own heart was yawning to the sense of its former pain and agony, and throbbing to lay its wounds at the feet of this new beloved. Dream-haze was upon him again as he drifted back toward the stall to claim his pigeons, if not his heart which was lost to him irretrievably. Man Singh and Abdur Rahim were following the emperor, as was customary, and keeping their silence. Abdur Rahim's expression was changing from one of despair to sorrow. Man Singh was trying to be cheerful, his gaze seeking some mute confirmation from Abdur Rahim. Their eyes met, and a pact of mutual understanding was exchanged between them. Man Singh, spurred by the silent support from Abdur Rahim, was framing his thoughts to discipline, as if to avert some doom or tragedy.

"Your Majesty, Mihrunnisa Begum has a daughter almost the age of Princess Bihar Banu." Man Singh ventured forth with a false note of cheerfulness.

"What's her name?" Jahangir could hear his heart weeping at the altar of Anarkali.

"Ladli, Your Majesty," was Man Singh's deflated murmur of a response.

Jahangir did not hear him. He was wading into the waters of pain and torment. His heart and limbs were heavy, his mind and body drowning into some whirlpool of chaos and confusion. The burden of his thoughts was pulling him back to some realms sacred, but his feet were inching closer toward the magic stall with poppies. He didn't even know that he was standing there, gazing at the miracle of his lost love with an intensity, profound and worshipful.

Mihrunnisa was all sunshine and laughter, arranging jewels on a gold tray and holding it out to her mother. Sensing the emperor's presence, she lifted her eyes, the laughing pools in them a dazzling blue. The emperor's gaze met hers, and their eyes were locked in one eternity of an embrace. *The silence itself is singing, the lover and the beloved*, Asmat Begum was thinking. The lover and the beloved were trying to glean and arrest the reflections of each other's thoughts, it seemed. Jahangir's senses were awakening to the pain of reality. The dream-oblivion was leaving him. The spell of her beauty's witchcraft was gone too. His thoughts were clearing the haze in memories lacerated by the reeds of time, and violating the sanctity of truth and passion.

Why am I standing here like a besotted lover? Jahangir's thoughts were pleading release from the pit of this confusion. *To desecrate the altar of my love? To woo this beauty incarnate? What should I say? Why did I come back? To see Anarkali in her lovely eyes? To make her the empress of my heart? No! To reclaim my pigeons.* His thoughts were rising on the heights of absurdity.

Mihrunnisa was holding only one pigeon, and whispering something to her mother. Asmat Begum was handing her a silk handkerchief, and Mihrunnisa seemed to be admiring the embroidery, ignoring the emperor completely.

"The emperor wishes to reclaim his pigeons..." Jahangir paused. His thoughts were goading him to add reclaim his heart, but he didn't. "But he sees only one pigeon?" His gaze was commanding her attention.

"That is true, Your Majesty. Only one pigeon is to be seen, as far as my sight confirms." Mihrunnisa raised her eyes, light and mirth shining in them with a quicksilver awakening.

"What happened to the other one?" Jahangir murmured under the spell of her beautiful eyes, the violence in his heart savage and stabbing.

"It flew away, Your Majesty," Mihrunnisa murmured back. Mirth dancing in her eyes, and spilling down her lips.

"How?" Jahangir's voice was choking, his heart lurching and somersaulting.

Mihrunnisa released her hold on the pigeon, letting it escape. Her hand was poised in the air, palm upward, her lips blowing a kiss after the bird, soaring higher and higher.

"Like this, Your Majesty," Mihrunnisa murmured, still watching the pigeon in its happy flight.

"A wit like yours can destroy the emperors as well the empires." Mirth and delirium came flooding through Jahangir's eyes and lips. "But you shall reign like a devi inside the sanctuary of the emperor's heart." The tempest of his mirth was uncontrollable.

The emperor was leaving the stall, the Mina Bazaar, the world, it seemed! Laughing still!

"Make preparations for a royal wedding, my viziers. The emperor's, if his fortunes permit," Jahangir commanded over his shoulders.

No response from behind grazed Jahangir's hysteria and delirium, for the viziers were stricken dumb with shock. The emperor needed no response, for he was gliding inside the oceans of his own joy and torment.

"And yes, the emperor commands an exquisite mausoleum to be erected over the tomb of Anarkali." Jahangir's mirth was subsiding. "I have found my living goddess after all. She might accompany me to Lahore to pray at the tomb of my beloved…for the peace in my heart." His very thoughts were commanding oblivion and surcease. All of a sudden, fatigue and lonesomeness were draining the bubbles of his delirium into the well of his practiced silence. His only need right this moment was to drain flagons of wine into the ocean-thirst of his dying hope and living torment.

Chapter Three

The vast library at Agra Palace was a sane refuge for Jahangir against the din of festivities where the entire palace was garlanded for Prince Khurram's wedding celebrations. But the volleys of laughter slashed with song and music from down the palace halls were still following him into the sanctuary of his solitude and contemplations. Prince Khurram was the happiest of bridegrooms, counting the ribbons of endless ceremonies till he could be alone with his bride, his beloved Arjumand Banu. The nuptial ceremonies had lasted one whole week, and today was the last day to seal the marriage vows. The emperor himself was a seven-month-old bridegroom, wedded to his idol of wit and beauty, Mihrunnisa. With this dream-vision of a beloved enriching his harem, he was still foundering inside the streams of love and pain…in love with his newly wedded bride, and suffering the pain of separation from Anarkali, though Anarkali was still the queen of his heart, beloved sweet and unforgettable.

The emperor's longings for Mihrunnisa were violent and insatiate, and he had named her *Nur Mahal*, meaning the Light of the Palace. But his soul was condemned eternally, hungering for the undying mystery within him, his unforgotten and unforgettable Anarkali. For him, Anarkali was merged body and soul with Nur Mahal, yet Nur Mahal's wit and beauty were bent on destroying the mystery of the mysterious within him, his own, very own Anarkali. The emperor's life was assuming the quality of a living charade, breathing the beauty of life and death in living, it seemed. He was thinking about Anarkali in the presence of Nur Mahal, and holding the portrait of Nur Mahal before his beloved's throne inside him, when free from the wit and the wisdom of his living bride. Rather, he was drowning his own inner torment into the rivers of wine, if not into the flagons of oblivion. Even now, while seated at his rosewood desk and concentrating on the verses of Talib Amuli, the face of Anarkali was surfacing into his thoughts.

The emperor was dressed in all the Moghul fineries of a wealthy monarch, especially so, to honor the wedding celebrations of his son Prince Khurram.

His pale silks were the color of citron, and his red turban studded with a large ruby in the middle. Seated in his gilded chair as his throne of solitude, he appeared to be some lone prince right out of the pages of the Arabian Nights, a young prince, not a forty-three-year-old emperor, whose bride of thirty-four was another beautiful bloom in his harem with the worthy title Nur Mahal. One gold flagon was keeping the emperor company, as he sat luxuriating in his gilded chair. Enjoying both his wine and the wealth of poetry by Talib Amuli, his two other companions, of whom he was oblivious, were Princess Bihar Banu and Princess Ladli, the latter, the daughter of Nur Mahal. Princess Ladli was of the same age as Princess Bihar Banu, and they had become the greatest of friends right after the emperor's marriage to Mihrunnisa. On this auspicious day of Prince Khurram's wedding, they were both swathed in brocades with matching ribbons in their hair and around their waists. Leaning against the window with crimson drapes, they were painting fields of poppies on the silk canvases. Both the princesses were aware of the privilege to be permitted to sit in the library, and worked quietly, so as not to disturb the emperor.

Were I glass instead of body. I will reveal thee to thyself without thy unveiling. Two lips have I, one for drinking. And one to apologize for drunkenness.

Jahangir's thoughts were trying to steal the nectar of music from this verse of Talib Amuli. A sudden fatigue was overpowering his senses. His thoughts were trooping along in one mournful procession to follow Talib Amuli, who had died recently.

So young, so young! Plucked out of the bower of this existence so suddenly. The greatest of poets. Jahangir's hand was reaching out to the gold flagon beside him.

His gaze was commencing a leisurely stroll over the inanimate splendor of this library, as he sipped his wine slowly and thoughtfully. The bookshelves with gilded volumes, and the chests with patterns of koftgari, were the objects of admiration where his gaze was lingering the most. The Moghul paintings with scenes of hunting and the European marvels with the depiction of Madonna and the Child were dissolving his sadness into pools of awe and veneration. His wine goblet was poised before him, and he appeared to be catching the scent of roses from the large floral arrangements.

Cradled between a pair of bookshelves on each side of the east wall was a masterpiece of art and sculpture, and Jahangir's gaze was arrested there involuntarily. This exquisite piece of ingenuity was presented to him on his birthday by one of his imperial artists. And it could never fail to evoke his awe and admiration whenever his attention was lured to it. Carved out of a solid block of marble, this wonder of inspiration housed spacious chambers with awnings in gold and ivory. The first chamber boasted three wrestlers, two engaged in a fierce fight, and the third one watching the other two, holding out a smooth stone on the palm of his hand. One spectator too, carved out of marble, could be seen lifelike, his bow and arrow abandoned beside a piece of log and one small pot. The second chamber was furnished with a throne and a canopy. A prince was seated on this throne with brocaded cushions at his back. The gaze of this prince was fixed to all five of his servants standing under the shade of a tree. It was a jacaranda tree, drawn and painted so craftily that it could be mistaken for a real tree. A large pavilion was carved out of the third chamber, displaying rope-dancers and men of learning. A trio of rope-dancers were performing together, one balancing a pole with three silken ropes, and the other swinging on the middle rope, sucking on his left foot which was held tight into his right hand. His left hand was stretched behind his back to keep the goat and the drum in balance, while the third companion on the adjoining rope stood beating the drum. Five men with staffs in their hands were the silent spectators in this chamber. The fourth chamber was smaller in contrast to the other three. In the middle of this chamber was Jesus Christ, facing two men. One man was kneeling at the feet of the Christ. The other, with his lips half parted, simply stood watching.

Jahangir's gaze was shifting from this masterpiece to the wall-to-wall bookshelves, bulging with volumes, all illumined and lacquered. Next, it was alighting on the two princesses, so serenely absorbed in their artistic endeavors. The fair profile of Princess Bihar Banu was carving rills of tenderness inside his heart, but his gaze was contemplating Princess Ladli whose back was toward him. The sheen of flax on her little head was jolting his thoughts in quest of his beloved empress Nur Mahal. His thoughts were stumbling into some den of absurdities.

How did my Nur consent to marry the emperor? Jahangir could hear his thoughts wading through the waters of disbelief and astonishment.

The emperor seemed to admire the colorful tapestries on the walls, but his thoughts were racing after Nur Mahal. A string of tragedies had been her only link to the emperor, even before she had met him. Her first husband, Sher Afghan, had killed the emperor's vizier, and in return was murdered by the imperial guards. Her father, with the grand title of Itmadudaula Khan, had been charged with the embezzlement of funds from the royal treasuries. He had been forgiven though, and later reinstated in the favor of the emperor. Her eldest brother, Sharif Muhammed, was charged with treason by joining hands with the royal rebel, Prince Khusrau. The prince's life was spared, but Sharif Muhammed was hanged by the emperor's own orders with no room for clemency.

A sad and ponderous smile was frozen on Jahangir's lips as he sat contemplating, his thoughts retracing the gullies of time. His features flushed with the warmth of wine were attaining the glow of sunsets, beautiful and mournful. The taste of sweet estrangement between him and Mihrunnisa, which he had tasted during the months of his wooing and courtship, was coming back to him. But nothing could have deterred him from marrying the lady of his love, he had told himself. Knowing the anguish and bitterness in her heart, he was longing to adopt her pain as a gift or dowry from the coffers of her beauty, where his own living torment could neither be gauged nor revealed. Mihrunnisa in return had been an angel of prudence, gentle in slicing the onslaught of the emperor's wooing, and concealing her pain within her, more graciously than he had ever hoped for or expected. But once she was married to the emperor, all her anguish and bitterness were dissolved into the vast ocean of her great love. She had given all to the emperor, her mind and body, and her soul and spirit too, loving him intensely and devotedly, and in exchange receiving nothing but the violence of his passion. The emperor's heart and soul were eternally lost to Anarkali; Jahangir was not blind to the unspoken thoughts of his living beloved. Anarkali was growing inside him more powerful in death than she had ever been in life. Now that the emperor was wedded to her semblance, Anarkali had begun to reign like a living, breathing tyrant. And not even the bewitching charms of Nur Mahal could rescue him from this undying torment. Anarkali had returned to rule and stay, assuming the role of an empress who was bent on taking vengeance for the loss of her love and life. The emperor had begun to drink heavily, more than ever before, though Nur Mahal's love alone was enough to drown him into the rivers of oblivion.

Paradoxically, Nur Mahal had become the emperor's sight and senses, and he too had given all to her whatever he could afford to part with. Since he could not bear to part with the aching wounds in his soul, he had given the bloom and prosperity of his whole empire to his one and only empress, Nur Mahal. He was moved to raptures by her beauty, but her wit and wisdom had soared his thoughts to such ecstatic heights, that he had begun to court freedom from the burdens of his royal duties.

Jahangir's hand reached for his gold flagon once again, a whimsical smile widening on his lips.

Even on this grand day of my son's wedding, my empress could not be detained from the cares of her royal duties? My beloved, receiving embassies from Surat, Turan and Deccan, I am sure. Jahangir's thoughts were a mockery of delight and indulgence.

Before he could taste the cherished sweetness from his cup, his sight was struck by the glow of an apparition drifting toward him. It was the living, breathing wraith of Anarkali-Nur Mahal, approaching closer and closer to where he sat gazing and pondering. *Not Anarkali!* One bubble of reality was bursting to nothingness inside the agonies of his awareness, but his heart was leaping with joy to greet the new beloved. Nur Mahal was haloed by the aura of grace and beauty. *The ghost of Anarkali!* Jahangir's thoughts were blinking away the sad illusion.

Nur Mahal was arrayed in shimmering brocades, slashed with blue velvets. The décolletage of pearls on her gown and a pearly sash at her waist were designed by her, to start a new trend in fashion. This gown called, *Nur Mahali*, was stitched with pearls, rippling and cascading. She was wearing a lavaliere of pearls around her throat in the pattern of dewdrop roses with interlocking vines, this too was her original design, which had become a vogue for the royal ladies in the Moghul court. She flashed a smile at the emperor before drifting toward the princesses.

"Now off with your indolence, my dears, and join the merriment down the halls." Nur Mahal beamed at the young princesses. "Your brother is getting married and you should be dancing your little feet off with joy and laughter." She left a little pause, and then swept Princess Ladli into one arm, cradling Princess Bihar Banu into her other. "The dancing girls themselves are waiting for the royal, little angels like you so that they could proceed with the *khattak* dance. Prince Perwiz has saved the gold and silver bhutans for you two, if you know how to whirl on your toes and tap your bhutans with your partners." She pinched their cheeks laughingly. "Now run off, while I goad the emperor to join me in dancing."

"I want the gold bhutan." Princess Bihar Banu shot for the door.

Jahangir sat sipping his wine, watching the velvet bundles flying out of this gilded chamber and disappearing down the hallway. His gaze was returning to his empress. This wraith of light and purity was sailing closer, radiant and glorious.

"Put your gold cup away, Your Majesty, I implore! Wine sits heavy on your pallor, and you mistake the color on your cheeks as a natural glow of health," Nur Mahal sang winsomely.

"This wine keeps me sober, my Nur, but the wine in your eyes is making me drunk." Jahangir smiled, relinquishing his goblet with a sigh.

"Then make merry, Your Majesty. The ocean of wine in my eyes never runs dry." Nur Jahan sank into the gilt chair beside him, mirth spilling from her lips.

"And yet the emperor needs only a flagon of wine and a piece of meat to make him merry." A spontaneous gale of mirth escaped Jahangir's lips. "And yet, my sweet, you have harnessed the emperor by the collar, and he obeys each little whim of yours with utmost devotion."

"The red, red rubies on your vest, Your Majesty, are in truth, the drops of my blood, holding each great whim of yours by the collar," Nur Mahal teased poetically.

"My whims are at your mercy, love!" Jahangir claimed her hand, kissing each finger with reverence. "Your beauty has chained me to subservience, Nur. Your wit and wisdom, to devotion. And now your poetry is robbing me of my own wit." His own thoughts were exploring the verses of Amir-ul-Amara.

Pass, O Messiah, o'er the heads of us slain by love. Thy restoring one life is worth a hundred murders.

"My wit, beauty and wisdom have failed to keep you away from your cup, Your Majesty," Nur Mahal murmured with a dint of sadness. "All those poets in your court with strings of poetry hanging from their lips, Your Majesty, if only they had the power to break all the gold flagons, and save you from the temptation of drinking."

"O censor, fear the weeping of the old vintner. Thy breaking one jar is equal to a hundred murders."

Another couplet broke forth on Jahangir's lips from the pen of Mulla Ali Ahmad. This poet too had retired to the abode of the dead two years from hence.

With this couplet still stinging his lips, Jahangir rose to his feet under some spell of desire which could not be postponed. Cupping Nur Mahal's face into his hands, he kissed her on the lips. Then he staggered back, and began to pace, his hands tied behind his back in a tight knot.

"Your Majesty." Nur Mahal gasped for breath. "How dismal this poetry! Two murders in two couplets...and tears and sadness...and on this auspicious day of your son's wedding too?" She was trying to discipline the violence inside her own heart. "Let us join the dancing and feasting, Your Majesty; the music is calling us."

"Dancing and feasting would last till dawn, sweet Nur. And the emperor rarely gets a moment of peace with you alone. All those intrigues and rebellions in his empire, leaving him no time to satisfy his great passion," Jahangir murmured, still pacing.

"All those viziers of yours, Your Majesty, the whole undisciplined lot. They are corrupt, conceited and avaricious," Nur Mahal intoned softly. "You should appoint men who are prudent and pure of heart, then there would be no intrigues or rebellions."

"Rebellions, my sweet rebel!" Jahangir exclaimed. "Didn't you rebel against the veil, and got the emperor's sanction to stay unveiled?"

"That sort of rebellion is favorable, Your Majesty, if I am to preside over the embassies to share the burden of your royal duties." Nur Mahal smiled to herself. "Did Khadija, Prophet Mohammed's wife, wear a veil when she conducted the business transactions?" Her eyes were questioning the veracity of her own thoughts.

"Ah, why connect religion with the foibles of mankind!" Jahangir intoned with a sudden interest. "Prophet Mohammed's other wives didn't veil themselves, either; the emperor is well versed in theology." He flashed her an adoring look. "Veiling is a mark of wealth and royalty, not the emblem of religion. And since you disdain this honor of wealth and royalty, the emperor respects your wishes."

"My wishes are to promote the health and wealth of the emperor and of his empire, drawing his attention toward appointing viziers who are skilled and judicious." Nur Mahal's tones were sad and dreamy.

"Didn't the emperor make your father the prime minister of Hind? With his title of Itmadudaula Khan alone, he could rule the whole world." Jahangir's look was ponderous. "And your brother, Sapur, receiving the title of Itaqid Khan, would he prove to be a great vizier? Asaf Khan, the youngest of your brothers, now the head of the imperial household. Of course, he is now the father-in-law of Prince Khurram."

"Just a fraction of devoted men to maintain repose and discipline, only in the capitol of Agra," Nur Mahal murmured profoundly.

"And the husbands of your sisters, Manija and Khadija! They could rise to higher ranks too, if you recommend them to the emperor, sweet Nur." Jahangir's eyes were shining with a subtle challenge.

"A handful of just men to fight cruelty and injustice in your empire, Your Majesty." Nur Mahal's eyes were unsheathing the daggers of mockery.

"Injustice!" Jahangir's feet were coming to a sudden halt by the mantel. "Are you inferring, Nur, that the emperor neglects the sprouting of cruelty and injustice in his empire?" His gaze was thoughtful and searching.

"Emperors are wont to carry the burdens of accusations, Your Majesty. The legacy of the royalty?" Nur Jahan began soothingly. "Prince Khusrau languishing in the prison. Your eldest son, Your Majesty? Is that an act of justice?"

"Ah, Prince Khusrau!" One flicker of a smile curled upon Jahangir's lips. "The traitor doesn't deserve even one patch of living space inside the royal palace, and all the emperor's wives are suing for his release. Including you, my beauty." He paused, his gaze profound. "In the scale of justice, neither laity nor royalty is permitted to claim special privileges," he murmured thoughtfully.

"The followers of Prince Khusrau impaled alive! Two of his men sown, one in the skin of an ox, and the other in the skin of a donkey. The one dying a wretched death, and the other surviving miraculously. Were those the acts of justice, Your Majesty?" was Nur Mahal's low comment.

"If you were to become the emperor's conscience, Nur, he would have no chance to delight in your beauty," Jahangir murmured to himself. "Traitors dying the treacherous deaths, those are the laws of the empire, Nur, not of the emperor's. You have yet to experience the puddles of tragedies in this world, if you are willing to share the emperor's burdens, along with his desire. This heart bruised and lacerated!"

"That Sikh Guru by the name of Arjun," Nur Mahal commenced heedlessly, "the one who favored Prince Khusrau and blessed the prince on his way to Lahore. Was he not executed, his property confiscated? In the name of justice, Your Majesty?"

"Treason demands not mercy, but vengeance, sweet inquisitor." Jahangir laughed suddenly. "When would this inquisition end?"

"As soon as I contrive to pull the chain of justice, Your Majesty, pleading for the release of Prince Khusrau." Nur Mahal laughed.

"The emperor would spare your lovely hands the labor of such an unbecoming task, my Nur," Jahangir quipped. "The emperor will sanction Prince Khusrau's release after the wedding ceremonies are over." He sought his chair, and sank into its velvety comfort. "And now let the emperor worship you. The witchcraft of your beauty is much more favorable to me than the shafts of your intellect and inquisition. They make me forget my desire." His eyes were lit up with the warmth of adoration. "I have ordered the construction of a grand palace at Lahore, just for you, my precious Nur. It would be named Nur Mahal."

"And the tomb of Anarkali, is that not in Lahore too?" An abrupt pang of jealousy escaped Nur Mahal's sense of euphoria.

"The Great Empress jealous of a dead beloved of the emperor?" Jahangir murmured sadly. "Can you heal the emperor's heart, love?" His voice was barely audible.

"She is more alive than the oceans of love throbbing inside my heart, Your Majesty. Do you think that my heart doesn't bleed?" Nur Mahal averted her gaze.

"Your heart is like a diamond, my love, with the power of cutting, but never receiving a scratch in return." Jahangir moaned with all the passion of a great lover.

"This diamond hides a ruby in its pulse, the color of blood, Your Majesty," Nur Mahal murmured.

"Turn not thy cheek, without thee I cannot live a moment. For thee to break one heart is equal to a hundred murders."

Jahangir laughed. "The couplets of the dead poets are still simmering in my head. But this one is my own creation, from the deepest deep within my soul."

"Your Majesty! An already broken heart, your heart, that is, needs mending, not breaking." Nur Mahal joined the emperor in his mirth. "Pour me a goblet of wine, Your Majesty, and I would drink to your health." Her voice was one ripple of a cataract.

"May the emperor share this toast of health with you, for he has only one goblet?" Jahangir reached out for the flagon eagerly, and filled the goblet to the brim. "The emperor will drink to your wit and beauty—and wisdom." He drained half the goblet before holding it out to her. "And what wise council did you lend to the ambassadors from Surat, Turan and Deccan?"

"The first embassy, Your Majesty, was from some T. Smith from London, the governor of the East India Company," Nur Mahal began avidly. "He requested a trade agreement between us and England. To this request, I granted their ships full sanction to land at the Moghul ports in compliance with the Moghul laws. Our dyes, spices, opium, ginger, pepper and textiles will fetch high prices if we trade with England. Very lucrative, in exchange for the worthless commodities which could be purchased from them at a low price. Of course, I had to use your royal seal, Your Majesty, to cement this agreement," she added cheerfully.

"You will have your own seal pretty soon, my beauty." Jahangir smiled, adoration shining in his eyes. "And coins will be struck in your name. You will be the empress of the world, love!" One ripple of a prophecy escaped his lips. "Feed me with the import of the other embassies as briefly as possible, my love. I can't fight the commands of my heart much longer; it is aching to hold you into its arms."

"I have a heart too, Your Majesty, remember? A diamond with a ruby in the middle," Nur Mahal murmured. "And if it keeps throbbing with the violence of love, you would never learn about the embassies."

"Your wit is greater than your passion, my love." Jahangir reclaimed his goblet, draining it quickly. "Proceed, my sweet, before the emperor carries you to his own royal bed. You might have to design another gown before the wedding ceremonies are over."

"Your Majesty!" Nur Mahal protested. "The embassy from Surat was folded shut by my own unwillingness to listen to their strings of apologies," she began sweetly. "The rest you know, Your Majesty. The Portuguese lamenting their folly after burning the Moghul vessels at Goa, all hundred and twenty of them. The burning of ship *Rhimi* was an accident, they still claim, and maintain the same story. Their offer of three *lakh* of rupees as compensation for the losses of Moghul ships is not accepted by me. The Portuguese ambassador had the audacity to request that the English be expelled from the Moghul ports. That is when I dismissed him with an explicit order to return to Goa till further orders from the emperor."

"And what are the emperor's orders, my Nur?" Jahangir asked amusedly.

"None, Your Majesty, so far," Nur Mahal quipped. "If I may suggest, Your Majesty, let the English and the Portuguese fight their own battles at the sea. Since you have banned the Portuguese from trade, they dare not attack the Moghul ships anymore."

"What fate befell, if I may ask, the Turani ambassador from the wand of your charming judgment, my love?" Jahangir's eyes were gathering warmth and wistfulness.

"All love and goodwill, Your Majesty." Nur Mahal's enthusiasm was ebbing and splintering. "Turan has Imam Quli Khan as its kind and generous monarch. He has sent us rare and precious gifts. Also, a letter from her mother, who is longing to meet me."

"And the emperor is longing to taste the wine of your beauty, my Nur." Jahangir eased himself up slowly and thoughtfully, his very gaze unrobing her.

"Your Majesty!" pleaded Nur Mahal. "Don't you wish to know about the Deccani embassy?"

"Deccan…" Jahangir's thoughts were left unuttered as his eunuch at the door sought his attention.

"What storms are brewing in your eyes, Itibar Khan? The emperor is not needed at the wedding festivities till late in the afternoon."

"No, Your Majesty." Itibar Khan fell into a hasty curtsy. "The Jain monk, Siddhichandra, is craving your audience, Your Majesty."

"Siddhichandra." An impatient murmur escaped Jahangir's lips, but then he smiled. "Send him in." His smile was whimsical and reminiscent.

Itibar Khan retraced his steps in a flurry of curtsies, and Jahangir rewarded him with a gracious smile. The emperor's hands were folding behind his back in a tight knot once again, as if he was restraining his passion to crush Nur Mahal into his arms. Nur Mahal's eyes and her cheeks, with a blush of rose, were making him giddy with desire. But since his thoughts had quickly arrested the young and handsome face of Siddhichandra, they were in mutiny against his heart, commanding him to test the chastity of this monk. His caprice was more overpowering than his passion, and he was tempted to indulge in a few moments of capricious interlude.

Siddhichandra was announced by the eunuch, and he stumbled into the library under some spell of shock and disbelief. His curtsy was impeccable though, after which he stood facing the emperor, his look still dazed.

"Sit at the feet of the empress, Siddhichandra. On this wedding day of our royal son, she is in a mood to receive embassies." Jahangir laughed, stealing a meaningful look at Nur Mahal.

Siddhichandra was startled to awareness. He had not noticed the empress right under his nose, and she was watching him with interest and kindness. Her eyes had sealed a pact of mischief with the emperor, and she was now smiling to herself. Siddhichandra's former disbelief in being admitted to the library was further heightened with astonishment in gaining this privilege to be with the empress. His curtsy was awkward, as he slumped at her feet as if kneeling before a goddess.

"Before you present your embassy to the empress, Siddhichandra, let the emperor persuade you to renounce your vow of asceticism." Jahangir was trying not to laugh. "You are handsome, Siddhichandra. Your youth is meant for the pleasure of contact with the bodies of young girls. Why, then, you waste it upon the desert of severe austerities?"

"Your Majesty!" Siddhichandra's cheeks were flushed with blotches of pink. "Your Majesty, the strength of a religious commitment counts not the years. In fact, young have more energy to discipline their minds, and to seek the treasures in their souls. As far as my handsomeness is concerned, it is insignificant. I have trained my mind not to be affected by vanity and to remain unattached. It stays unaffected by the worldly pleasures." He lowered his eyes.

"You are well versed in the doctrines of Hindu ashrama, I am sure, Siddhichandra," Nur Mahal began softly. "Initial renunciation, then indulgence, and final renunciation." She watched Siddhichandra lift his eyes, and continued. "Asceticism is meant for those who have sated their desires with pleasure and incontinence, not for those who have yet to experience them. You are young, almost twenty-five, you told me yourself. Don't you wish to have a wife, and children of your own?" she coaxed gently.

"I am wedded to my religion, Great Empress," was Siddhichandra's choked confession.

"You are drunk by the wine of your own austerities, my young monk," Jahangir teased happily. "The emperor is going to banish you to the forest, where the celibate trees woo not the vestal lilies. But tell me, what made you seek the emperor's audience on this great day of his son's wedding?" Edicts of dismissal were shining in his eyes.

"My guru, Your Majesty, he is ill. Feverish and delirious," Siddhichandra began all flustered. "So far none of the remedies prescribed by the physicians have helped him. I pleaded for an audience, Your Majesty, hoping that your generosity...that you may send your physician from Persia to attend my guru." His very eyes were pleading.

"And you have trained your mind not to be affected by anything?" Jahangir smiled sadly. "You have my permission to talk with Mahabat Khan. Inform him that by the emperor's orders he is to send Hakim Sadra to your guru." He waved dismissal.

Siddhichandra rose to his feet in some daze of joy and gratitude, bowing low before the emperor and the empress, and then fleeing as if pressed by the very hands of fates to save the life of his guru.

"He has a noble and virtuous heart, Your Majesty, endowed with strength and discipline," Nur Mahal sang mirthfully. "It is wrong of us to goad him to renounce his vow of chastity."

"Celibacy is not a virtue but a curse from the very gods, my love. Rather a temptation for the fools to renounce all joys in life in hope of gaining bliss in the life hereafter." Jahangir assisted her to her feet, catching her into one eager embrace, and kissing passionately.

"Your Majesty." Nur Mahal could barely murmur, as if swooning. "Such impropriety! Eunuchs have eyes on the back of their heads…" Her words as well as her thoughts were a tremor of appeals. "Feasting and celebrations await us downstairs."

"The emperor is accustomed to feasting before the feasting, love." Jahangir released her laughingly. "Your most obedient slave, my Nur." He spirited her out of the library most gallantly.

The hall of mirrors spruced with garlands was the abode of the wedding ceremonies, where Jahangir and Nur Mahal landed without ceremony. The khattak dance was at its culmination, the bhutans tapping and twirling, while the dancers swirled on their feet in rhythm with the music. Farther down the hall was a stage furnished with ferns in brass pots and tall floral arrangements. The musicians on this stage were testing their instruments to evoke bhangra tunes for the next dance. But the khattak dance was the frenzy of the moment. The ladies in velvet and brocade gowns with their partners in silken robes and jeweled turbans were creating a tapestry of colors while twirling and pirouetting.

Amidst this ocean of music and festivity, the royal servants in white robes and crimson turbans were scurrying back and forth, serving sweets and fruits. The wine-bearers too, with gold flagons in their arms, were eager to replenish the jeweled cups. The aunts, the mothers, the daughters, and all the emperor's wives were there too, their coiffeurs blazing with jewels and flowers.

The low stage, smothered in velvets with a gold canopy overhead, was offering a pleasant refuge to the bride and the bridegroom. Arjumand Banu was wearing a gown of white silk, clustered with rubies in the pattern of roses. A tiara of rubies and diamonds was glowing over her black, pleated hair with its own blaze of glory and radiance. Her delicate eyebrows were penciled, and her long, raven eyelashes were lending her the appearance of a sleeping beauty, much younger than her nineteen springs of youth and girlhood. Prince Khurram, seated beside her, was no less an object of admiration in youth and handsomeness. In contrast to his bride, he was looking older than his twenty years of princely bearing, stumbling on the verge of manhood. His white turban with a red plume was studded with rubies and diamonds.

Jahangir and Nur Mahal were lost into the melee of music and festivity, fluttering from one end of the hall to the other with a thousand interruptions on the way, greeting and laughing like the two young lovers caught in the serenade of royal amenities. All hearts could be felt throbbing in envy at Nur Mahal's rare gown and jewels, for no one in this royal household had the skill or the courage in designing or flaunting such exquisite designs. The other wives of the emperor were too proud to acknowledge her talents, though complimenting her only to please the emperor.

Amidst a whirlwind of greetings, Jahangir had lost sight of Nur Mahal. He had barely dismissed a beau of princes when he found himself standing close to a circle of dancers, alone and unattended. The young dancers were caught into a frenzy of rhythm as he stood watching, fascinated by the tilaks on their foreheads and studs in their noses, which seemed to follow their own tunes in blaze and intensity. All of a sudden, he felt cold and abandoned. Slowly and gradually, he was being sucked into a world where there was nothing but loneliness and desolation. The stark naked vacuum of silence, utter and absolute. A shuddering canvas on the very waves of sand-dunes was etching a face, Anarkali. The emperor with his cup of wine poised before him was defacing that vision. His gaze was searching Nur Mahal, his mind bent on destroying the portrait of Anarkali. A strip of reality was emerging before his sight against some haze of memory and nostalgia. Inside him were silence and darkness, but the face of Nur Mahal's cousin, Jafar Beg, was bobbing up and down before his eyes like a rude intrusion. Jafar Beg was wending his way toward the emperor, his face wreathed in smiles.

"Your Majesty, I regret I didn't get the honor of greeting you at the wedding celebrations in the palace of Asaf Khan," Jafar Beg declared. "Please accept my deepest gratitude for raising my standard to three hundred horse and men." He bowed his head.

"One of these days you might be trooping down the jungles of Bengal on lengthy campaigns, Jafar. Then, you won't feel so grateful." Jahangir laughed. "Any news of importance, Jafar, great or small, that you might wish to share with the emperor?"

"Muqarab Khan is converted to Christianity, Your Majesty." Jafar Beg was quick to release this bit of information. "By Father Corsi or by Father Xavier, I am not sure."

"Muqarab Khan, the greatest of surgeons, and my own personal vizier!" Jahangir's eyes were kindling a blaze of mirth. "How the Great Providence works is beyond our mortal understanding. Maybe he will be more skilled in healing the emperor now that he is under the shadow of the healer, Jesus Christ." He laughed.

Asaf Khan, standing not too far, was quick to join the emperor. He was endowed with a nature quite bold and vivacious. But he had grown more bold now that his daughter was being wedded to the emperor's son.

"May I join the emperor and share his happiness, Your Majesty?" Asaf Khan's eyes were changing colors like the opals in his mauve turban.

"With great pleasure, the emperor welcomes you, Asaf. Especially now that your jewel of a daughter has become a precious ornament in the crown of my beloved son." Jahangir smiled affably. "My son, he is so much in love with your daughter that he seems drowned inside the ocean of his own longings sweet and ineffable!"

More royalty were gathering around the emperor. Asmat Begum and Itmadudaula Khan were not far behind, lured toward this royal circle by the mirth and gaiety of the emperor. Jahangir's gaze was welcoming the parents of his Nur Mahal, and his thoughts were bursting forth into tides of raillery.

"I hear you are practicing the arts of necromancy, Asmat Begum?" Jahangir's gaze was teasing Asmat Begum.

"Who dared make such a vile accusation against me, Your Majesty?" Asmat Begum beamed with much pleasure.

"The emperor himself!" Jahangir laughed. "The emperor's heart could not be slain by the beauty of your daughter alone, unless it was bewitched by the charms and amulets crafted by her mother." His thoughts were effacing the vision of Anarkali.

"I am testing my skills in making perfumes, Your Majesty, if this talent falls under the category of necromancy," Asmat Begum quipped brightly.

"No one knows my plight!" Itaqid Khan protested from behind, flashing a warm look at his mother. "I am the one commanded to gather roses from the gardens."

"And who is assigned the job of watching the rose petals boil and simmer all night? Who else, but me." Itmadudaula Khan sought his wife's attention.

"Besides roses, Itaqid, didn't you gather precious gifts from all over the empire?" Jahangir asked. "When are you going to parade them before the emperor?"

"Whenever you command, Your Majesty." Itaqid Khan smiled broadly. "The rarities which I have chosen to present to you as gifts, I have brought with me, only awaiting your permission to be paraded before you, Your Majesty."

"What are those rarities, my gallant vizier, if the emperor may ask?" Jahangir's eyes were shining with interest.

"The birds of prey, such as Yaks, hawks and falcons, Your Majesty. And the ponies of the most exquisite breed," Itaqid Khan began with the pride of an adventurer. "The jade inkpots and the alabaster vases. The chests of ebony with koftgari designs. The sandalwood tables with the inlay of lapis lazuli. Musk bags, navels of musk, and the skins of musk antelopes. Daggers of gold, and jeweled swords. Many, many more rarities, Your Majesty, just to name a few." He was getting flustered.

"And no zebras, whom the painter of fate has colored with a strange brush?" Jahangir teased. "Don't forget to summon the court painters when those birds of prey are presented to the emperor, especially Mansard; he has a great skill in painting the colorful plumage. These birds must be preserved for posterity." His aesthetic senses were soaring, but getting caught midway at the appearance of Sahiba Jamali.

Sahiba Jamali's high coiffure decked with pearls and rosebuds could not be missed by the emperor, as she sailed closer in her gown of pink silks. Her hazel eyes were glinting accusations, though she chirped happily.

"Since the emperor is not requesting his wives to dance with him, they have decided to honor him with their own requests." Sahiba Jamali offered her arm.

"To dance with you, my mistress of beauty, is the emperor's honor, entirely, if he can get away from his royal brood." Jahangir's attention was diverted to his son, Prince Perwiz. "Come here, my besotted prince, and seek guidance from the emperor."

Prince Perwiz stumbled forward. He was quick to notice his mother beside the emperor, and steadied his step, his eyes pleading some sort of favors. Sahiba Jamali stood smoothing her gown, her own gaze tender and comforting.

"You are espoused to your gold cup, my heedless prince, while your wife languishes in utter neglect," Jahangir chided, no rebuke shining in his eyes.

"Your Majesty!" Prince Perwiz laughed. "This is the occasion for drinking and feasting, Your Majesty."

"Every blithering day is a holy feast for you, my drunken lout of a prince. An orgy of oblivion and drunkenness!" Jahangir declared with the mingling of rage and sympathy. "You are to be dispatched on a Deccani campaign since Prince Khurram must stay with his newly wedded bride, for a few months at least."

"I would exchange my cup for a sword, Your Majesty," Prince Perwiz murmured contritely.

The emperor was about to shoot another command, but the sudden appearance of Jagat Gosaini was checking his thoughts. She was haloed by the light of *naurattan*, a tiara of nine jewels, her brocades rustling. Her agate eyes were attaining the color of wine, as if spilling joy from the very font of celebration on this day of her son's wedding.

"Your Majesty, on this auspicious day of our son's wedding, you should be dancing and scattering gold, not wasting these precious moments in idle gossip." Jagat Gosaini sailed closer.

"You have scattered enough gold already from your lovely eyes, my white rose! Or, should the emperor say, Bilqis Makani, since this title becomes you, the lady of pure abode?" Jahangir could not help laughing. "And as for the dance, my love, the emperor is engaged for the first dance." He snatched Sahiba Jamali's hand and whirled her away.

The gleam and ripple in silks and jewels were merging with the tides of bhangra music amidst its frenzied beats. The snapping of the fingers and the clapping of the hands were shooting forth waves of colors from jeweled rings and armlets. The partners were taking turns, clapping and whirling. The emperor's red turban with a large ruby in the middle could be seen undulating in waves upon waves of colors as he danced and changed partners. His tall figure with graceful movements was floating like a painted shadow, following his partners with the quicksilver ease of an adept dancer. The *bhangra* tunes were ebbing to a culmination. The men were standing and clapping, while the ladies were pirouetting on their toes, circling around their partners. This scene was changing, now the ladies were clapping, and the men wooing the ladies with the athletic zest of the acrobats. The drums were sounding a crescendo, and the feet of the dancers were shot in the air before landing on the floor with the fury of a thunder. The arms of the men were looping around the waists of the ladies, while they stood there with their backs arched and heads thrown back in a gesture of swooning.

The emperor's hands were locked behind his back, as he danced his way out of the bhangra circle. Sahiba Jamali behind him, panting and breathless. More of the emperor's wives were crowding around him, demanding the pleasure of dancing with him. But he was evading them all, blowing kisses at them, and escaping their protests and demands. He was drifting farther and farther away from the realm of music and dancing.

Finding his wine-bearer at his elbow, Jahangir snatched a goblet from him, and quaffed it thirstily. He was about to demand more, when he caught sight of his mother approaching him imperiously. She was followed by Nur Mahal who was entertaining her with wit and humor, it was obvious, for Mirayam Uzzmanni had begun to smile.

"Ah, Miryam Uzzmanni! No wonder your title means the Mother of the Universe," Jahangir exclaimed happily. "You have brought back my jewel, my own Nur Mahal. I had lost her into the clouds of merriment." He claimed her hands into his own, and kissed her on the cheek. "All the fortunes smile on you, this auspicious day, dear Mamma. The wedding of your grandson, and the empire of Hind at your feet." He stole a glance at Nur Mahal before returning his gaze to his mother.

"While my other best loved grandson sits forlorn inside the royal prison of his own palace, Your Majesty." Miryam Uzzmanni sighed to herself.

"Prince Khusrau would be permitted to visit me as often as he wishes, dear Mamma. Soon, very soon." Jahangir breathed quickly, noticing, with relief, the approach of Salima Sultan.

Salima Sultan was another surviving wife of the late emperor, the father of Jahangir, the Great Akbar. She was styled Padishah Begum after Akbar's death, and still retained that title and status. Salima Sultan flashed a kind smile at Nur Mahal, and bestowed upon the emperor the sweetest of smiles reserved for him alone. Then she turned to Miryam Uzzmanni.

"That endless parade of wedding ceremonies, Miryam Uzzmanni, everyone is missing you and wondering," Salima Sultan began softly. "They are right in wondering that you must be indulging in the pleasure of talking with your son, and neglecting to be with your grandson who needs your blessings." A shadow of pain crossed her features all of a sudden, accentuating her pallor.

"It is no pleasure talking with the emperor when he carries the weight of farmans in his very eyes," Miryam Uzzmanni responded with a dint of regret.

"Mamma!" Jahangir exclaimed, shifting his attention to Salima Sultan. "Don't heed Mamma, she has nothing but criticism for the emperor. But how pale you look? Even the fire of jewels is not lending any color to your cheeks. I must command Hakim Sadra to tend to your health," he demurred aloud.

"It is nothing, Your Majesty. Just plain fatigue. After the wedding, I will have blooms on my cheeks," Salima Sultan murmured soothingly. She slipped her arm around Miryam Uzzmanni's waist, and led her away quietly.

"Where did you fly off, my Nur? Leaving the emperor alone and desolate," Jahangir chanted merrily, as soon as the royal ladies had left.

"Dancing is not exactly a lonesome indulgence, Your Majesty." Laughter bubbled in Nur Mahal's eyes, as she added, "Quite far from being desolate."

"So, you have been spying on the emperor, my wicked beauty." Jahangir laughed.

"Who could miss the tall, handsome emperor wearing my heart as a teardrop ruby in his red turban, Your Majesty?" Nur Mahal joined him in his mirth.

"Centuries of wait, and continents apart you have stayed away from me, my love, and now you jest," Jahangir intoned hoarsely.

"We should not let more centuries slip past, Your Majesty, lest the royal couple miss your blessings." Nur Mahal shifted her attention to the garlanded stage.

She stood watching the bride, her lovely niece, whom she adored with all her heart and soul, though her heart right this moment was praying for the sprigs of joy and peace inside the heart of the emperor. Her marble profile appeared cold as ice, and the jewels radiating fire around her face could not dissolve the chill and pallor in her features. Even the flames of ardor and intensity in Jahangir's eyes were lending no warmth to her cheeks, his gaze following hers, feverish and unseeing.

To the left of the garlanded stage, a group of young dancers were pirouetting on their feet. These lithe dancers with bare waists and layers upon layers of chiffon draped over their hips, were lending the whole scene a semblance of some dream where mists could be seen merging with colors, ethereal and shifting. The guests were standing there entranced, their eyes following each little movement of the dancers, perfumed and bejeweled. A bevy of singers in the background with gleaming studs in their noses were absorbed in such artistry of song and music that no musician could vie with their talents. They were playing thirteen pairs of talas at once and in unison. All fair musicians of this fairest sex had two cymbals on each wrist, two on each shoulders, one on each breast, and two on the fingers of each hand.

Nur Mahal's thoughts were swept into the tempest of this music as she stood there rapt, oblivious even to the presence of the emperor beside him. Jahangir too was stricken with awe and admiration, his aesthetic senses not only arresting the tunes, but the loveliness of art with all its perfection. For some strange reason, his sight and senses were rejecting this artistic vision of beauty and harmony, all of a sudden. He was lonesome, his gaze restless and wandering, finally settling on the bride and the bridegroom. The bride's eyes were closing, as if contemplating bliss, if not the joys of her wedding night. Prince Khurram was admiring the jewels presented to him by Itmadudaula Khan. The belly dancers before him were trying to attract his attention, but nothing could entice him away from the sparkling gems in his possession. *Not even the beauty of his young bride!* Jahangir was thinking.

"My son, another Jain monk!" Jahangir exclaimed abruptly. "Look, Nur, how he admires the jewels? Assessing their worth, while the jewel-like dancers tempt not his ascetic heart. Not even the lily-white purity of his bride, the emperor thinks?"

"Ascetic, Your Majesty, I disagree," Nur Mahal murmured softly. "He has the most passionate of hearts ever found throbbing inside the bosom of any young man. He has great reverence for form and color in jewels, I admit, and is admiring their beauty, not their worth." Her look was dreamy as she turned to face the emperor.

"The same as the emperor's heart! My own heart throbbing in his bosom, then? And a part of it which is left in me, not quite young, but passionate just the same." Jahangir smiled. "Come, love, the emperor must look into the passionate heart of his son, before he dares discover his own." He offered her his arm.

The emperor and Nur Mahal had reached the garlanded stage with only a few interruptions on the way. At their intended approach, the sea of guests was parting to carve a path for the royal couple. Prince Khurram had abandoned his jewels, and was now enamored by his jewel of a bride. The nuptial ceremonies were coming close to a blessed conclusion, for the court maulvi had closed his holy book and was reciting no more suras from the Quran. Two servants in crimson robes, carrying gold bowls, were offering rosewater to the bride and the bridegroom. After the ceremonial washing of their hands in rosewater, the royal couple had signed their marriage contract, and were showered with applause with a mingling of blessings and felicitations.

The showers of rose petals from the balconies above were bathing all in color and perfume, especially the bride and the bridegroom. The wedding songs were bursting forth afresh with tunes sweet and nostalgic. An ocean of dancing girls with silver trays balanced on their arms were floating toward the royal couple with gifts and felicitations. First and foremost, the wedding gifts of the emperor were presented to the newlyweds by the very hands of the dancers. They were quick to empty their silver trays laden with rings, the armlets, the necklaces, all gleaming in gold settings, all flawless and exquisite.

The newlyweds were dismounting the garlanded stage, the emperor scattering gold and silver coins at their feet. Prince Khurram was in raptures, his arm slipped around the waist of his bride most possessively. He was pressing her close to him, as if holding on to a dream, his eyes feverish and glowing. The look on his young face was almost of agony and rapture, as if he was afraid that this happy dream would fade if he relinquished his hold on his bride.

"Soon, you would be whirled into the frenzy of wedding dances, Khurram Baba, and they would drain your energy and passion, if you do not replenish them with wine!" Jahangir's eyes were lit up with a buoyant smile "A cup of wine on your wedding day, and you would be soaring to the very gates of the heavens."

"I am in heaven, Your Majesty," Prince Khurram declared passionately. "Besides, Your Majesty, I consider wine my enemy," was his giddy comment.

Jahangir began to laugh uncontrollably. His eyes sparkling with a poetic gleam. One quatrain by Avicenna was uncurling its lips in his thoughts, and he began to recite as if it was his own mad inspiration.

"Wine is a raging enemy, a prudent friend. A little is an antidote, but much a snake's poison. In much there is no little injury. In a little there is much profit."

Jahangir turned to Nur Mahal. "What do you say in defense of our wedded prince, my lovely empress?" he asked laughingly.

"That our prince is most prudent." Nur Mahal laughed.

The festive dances were sprouting and expanding in tides upon tides of music and gaiety. Prince Khurram was drifting into the rhythms of music and dancing irresistibly, but relinquishing not his hold on his lovely bride. The other princes requesting a dance with his bride were turned away by the sheer violence of fever and denial in his eyes, and they were pleading no more. Only the emperor had the privilege of claiming one dance with his daughter-in-law. He had indulged in a few more dances with his other wives and with Nur Mahal, but now he was getting wearied of all dances and festive celebrations. Caught unawares, Jahangir was whirled into the bhangra circle once again by the witchcraft of Nur Mahal, though she herself was whirling away with other partners. The wedding feast was being announced amidst the thunder of clapping and dancing, but Jahangir's thoughts were bent on escaping this dancing and feasting. He was moving in flow with the dancers, his eyes following Nur Mahal. The ladies were clapping now, and the men circling around them with their fingers snapping and their backs swinging. Waiting for such an opportunity, Jahangir floated toward Nur Mahal, his feet tapping and his arms swinging, and he snatched her away from this bhangra madness.

"The emperor needs fresh air, love." Jahangir pulled her along, his expression urgent and desperate. "The feasting would last till midnight, if not till dawn! And yet, the emperor needs to feast on your beauty alone," he murmured.

"The begums will send an arrest warrant for the emperor, if they didn't see him in the feasting hall," Nur Mahal murmured back.

Endowed with the nobility of her heart and with a clear perception, Nur Mahal had sensed the emperor's sadness even before he had come gliding to snatch her away from the tempest of music and dance. Nur Mahal allowed herself the luxury of being snatched away from this arena of music and dancing, though thinking sadly to herself, *sadness has made a permanent abode inside the heart of the emperor.* But once they had stepped out on to the verandah of this red sandstone palace, both were quiet in their own separate worlds. Nur Mahal was feeling a nameless sting inside the very fabric of her silence, the ache of sadness inside her reaching the very cores of her soul. Rarely would she feel sad, and that too in brief interludes. Her sadness, though numbered few, was of cosmic revelations, when her heart would yearn to fathom the mystery of injustices done to one in one's short life. And right now, without any rhyme or reason, she was aware of many injustices done to mankind by mankind. Her thoughts were holding on to one spike of an injustice done to her. *The emperor professes to love me, but he is in love with the apparition of Anarkali,* Nur Mahal was thinking. She could peer into the soul of the emperor with much more ease than into her own; she could hear her thoughts.

Jahangir's thoughts were in rapport with Nur Mahal's. They too were professing clarity of vision in knowing the heart of his beloved. Both were unaware that they were claiming the gift of clairvoyance, though they could not divine the needs of their own souls, much less enter the psyche of each other.

The royal gardens were welcoming his sight, and his mood was of quiet and reverie, nurturing not sadness, but solitude. They were both lonely, utterly and absolutely lonely, and that was the only truth they knew about each other. That alone, and nothing more! The emperor loved Nur Mahal the only way he knew he was capable of loving her. There was only one altar in his soul, where both Nur Mahal and Anarkali reigned supreme. The latter was the goddess of his loss and the former, the goddess of his love. Both the dearest and profoundest of his loves, and both irreplaceable and unforgettable.

The red sandstone palace looming above the gardens appeared to follow the royal couple as they promenaded toward the terraces in utmost silence. The eaves, the domes and the cupolas were spangled with colorful streamers. Even the Moghul standards with couchant lion shadowing a part of the body of the sun were unfurled on stately pillars as a part of the embellishments to honor Prince Khurram's wedding. The marble fountains were gurgling in the distance. The emperor and Nur Mahal were living their own dreams inside the quiet hush of their own hearts and thoughts. The heavy perfume of the Indian roses was drugging their senses, and they could not help but savor it passionately.

The gardens were quiet and dreamy. Even the gardeners had retired to their humble abodes, awaiting the promise of a magnificent feast from the royal kitchens. Only the finches and the hoopoes had stayed, celebrating their own freedom, and caring not for the sumptuous feasts. They could be seen frolicking in the wind, or gliding down to rest into the arms of the poplars.

The emperor was choosing not to follow the manicured paths, but straying farther from the palace and the gardens. One familiar moat with its goldfish protected by a fringe of reeds had attracted his attention, and he was lured toward it as if drifting in a dream. Claiming Nur Mahal's hand absently, he was climbing the quaint, little bridge splashed with wild ivy and bridal creeper. The moat was small, and it was left behind as if vanishing in a flash without their ever crossing it. The grass was tall here, and farther down were the mighty oaks and jacaranda trees, tracing a path toward the palace gates. The gateway itself was strewn with garlands from the very bower of roses.

Jahangir's gaze was fixed to the front gateway where his feet had come to a sudden halt, involuntarily. Nur Mahal was standing beside him quiet and contemplative. Her gaze too was arrested to the gateway where two majestic elephants carved in stone, bearing the life-size statues of the Rajput heroes, Patta and Jaimal, were staring back at her. Jahangir's gaze was kindling to awareness. He turned suddenly, breaking Nur Mahal's contemplative silence with a declaration of his own.

"Who are these men, my Nur? Do you know? The dust of their bodies is cemented in these stones till eternity, for us to behold and admire," Jahangir reminisced aloud.

"The Rajput heroes, Your Majesty," Nur Mahal intoned softly, her look sad and profound. "Your father, didn't he kill them at the battle of Chitor?"

"They were the mighty foes of the mighty Moghuls, my love," Jahangir began whimsically. "Yes, my father killed them, but he admired their valor and might. And after his victory at Chitor, he ordered these statues to be built in honor of their courage in battles. Carved in the book of history, these Rajputs would outlive the Moghuls, my love." He claimed her hand, making her walk beside him. "What sadness weighs heavy in our hearts and on our shoulders, love?" he murmured to himself.

"Your sadness becomes mine, Your Majesty," Nur Mahal murmured back.

"Leave the emperor's sadness to its own mute misery, love! It is a sickness no physician on this earth can ever heal, not even your love and beauty, the pearl of my harem." Jahangir elicited one sliver of a mirth.

"Afflicted with love as I am, Your Majesty, I can be a great physician to cure all ailments with love," Nur Mahal commented unconvincingly.

"Your most obedient patient, my love." Jahangir laughed, cantering ahead of her with the caprice of an adventurer.

Nur Mahal had ceased to think, only drifting along in conformity with the emperor's moods, shifting from one of caprice to quietude. They were standing at the other side of the moat once again. Nur Mahal was straggling a little apart, and the emperor was standing in one spot, rapt and oblivious. He was watching the mating of a pair of cranes. The naturalist inside him was filled with awe as if the treasures of the seven worlds were laid at his feet by the magic wand of nature's own munificence.

"Look, Nur, nature's miracle! A rare sight observed only by a privileged few," Jahangir declared without taking his eyes off the amorous birds.

Nur Mahal stirred, following the emperor's gaze, and stepping closer. Her sadness had left, but a nameless languor had clamped her senses to silence. The emperor's arm was slipping around her waist and drawing her closer, though he was still rapt in admiring the incontinence of the heedless birds.

"Have you ever seen such tenderness in love, my Nur, such wildness too?" Jahangir was murmuring. His lips were grazing against her cheek, but his eyes were locked to the cranes. "How the male is proud and aggressive? Yet, his kisses are tender. Watch his passionate attempts in taming his mate. Tender, yet wild. Ah, the spilling of passion, the culmination! Look, how the female swoons. The consummation of two tiny souls. In her eyes…small, beady eyes, you can see the bliss…the pain…and light supreme…. Yet, the mating of our own souls, is it any different…" He pressed her to him.

"The beauty of our gardens might reveal our hearts to each other. Let us explore their hearts before we discover ours."

The white, gleaming terraces were the companions of the emperor and Nur Mahal, as they lingered along the paths edged with moss roses. Behind them were the marble fountains cascading into ripples of light and music. They seemed to be drunk with the wine of nature and savoring each drop into the cups of their silence and nearness. Feeling closer than ever before, they were drifting together in some dream-haze of a paradise newly discovered. More like the night-lovers, they were exchanging confidences, their voices low and tremulous, as if they had just escaped from the jungles of a prying world, and had discovered these gardens as their perfect refuge.

A few gardeners were coming into view with lamps in their arms to light more paths and terraces which were left neglected. From the distance, they could see the blaze of red ruby in the emperor's turban and a halo of diamonds on Nur Mahal's head. But the emperor and Nur Mahal were entering the grove of pipals, interspersed with pomelo and jacaranda trees. They could inhale the scent of jasmine there, with the mingling of perfume from rat-ki-rani. Fields upon fields of more aromatic flowers were coming into view, *juhi, ketki, nargis* and *molsari*, just to name a few. The red and white *kaner* and the bright red *ratan manjari* appeared to wave at the royal couple, while swaying and swinging in the wind.

One small courtyard amidst sprawling lawns was the only vantage point where Jahangir halted to admire the glory of his gardens. He was holding Nur Mahal's hand, and his gaze penciling the scenic splendor inside the very canvas of his heart. There were no terraces here, but the neat, round beds of white tuberoses. Jahangir was leaving the courtyard, still holding Nur Mahal's hand. He could see the large cistern in the distance. He himself had ordered this cistern to be hewn out of a single block of sandstone, and to be filled with clear water. This cistern was Nur Mahal's talisman, as much a part of her as of the emperor. But right now as the emperor was literally dragging her toward it, her heart was breaking under the weight of sadness once again. His gaze was arrested to the carved numbers on the cistern wall, his name engraved in there, and the year 1611 chiseled in large, bold letters.

"Do you remember this, my love?" Jahangir's gaze was arrested to the carved letters. "The monument of our love and marriage. My humble wedding present to you, commemorating the year of our marriage." His voice was low and tender.

"Yes, Your Majesty." Nur Mahal's eyes were brimming with tears. "And the monument of love in Lahore, Anarkali's." One cry of pain was stifled inside her heart.

"Love!" Jahangir was startled to awareness. "My pearl, my soul." The kindling of fire and agony in his heart was enough to hurl him toward his beloved. "Our bridal night once more, love, this very night, and tears in your eyes." He held her into his arms, kissing away her tears. "For how long will you stay jealous of the dead, my love?"

"As long as you drown your anguish in wine, Your Majesty, seeking bliss in oblivion." Nur Mahal smiled through her tears.

"The slayer of my torment, you have slain my heart!" Jahangir declared under some spell of delirium. "And as for wine, my love, it matches not the sweetness on your lips. This ruby nectar, which serves not the emperor's needs when he needs it the most." His lips were scorching hers, the agony of his soul a blaze most savage.

Chapter Four

The four storey palace at Ajmer with its lofty chambers was bathed in a hush so profound, that not even a whiff of breeze dared make a whisper. Jahangir, seated at his rosewood desk, was making entries in his journal, the jeweled pen in his hand making long strokes as soundless as the profound hush inside this room. He had moved his court to Ajmer a year ago, now almost two years after the wedding of Prince Khurram. This particular afternoon, Jahangir had chosen this bedroom as his study to write down his impressions of the birds and the beasts, which his instincts as a naturalist had moved him to study during his pleasure excursions. The large bath with blue tiles and rose decor adjacent to this bedroom was occupied by Nur Mahal, who was finishing her toilette.

Almost three frolicking years had elapsed since Jahangir had wedded Nur Mahal, and he was still floating inside the mists of love lost and love gained. The tomb of Anarkali as well as Nur Mahal's palace at Lahore were complete, and both the emperor and the empress had visited these places at brief intervals of time. Jahangir had prayed earnestly at the tomb of Anarkali, but the dead beloved had no wish to leave the hedonist emperor to his hope of joy in living. She had come back, indeed, to torment the emperor! Alive and beautiful in the semblance of Nur Mahal, she had made a permanent abode inside the heart and soul of the emperor. Now that he was wedded to his living love, she was materialized like a tyrant to reign over his passions as the queen of agony. He could see nothing but Anarkali in the face of nature and into the eyes of Nur Mahal. Though possessed by the memory of Anarkali, he was hopelessly in love with Nur Mahal, loving both in the everlasting torment of his dreams and reveries. Nur Mahal, in return, was tormented by the duplicity of his love and despair. Each moment of her married life unfolded before her the cruel truth, that the emperor was capable only of loving the unforgotten and the unforgettable. Paradoxically, at the inception of such a loss when Jahangir was young and vulnerable, hope had become his foe and friend. And now that the hope had revealed itself in the guise of benevolence, it had plunged him deep into a pit of utter hopelessness.

All was not entirely hopeless, though. Jahangir was too much of a hedonist to even think of relinquishing the pleasures in living, or of letting his beloved suffer the dearth of feasting and entertainment. He was destined to love life as intensely as Nur Mahal herself, gathering both joys and pains out of the very husks of life. His need for oblivion had become stronger than ever before though, and inebriation itself was his sanctuary to numb the ache and yearning inside his heart, wild and passionate. He could not visit this sanctuary often, for Nur Mahal was always there to defeat his need with the ocean of her own love, always sweet, always irresistible. If wine was denied to him as a result of the charming appeals from the empress, her wit and beauty were enough to reward him with bounties of love. Besides, both loved sports and hunting, and pomp and ceremony, and Nur Mahal was getting skilled in planning such excursions in advance even before the emperor's mood, rather his need, could tempt him toward the rungs of inebriation. The emperor had relinquished all his power into the hands of this bewitching empress who reigned over his own joy and torment too, much like the Goddess of Love. A few of the royal duties, which he could not abandon, were performed by him with a feeling of disinterest and obligation. *Receiving embassies and issuing farmans to maintain peace and justice in his empire.* Even now as he sat delineating his impressions about the albino species of the birds, his thoughts were lumbering toward his throne outside this palace where he had to preside over the embassies, *joylessly.*

Jahangir's gaze as well as his thoughts were straying, before he could seal his well-cherished expressions with authenticity. His desk was facing the great window with damask drapes, the color of old rose, the gold tassels sweeping them back in neat folds. From where he sat he could see the abundance of early spring in foliage and flowers, against which the fountains stood bubbling. The day was much too lovely to be ignored, and the pen slipped from his hand, his gaze devouring the hush and beauty of his gardens with an aching tenderness. Before Anarkali could pervade his senses to dull misery, he whirled his chair around, the Bokhara carpet under his feet soft and protesting. The first thing which arrested his attention in this room was the large mahogany bed, with a canopy of rose and ivory. He was forcing his attention on the rosewood shelf where Nur Mahal had arranged his favorite poetry books. Several volumes were peering back at him, along with the marble vases and cedar boxes so craftily displayed. But Jahangir's gaze was shifting to the bedside table, its mother-of-pearl glistening in patterns of vines and flowers. A silver candelabrum and several clusters of tuberoses in a glass bowl were gracing this table. Right below the candelabrum was a book by Omar Khayyam, its green binding hugging the polished wood.

My Nur, how unpredictable, didn't take Omar Khayyam with her to the bath. Jahangir's eyes were closing shut at the inception of this thought alone.

Absurdly and inexplicably, he could hear laughter in his thoughts, which were unfolding a scene, arresting the form of one mad dog who had inflicted fatal wounds on two of his royal elephants. Then his thoughts were hovering over the deathbed of Inyat Khan. Inyat Khan was one of his courtiers, whom he had ordered to be brought to his presence so that he could observe the expressions of a man in his final stages of demise. He could hear the laughter in his thoughts as they sprang forth to embrace another memory which had nothing to do with death and dying. One daughter of a gardener was coming into view. She had no breasts and had hair on her chest, though in any other way she was an ordinary woman. The laughter was leaving Jahangir's thoughts at the sudden assault of another recollection—that of his own illness. He could vividly imagine his body burning with fever, his lips thirsting for wine, and Nur Mahal snatching the gold cup away form his trembling hands.

The taste of that fever and thirst was relinquished by Jahangir's thoughts, as more memories were sprouting forth to make him opiate and listless. While his thoughts were bound to tease and frolic, his hands had a mind of their own, feeling the smooth, round pearls in his ears. He had holes bored in his ears right after his recovery from that illness. *It was not caprice*, Jahangir's thoughts even now were adamant in professing, but *gratitude* to the saint who had bestowed upon him the gift of health. The fact was that while despairing of his health, the emperor had visited the tomb of Muinuddin Chishti, and had prayed fervently. Ill and desperate, the emperor had made a solemn vow at the grave of the dead saint that if his health was restored, he would bore holes in his ears in the fashion of the true disciples. His recovery was quick, and he had fulfilled his vow. After that, the emperor had become a frequent visitor to the tomb of Muinuddin Chishti.

Jahangir's eyes were still closed, his hands now limp into his lap, but his thoughts were feeling the fineries on his royal person. One great, uncut ruby in the middle of his turban was encircled with emeralds and diamonds. A jeweled dagger was slung at his waist, radiating its own fire of jewels. His thoughts now were crawling over the mounds of duties which he could not avoid, though Nur Mahal shared half the burden.

Nur Mahal? Nur Jahan, now! The light of the world! Didn't I bestow this title on her...after the death of Salima Sultan? Jahangir's thoughts were a volley of exclamations. *Salima Sultan! Had my father been alive, he would have mourned her death with ashes in his hair...to heal the bleeding wounds in his heart.*

Jahangir's thoughts were poetic, and gathering the mists of forgetfulness. He could hear his thoughts as if they were a string of hearts, throbbing away to cling to the mists of awareness. He had to attend a few embassies this afternoon, then visit the tomb of Muinuddin Chishti to participate in the ritual of feeding the poor. Beyond the limit of these two facts, Jahangir's thoughts were getting lost against the islands of clouds, gray and billowing. Reality was somewhere in abeyance, turning to ashes inside the flames of unreality. So absorbed was he inside the void of his thoughts, that he didn't even notice the rustle of silks, as Nur Jahan approached.

Nur Jahan was all perfumed and bejeweled. Her red silks broidered with silver rosettes appeared to cling to her tiny waist and ample bosom with a caressive softness. She was wearing the empire-style gown of her own design. It was open at the breast, artfully held together in ribbons of lace and satin. This entire gown was splashed with diamonds, each rosette boasting its own precious jewel in the middle. Noticing the emperor lost in reveries, she had paused in the middle of the room, folding her hands behind her back. She was holding a pair of ruby earrings in the palm of her right hand. Her fingers were closing around them as she floated closer. Standing behind the emperor's chair, she covered his eyes with her left hand.

"Who am I, Your Majesty? If you could guess, you would be rewarded with a set of ruby earrings," Nur Jahan murmured.

"How could I go wrong, my light of the world? Your very breath wafts the scent of roses," Jahangir laughed.

"Just because I *am* wearing the scent of roses!" Nur Jahan murmured. "This *itr*, the scent of roses, which Mamma invented. And what did she get in return?" She held out the rubies in the palm of her hand.

"My genius of a mother-in-law! I bestowed upon her a string of pearls. She was so grateful, she rewarded the emperor with the burden of her own gratitude? By naming her invention after me, itr-i-Jahangiri, is that what she said?" Jahangir claimed the earrings dreamily. "And the emperor, in return of her gratitude, my love, bestowed upon her daughter the title of Nur Jahan. My Nur." His voice was low and tender. "You deserve this title absolutely. Though it came late, only after the death of Salima Sultan styled as Padishah

Begum. Now the whole world bows before you! You are Padishah Begum and Nur Jahan, light of the world, my own Nur."

"Nur Jahan known only to you, Your Majesty. And Padishah Begum to the ladies of the harem alone." Nur Jahan was removing the pearl earrings off the emperor's ears.

"Ah, the emperor has neglected to proclaim this title to the world, is that so? It shall be done. You are the empress, love, you have to remind the emperor. He is extremely forgetful." Jahangir claimed her hand, kissing each finger blissfully. "And why must the emperor wear rubies instead of the pearls?" he asked capriciously.

"For two most significant reasons, Your Majesty." Nur Jahan stood admiring the rubies in his ears, which she had just replaced with the pearl ones. "First, the smooth, little pearls do not complement the uncut ruby in your turban. Secondly, since all the courtiers copy the emperor and are wearing pearl earrings, the emperor needs to steer them toward variety."

"And next time, you would be designing the empire-style robe for the emperor?" Jahangir laughed.

"If you could be persuaded to wear it, Your Majesty. It might start a new vogue in the court. But then I would have to invent an entirely new style of gowns to suit the ladies of the harem," Nur Jahan quipped brightly.

"Come, sweet, your wit alone is the occasion to celebrate. The emperor is thirsting for wine." Jahangir's sudden urge for wine was like one of his capricious moods. "Pour some for the emperor. Where did you hide the gold flagon?"

"Beyond your reach, and your imagination, Your Majesty!" Nur Jahan declared sweetly. "Besides, you have already exhausted your allowance of two cups in the morning, Your Majesty. And if you wish to drink one now, you won't get any in the afternoon." Her eyes were flashing mirth and rebuke.

"From your lips divine then. Much sweeter than the wine." Jahangir stumbled to his feet. He snatched her to him, crushing her lips with kisses wild and feverish.

All of a sudden, his thirst for love and wine was like fire inside him. It was rising to his lips, singeing them with the parched hungers of the soul, wild and turbulent. His thoughts too were hungering for violence, courting some hurricane of hatred which he had never seen before inside the storm clouds of his mind. He could feel the serpent of agony and torment inside him, revealing its own volcano of odium. The reek of desire oozing forth from its lips, to disfigure this beauty, to maim and destroy his love. Such savagery in pain! Such devastating rage and misery! He could feel it all, the pain and the paralysis. Wrenching himself free from his own violence, he swayed back. Stricken afresh by the witchcraft of her beauty, he stood there in awe, humbled, dazzled, gazing at her, absorbing the flash of diamonds in her eyes and on her royal person. His own mind was flashing the portrait of Anarkali, the author of hatred and violence. The lake-blue eyes of Anarkali were shining through the blue pools of Nur Jahan's.

"You need to lie down and catch your breath, my Nur, while the emperor tries to curb his passion for more wine." Jahangir began to pace in some stupor of pain and giddiness. "If the emperor wishes, he will have a reservoir of wine in this very room. And your beautiful eyes have to drain it every night, so that the emperor may drink from them even in his sleep."

"Remember, Your Majesty, the fever and the headaches? If I had not taken the wine away from you, you would have suffered more than want and craving." Nur Jahan could barely murmur, sinking into a chair beside the desk. "The health of the empire depends upon the health of the emperor, everyone knows that! If you don't trust me, ask your politicians and physicians, Your Majesty."

"Trust, my love, is an inadequate word in comparison with the physician who saved my life, *you*. And that's you and you alone. You are my saint and healer both!" Jahangir recalled under some spell of delirium. "Absolute surrender to your advice and judgment, that's how the emperor feels. Yes, surrender is the right word, branded on the lips of my heart and soul with the pen of love and gratitude. Imagine, you, the empress, treating me to all the healthy meals cooked by your own hands! And diverting my attention from wine with tales delicious and enchanting."

"And to soothe the rashes, rubbing your face with sweet unguents, Your Majesty! Just to raise your gall and fever, I suppose?" Nur Jahan resorted to wit.

Her lips were still smarting against the sting of hatred which she could not help but feel against the pools of frenzy and violence in the emperor's kisses, this hatred which she too had not ever noticed before during this brief period of love and conflict in marriage. True, his bouts in lovemaking, at times, could rise to the heights of brutal hungers, but not ever before had she felt this weight of hatred with all its fever of madness and violence. This strange discovery was numbing her senses and chilling her thoughts. She could feel the ache of loneliness inside the very silence of her soul and psyche. Though lonely herself, she could feel the pain and loneliness of the emperor. He was mired deep in sorrow, reliving the dead past, inside the very grave of Anarkali. Nur Jahan's thoughts were following the emperor in the ritual of his pacing.

"Had the burden of royal duties not compelled me to appear before my subjects, morning, noon and evening, I would have peeled those rashes off my face with my own hands. Permitting no physicians to tend me, but you, my sweet," Jahangir was saying.

Nur Jahan had fallen prey to her own reveries, but this confession of the emperor was reaching her awareness. In fact, it was having a startling affect upon her mute sufferings. She was stirring in her chair, the night-blue in her eyes stark and profound.

"That illness has passed, and so has the emperor's gall," Jahangir continued. "And now the emperor wishes to share this peace of good news with you. To burden you more with duties than love, my Nur." He was still pacing. "Our empire is mounting the rungs of peace, justice and prosperity. Ahad, the Afghan, was defeated on the very borders of Jalalabad. Rana Amar Singh of Mewar, he has submitted before our fortunate Prince Khurram without a fight. God of Mercy has destroyed Bahadur, the chief of Gujrat, though he died peacefully in his bed, taking along with him the leaven of turbulence and insubordination. The Portuguese were defeated by the hands of the English on the very port of Surat. Most of their vessels were burnt. The Portuguese, what tenacious spirits rule them? In their flight, they had the audacity to send a message to Muqarab Khan to sue for peace and intervention, claiming that they had come to the port with peaceful intentions, and that the English were the first ones to start the fight..." His feet were coming to a slow halt before his desk where Nur Jahan sat absorbed in admiring the bust of St. John's head cut in gold and amber. "You have not even caught one word out of the bulletin of my news, my Nur?" he murmured rather dolefully.

"Each word is engraved inside the tablets of my heart, Your Majesty." Nur Jahan turned her head slowly. "Your Majesty, the English are gaining too much power, I fear. They are assuming utmost authority over the ports and the cities, as if the whole empire belongs to them." Some alien fears and doubts were surfacing in her eyes.

"And what more do you fear, the light of my soul?" Jahangir asked quickly, lowering himself into his own gilt chair, and puzzled by the clouds of fears in her eyes.

"Your reputation, Your Majesty. Most of all, your whims and caprice," Nur Jahan responded serenely.

"The reputation of the emperors is tarnished if they are cruel, unjust or bigoted? Or malefic, or avaricious?" Jahangir began ponderously. "Do you think, my Nur, that any of those formidable vices are a part of the emperor's character?"

"None, Your Majesty," was Nur Jahan's evasive murmur of a response. "Yet cruelty and kindness, and all the conflicting vices and virtues reside in all of us."

"Honesty is dear to my heart, my precious Nur. Do you find the emperor cruel?" Jahangir's eyes appeared to search the very essence of beauty concealed within her.

"Yes, Your Majesty," Nur Jahan murmured reluctantly.

"What inspires you to accuse the emperor of cruelty?" Jahangir goaded softly.

"The demolition of that temple near Ajmer." Nur Jahan averted her gaze.

"Oh, that hideous monument! That emblem of ugliness and deformity." One snort of a laughter escaped Jahangir's lips. "A sore sight to my aesthetic senses! Are you talking about the same temple dedicated to Vishnu? Displaying an idol cut out of a black stone with a pig's head and the body of a man? My senses revolt at the mere thought of it. Had I not seen it, I would not have ordered it destroyed."

"Beauty and ugliness are relative terms, Your Majesty. If you destroy everything which offends your sight, you would attract a horde of enemies." Nur Jahan's eyes were now flashing. "What appears ugly to one may be a paragon of beauty to the other. Since one cannot preserve beauty from turning into ugliness, one has no right to turn ugliness into a heap of ruins. Besides, idols and temples are as sacred to the Hindus as mosques and gardens are to the Muslims."

"I have no theological abhorrence of idolatry in Hinduism, my Nur, but a visual repulsion of specific forms which thwart my personal sense of beauty," Jahangir thought aloud, a flood of interest shining in his eyes.

"Who would believe you, Your Majesty? Not your courtiers, who heard you declaring aloud, 'worthless religion of the Hindus!' And that too, when Hindus were not far behind in the assembly." Nur Jahan's eyes were gathering rills of mirth and raillery.

"And that too, my sweet, was the result of my indignation at the site of ugliness, with no hint of cruelty in my acts or expressions. Your accusations are proving wrong and worthless." Jahangir smiled, his own eyes gathering mischief.

"Whim and caprice then," Nur Jahan muttered sweetly. "No one can tell that you don't have a grain of bigotry in you when you say such things, Your Majesty. That's what I mean, when I say I fear your whims and caprice."

"Everyone should know, each and every blathering fool of them. Yes, my lone inquisitor, everyone should know," Jahangir began vehemently, "I respect and revere the gods of the Hindus. Especially their goddesses. Of course, not Kali, the goddess of creation and destruction, but Sita, the Helen of Hind. Shri, Durga and Parvati too. And most certainly Lakshami, the goddess of beauty and wealth. The emperor adores and worships them all. Does the emperor not celebrate all the Hindu festivals with as much pomp as all the Muslim festivals?" His gaze was contemplating the masterpiece of the Virgin Mary over the mantel. "And the emperor idolizes the Virgin Mary."

"And Khadija?" Nur Jahan queried softly.

"Yes, Khadija, the beloved wife of Prophet Muhammed. You are much like Khadija, my love, though I am no prophet. You have made the emperor forget all his other wives," Jahangir teased. "Do they live in this palace? Are they alive?"

"Yes, Your Majesty. They are intriguingly alive and deliciously happy." Nur Jahan laughed. "You should have their portraits drawn by the court painters. All those portraits could grace these walls, and you would never miss them. This bedroom looks depressing with the paintings of turbaned men and hunting scenes. Time and age demand the depiction of harem scenes, and harem ladies. Such art and beauty in a woman's form, and the Moghul painters don't capture it on the canvas. All the reflections of beautiful imagery missing in your palaces, Your Majesty, and your aesthetic senses do not revolt against such negligence?"

"Because the emperor prefers the living, breathing art in beauty and youth, my sweet rebel." Jahangir laughed. "You yourself dabble in painting, my Nur, don't you? Arrest your youth and beauty in a self-portrait, and leave the turbaned emperor to his own depressing fate."

"Now don't accuse the empress of such indelicacy, Your Majesty. I don't find turbaned men depressing, as long as they are the living, breathing emblems of grace and courtesy." Nur Jahan joined him in his mirth.

"Only the emperor can withstand accusations and inquisitions, and he alone, not you! Have you exhausted your source of accusations yet? Entirely, I mean?" was Jahangir's wistful provocation.

"Not quite, Your Majesty! Not entirely, either. Since your whims carry you to the oceans of rage and forgetfulness, someone has to row your boat to the shore of awareness," Nur Jahan sang poetically. "Isn't it wrong to destroy the hermitage of a yogi whose entire life is devoted to the service of God? White domed abode of the yogi, it was not hideous, but serene and comely. And yet, you ordered its destruction! Homes are sacred too, Your Majesty, and their sanctity must be preserved under all circumstances."

"That holy imposter, oh, my righteous love!" Jahangir declared with a mingling of mirth and vehemence. "How can you defend such a mad reptile who earns his living by evil means? Pretending to devote his life to God alone, does he? Don't you know what practice of his incited my rage the most? A part of his act in worshiping God, as you say, was to stuff flour into his mouth and imitate the cry of an animal. He was the architect of lies, and of the great ones too. Spreading rumors that the tank beside his white domed building, the serene and comely one in your estimation, was bottomless. I had it measured before I ordered it demolished. It came to exactly twelve cubits deep and one and a half mile in circumference."

"Lies can be remedied with reprimands, Your Majesty, not with destruction," Nur Jahan murmured dreamily.

"Not when they rise higher than the mountains, love! Then they become a giant hurdle in the face of truth, immovable and immutable," Jahangir intoned unconvincingly. "So far you have only recounted the emperor's cruelties, my love, and his whims and caprices too! Any kindness which you might like to conjure up?"

"Many, Your Majesty, and your love, if I may dwell on that for a moment," Nur Jahan began intensely. "Especially since you have become a grandfather. No father in this whole world could love his daughter more as Prince Khurram does, but you love your granddaughter more, even Arjumand Banu confesses. Well, who can resist loving Princess Jahanara? A bloom of only one fleeting summer, and charming as a rosebud. I digress, but kindness like the charities begin at home, or they should, I should say. Your kindness to Prince Khusrau, for one, allowing him to visit you as often as he pleases."

"Ah, Khusrau, my unfortunate son!" Jahangir stifled a sigh of regret. "If he was just plain maudlin, I could be moved to sympathy, trying my best to make those visits pleasant and endurable. But he is so aloof, so doleful, that he leaves me in the gloomiest of moods after each visit."

"I have tried to dispel his gloom, Your Majesty. God knows, I still try," Nur Jahan began intensely. "I even offered him the hand of my sweet Ladli in marriage, but he will have none of her. He says he is in love with his wife, and has no wish to acquire more," she commented without bitterness.

"Princess Ladli. She is beautiful!" Jahangir reminisced aloud. "And my son, he is much like me in that respect. Utterly and absolutely in love with his wife…" He paused, mischief alighting in his eyes with a quicksilver haste. "How would you feel, Nur, if the emperor took another bride while still professing to be madly in love with you?"

"My charm and beauty would dissolve any new bride of yours to oblivion, Your Majesty, like the rest of them," Nur Jahan chanted mirthfully.

"The emperor dares not disagree, my Nur. For your beauty and witchcraft might turn him into a toad." Jahangir laughed. "I have this great urge to go to *Nur Chashma* right now, the only fountain named after you, my Nur. And then go hunting. Just the two of us. No guards, no courtiers! No pomp, no ceremony."

"Right on the dot when it is time to receive the embassies, Your Majesty?" Nur Jahan teased. "Especially today, when another English ambassador is to present himself before you. He had been ill before he reached Ajmer. My only hope is that he can prove himself to be less proud than the rest of them whom we have received so far. And less bigoted, and less avaricious! All the shopkeepers of London are gathering here. Disdaining the Hindu gods, and uttering blasphemies when the name of Islam is mentioned. Shrewd merchants though, and that is a compliment, not the measure of their greed!"

"Wearing a noose of ignorance around their necks, they are still not as besotted as they seem, my Nur," Jahangir began happily. "Besides, freedom of speech is dear to the emperor. Secular, or religious, as far as there is tolerance for all religions in his empire."

"Your kindnesses and generosities, Your Majesty, which I neglected to mention. You pardon and condone all the offences of the priests, the padres and the pundits. Your rod of justice and your sense of tolerance for all religions." Nur Jahan breathed under the spell of her own generous spirit. "Justice and tolerance! Two of the most highly prized virtues in this age and time," she added intensely.

"Since you are in a mood to flatter the emperor, Nur, flatter him more with a goblet of wine." Jahangir's urge to drink was surfacing again.

"Are you not drunk with the wine from my eyes yet, Your Majesty?" Nur Jahan eased herself up gracefully.

"If I was, I would be uttering inanities. Or was I?" Jahangir quipped brightly.

"At times, inanities are much more profound than the profundities, Your Majesty. The profundities, which fall like the pieces of a puzzle on untrained ears, or hitting one on the head who are not perceptive enough to catch subtleties in each word and gesture." Nur Jahan sailed away to fetch the most coveted flagon of wine.

"My profound empress! You would be wise to serve the emperor quickly, before he could claim your beauty to satisfy the hungers of his soul." Jahangir laughed to himself, watching her disappear into the dressing-room.

Jahangir was up on his feet with the alacrity of a young man, as soon as the empress had disappeared behind the sandalwood screen. He was feeling sprightful, delighted by the prospect of quenching his thirst for wine. Addicted as he was to wine and Nur Jahan, he couldn't stay away from both for long. His addictions could not be cured, his very own soul had attested to this truth which he could neither deny nor defy. One more truth to which his soul was shackled, was that it could not kill the memory of Anarkali. Though it had tried, inflicting the most excruciating of punishments upon itself and upon the body which held it prisoner. Even now, the same soul was pleading mercy from the beautiful dead, as Jahangir stood awaiting the nectar of oblivion, surrendering himself to receive the offering of wine and love from the hands of his living beloved. The living beloved was returning. She had filled two jeweled goblets, and was drifting toward the emperor like a wraith of light and purity.

"Celebrating your health, Your Majesty, with the wine from my eyes and from my heart." Nur Jahan offered one goblet to the emperor. Facing him, she stood sipping her own daintily and merrily.

"To your beauty, love! And to your wit and youth. And to our anguished love." Jahangir drank thirstily.

The emperor's joy was disrupted by the sound of the gold bell. Mehr Harwi, Nur Jahan's lady-in-waiting, was not far behind to seek audience from the emperor and the empress. Jahangir was announcing his consent to receive her with a gesture so impatient that it could slice the thin air to smithereens.

"Your Majesty. Padishah Begum." Mehr Harwi fell into two consecutive curtsies. "Prince Khusrau requests the honor of a brief visit."

"He is welcome to join us." Jahangir boomed an impatient consent.

Mehr Harwi retraced her steps, bowing and stumbling. Her satin gown, the color of citron, could be heard rustling behind the gilded portals. Nur Jahan was sinking back into her own chair, donning a mask of serenity and cheerfulness. Jahangir was standing with his back toward her, contemplating his empty cup, as if reading his fortunes inside the chasms of emptiness. Prince Khusrau was making his appearance slowly and reluctantly. His young, handsome features were swathed in a cloak of despair, it seemed. He was dressed in all white, the pure silks accentuating his vow of misery and austerity. A green cummerbund and a matching turban were his only adornments. He curtsied gracefully, waiting for the emperor to speak.

"Welcome, my prince," Jahangir murmured, rather than greeted. "Are your Sanskrit studies faring well? I hear you have become quite a scholar."

"Not so well, Your Majesty. Not since the death of Naqib Khan. He was my guru." Prince Khusrau appeared to protest rather than respond.

"Is not your ward, Rai singh Dalan, well versed in Sanskrit to tutor you further?" Jahangir's thoughts were diving into some pit of grief.

"A little, Your Majesty. Devoted as he is to me, he is visited by melancholia these days. He thinks that soon I would be sent away somewhere, where he will not be permitted to see me," Prince Khusrau offered reluctantly.

"Vile rumors, my besotted prince!" Jahangir declared, flitting a glance at Nur Jahan.

Nur Jahan was sitting there in a world of her own, her heart attentive, and her expression inscrutable. Her white profile was smooth and glistening against the flames of her red silks. Prince Khusrau also stole a glance at her, and she smiled. Jahangir had lost his chain of thought. He was only aware of the portrait of tragedy before him, his firstborn son. *My own beloved son, the victim of intrigue and rebellion.* Jahangir was thinking. *My own unfortunate son! Tormented by his own sufferings, and in return tormenting me with his dejected looks and witless tenacity.*

"Such pallor! You are on the verge of emaciation," Jahangir began indulgently. "Do the royal cooks have dearth of delicacies to tempt the son of the emperor?" His very soul was grieving, as if he would never see his son again.

"Confinement doesn't suit my health, Your Majesty," Prince Khusrau murmured.

"Do you wish to ride and hunt, Khusrau Baba?" The very shadow of storm clouds in Jahangir's thoughts had elicited this endearment, *Khusrau Baba.*

"With your gracious permission, yes, Your Majesty." Prince Khusrau could barely conceal the disdain in his dull utterance.

"With my permission, if you heed, my rebel prince." Jahangir's ocean of love was gathering a tempest of rage and impatience. "And did you not reject the honor of marrying Princess Ladli?" he asked impatiently.

"It is my earnest wish to save her from the unhappiness of marrying an unhappy and undeserving man," Prince Khusrau murmured wretchedly.

"Unhappy! And why must you stay unhappy? The palace and the gardens at your disposal, and the music and the dancers…" Jahangir's rage was mounting. "And why must you dress like a minstrel? Wearing the mantle of mourning in your eyes and on your shoulders? Why can't you smile? Are the royal treasuries robbed of all the jewels that they can't lend you one small ruby or a teardrop diamond?"

"I covet only the jewels of wisdom, Your Majesty," was Prince Khusrau's low response. "Against wisdom, jewels are nothing but pebbles. Glittering. Worthless."

"And where could you find wisdom, my prudent scholar?" Jahangir asked.

"Inside the hearts where love and forgiveness reside, Your Majesty," Prince Khusrau murmured against the daggers of rage in the emperor's eyes.

"And the emperor's heart is unloving, unforgiving?" was Jahangir's incensed exclamation. "Begone! Begone, my unhappy, besotted prince. The emperor can't endure the flood of misery and despair in your eyes and on your lips. You annoy the emperor. Your unhappiness is contagious." He waved dismissal with an impatient wave of his arm.

Prince Khusrau offered a stiff curtsy, fleeing in haste, no word of plea or apology gracing his lips. He was vanished behind the portals like an avenging ghost.

"The emperor is going to forbid him the privilege of such visits. The prince is doleful and impertinent. He succeeds in plunging the emperor into the insanest of moods." Jahangir's fury was volcanic.

"Prince Khusrau has been most unfortunate in choosing his friends, Your Majesty. They are the ones who tutor him in the art of rebellion. He deserves your pity, not harshness. Forgiveness too, yes," Nur Jahan pleaded, floating toward him like a beautiful dream. "And love and wisdom…" Her pleas and thoughts were silenced by an abrupt exclamation from the emperor.

"Your royal inquisition once more, Nur? Does the emperor lack love and wisdom?" Jahangir's heart was throbbing to challenge its own rage and frenzy.

"I didn't say that, Your Majesty!" The blue stars in Nur Jahan's eyes were twinkling protests. "Your love is bounteous and your wisdom boundless. If you were not wise, there would be no peace and justice in your empire. And if you were not loving, your wives would burn me alive on the pyre of their own intrigues lit by the fires of envy and jealousy." Her wit alone was soothing the emperor's grief and anger.

"Your wit and beauty confound the emperor's sense of reason and justice, my Nur," Jahangir murmured with an attempt at buoyancy. "And your flattery and witchcraft." He began to laugh. "A fool in me knows, my Nur, that your wisdom and understanding alone are my talisman. And don't tell me you are not striving to mount the rungs of enlightenment. If you stumble in this noble quest, the emperor would not be far behind to fall into the pit of darkness."

"No burdens of wisdom or understanding I claim to carry on my weak shoulders, Your Majesty," Nur Jahan murmured profoundly. "Silence is wisdom, and I say too much. Nothingness is understanding, and I surround myself with everything, holding on to illusion as reality. Not knowing is the first step toward enlightenment, and I want to know the mysteries of the seven worlds…" Her thoughts were scattered by the intrusive chimes from the gold bell.

Mehr Harwi was craving the royal couple's audience once again. This time, she was announcing the arrival of Prince Khurram. In contrast to his older brother, Prince Khurram's visit was marked by the breeze of joy and hope. He was greeted by both the emperor and the empress with cheers of welcome.

Though bathed with the aura of warmth and sunshine, Prince Khurram sauntered into the room with the royal hauteur of a proud Assyrian. His firm nose with flared nostrils was accentuating the transparency of ivory in his features. He was wearing a jacket of brocade with jeweled flowers edged with round, smooth pearls. His eyes, the color of almonds, were liquid and bright, as if they were reflecting all the warmth of the jewels in their slanted cups. He was holding a large, glittering diamond on the palm of his hand, his fingers cupping this jewel most tenderly.

"Ah, my handsome, fortunate son! What happy news await the emperor from the joy in your eyes?" Jahangir's eyes were spilling mirth.

"A treasure of joys for you, Your Majesty, with tidings glad and comforting." Prince Khurram smiled. "But first, a rare treasure for the empress. A gift of love from the shining abyss in my very soul." His poetic expression itself was uncurling his fingers to reveal the diamond.

"My own treasure, my Prince Khurram! If only I could claim you, forever and forever, as my own son." Nur Jahan claimed the jewel most reverently.

"A worthless pebble by the looks of it!" Jahangir teased. "A jeweler might cut and hone it to some semblance of perfection. Then and then only it could be worthy to grace the bosom of my empress." His eyes were kindling amusement.

"It is perfect," Nur Jahan murmured to herself. "Love is blind to imperfections, and the gift of love is priceless."

"Only a jeweler's skill can make it worth the prize for royalty. Otherwise, it is worthless," Jahangir intoned assiduously.

"Even now, Your Majesty, as it is, it can fetch fifty thousand rupees, and claim its seat as worthy to be displayed before the kings." Prince Khurram laughed.

"In fact, the emperor is jealous, Khurram Baba." Jahangir joined his son in his mirth. "Now dole out all the treasures of your glad tidings, and the emperor would try to sift jewels out of some sad-happy news which always happen to lurk in the distance."

"May I sit, Your Majesty?" Prince Khurram drifted toward the empress' side, where she had seated herself in some daze of joy and admiration.

"How dare you sit, my young, heedless charmer, before the emperor has not seated himself?" Jahangir sought his own gilt chair laughingly. "And leave out the perilous details out of your grand eloquence." His own thoughts were melting in the poetry of joy and anticipation.

"More so comical and pitiful, Your Majesty." Prince Khurram launched his missile of news with the élan of a happy general. "Ambar Malik, that ill-starred rebel as you remember him, Your Majesty, is totally routed and defeated. The battle was fought at Bahaman, as if the armies of light and darkness were confronting each other. Our Moghul troops were commanded by Ali Khan, Ray Chand, Beg Turkman, and Bir Singh Deo, and they all displayed great valor, though the fighting was fierce. Against their might, the enemy were reduced to scattered heaps—the wounded and the dying. Ambar Malik, unable to maintain his stand at opposition, was the first one to flee to safety."

"Ah, that black-faced reptile with black fortunes following at his heels!" Jahangir exclaimed without waiting to hear more. "The emperor can picture that whole bloody scene with his mind's eye, Khurram Baba! How strange, my mind is spilling verses where blood has been spilt.

"With broken arms and loosened loins. No strength in their feet, no sense in their heads."

"There are hope and peace in the hearts of few, and misery and despair inside the hearts of many," Nur Jahan murmured to herself.

"Padishah Begum!" One gentle protest fluttered on the lips of Prince Khurram.

"Poetry doesn't mix with politics, that's the emperor's sad regret."

Jahangir flashed her a searching look. "What poetic thoughts and sadnesses are stealing the sparkle from your eyes, my Nur?"

"Not poetry, but philosophy, Your Majesty," Nur Jahan murmured under the weight of her own mute profundities. "Though your couplet mingled well with war, if I may be as bold as to agree…or contradict, considering your assertion," she smiled, "I was thinking about Ambar Malik, your Abyssinian slave, Your Majesty. What irony, the emperor's own slave leading the army of darkness, if I presume right? Against the army of light, our own Moghul army, jubilant and victorious. I don't know what I am thinking, or saying…" She paused, flashing an abrupt query at Prince Khurram. "I don't like the idea of Ambar Malik's flight to safety, though. How did he escape?"

"Padishah Begum, how can I best explain!" Prince Khurram's arms were shot up in one hopeless gesture. "If gloom and darkness had not lowered their banners at the cries of those black-fortuned ones, not one of them would have found any road to the valley of safety." His eyes were now lit up with the stars of poetry and sarcasm.

"Oh, that poor wretch, and all those miserable fugitives!" Nur Jahan declared with mock sympathy.

"How your sympathies split, my empress, between the emperor and his inveterate rebels," Jahangir mocked.

"How can my sympathies be divided, Your Majesty, when the prince and the emperor, the two dearest ones to my heart, are right by my side?" Nur Jahan's sing-song voice trembled on a verge of mirth. "As for that ill-starred rebel, he reminds me of a crocodile, and my sympathies brand him as a traitor. Black as the night himself, his heart must be black too with a river of conflict so thick that it confounds his sight to discern which way his allegiance should flow."

"Might as well converse with the empress, Khurram Baba. Her wit and poetry in rapport with war and politics, dig deep trenches inside her very veins to reach the channels of prudence and perception. All manner of intrigue or sedition crumble before the shafts of her wisdom," Jahangir suggested joyfully. "And yet, spill all your good news at once, before the emperor gets wearied of wars and rebellions."

"Wars and conquests, Your Majesty, if that sounds more appealing." Prince Khurram obeyed with a smile most winsome. "And yet, more good news are to follow. I am saving such a *one* till the very end. But first, another seed of conquest. The province of Khokhar was won by the brilliant strategies of Ibrahim Khan. Darjan Sal was captured, its neighboring states succumbing to our rule too, and the diamond mines are in our possession."

"So, that's from where this pebble was retrieved?" Jahangir laughed.

"A gem of most exquisite beauty, Your Majesty, and worth many a kingdoms," Prince Khurram quipped warmly.

"And now, where is that gem of good news you have been saving for us as the last *one*?" Jahangir's tone was more of a command than an inquiry. "The emperor doesn't recall sending any more emissaries or contingents to quell the rebellions."

"None that I am aware of either, Your Majesty," Prince Khurram beamed. "Ah, the good news! My most beloved princess, my one and only Jahanara, is now blessed with the company of a prince-brother." His features were transfigured with joy. "This very morning, Your Majesty, I held my son into my arms. A more comely prince I have not ever seen before," he murmured as if to himself.

"Arjumand Banu, already the mother of two royal blooms." An ecstatic cry blossomed on Nur Jahan's own lips.

"And you, my wicked prince, what prompted you to make us suffer this delay in happiness?" Jahangir declared. "And what have you named your comely prince, ah, my grandson, my grandson?" He got to his feet, his eyes shining.

"I am hoping for this honor from you, Your Majesty," was Prince Khurram's suave appeal.

"What do you suggest, my Nur?" Jahangir sought Nur Jahan's attention.

"I have always favored the name Dara for boys, as long as I can remember, Your Majesty," Nur Jahan offered quickly.

"And the emperor wanted to name one of his sons Shikoh," Jahangir murmured.

"Dara Shikoh, that's it! A propitious name, Your Majesty! Padishah Begum! We will name him Dara Shikoh," Prince Khurram chanted wistfully.

"A beautiful name! Worthy of a royal prince, the son of my most beloved son." Jahangir's joy was deflated at the sound of the trumpets, blaring forth in anticipation of the court session over which he was to preside. "And if these embassies were not to pilfer the emperor's time and pleasure, he would have the grand pleasure of seeing his grandson right this minute." A mock lament escaped his lips. "Any blistering embassies, for which the emperor should be warned, Khurram Baba?" he inquired.

"Only the ones presented by the priests, Your Majesty." Prince Khurram's expression was dry all of a sudden. "If I may suggest, Your Majesty, do not admit that maverick Englishman, Coryat, in your court. He has been acting demented lately. His eccentricities guide him to rant and blaspheme. Another one to watch, Your Majesty, is Thomas Roe. He reeks of pride, if not of bigotry," he added thoughtfully.

"Fair warnings, fair prince." Jahangir laughed. The next minute he was bowing before Nur Jahan, his eyes lit up with the stars of mockery and tenderness. "The prince and the emperor beg leave of the empress." With a gallant sweep of his arm he was turning away.

"And the empress commands, Your Majesty, not to delay our royal pleasure in serving alms at the tomb of Muinuddin Chishti this evening." Nur Jahan eased herself up gracefully.

"The prince too would offer alms at the tomb of that revered saint to celebrate the birth of his son, Padishah Begum, whether she commands it or not," was Prince Khurram's joyful confession.

"Even the showers of gold and silver would not be enough to celebrate the birth of our grandson!" Jahangir's joy itself was beckoning Prince Khurram to follow him.

Chapter Five

The palace gardens at Ajmer were famous for their lush, silken grandeur. This late afternoon, they were a bazaar of music and festivity where Jahangir sat on his throne receiving embassies. From the palace windows, the ladies of the harem could watch all this pomp and ceremony if they needed such diversion, or if their needs were as varied as Nur Jahan's. Nur Jahan would often stand by her bedroom window, absorbing not only the color and pageantry of such scenes, but the import and execution of the emperor's commands. This was no secret to Jahangir, but right now the beautiful eyes of Anarkali were spilling wine from the very ocean of clear blue skies into his heart as he sat receiving embassies. His beloved Nur Jahan was continents apart from him, yet his beloved Anarkali was so tenderly close to him, so achingly near. He was not seated on his throne of mother-of-pearl, flanked by a canopy of gold and brocade, but at the altar of his beloved, spilling libations of worship before her presence, and drinking draughts of pain-bliss from her absence-nearness.

This pain-bliss was Jahangir's companion as he dismissed one embassy, stalling the others with an imperious wave of his arm. He was leaning back against the velvety softness of his chair, luxuriating in the sense of his power and might. His aesthetic senses were arresting the beauty of his gardens, before it could be dimmed against the dull haze of embassies. The *makrana* fountains could be seen sprinkling the marble terraces with gleams of pearl in sunshine. Beyond the bower of roses were an exquisite array of bushes pruned in shapes of gazelles and peacocks. The scent of jasmine and Indian roses was in the air, and Jahangir inhaled it deeply. His gaze was sweeping over the flood of princes and courtiers, before settling on a group of singers and musicians on the white stage. This stage was garlanded with white tuberoses, shuddering with the beat of *qawwali*, it seemed. The ecstatic refrain in this qawwali was from the verse by a late poet by the name of Amir Khusrau.

Jahangir was familiar with this famous verse as he had heard it quite often, recited by his own court poets when they lacked inspiration. His attention now was diverted to Sayyid Shah, who was mimicking a religious dance to the refrain of this verse. Sayyid Shah was Jahangir's courtier; a maverick who was wont to act as a buffoon whenever a chance presented him this luxury. Right now, he was indulging in such a luxury, dancing and whirling like a dervish.

"Each nation has its right road of faith and its shrine—qibla-gahi. I have set up my shrine on the path of him with a crooked cap."

Laughter was alighting in Jahangir's eyes, as he crushed the madness of his courtier with a loud command. He summoned Sayyid Shah to his presence, before he could whirl himself to absolute giddiness. Obeying the emperor's command, he was whirling his way toward the throne. His multicolored turban had fallen awry as he himself fell into one heap of a curtsy.

"Satisfy the emperor's curiosity, my court fool, what does this verse mean?" Jahangir demanded capriciously.

"Your Majesty!" Sayyid Shah's hands were fumbling to adjust his turban. "This verse has a history of being misconstrued and misinterpreted. But I would relate a true account which made it possible to survive distortions. Here it goes, if you bear with me, Your Majesty. One old saint, now retired to the abode of the dead, by the name of Shaikh Auliya, was once sitting on a terraced roof. His house was by the bank of Jamna, and he was watching with devotion the ritual bathing of the Hindus. He was wearing a cap tilted to one side of his head. He seemed to be deeply immersed in his quiet contemplations until he espied Amir Khusrau on the street. Suddenly, he was heard reciting, 'Each race has its right road of faith and its shrine—qibla-gahi,' and waving and drawing Amir Khusrau's attention to him. Amir Khusrau in return was heard paying homage to the saint by reciting this line, 'I have set up my shrine on the path of him with the crooked cap.' Shaikh Auliya, hearing this hemistich, fell senseless and delivered his soul to the Creator. No true account such as this would you ever hear from another, Your Majesty." He sprang to his feet jauntily.

"The saint must have mistaken the poet's reed of inspiration, ascribing it to his own crooked cap." Jahangir's gaze was intense and piercing. "Crooked cap has gone through many transformations in relation to its meaning and connotation. Being presumptuous is one, or the one who has left the true path of religion. It is known to connote beloved also, one's own spiritual mentor."

He smiled. "Yet, begone, my fool of a courtier, before the emperor falls senseless on his own throne?"

One Persian ambassador was being heralded toward the throne, who could not be stalled in making his presence known to the emperor. This proud ambassador was Muhammad Riza Beg, sent by the Persian monarch himself, Shah Abbas of Persia. He was approaching closer with a sea of colorful pennants behind him, and a marching band following at his heels. He had just abandoned his train of fifty horses saddled in shimmering gold, and was now attended by a coterie of men, all turbaned and bejeweled. These men were carrying gifts, to be offered to the emperor. The Moghul viziers and courtiers in disciplined ranks were making way for this illustrious guest, though not quite graciously. Prince Khurram, Asaf Khan and Itmadudaula Khan had already moved to their assigned posts close to the emperor.

Itibar Khan, the governor of Agra, was the first one to greet Muhammad Riza Beg. The governor of Orissa, Ahmed Beg, was craning his neck to have a better view of this haughty Persian with a six-pointed turban in red. Ibrahim Khan, the governor of Bengal, was the next one to receive the Persian ambassador. Khan Jahan, the governor of Multan, was next in line, greeting the Persian ambassador with merely a nod of his head.

Asaf Khan, standing behind the emperor, was watching this whole show with smiles both amused and condescending. Itmadudaula Khan beside him was simply indifferent. Prince Khurram, beside the emperor, was ignoring the Persian's haughty approach, and exchanging amenities with his own attendant, Salih. The first and second row closer to the throne were teeming with the emperor's own viziers and courtiers. Amongst them, Nahir Khan, Sayyid Dilir, Afzal Khan, Abul Hasan, Fadai Khan, Muqarab Khan, Mukhlis Khan, just to name a few. They were marked for prominence, more so by the shining agog in their eyes, than by the badges of rank on their arms. The seventh row was reserved for the royal princes, both young and old. They too were all agog, watching this Persian galore with much interest. Asaf Khan's son, Abu Talib, was the only demure one amongst the rest of the princes. Prince Hoshang and Prince Tahmuras, the sons of late Prince Daniyal, were seen whispering amongst themselves. Prince Khusrau's son, Prince Balaqi, was squeezed in there, rapt and speechless. Prince Jahandar and Prince Shahriyar were attracting the attention of all with their loud banter.

Mahabat Khan was the one to present the Persian ambassador before the emperor. He was skilled in such a task, and after one flourish of a curtsy, was retiring into the background. Muhammed Riza Beg was left alone, bowing before the emperor twice and murmuring his greetings. He was quick to flaunt his gifts by commanding his men with a stiff wave of his arm.

The attendants wearing conical hats, obeying this signal, were quick to parade those gifts before the emperor. Five gold clocks embedded with jewels. Five swords studded with precious gems. Several boxes, open at the top, revealing a wealth of Venetian glasses. One cabinet rich with cloth of gold was lowered reverently. Two chests holding exquisite sets of Persian hangings were unburdened. Eight carpets of silk were a tapestry of flowers. A chest of mother-of-pearl was housing clusters of rubies.

"Twenty-seven Arabian and Persian horses." One Persian attendant had begun to read the list of the gifts which were brought for the emperor, but could not be presented while the court was in session. "Nine mules, fair and large. Seven camels laden with velvets. Twenty-one camels carrying gold flagons brimming with Persian wines. Seven more camels loaded with bottles of rose-water. One large cabinet containing forty muskets..." His boastful recital was cut short by one impatient wave of the emperor's arm.

"How does my *brother*?" Jahangir's abrupt inquiry was directed toward Muhammed Riza Beg.

Muhammed Riza Beg stood abashed for a moment, understanding perfectly well the emperor's expression *brother,* meaning Shah Abbas, yet he was taken aback. He appeared to be expecting to hear from the emperor the title *the King of Persia,* but was disappointed. Since the emperor's gaze was stern and commanding, he breathed quickly.

"Shah Abbas, His Majesty, the King of Persia, is in splendid health, Your Majesty," was Muhammed Riza Beg's flustered response.

"And what brings you to our court with such pomp and ceremony?" Jahangir asked amusedly.

"To bring greetings, Your Majesty, from our King of Persia. And to..." Muhammed Riza Beg was stung to silence, more so by the flashing intensity in the emperor's eyes than by the imperious wave of his arm.

"And to win back Kandahar from us!" Jahangir declared.

"No, Your Majesty." Muhammed Riza Beg lowered his eyes. "The King of Persia seeks your alliance against the Turkish King," he murmured low.

"Concerning that, the emperor would convey his decision to you in a matter of time." Jahangir waved dismissal. "And send my *brother* my profoundest of thanks for the precious gifts," he added.

Muhammed Riza Beg performed three consecutive curtsies without flinching, his look dazed. Jahangir was commanding Iradat Khan to escort the

Persian ambassador to the aisle of the younger princes. Muhammed Riza Beg was being conducted to the seventh row, his face now ashen and seething with chagrin. He could not fail to notice the emperor's disfavor while being escorted to the inferior row where only younger princes indulged in fun and sport, besides making sport of the ones burdened with humiliation.

Jahangir, with his cup replenished to the brim, was willing the embassies to cease their assault. His gaze was warm and thoughtful though, bestowing smiles upon his viziers and courtiers whose faces shone with the light of ardor and expectancy. Catching one of Prince Khurram's comments, he was about to voice his own thoughts, when he espied Mir Ali edging closer to the throne. He was holding, rather hugging, a large book with exquisite gilt binding. His eyes were shining, as if craving audience just to lay his treasure at the feet of the emperor. The large book itself had arrested Jahangir's attention, and his own eyes were glowing with interest.

"What do we have here, my crafty calligrapher?" Jahangir flashed him a smile.

"A gift for you, Your Majesty, from Abdur Rahim," Mir Ali beamed with excitement. "He has sent you his own version of the story *Yusuf and Zulaikha* from the Quran." He held out the book to the emperor.

"A rare and most precious gift, which the emperor welcomes with a loving heart." Jahangir claimed the book with utmost reverence. He began flitting the pages with awe and wonder.

"Your Majesty." Mir Ali sought the emperor's attention. "May I present my own gift, if you permit it, Your Majesty? I will have it fetched."

"Yes, yes, Mir Ali," Jahangir consented, his eyes still glued to the book.

Mir Ali was too overwhelmed to speak, motioning Arab Dost with his eyes alone to fetch his much cherished work of art. Arab Dost was the imperial agent entrusted with this gift beforehand, and was quick to carry out this happy errand without delay. Mir Ali, the artist and the calligraphist, stood watching the emperor with devotion and reverence. A thin, beatific smile curled on Jahangir's lips as he closed the book with a thoughtful reluctance. His gaze returning to Mir Ali with the intensity of warmth and admiration.

"This script is illumined by you, my genius of an artist? The emperor cannot mistake your unique style for another," Jahangir complimented profusely.

"Yes, Your Majesty," Mir Ali admitted happily. "Abdur Rahim wrote the story, and I copied it with my own hand. The binding and illumination, Your Majesty, are my own design, as you judged it correctly," he murmured.

"This would grace our royal library after the emperor has had his fill. No other library could boast such a treasure. The work is noble and exquisite. Both in writing and depiction…" Jahangir's attention was diverted to a miracle of wonder floating in the air.

A silver throne hoisted on the heads of Arab Dost and Jawahir Khan appeared ethereal. It was supported in the back by Buland Khan and Hushiyar Khan. A little distance from the present throne, it was being lowered slowly and carefully, then adjusted to a position so as to reveal its splendor directly under the gaze of the emperor.

"What splendid miracle has landed in our garden?" Jahangir exclaimed.

"My gift for you, Your Majesty." Mir Ali could barely breathe.

"A silver throne! The handiwork of a genius. Such wonder of art I have not ever seen before," Jahangir murmured, absorbing each little detail intensely.

This silver throne appeared to breathe on its own. Inlaid with naurattan, its nine precious jewels in each cluster were blazing and throbbing with life. The legs painted with rosebuds and bridal vines were vivid and alive. Its velvety seat was meadow-soft, and gleaming like a large emerald.

"The emperor offers you his heartfelt thanks, Mir Ali." Jahangir bestowed upon him the warmest of smiles. "For this wondrous gift of yours, you are to receive one lakh of rupees in cash and trays laden with pearls and rubies. This one is more beautiful than the gold one which you designed." He paused, his look dreamy and reminiscent. "The gold throne which I ordered to be sent to Prince Perwiz. Did it ever reach him in Burhanpur, along with my gifts of pearls and rubies?" He retrieved a silk purse out of the coffer beside him, and offered it to Mir Ali.

"Yes, Your Majesty." Mir Ali bowed double after claiming the purse. The gold and silver ashrafis in there whispering to him the fortunes of the fortunate. "Prince Perwiz, Your Majesty, sends his warmest thanks…wrapped in silks of gratitude, says the happy prince. Your express runner Banarasi himself, Your Majesty, brought this ecstatic reply from Prince Perwiz."

"Why use the express runner, if news reaches the emperor a decade later?" Jahangir laughed.

"Only this morning, Your Majesty, I…" Mir Ali's incoherence was stalled by an abrupt wave of dismissal from the emperor.

"Repair to the streets paved with gold, my genius friend, for the emperor would shower riches and honors upon you much earlier than a decade. But he must attend to his embassies, lest he is late in praying and serving at the tomb of Muinuddin Chishti."

Mir Ali retraced his steps, bowing and curtsying, his eyes spilling joy into the very breath of air. Before further embassies could be announced, Itmadudaula Khan sought the emperor's attention.

"Your Majesty, may I look at this work of holiness?" Itmadudaula Khan's gaze was fixed to the book in the emperor's lap. "For all art is holy, and authorship a divine inspiration from the very lips of God."

"Holy stars in your eyes, Father, and holiness in the beautiful eyes of your daughter are the only two treasures which the emperor wishes to keep and cherish," Jahangir murmured, relinquishing the book into his hands.

"Taking advantage of your happiness, Your Majesty, may I lay these holy stars at your feet, and request a boon?" Itmadudaula Khan requested humbly.

"Any boon, my worthy father-in-law, any boon! The emperor can deny you nothing." Jahangir's eyes were gathering rills of laughter and premonition.

"Then, may I be as bold as to request that Prince Khusrau be left under the charge of Prince Khurram, for the reason of his own safety and well-being?" Itmadudaula Khan pleaded softly.

"Safety!" Laughter was gone from Jahangir's eyes. His eyes as well as his thoughts were searching the faces of Asaf Khan and Prince Khurram before returning to Itmadudaula Khan. "My prince! Is he not safe under the care of Rai Singh Dalan?"

"He is, Your Majesty, he is," Itmadudaula Khan agreed affably. "But since his thoughts favor gloom and depression, he is tempted to conspire, and might become the victim of rebellion once again. If he has your permission, Your Majesty, to accompany Prince Khurram on the campaigns, he might be cured of his dark moods and scheming thoughts. Prince Khurram would keep a close watch over him, keeping him away from the influence of his evil companions."

"The emperor would have denied you no other boon but this, my kind father." A volley of mirth escaped Jahangir's, spilling only pain and hysteria.

Against this ocean of the emperor's mirth, another raucous din was circling high down the courtyard below. The mad Englishman, Coryat, as prophesied by Prince Khurram, was having a verbal tirade with a laundress. He had such perfect command of the native language, that he was drowning the voice of the laundress in colloquial Hindi with a shower of epithets she herself had not ever heard. The poor laundress was so flustered, that she was resorting to prayers and exclamations. Forgetting all about her arguments, she was seen fleeing toward the palace mosque, as if pursued by the demons.

One demon was sure following her, no other than Coryat himself. Bounding past her, he was lost inside the white serenity of this mosque, not for long though. He had climbed the minaret reserved only for the muezzin. Muezzin was not even inside the mosque. Coryat was seen waving his arms, and singing some litany of a prayer-madness.

"There is no God, but one God, and Jesus Christ is the son of God," Coryat was reciting with all the force of bellows in his lungs.

Jahangir was not laughing, but mirth was shining in his eyes. Prince Khurram, though not orthodox himself, was afraid that the Muslims would cut this man to pieces, if he repeated his litany *Son of God*. Asaf Khan was outraged, sentencing Coryat to death in his thoughts, even before he could voice his plea for such a sentence to the emperor. Itmadudaula Khan was vehement in his condemnation, urging the emperor to send this heathen to the gallows for uttering such blasphemy. The royal guards were dragging Coryat down the minaret steps as some burden most foul to be cast into the darkest of dungeons. They were literally hauling him before the emperor, their eyes flaming.

Coryat was bowing before the emperor most gallantly. Wearing the rags of dignity in his eyes, he was lowering a string of flattering speech in Persian, his accent fluid and eloquent. His eyes were feverish, but his oration was as refined as of any of the Persian scholars the emperor held in great esteem. So impressed was the emperor by Coryat's command of Persian language, that he had made a swift decision not to punish this madman. Coryat was rising in his esteem as a genius who had accomplished the most difficult of tasks in mastering both Hindi and Persian during his brief stay in India.

"You are a genius, Coryat! In speech, madness and syllogism!" Jahangir laughed, snatching another heavy purse from his coffer, and flinging it to Coryat.

Coryat caught this rich gift in the midair with the agility of an acrobat. He was bowing before the emperor once again, and thanking him profusely in Persian. The courtiers were abashed, holding their breaths as well as their thoughts on a verge of sedition. No one had noticed Sir Thomas Roe who had edged closer. He had been waiting patiently and with utmost grace to be announced to the emperor. Being a man of somewhat shallow intellect, he was finding Coryat's behavior most unbecoming, and an involuntary comment on his lips was enough to shatter the mask of his arrogance.

"How degrading for an Englishman to act as a beggar!" Thomas Roe exclaimed. His very gaze was holding his fellow countryman in contempt, as if saying, *you have demeaned yourself by accepting a gift from the emperor in such a lowly manner.*

"Another mad Englishman ignorant of the etiquettes of the Moghul court?" Jahangir thundered, rage kindling in his eyes suddenly.

"Sir Thomas Roe, Your Majesty, the ambassador from England. He is entrusted with a letter from King James to be delivered to you, Your Majesty," Reverend John interceded on behalf of Thomas Roe.

Sir Thomas Roe stood there stiff and proud. His hose and doublet of metallic gray were clinging to his body, lending him the semblance of an invader who had lost his weapons. His long, sharp nose appeared to be jutting over his paper-thin moustache, which was curled and joined to his whiskers. Only his large eyes with liquid warmth were revealing the glints of misery and discomfiture.

"He can pocket that English title in his doublet and return to England, my good Chaplin." Jahangir flashed a mild reproof at Reverend John.

"Prostrate yourself before the emperor, you mannerless cur," Reverend Terry from behind whispered to Thomas Roe with the indignation of a school teacher.

"I am an English ambassador, and I will not kneel before the emperor like a servant," Thomas Roe murmured back.

"For this breach of etiquette, you could be sent to the tower, and spend the rest of your days in abject misery." Jahangir's gaze held Thomas Roe captive in its searching intensity. His very eyes were spilling commands, if not dismissal.

"Your Majesty, I have already suffered great miseries and indignities by the hands of your Moghul viziers, during my journey from Surat to Ajmer, Your Majesty," Thomas Roe murmured with a slight bow of his head. "May I plead the emperor's justice, Your Majesty, against those injuries?" he asked quite humbly.

"The emperor's justice erects no barriers between a friend or a foe, bold ambassador," Jahangir intoned. His rage was now channeled toward those viziers who were being accused of treating this guest unjustly. "State your grievances with due courtesy, proud victim, for the emperor forgives not mannerless guests who choose ignorance as their defense to defy the Moghul etiquettes," he warned kindly.

"The etiquettes of my own country demand my utmost obedience, Your Majesty." Thomas Roe curtsied with a flourish of his arm. "And I come as a friend, not as a foe, Your Majesty," he added.

"You are not only bold, but witless, Thomas." Jahangir smiled. "With your courage, rather audacity, you are winning the favor of the emperor. If only you could soften the glints of pride and arrogance in your eyes, you might win the friendships of the Moghul viziers." He paused, overwhelmed by fatigue all of a sudden. "But do state your grievances, Thomas. Briefly, I command! For the emperor has other duties to perform."

"Pardon me, Your Majesty," was Thomas Roe's low response. "My grievances are of no consequence, since I have gained Your Majesty's favor." He hesitated, but then continued. "Though I was treated rudely and roughly by your officials, Your Majesty, at the ports of Surat. All those officers insisting and demanding to search me personally. Then commanding me to visit the governor of Surat before proceeding to crave your audience, Your Majesty. When I didn't agree to this, your Governor Zulfiqar Khan stormed into my house uninvited. I greeted him as if his rudeness didn't affect me in the least, showing him that I was privileged to be his host as I led him into my courtyard."

"Guilty as ever for the breech of etiquettes, Thomas! And that's you, willfully remaining ignorant of the Moghul etiquettes." Jahangir laughed without joy.

"Your Majesty, permit me to speak with this proud ambassador of the King James." Prince Khurram sought the emperor's attention.

"Just to question his pride, that's your only privilege, my handsome prince," Jahangir consented.

"Thank you, Your Majesty." Prince Khurram bowed before the emperor, returning his attention to Thomas Roe. "Didn't you, Sir Thomas, assert your authority at the port of Surat, defying the regulations of the Moghul customs? And didn't you rally your men to fire pistols when the Moghul officers, according to the law of our empire, attempted to search you and your men?" His very gaze was challenging.

"To keep the dignity of England in view, I was constrained to act that way, royal prince," was Thomas Roe's crafty response.

"Such pretensions ought to be left in England, haughty ambassador," Jahangir shot a quick reprimand. "State your errand, Thomas. You must cast off this mantle of pride. It doesn't fetch an ounce of gain to anyone in the Moghul courts, especially to the foreigners who are steeped in false dignity of their country's prides and honors."

"I have a letter from King James, Your Majesty, requesting trade treaty with England." Thomas Roe was quick to procure the letter from his pocket.

"An insignificant request before the eyes of the emperor. This must be left to the attention of my viziers." Jahangir waved dismissal, motioning his attendant Jahu to claim the missive for later perusal.

"Please, Your Majesty, may I present the gifts from King James?" Thomas Roe snatched the gifts from the hands of his footman. He held out one richly embroidered scarf and an English sword to the emperor.

"These gifts would be displayed in our royal palace as the ornaments of pride." Jahangir got to his feet, his gaze flashing scorn and mirth.

"Your Majesty, if you deign to see the English coach sent by King James, it stands by the palace gates for Your Majesty's approval," Thomas Roe pleaded quickly, urging his footman to display other gifts. A pair of virginals, silver knives and gilded goblets were pouring forth from the chest unlidded by the footman.

"Then the emperor will deck himself with the silk scarf and wear the English sword to see this rare gift of King James." Jahangir dismounted his throne thoughtfully.

The English coach all gilded and slashed with red velvet was a curious enormity to test and behold. Jahangir was delighted by its size and glamour, his aesthetic senses searching for beauty and grace, and divining improvements. Though impressed by the design and contour of the carriage, he wished the Chinese velvet to be replaced by Persian velvet with matching cushions. He didn't like the brass nails, and was ordering those to be replaced with the silver ones. As a mark of his gratitude, he was ordering his own vizier and physician Muqarab Khan to attend to the needs of Thomas Roe, and bestowing another favor upon the English ambassador by inviting him to join the emperor for celebration and almsgiving at the tomb of Muinuddin Chishti.

"Harness this coach with four Arabian horses, and the emperor would be delighted to ride in it this evening to the tomb of the saint," Jahangir announced before trooping ahead toward his own palace.

A cavalcade of royal guards had reached the shrine of Muinuddin Chishti with all the pomp and splendor of a Moghul pageantry. Jahangir and Nur Jahan had journeyed in the English coach embellished with silk trappings on which were embedded precious gems in patterns of vines and flowers. The caparisoned horses and elephants with the gilded howdahs had carried the viziers and the courtiers in a rich procession following the emperor's coach. The tomb of the saint was welcoming the pageant of the Moghuls, who were longing to participate in the night-long rituals of festivities and alms-giving.

Muinuddin Chishti's shrine, immersed in a flood of song and music, was teeming with devotees of all sects and faiths. The Sufis were dancing in ecstatic abandon, and the dervishes whirling on their toes in oblivion to their own devotion. The Qawwals were drunk with the spiritual songs of their own qawwalis, and beating drums in rhythm with their hearts. The tomb of the saint was garlanded with roses and marigolds. The courtyard next to it was inlaid with mother-of-pearl and changing colors against the rush of plumed turbans. The ladies were weighed down with gold in their ears and around their throats, their arms glittering with gold bracelets squeezed clear to their elbows. The poor and the needy were assembled in the three large courtyards on the east side of the shrine, coveting for the bounties in food, not in gold. Jahangir and Nur Jahan were secluded in the fourth courtyard by a railing of latticework in gold. Several cauldrons heaped with cooked rice, lentils and vegetables were at their disposal to serve the needy with royal portions.

Jahangir, Nur Jahan and all the emperor's wives, surrounded by cauldrons of food, were standing in the middle of the courtyard under a gazebo wrought in solid sandstone. A large chandelier was hanging low from the ceiling, bathing all in a frolic of light and shadows. The emperor was the first one to ladle out a platter of rice, which was entrusted to the care of Jahu to be served promptly. Nur Jahan followed suit, spooning out lentils in large bowls. Then the emperor's other wives were taking turns in heaping the dishes with steaming vegetables. Soon, other begums had joined and there was an assembly-line of bowls and platters to be carried away. Jahangir and Nur Jahan were slipping away on their own at the first opportunity after the ladling and spooning were in full swing under the care of the Begums. They had found a refuge near the gilded lattice where tuberoses appeared to unfold their lips to greet the emperor and the empress.

"Is the emperor's health worth all this serving and alms-giving? Serving those who are hungering more for riotous festivity than for viands cooked and garnished?" Jahangir commented.

"The viands are to be served at night, Your Majesty. More appropriately, when hungers gnaw at the soul rather than the stomach." Nur Jahan laughed. "And the emperor's health is worth many empires! Without which, the peace and justice in his empire would dissolve into chaos and rebellion."

"Rebellion, if not chaos, still abound in his empire, my lovely Nur," Jahangir quipped brightly. "Early next morning, my adored prince, Prince Khurram, has to march straight to Deccan to chastise the warring lords. If the emperor is fortunate in not encountering more rebellions, he would repair to

Mandu to hunt. Ah, the beautiful gardens over there, and with you as the most beautiful of my flowers."

"Your Majesty! The gardens in Kashmir are much more beautiful than all the gardens in the whole wide world, I have heard," Nur Jahan murmured. "I have a liking for chenar trees though, and Kashmir, I hear, boasts only of pines, cedars and spruces."

"The emperor would import chenar trees from Iran to adorn the gardens of Kashmir for you alone, my Nur," Jahangir murmured back.

"In that case, Your Majesty, I might not live to see them bloom," Nur Jahan chanted happily. "But I do suggest, Your Majesty, that you celebrate your birthday and weighing ceremony in Ajmer before repairing to any of the heavenly gardens." Her joy was tarnished, for she could sense the emperor's sadness.

"The anniversary of my late father comes a few months earlier than my own birthday," Jahangir reminisced aloud. "I wish to mark that day with celebrations, much in the manner of my own birthday. My dear father, he can't come back, but his memory can be weighed with the pearls of his wisdom." His thoughts were creating illusions where only Anarkali reigned. "Did I tell you about my dream, last night's dream?" he asked abruptly.

"Your dreams, Your Majesty, I dare not explore." Nur Jahan smiled.

"Yes, I saw my father in my dream, alive and majestic," Jahangir continued heedlessly. "He spoke to me endearingly. 'Shaikhu Baba, forgive for my sake the fault of Khan Azam,' he told me clearly. It was rather a command," he demurred. "Remind me, Nur, the first thing in the morning, I must summon Khan Azam from the fort of Gwalior, and grant him his freedom."

"And reward him with kindness, Your Majesty, the kindness which he cannot help but drown into the rivers of his own ingratitude," Nur Jahan warned.

"If you only knew my father, Nur, if you only knew." Jahangir's tone was dreamy, his heart weeping at the tomb of Anarkali. "With the pearls of his wisdom and kindness, he could command obedience of any man, even from his grave."

"And how do you wish to celebrate the anniversary of your great, great father this year, Your Majesty?" Nur Jahan's gaze was warm and searching.

"By offering gifts rich and precious, which would adorn the tomb of Muinuddin Chishti with sparkling gems." Jahangir could barely murmur. "And by feeding the poor and the sick with the milk of the antelopes. How long has it been, Nur, do you remember? The same day when I had bestowed a jagir on Khan Azam, an antelope was brought to my presence. It was kept in our palace for a week, while I couldn't get over my surprise by the buckets full of milk it could give each day."

"The healing powers of the milk of that antelope, how can I forget, Your Majesty?" Nur Jahan's wit and optimism were returning "It cured many a victims of their asthma. Including you, Your Majesty, the royal victim!"

"Ah, my sweet Nur." Jahangir snatched her hand into his own, pressing it absently. "Let us return to the tomb of the revered saint, my pearl. Will you pray with the emperor once again? For the peace in his heart…and for our love and happiness, together." His gaze was sailing toward the vaulted sepulcher of the saint.

"And to neglect to serve the alms to the poor," Nur Jahan quipped.

"Has Hind ever seen an emperor serving the alms? Or a goddess as his consort?" was Jahangir's delirious response. The ecstasy of Sufi music was reaching his own heart. And his soul was keeping rhythm with the whirling dervishes.

Chapter Six

Another time, another music! The night-madness of that Sufic ecstasy was lost to Jahangir for three whole years. And it was resurrected this year, this day, as he sat in his garden palace at Mandu, watching the mystical dancing of the Sufis. These Sufis were much different than the ones he had seen at the shrine of Muinuddin Chishti. Trained as they were by their own mystical and spiritual needs, they were summoned by his viziers to commemorate the forty-eighth birthday of the emperor. Almost three sad-happy years had flitted past since he had prayed with Nur Jahan at the tomb of Muinuddin Chishti. Sad in a sense that Prince Khusrau was given into the custody of Prince Khurram despite the emperor's wish to keep the prince at Agra. Jahangir had let the prince go most reluctantly, with a sense of foreboding inside his heart which could not be pacified. This farewell with his unfortunate son had been most heartrending for him, since it was against his will and in league with his sense of foreboding. Prince Khurram, against the veil of his own covert demands, had requested the emperor for the company of Prince Khusrau during his Deccani campaigns. Sensing the emperor's reluctance and indecision, Prince Khurram was bold enough to assert that he would be unwilling to fight the enemy if Prince Khusrau was not entrusted to his charge. The emperor had no choice but to favor his beloved son with his unfortunate one, whose rebellious nature itself had condemned him to such a state of misery and incarceration. Before their march to Deccan, Jahangir had commanded Prince Khurram to treat his unfortunate brother kindly and with utmost solicitude, since he was prone to bouts of depression and melancholia. Jahangir had further commanded Prince Khurram to write to him, but since his departure the prince had not once sent a letter to the emperor.

During these past three years, the sadness was numbered few as compared to the joys which had become a constant source of delight to his royal household and prosperous reign. All the emperor's sons and daughters were married now, with the exception of the twin princes. Bihar Banu, being the youngest daughter, was married to Prince Tahmuras the year before last. Prince Khurram had been successful in all campaigns, quelling rebellions and gaining allies with his charm and valor both. Recently, he had returned to Mandu with the laurels of victories on his shoulders, but the emperor had not the chance to receive him yet. He had still not heard any news of Prince Khusrau, but was yearning to see both his sons after the completion of his weighing ceremony. He was postponing his pain and pleasure for such a reunion until after the twin celebrations on this auspicious day. One of the celebration was for his birthday, and the other one for the victory over Deccan by his son Prince Khurram.

To commemorate the grand celebrations of his birthday, the emperor was seated on a gold scale to be weighed six times in conformity with the Moghul custom of celebrating imperial birthdays. He was to be weighed against gold, silver, gems, cloth of gold, silk and linen, spice, and finally against corn, grain and butter. All those items were to be distributed amongst the poor, and this ritual was performed twice a year, both on his solar and lunar birthdays. Right now, seated rather uncomfortably, the emperor was watching the glittering heaps of gold on the other end of the scale, which were rising high by the swift hands of the servants in calico robes and colorful turbans. The emperor himself was glittering with jewels. Pearls and rubies on his fingers appeared to vie with the strings of pearls around his neck. Diamond bracelets on his arms were glittering, and big diamonds sparkled in his ears with the fire of their own brilliance.

The gold scale itself was encrusted with rubies and turquoises. It was hoisted on a gold pole under a large canopy with meadow-green silks and brocades. The emperor was seated cross-legged, his gold stockings matching the purest gold with which the scale was wrought and fashioned.

The entire garden was teeming with guests. Most of them were lolling against satiny pillows on rich carpets, indulging in drinks and merriment, and ogling the dancing girls in drunken reverie. For the emperor's sole pleasure amidst this cumbersome ceremony, a rank of elephants with gold chains and silver bells were being paraded with all pomp and glory. Some of the elephants were wearing mantles of silk, their breastplates studded with jewels. The emperor was longing to get back to his throne under the canopy of gold and silver where he could drink in the company of his viziers and courtiers, and receive his victorious son Prince Khurram.

The garden itself was efflorescent with happy blooms, where all the princes and guests had assembled to celebrate the emperor's birthday. The

Persian and Bokhara carpets were unrolled in tides upon tides of color from the palace gates to the imposing facade of the palace. The tablas were evoking the tunes most wild and the sitars were trying to subdue their violence on the strings of peace, much like the changing of rhythms, of peace and violence inside the heart of the emperor. His thoughts were entering the harem of his palace to be with Nur Jahan, paying homage to her beauty, and kneeling in gratitude before Brenier. Brenier was the English physician who had recently and miraculously cured Nur Jahan of her fevers and violent headaches.

Am I going to lose my beloved a second time? Is she not the one and the same...beloved...Anarkali? One and the same! Tormented and tormenting. Jahangir's thoughts were gathering the rills of joy and sadness.

Anarkali was offering the emperor her gift of love on his birthday. Her own death and tragedy? But the emperor didn't wish to be sad on his birthday, Jahangir could hear one agonized groan inside the blister of his thoughts. The silence of agony in his soul was pleading with Anarkali, requesting a boon of freedom from his dead beloved. Freedom from pain, from memory, from love unforgettable! He was becoming oblivious to all.

The rounds of weighing were banished from his sight and senses. Only the last round with the jars of melted butter and sacks of corn and grain, were transporting him back to the world of celebrations. *Free at last from this ritual of a birthday celebration.* Jahangir's thoughts were heaving a sigh of relief. *Free at last, and still shackled to Anarkali's love in memories.* Jahangir was proceeding toward his throne.

How can I carry this burden of loss and grief in my soul, and still live to love another? Jahangir's thoughts were jolted to awakening by this lament from within.

The gold throne encrusted with jewels where Jahangir sat sipping his wine was his sanctuary outside the prison of pain and memory. He was fascinated by the scintillating glow of lace-patterns from the poplars where they danced and trembled like the turbulent waves. His aesthetic senses were courting bliss, and alighting on Prince Khurram in this sea of color and sparkle. The prince was appareled in purple silks, and sailing toward the throne like a devotee, followed by a stream of his companions.

"Your Majesty," Prince Khurram curtsied, "may I present Rana Amar and Kunwar Karan of Mewar? They have journeyed with me, Your Majesty, to offer their allegiance to the emperor."

"Foes turned friends are most welcome in our court." Jahangir laughed. "Surrender is an act of valor most sublime, requiring much more courage than a will to fight and win." He beamed at his new allies. "You would be equipped with Iraqi horses to enjoy the hunt in Mandu as a reward of your valor and courage."

"Thank you, Your Majesty. We are already indebted to your generosities." Kunwar Karan was the bold one to respond with utmost candor.

Rana Kamar, the bashful one, curtsied low once again, his very gaze offering gratitude, as if overwhelmed by the pools of warmth in the eyes of the emperor.

"Such rare, charming manners in this time and age when intrigues and rebellions breed more foes than friends. The emperor is greatly pleased," Jahangir commented, turning his attention to his son. "Khurram Baba, you are to command Abul Hakim to carve two life-size statues of Rana Amar and Kunwar Karan. Each one on horseback carved out of smooth, unblemished rocks. Those statues will adorn the emperor's garden at Agra right below his balcony—the seat of *jharoka*."

"I have been waiting to make a request, Your Majesty," Prince Khurram began charmingly. "Since the keys of Ahmednagar fort and other strongholds have been delivered into your hands, Your Majesty, I feel bold to make such a request. Adil Khan, as you know, Your Majesty, has had great influence in making his ambassadors, Afzal Khan and Ray Rayan, submit to the authority of your sovereign rule. Considering this, may I request that Adil Khan be bestowed with the title of *farzand*, 'son'?" He smiled.

"Summon the orphanous youth to my presence, Khurram Baba. The emperor can deny you nothing on this auspicious day of his birthday. Though its grandeur, truly but sadly, pales before the laurels of your victories." His very gaze was paying compliments.

Adil Khan was summoned from behind by the imperial agent. Since Adil Khan was expecting such summons, he was quick to hurl himself forward, prostrating himself before the emperor, all flushed and overwhelmed.

"You will become, at Shah Khurram's, request renowned in the world as my son."

Jahangir was inspired with this gift of a couplet. "The emperor bestows upon you the title of farzand," he sang happily.

"Thank you, Your Majesty. Such great honor…" Adil Khan could barely murmur. Before he could loosen the string of joy in his heart, the *kanchanis*, the dancing girls, whirled closer to the throne in a rainbow of colors.

These kanchanis were urged by the giddy viziers to offer felicitations to the emperor with song and dancing. Their voices were sailing on the strings of a lovelorn. With half-naked bellies and layers of chiffons over their waists, their jeweled hands could be seen slithering down their hips in movements both lurid and provocative. The viziers and courtiers, with their eyes shining and their faces flushed, were transfixed. Jahangir was amused, only his aesthetic senses gathering shimmering folds in color and sparkle where bodies were lost in the insignificant details of rhythm and balance. His pleasure now sated, the emperor's gaze was sweeping over the sea of his courtiers, and getting arrested to Brenier where he stood earthed. Brenier was watching this orgy of dance and revelry with a melancholy absorption. Jahangir was smiling to himself, his thoughts branding this strange physician with the epithet of a warlock, whose magic and necromancy had cured his beloved, not his medical skills. A curious, little magic wand was whistling in his own head, summoning Nur Jahan, her feverish eyes cutting his heart to pieces. His heart was too joyful this very moment to court sad illusions though, and his thoughts were blooming forth to bestow gifts upon this lone physician who appeared smitten with love and melancholia. Trays upon trays of gold and jewels were glittering in the emperor's head as magnanimous gifts, but his thoughts were bent on dissolving Brenier's melancholia with a wand of magic. Such a wand of magic-inspiration was swinging down his thoughts like a bolt of lightning. Choosing one kanchani with his gaze alone, the emperor had made his decision, not in the least aware of Brenier's own passionate heart which was lost to another kanchani, not chosen by the emperor.

"Summon Brenier to the emperor's presence," Jahangir commanded over his shoulders to Asaf Khan. "The emperor wishes to bestow a gift upon him." His gaze was fixed to the goddesses of song and dance.

Brenier was summoned quickly amidst the frenzy of music and dancing. He was stumbling forth in some daze of joy and melancholy. His expression was one of a lover in great misery, as if shot by the arrows of cupid. Jahangir's thoughts were snatched into the whimsical circle of their own wonder and curiosity.

"Brenier, you are a great physician. In recompense to your miraculous healing of the empress, the emperor is going to reward you with many a boons." Jahangir smiled. "As a first boon, the emperor bestows upon you the kanchani in shimmering chiffons of green." He indicated the lead dancer. The girl was frozen midway in her act of swirling.

"Your Majesty," muttered Brenier in all consternation. "I hope, Your Majesty, you would not be offended, if I decline this gift so munificently offered." He could not breathe. His gaze was lured to the other kanchani beside the one chosen by the emperor, with the mute appeal of a wounded lover. He had fallen in love with that particular kanchani, but his confession had brought only rejections, and now he seemed to be sinking deeper into the rivers of agony, his gaze appealing his beloved in silence. "In lieu thereof, Your Majesty." His gaze returned to the emperor. "Would your generosity permit me to claim the kanchani in crimson chiffons stitched with little stars…" He could not speak, fright and delirium choking his voice.

For one brief moment, the air itself was charged with fear and astonishment. The hush was complete and absolute, even the rhythm of music swallowed by silence. No one had ever dared decline the emperor's gift in hope of substituting for another! Besides, the girl whom Brenier had indicated was a Muslim and the physician himself a Christian. This fact alone had stricken the courtiers dumb with shock and disbelief. Soon, their shock and disbelief were dissolved; they had begun to consult each other in subdued tones. Their eyes were shining, as if saying that the emperor would be angry, and would not ever grant his consent to this ludicrous plea of the physician.

Jahangir, on the contrary, was calm and contemplative. Far from getting angry, he was not even feeling offended by the genuine request of the physician. Since he himself was not the one to entertain any religious scruples, permitting only the purity of his heart to dictate his moods and whims, he was not thinking about the disparity of religions between kanchani and the physician. He was greatly amused, rather feeling a tenderness toward this physician, who seemed to be smitten by love and suffering.

"Hushiyar Khan," Jahangir commanded Nur Jahan's eunuch in sight. "Be as gallant as to carry that kanchani in crimson chiffons into your arms, and lower her gently into the lap of Brenier. The emperor's gift to the good physician." He began to laugh.

Hushiyar Khan was quick to obey the emperor's orders. Brenier, recovering from his painful stupor, was now kissing the girl's feet. The courtiers were whispering no more, but joining the emperor in his mirth to please him. This din of mirth and revelry was slashed suddenly, as the two mastiffs sent to the emperor as gifts by the East India Company had bounded loose of Thomas Roe's vigil and restraint. They were attacking one elephant and fastening their teeth into its trunk. The emperor's mirth was now uncontrollable, as if the circus beasts had entered the arena of his own palace gardens. Thomas Roe was desperate, trying to restrain the mastiffs with the help of the royal guards. After accomplishing this task, he was plodding toward the throne, all flustered.

"The emperor would feed these mastiffs with silver tongs, Roe, and they would learn the etiquettes of the Moghul court!" Jahangir declared laughingly.

"Your Majesty, I am glad you are pleased with these gifts." One murmur of an apology escaped Thomas Roe's taut lips. "The East India company is fortunate in winning the emperor's favor. The English coach, which our King James sent, didn't meet Your Majesty's approval. Alas, the Chinese velvet was stripped and replaced with Persian velvet, the brass nails abandoned for the silver ones." His laments were burdened with the weight of remorse and apology.

"Yes, these rude mastiffs have proved to be a rare delight for the emperor on his birthday." Jahangir's mirth was dwindling. "My royal elephant, the victim of such a brutal attack! He needs hot spray to ease the discomfort inflicted by these savage beasts. This hot spray, emperor's own invention, mark you. I devised this method so that they don't suffer cold in the winters. All the royal elephants get this special treatment. And these mastiffs would be doused in cold water as well, as a reward for their violent behavior." The mists of sadness were alighting in his eyes all of a sudden.

"May I present a few portraits, Your Majesty? They are painted by the gentle hands, and no rude colors taint the beauty of their subjects." Thomas Roe was regaining his sense of wit and decorum.

"No treasures in the world are more precious to the emperor than the treasures of art, especially, if they arrest nature and mankind in colors most vivid, which have the power to throb with the life of their own." Jahangir granted his consent.

Thomas Roe's footman was at his master's side with the alacrity of Sancho Panza, carrying a bundle of portraits, and revealing one at a time with the pride of an artist. The portraits were delivered to the emperor through Asaf Khan, who could not help steal a look at them with the skepticism of an art connoisseur. Two of these portraits were of some fair and beautiful English women. One was of a woman at her toilette, and the other was of a woman seated in a parlor busy at her embroidery. The third one was of Venus and Satyr. The emperor's gaze was lingering the most on the third portrait. It sure was vivid and throbbing with life. Venus appeared to be mocking the naked Satyr, and pressing her white hand against his nose.

"A Sylvan demigod and the Italian goddess of bloom and beauty," Jahangir murmured to himself, his thoughts resurrecting the deities dead and forgotten. "The emperor likes the portrait of Jesus and the Virgin Mary the best, Roe, the one you presented last time." He lifted his gaze slowly. "This portrait here, somehow, is proclaiming loudly the superiority of white race. White Venus suspending the brown demigod by the nose? But the emperor welcomes these gifts most heartily." He smiled, waving dismissal.

"May I please, Your Majesty, once again submit my proposal about the treaty between India and England? Before I leave, Your Majesty," Thomas Roe pleaded.

"Oh, yes, you are deserting us, Roe, leaving us soon, much too soon. This very evening, to be precise, how the emperor forgets. Leaving the gold-paved streets of Hind for the dusty roads of England. This is the land of the heathens, you think?" Jahangir's tone was light and bantering. "You have been unhappy in Hind, the emperor regrets. Your chaplain, John Hall, died, didn't he? And didn't you send a letter to someone in Surat requesting another clergyman? Don't be surprised as to how, but the emperor knows the import of your letter. 'I can't live here without the comfort of God's word and heavenly sacraments.' Didn't you write that?"

"True to my own God, as you are to your own, Your Majesty," Thomas Roe murmured humbly. "May I get your consent to that trade treaty, Your Majesty, before I leave?" he pleaded assiduously.

"The emperor doesn't deal with these insignificant matters, Roe. Though he has assigned Asaf Khan to deliver a letter of agreement into your hands," Jahangir intoned thoughtfully. "I have also left with him a letter to King James, penned by my own hands. You may recite my greetings to your king in my own words: when Your Majesty shall open this letter, let your heart be as fresh as a sweet garden. Gifts to your king are in safe keeping with Asaf Khan too. An exquisite tent in a rainbow of colors. A royal silk umbrella. Silk-wool Bokhara carpets. Several caskets laden with jewels. A rare breed of red deer. And a pair of antelopes. Don't forget to take special care of the antelopes."

"Thank you, Your Majesty. I will guard them with my life," Thomas Roe breathed happily. "If I may, Your Majesty? May I ask if those antelopes are tame?"

"One is perfectly tamed, as far as the emperor knows. He is my personal friend, and the emperor has assigned a monument to him at Agra." Jahangir beamed congenially. "And now as a token of our own friendship and farewell, share a cup of wine with the emperor." He was holding out his own cup to Jawahir Khan, his very gaze commanding him to fill another one for Thomas Roe.

The strong Indian wine was offered to Thomas Roe in a cup of gold encrusted with rubies. A few sips, and his eyes were watery. The astringent taste was burning through his throat like hot lava. Since the emperor was in a jovial mood, he was commanding Jawahir Khan to replenish the ambassador's cup as soon as it was empty, further commanding Thomas Roe to drink to the emperor's health and for the prosperity of his empire. Over the fifth cup, Thomas Roe was caught under the assault of sneezes most violent and painful. Hot tears were running down his eyes, his lips dry and stinging. This wild spectacle of a big man sneezing over his wine was plunging the emperor into a violent fit of mirth. The emperor was laughing uncontrollably. His hands pressed against his ribs, he was hauling himself up with a desperate attempt at controlling his laughter. Finally, his mirth was subsided, and he was able to wave dismissal in a dignified manner. Before leaving his throne, he was shooting one last command at Jawahir Khan.

"Bestow this gold flagon and the jeweled cup, as gifts, upon this distinguished ambassador as the tokens of remembrance for my birthday." Jahangir was sailing on the clouds of mirth toward his palace.

Since Prince Khurram claimed his place beside the emperor in his merry sailing, Jahangir tossed a benevolent invitation at the prince.

"Invite Kunwar Karan to the palace, Khurram Baba. His wit and valor will gather bounteous gifts from the empress, I am sure." Jahangir's mirth was gathering more bubbles of joy. "No more Khurram Baba? *Shah Jahan*, should the emperor say, to exalt your blessed title with his royal lips."

"Shah Jahan, Your Majesty, is blessed with another princely son! He will be the one receiving bounteous gifts from the empress for himself and for his royal son," Prince Khurram announced happily.

"Are you always in the habit of postponing the happiest of news till the end?" Jahangir exclaimed, his eyes spilling joy, and his feet floating over the marble steps in his haste to reach the gilded portals.

Seated on a gold couch with Nur Jahan beside him, Jahangir was still celebrating his birthday with wine and gifts. All the royal household had assembled in this room, including the guests invited by the emperor. This palace at Mundu could boast of large, spacious rooms, but this one chosen by the emperor for his birthday celebrations was the largest of them all, with tall ceilings and the size of several courtyards. On all sides, it was flanked by imposing windows in latticework, which were left curtainless to absorb the glory of the gardens. Some of the begums were lolling against the brocaded pillows, and some were sitting couchant on the gold davenports. The emperor's wives were wafting their own scents of joy and perfume, and heaping gifts at the emperor's feet with cries of great felicitations. The young princes and princesses were happy and heedless in their own world of cards and jests. The younger ones attended by the royal ayahs were the center of attraction for everyone, smothered with hugs and kisses, and shifted from lap to lap with the warmth of love and tenderness. Jahangir himself had hugged his newly born grandson, Prince Shah Shuja, bestowing upon him the strings of pearls, and cradling him into the warmth of his love and endearments. After this he was surrounded by his wives and flooded with gifts. Finally, he had sought refuge on the gold couch beside Nur Jahan, pleading reprieve from gifts and felicitations.

"On your birthday, Your Majesty, the fortunate ones are favored with great titles," Nur Jahan teased softly. "Prince Khurram, now Shah Jahan. The ruler of the world! What an envious title to hold and cherish." Her eyes were shining.

"And didn't the emperor bestow on you the title of Padishah Begum? This very morning, officially and in the presence of all?" was Jahangir's tender exclamation.

"Then Padishah Begum is going to bestow precious gifts on valorous Shah Jahan, if not titles." Nur Jahan eased herself up gracefully. She clapped her hands for her lady-in-waiting to fetch the gifts. "Come, my handsome prince. Receive your gifts from the empress, if not from Padishah Begum."

"From Mamma, Empress, Padishah Begum, all in one," Shah Jahan murmured.

"A jeweled sword and a dress of honor for right now, my gallant prince." Nur Jahan held out the gifts to the prince. "And an Arabian horse with a rich saddle, and an elephant with gilded howdah are waiting for your pleasure in the palace gardens." Her eyes were brimming with love and adoration.

"My deepest thanks and gratitude to the empress." Shah Jahan fell into another flourish of a curtsy. "May I, Padishah Begum, request that you bestow gifts on Kunwar Karan with your own gracious hands?"

"With the delight of an empress, and with the munificence of a Padishah Begum," Nur Jahan chanted happily, her gaze selecting a couple of gifts displayed by her lady-in-waiting, Mehr Harwi.

Kunwar Karan was summoned promptly, who was lingering behind not very far, expecting such an honor, his heart dithering.

"Padishah Begum." Kunwar Karan succeeded in offering one awkward curtsy.

"A rosary of pearls. One jeweled sword and a dress of honor for the valorous friend of Shah Jahan." Nur Jahan beamed.

"And the emperor has nothing to offer you, Karan, but a promise of hawks. Falcons, horses and elephants!" Jahangir declared suddenly.

"You may offer him, Your Majesty, your coat-of-mail. It is hanging right below the portrait of Jesus and the Virgin Mary, where your royal gaze can touch and possess it," Nur Jahan challenged mirthfully. "And a couple of rings from your fingers, perhaps? The one with the ruby, and the other with the large emerald?"

"The emperor would be robbed of all his treasures on his birthday." Jahangir slipped off the rings from his fingers, holding them out to Kunwar Karan, who edged closer, bowing and stumbling.

"Better check the generosity of the emperor, Padishah Begum." Shah Jahan shot a sweet warning at Nur Jahan. "His Majesty has given away Hind to Thomas Roe in some sort of trade agreement in his letter to King James, it seems."

"A letter to King James!" Nur Jahan exclaimed, her gaze shifting from the prince to the emperor with a flashing intensity. "May we hear its import, Your Majesty?"

"It is of no interest to any of the ladies, my Nur." Jahangir drained his cup.

"Yes, it's of great interest to us, Your Majesty." Jagat Gosaini floated closer, concealing the stars of jealousy in her agate eyes. "The account of the titles needs to be settled first, though. Since my son can boast of his title, Shah Jahan, as the ruler of the world; his mother, doesn't she deserve a worthy title?"

"You are the empress of my heart, my white rose." Jahangir laughed. "Why do all the emperor's wives forget their titles? Didn't the emperor bestow on you the title of Bilqis Makani, Lady of the Pure Abode? Your heart is pure as snow, my love, though, jealousy, at times, tarnishes its purity." His gaze was intense and caressive.

"Your jests and flatteries, Your Majesty, corrupt my heart more than any pools of jealousy in my own thoughts," Jagat Gosaini quipped. "And yet thank you, Your Majesty, for this old, worthy title which I would be proud to take to my grave."

"That letter, Your Majesty, must not be forgotten in this war of titles. Yet, I too request a title, since you are in a generous mood on this auspicious day of your birthday." Sahiba Jamali floated close to the royal circle.

"Another forgetful wife! The emperor is under siege," Jahangir murmured, mock disbelief shining in his eyes. "You are the emperor's mistress of beauty, love. How quickly you forget of your beautiful title." His gaze was alighting on Prince Perwiz, trailing behind her as some shadow of love and devotion. "Come forward, my invisible prince," he commanded suddenly. "Since your mamma is the mistress of beauty, are you the prince of peace, in Burhanpur, I mean?"

"Yes, Your Majesty," was Prince Perwiz's laconic response.

Prince Perwiz was saved of a royal inquisition by the fortunate intervention of Malika Jahan. She had come upon this royal circle like the breath of perfumed air, her eyes shining with mirth, and her lavender gown evoking more attention than her beauty.

"I don't need a title, Your Majesty. I am the lady of the world, as my name itself proclaims," Malika Jahan sang happily. She was forgetting why she had bounded into this circle with such tumultuous glee. "Oh, yes, the lady of the world has to know each word and each detail in that letter, Your Majesty." Her eyes were sparkling with mirth.

"Yes, that letter is getting lost in this melee of titles, Your Majesty." One loud chorus was rippling forth from the lips of the other wives. Amongst them, the voices of Nurunnisa, Khairunnisa and Salihah Banu were more urgent and demanding.

"How fortunate for you, Your Majesty! You can keep the contents of the letter sealed, while we chant and sue for titles." Karamasi Begum's sing-song voice was rising above the crescendo of appeals. She was hugging her daughter, Princess Bihar Banu, who was seated not far from her husband, Prince Tahmuras. In the background, Prince Jahandar and Prince Shahriyar could be heard laughing.

"Your sweet rebellion has plunged the emperor into a pit of quandary, my Nur," Jahangir chided. "How is he going to construct this missive in his head now?" He was succeeding in eliciting a frown amidst the star-dance of mirth in her eyes.

"You better breathe life into that missive, Your Majesty, before the insurrection really begins." Nur Jahan sank into the golden depths of her couch laughingly.

"Shah Jahan, the instigator of this clamor, stands witness to my greetings to King James." Jahangir flashed his son a mirthful rebuke. "Since he is the chief rebel, he would have to recite that…when the leisure permits him." His rebuke was unnoticed by Shah Jahan, who had installed himself at the feet of his adored wife, Arjumand Banu.

Shah Jahan was arrested in a world of his own, oblivious to everyone and everything with the exception of his beloved. He was gazing into the dark eyes of his wife, as if worshiping a goddess, oblivious even of his two royal children who had bounced right into his lap, now snuggled blissfully. His one arm was cradling his two-year-old daughter, Princess Jahanara, and the other stroking absently the head of his one-year-old son, Prince Dara Shikoh. Behind them, their royal ayah could be seen dozing off with the newly born prince, Prince Shah Shuja in her lap. But Jahangir's gaze was riveted to the rapt expression on his son's face. So tender and sublime it was, that he was awed by the purity of his son's love for his wife. Tearing his gaze away, he was returning his attention to the circle of his own wives, his look dreamy and profound.

"Where to begin?" Jahangir waved his arms helplessly. "Ah, yes, it is coming to me in rags royal and bleating." His heart was melting by the warmth of eagerness in the eyes of his wives. "Make of it what you may, and leave the rest to your sweet imaginations, my sweets. King James must be sneezing his heart out to be remembered by so many royal ladies all at once." He paused before reciting his missive in bits and shreds. *"The letter of love and friendship which you sent and the presents, tokens of your good affection toward me, I have received by the hands of your ambassador, Sir Thomas Roe. He well deserves to be your trusted servant. I have given my general command to all the ports and kingdoms of my dominions to receive merchants of the English nation as my friends and subjects. So that, in what place whatsoever they choose to live, they may have reception and residence to their own satisfaction, concerning safety and comfort. And what goods whatsoever they desire to buy or sell, they may have free liberty without any restraint."* He closed his eyes, as if trying to remember more.

"What goods whatsoever, Your Majesty?" Miryam Uzzmanni broke her silence. "The English goods are not worth trading, Your Majesty. How could you sanction such a privilege? Have you forgotten the gilded mirrors? They arrived here unglued and unpolished, falling to pieces in the very process of unpacking!"

"And the leather cases, Your Majesty!" Shah Jahan was awakening to join his grandmother and to voice his opposition against this trade treaty. "All shipments gathering mold outside, and decaying from within."

"And the rings of most atrocious quality and design, Your Majesty." Asmat Begum could not help joining in this tirade.

"And cheap velvet, Your Majesty!" Asaf Khan too was leaping into this arena of protests with the bravado of a soldier.

"And the English coach with brass nails, Your Majesty." Itmadudaula Khan was the next one to jump into this sea of discontent.

"Not to mention the Mercator's map, which depicted India as the smallest of the continents, Your Majesty." Nur Jahan was not to be left behind.

Jahangir was absorbing all with an air of self-pity and self-resignation. A thin smile was curling on his lips, and his gaze sweeping from one to the other dreamily and indulgently. The serenity in his gaze and thoughts was reaching out to his daughter Princess Bihar Banu, who stood by the latticework window, whispering to her husband, Prince Tahmuras. Princess Sultanunissa was standing close by, her own gaze wandering. This eldest daughter of the emperor, the sister of Prince Khusrau, was pressing her niece, Princess Jahanara, to her breast. Prince Balaqi, her darling nephew as being the son of Prince Khusrau, was watching her under some spell of mute adoration. The smile on the emperor's lips was fading, his own gaze now in wild pursuit to find Prince Khusrau. His heart was aching and throbbing, all of a sudden, longing for one glimpse of his unfortunate son. His gaze was returning to the ocean of his sweet rebels, no pain surfacing in his eyes, but the warmth of mockery and indulgence.

"This is the night of sweet forgetfulness! How you all sweetly forget, especially, my sweet mamma." Jahangir's tone was a ripple of half rebuke, half regret. "The ladies of my harem, their love for table knives, ostrich plumes, cloth of gold, just to name a few. All these we import from England; why? Simply to sweeten the wants with precious needs nurtured by the royal ladies. And England, craving our own goods with the greed of a lion's share."

"And the lamb of the lion, Thomas Roe! Will he stay in Hind forever, Your Majesty?" Miryam Uzzmanni shot her disapproval.

"It is insignificant to the emperor whether he stays or leaves, dear Mamma," Jahangir murmured patiently. "Though, he is leaving!"

"I have a feeling, Your Majesty, he will be following you to Gujrat where you plan to hunt," Shah Jahan predicted prophetically.

"And if he plays his viol before you, Your Majesty, you will be inviting him to Kashmir where we journey next," Nur Jahan teased brightly.

"My sweet rebel and my sweet tormentor." Jahangir flashed a warm challenge at her. "You will yet hear to…" He paused, noticing a coterie of servants carrying silver trays laden with fresh fruits. "Ah, the most precious of birthday gifts, and the most delicious too, the emperor can predict." His eyes were lit up with joy at the sudden remembrance of these gifts promised to him at the dinner table. "These rare gems from lands far and undefiled by greed." His very gaze was tasting these fruits and the lips of the beloved lands. "The celebrated melons from Karez and Badakhshan." His eyes were following each tray, as it was being lowered on the table with a cloth of gold. "Grapes from Kabul and Samarkand. The sweet pomegranates from Yazd and Farrah. Pears from Samarkand and Badakhshan. Apples from Kabul and Kashmir. Pineapples from Cambay." He was watching the servants retrace their steps, catching sight of Shah Jahan on the way. The prince in return was watching his stepsister Princess Sultanunissa. A familiar ache was uncurling its lips in Jahangir's heart once again, and his own lips were voicing its sudden violence. "Shah Jahan, where is Prince Khusrau?"

"My wise brother, Your Majesty, didn't wish to sadden you with his state of melancholy on this auspicious day of your birthday," was Shah Jahan's suave, yet flustered response. "He is languishing in his own apartments with his beloved wife," he added winsomely, as if awakening from a shock by this abrupt query.

"And yet, the emperor is sad," Jahangir murmured to himself. He was heaving himself up slowly and ponderously. "Come, Nur, delight the emperor with tales wild from Gujrat and Kashmir since you have gathered much from books and dreams, all ethereal, all phantasmagoric." He assisted her to her feet. He was turning his back on all, seeking the polished rungs of the staircase, winding up toward the royal bedrooms.

Inside the vast bedroom with Persian carpets and gilded paintings, Jahangir stood pondering with his back toward Nur Jahan. He had just picked a copy of Hafiz's diwan from his desk and was holding it wistfully. Turning suddenly, he held out this book of poetry to Nur Jahan, as if offering her the world.

"My own birthday gift from the emperor to you for your love for the tormented child in him." Jahangir's eyes were lit up with love and sadness.

"Your Majesty!" Nur Jahan was overwhelmed, claiming the book, and hugging it to her breast in mute reverence.

She was in a daze. Receiving such a gift from the emperor was like possessing the kingdoms. For once in her life, words failed her. Her very thoughts were bereft of speech even in her head where they stood lurching and swooning. The sapphire stars in her eyes were twinkling a mist of tears. Her white face, with the touch of ivory, was glowing, turning luminescent. The bluest of blue silks gathered at her waist in a jeweled sash had planted her there in the semblance of a marble figurine who would outlive the ravages of time, eternally young, eternally beautiful.

"You love poetry, the light of my soul." Jahangir was smiling into the eyes of his own cruel past where Anarkali was much like Nur Jahan. He had parted from her once and forever with the sparkle of dewdrops in her eyes as tears; the emperor was blinking away this vision. "You are the emperor's love poem, so the emperor presents you a wealth in poetry, instead of riches in gold and jewels." His heart was thundering to absorb Anarkali and Nur Jahan into the very oceans of his numb, chilling soul.

"Such riches as gold and jewels are not coveted by Nur Jahan, Your Majesty." Nur Jahan could barely murmur. "And yet, such riches too have made my dreams flower into gardens and rest-houses." She smiled through the mists of her tears. "Shaddara garden in Lahore, for one. Nur sarai…and another one in Patna…" Her sweet reminiscences were silenced by a sudden shower of kisses from the lips of the emperor.

"Your dreams, my Nur, would flower eternally into the gardens of Kashmir when we go there…" Jahangir was kissing her under some spell of hunger and violence.

The emperor was crushing Nur Jahan to him, hurting her lips, yet holding Anarkali tenderly into the ravished folds of his soul. He appeared to be draining the beauty of both his loves inside the chalice of his parched, hungry kisses. His heart was swollen like the river of pain and turbulence, longing to find his love inside some abyss profound and bottomless, clinging to the beauty of this terrible love, who was his torment and beloved both. The large, canopied bed before his sight was rising like the tomb of Anarkali, a sacred tomb, which he must defile by the raging lust in his loins and inside the vaults of his psyche.

Chapter Seven

The fragrant valley of Kashmir was welcoming the royal guests, as Jahangir and Nur Jahan rode side-by-side in utmost luxury, which the Moghul pomp and splendor could boast and provide. Ahead of the royal couple was a procession of the Kashmiri girls with flowers in their hair. They were singing and dancing in wild abandon to the nature's own rhythm. Nur Jahan had chosen to ride an Arabian steed with a white mane, while the emperor was riding his favorite piebald with patches of black. Their caparisoned horses with red velvet saddles were as royally decked as the royal couple splashed with the colors in silks and jewels. Nur Jahan's blue silks were strewn with diamonds. The large amethyst in Jahangir's turban was spilling its own dazzling colors.

This pine-valley itself was adorned with beautiful vistas to complement the royal couple with its own abundance of color and wealth. The wild flowers in thick clusters were a colorful tapestry, filling the air with their scent and scenic splendor. Nur Jahan was awed by the vibrant colors, cherishing each bloom as if they were some jewels in the royal treasuries than silken wonders inside the hearts of these pine-valleys. Peace and serenity were all around them, she was thinking, but their hearts were tainted with the sorrows of the past, and with apprehensions for the future. Nur Jahan, blessed with the spirit of joy and vivacity, could forget all with the exception of Anarkali's demon inside the emperor's heart, and of his health on the verge of collapse. And the emperor could remember nothing but the shadows of death arrested somewhere between the bubbles of time where recent past could not be torn away form the years long departed. Four years with the glare of joys and tragedies had hissed past since Prince Shah Jahan's return from Deccan. And now the emperor himself was caught amidst the whirlwind of his own ailments and recoveries.

The emperor's birthday celebrations had ended with his excesses in drinking and feasting. He was still celebrating the valor and victory of Shah

Jahan. The emperor was always trying to convince the empress and his other wives when under the assault of the temptations to drink himself to oblivion. Oblivion didn't come to him easy though. He could imbibe wine by the flagons for weeks and months before it would obey the commands of his drunken stupor. Against his whims and temptations, he had interludes of light-hearted gaiety when he would be visited by a false sense of euphoria and buoyancy. The same sense of euphoria and buoyancy had been his companion when he had moved his court to Ahmadabad, the capital of Gujrat. Here, he was greeted with the news that Prince Shah Jahan was blessed with a daughter whom he had named Roshanara. And then he had plunged himself headlong into hunting excursions, spruced with wine parties in the evenings. Fatigue from hunting and drunkenness were taking their toll on his body, and within a few weeks of his stay at Ahmadabad, he had become the victim of asthma. Nur Jahan, guided by the royal physicians, had pleaded with the emperor to cut down on his drinking, making a slow and steady progress in her endeavor, more so by her wit and wisdom than by her pleas followed by restrictions. For almost a year, Jahangir's health was balanced on the scale of asthma attacks and recoveries, but he had not fully recovered. Within that year, as the emperor had moved to Gujrat, he had heard about the death of Man Singh.

Man Singh, though the emperor's maternal uncle, had had a major part in inciting Prince Khusrau to rebellion. Right after Jahangir's accession, Man Singh had been bold enough to predict that the emperor's reign would last only two years. Jahangir had merely laughed himself to forgetfulness, condoning Man Singh's divinations, which were based on astrological misconceptions, the emperor had asserted. After two years, while the emperor's reign was still prosperous and flourishing, Man Singh's own heart had begun to court fears and doubts. He had decided to flee to Bikaner, pressed by his own fears that the emperor's rage would surely fall on him sooner or later. Since then he had been living there in seclusion and obscurity. Several years of self-exile, and Man Singh's name was never mentioned to the emperor until now when the royal entourage had halted at Gujrat. The emperor was informed that Man Singh had contracted leprosy, but was now completely healed. Jahangir was curious to witness this miracle with his own eyes, and had sent orders for Man Singh to appear before him. Man Singh, receiving these summons, had become so overcome with fear that he had died of sheer fright on his way from Bikaner to Gujrat.

Gujrat had become a haven for hunting for both the emperor and the empress, Ahmadabad their favorite resort for hunting and exploring. Nur

Jahan could boast of hunting many a birds and tigers, while honing her skills to perfection. She was close to perfecting her skills when the royal entourage had to return to Agra. More than a year had flitted past on the wings of heedless time since their visit to Gujrat, the emperor had to remind the empress, though both were equally baffled by the flight of time unnoticed by them. Only Thomas Roe's final departure to England was noticed in Gujrat. He had followed the emperor from Mandu to Gujrat as predicted by Prince Shah Jahan. He had stayed in Gujrat only a few months, exploring on his own, and languishing on the ports for fun and pleasure. Before sailing on his good ship *Anne*, he had imparted his last bulletin of news from England that a great bard by the name of Shakespeare had died.

The journey back to Agra had been swift and frolicsome, enhanced by the breeze of good news that Prince Shah Jahan was blessed with another princely son. This third prince of Arjumand Banu was born in the village of Dauhad and named Aurangzeb. Upon reaching Agra, the royal entourage were awed by the ecliptic manifestation between Libra and Scorpio. Gazing at the sky, Jahangir had thought that the eclipse looked like a javelin, but then he had exclaimed under some spell of disbelief, "It has the perfect shape of a porcupine!"

Sixteen days later, Agra had been visited by another wondrous manifestation. In the same quarter of the sky, a comet with long tail had made its appearance. By now the astrologers were quivering with fear, divining portents and foretelling misfortunes.

Most of the misfortunes had fallen on the royal household, though much later than predicted. Jahangir had to leave the sanctuary of Agra to quell rebellions in Lahore. Soon, he had succeeded in obtaining submission from the proud lord of this rich and warring province. Amidst these battles of pride and politics, Jahangir had not neglected to indulge in the pleasures of hunting and exploring. He was much enamored by one wild antelope which he had hunted without causing much injury to the beast. This antelope had become his companion of the wars and intrigues, and with much patience and affection, he had succeeded in taming it. So delighted was he after this task was accomplished that he had ordered a house to be built for this antelope inside the very precincts of Lahore, which would be called *Hiran Minar*. No sooner had he returned to Agra, that he was stricken with grief by the most tragic of news.

The emperor's wife, Bilqis Makani, the mother of his beloved son Prince Shah Jahan, had died suddenly. Jahangir's own grief at his wife's death was doubled by the grief of his grieving son. Shah Jahan had loved and revered his mother with the passion of an innocent child who could never imagine such a loss, save alone its crushing impact on his passionate heart. Such hopeless, helpless pain had taken hold of Jahangir's own mind at the grief of his beloved son, that he had begun searching for antidotes and diversions to ease Shah Jahan's suffering. Thinking about Prince Shah Jahan's artistic temperament and of his passionate devotion to gardens, the name of Fatehpur Sikri had come to Jahangir's mind like a godsend prayer and revelation. Fatehpur Sikri had beautiful gardens built by Akbar, and Jahangir had thought of transporting his entire household to Fatehpur Sikri for the sole comfort and diversion of Shah Jahan. He himself had found comfort in such thoughts and had decided to move to Fatehpur Sikri before embarking on his long journey to Kashmir. Prince Shah Jahan's sufferings were visible in tears and laments, while the emperor's were mute and stabbing like the blades of ice, though he had begun to pray and meditate, praying to his father, the Great Akbar, not to God, as if seeking justice for the injuries done by God to mankind.

 No intercession from man or God had come to the emperor to console him in his sufferings. His own grief was unmitigated, and he could find no magic potions to pacify the grief of his son. While the preparations of journey to Fatehpur Sikri were being finalized, the emperor had fallen victim to his own bouts of drinking and forgetting. He was drinking heavily, and defying the onslaught of asthma, naming such attacks as insignificant tremors of the body and soul. Before the royal household could embark on their journey to Fatehpur Sikri, Prince Jahandar was struck with yellow fever. This handsome prince was sucked into the furnace of death, and Agra was once again the house of mourning under the weight of this fresh tragedy.

 The veil of mourning was not to leave the royal family, every scalding hour of the day and night, it was becoming obvious. After much delay, on their way to Fatehpur Sikri, they were confronted with evil news if not with misfortunes. Bubonic plague had broken out in Doab, inching its way to the very destination where they had hoped to find refuge from pain and sorrow. Even before the royal entourage could reach the precincts of Fatehpur Sikri, the plague had spread as far as Lahore and Sirhind. It had enveloped Agra, Delhi and the entire population of Doab into mists of shock and horror, where death stood looming and grinning. To fight this epidemic was a lost cause, but to provide relief to the living victims was one imperative need which had possessed the emperor's mind like an eternal conflagration. Some cosmic energy was poured into his body to fight death, and to release life from the clutches of this foul murrain. After installing his royal family in the palace at Fatehpur Sikri, he had immersed himself in all possible endeavors to defeat this pestilence and to provide aid to the families of the victims.

The emperor had banished his own sorrow to crusade against death, disease and suffering. He was quick to devise a plan which could accelerate the supply of food and medicine to all, even in the remotest of villages in Hind. This plan was conceived with the swiftness of lightning, and executed with the precision of an arrow. The emperor was bursting with cosmic energy, and Anarkali had become his healer and comforter both, where no grief or despair could be seen inside the vast misery of this earth blackened with the soot of death. She was his love and salvation, comforting him, and visiting with him the families of the afflicted and the suffering. By the time the epidemic was disappearing by the virtue of its own havoc and culmination, the cosmic energy of the emperor was draining. He was seeking bliss in oblivion. Anarkali had left him. Wine was the panacea to all his sufferings. He had succumbed to the violence of asthma.

Fever, lethargy and shortness of breath had become the emperor's legacy from the violence of asthma attacks. He was further afflicted with a pressure around the temples and in the middle of his forehead. This pressure alone was enough to affect his sight with the onslaught of severe headaches. The royal physician Hakim Rukna, with his skillful ministrations, had been able to cure the emperor's headaches, and his sight was restored to normal. Hakim Rukna was an expert surgeon; he had cut open the vein in the emperor's head, draining out several ounces of blood to ease the pressure. After that surgical procedure, the pressure around the emperor's temples was immediately reduced, and he could feel instant relief from the pressure and congestion. For his asthma attacks, the emperor was advised not to drink, or to reduce the consumption of wine for a few months at least. Feeling reprieve from his physical sufferings and to ward off his mental ones, he had turned his thoughts toward his son, Shah Jahan. Fatehpur Sikri was recovered from the ravages of plague, and the emperor had ordered several excursions to this city to divert his son's attention from grief and mourning. The prince and the emperor had visited the shrines and the architectural wonders which Akbar had had built during his reign of forty-nine years. Anarkali was the emperor's guide wherever he went, but in truth Nur Jahan was with him at all times, the empress incarnate to allot small portions of wine to the emperor, and to delight both the prince and the emperor with her wit and wisdom. Shah Jahan was consoled, more truthfully so after reading the inscription which Akbar had inscribed on the victory gate of Fatehpur Sikri.

The world is a bridge. Pass over it, but do not build upon it. He who hopes for an hour may hope for an eternity. The world is but an hour. Spend it in devotion, the rest is unseen.

Jahangir had learned to nurture hopes like a gardener whose labor and patience could be rewarded with scented blooms in the future. And the road to Kashmir was a journey of hope, indeed. The emperor was drinking only the allotted portions of wine in perfect obedience to the advice of his royal physicians. His mental and physical sufferings of the past few months had honed his features to pale ivory, but his wit was returning, along with his love for life. Before continuing his journey, he had celebrated his fiftieth birthday with the usual pomp and weighing ceremonies as befitting the emperor of Hind. He had also visited the tomb of Muinuddin Chishti to make a solemn vow not to shoot with gun and bullet, and not to injure any living thing with his own hands. Nur Jahan had watched him take that vow of nonviolence, and could not help but inquire the logic behind this vow. Jahangir was quick to satisfy her curiosity.

"If you already don't know, my pearl, my grandson Prince Shuja is ill. I am making this vow with a prayer that he gets well. Besides, at Allahabad, my lovely Nur, when I was a young prince and had set up my own court, I had vowed to myself that on my fiftieth birthday I would cease the practice of hunting and shooting any living creature with my own hands," Jahangir responded effusively.

The wholesome air of Kashmir had worked wonders on the emperor's health, though his features were still pale and gaunt. Even his pallor had a subtle glow in it, shining with the vitality of youth, as if the emperor was transformed into a young prince once again. He was forever bestowing presents on Nur Jahan, and showering her with compliments. His aesthetic senses were not content alone with the beauty in nature, but with the beauty of the cosmic mind. Well versed in the doctrines of religion and philosophy, he was striving to learn more to quench the inner hungers of his body and soul. In his eagerness to feed his mind with the fresh morsels of spirituality, he had sought the company of one Jain monk, Jadhrup, in his own hermitage, instead of summoning him to his palace. He had spent many a cherished hours with him to gain some sort of understanding in the science of Vedanta. After returning to his palace, he would share this knowledge with Nur Jahan, goading her to argument and discussion as to the similarities between the two sciences, that of Sufism and of Vedanta.

Nur Jahan's own mind was quite sharp to absorb and dissect each word, and she would get into heated discussions with the emperor. Theology was not her forte though, and while riding through the hunting grounds, she would implore the emperor to let her hunt and shoot the tigers. Rather, mocking gently for his vow of nonviolence, which would not permit him the pleasure of hunting. The emperor would always consent most heartily, wearing her mockery in his own eyes and admiring her skills in hunting. Once she had killed one ferocious tiger with one single shot, and the emperor had been in raptures over her prowess in hunting and shooting. On another occasion, she had shot two tigers with one shot each, straight from her howdah, and had knocked two more insensible with four shots. Jahangir was more awed than impressed, and had given her a pair of diamond bracelets as a reward for her unerring skills.

Nur Jahan was wearing those bracelets even today while riding beside the emperor, their royal steeds enjoying a leisurely canter. She was quiet and content. At this particular moment, she was gazing at her diamond bracelets wistfully. Her thoughts were recollecting the words of a poet who had penned an impromptu couplet at the scene of hunting, where she had shot two tigers.

Though Nur Jahan in form be a woman. In the ranks of men, she is a tiger-slayer.

A beatific smile was curling on Nur Jahan's lips at the thought of this cherished memory. The valleys of Kashmir had risen to greet her with the soma of youth, and she had drunk deep of its nectar—blossoming like a *flower*. The scented flowers in these pine-valleys had the power to turn any couple into romantic lovers, and Jahangir was the first to be smitten afresh with love, loving his beloved Nur with the passion of a youthful prince, and granting her the freedom to build palaces, mosques and gardens inside the very heart of Kashmir.

Jahangir was riding quietly, enjoying the bliss and peace in nature, and of the valleys. His aesthetic senses were absorbing all colors, and grateful for the beautiful companion beside him. Anarkali was resting sweetly in her tomb at Lahore, leaving the royal couple alone to the indulgence of their own bliss and ecstasy. Nur Jahan's thoughts were getting entangled inside the wonderworks of her own design and architecture, though she was becoming aware of the emperor's silence, sensing his sadness even before he himself could catch its scent and stealth. His thoughts were looking back at the shades and shadows of death. His beloved son, Jahandar! His beloved wife, Bilqis Makani! Something deep within him was entombing him in peace with Anarkali.

The Kashmiri girls were still singing and dancing ahead of the royal couple. They were caught in their own mood of joy and festivity with a carefree abandon. Jahangir was not watching the dancers though; his gaze was unveiling the vistas as if seeing the bride of nature for the very first time. Nur Jahan's gaze was unfolding fields upon fields of saffron, which were coming into view against the undulating contours of the valleys. Saffron and other wild flowers were wafting such an overpowering scent that Jahangir could feel the vein in his forehead throbbing with the threat of a headache. He pressed his temples, sneezing violently, his eyes stinging. The strong scent pervading the glens and the valleys was now seething in his very veins, and he appeared to be gasping for breath.

"Your Majesty, you should have permitted Hakim Rukna to accompany us," Nur Jahan commented, concealing her fear inside the blue pools of her eyes.

"Ah, that messiah of age! He has cured the emperor completely, my Nur." Jahangir was feeling a sudden relief. "This perfume from saffron is overpowering." His eyes were absorbing sparkle from the amethyst in his turban. "The emperor will suffer the siege of a headache, not the shortness of breath, if he doesn't flee from this valley of perfume and enchantment." He spurred his horse, joining the bevy of Kashmiri girls. "Don't you get headaches from this strong scent of saffron, my pretty damsels?"

"What is a headache, Your Majesty?" was one baffled exclamation from the lips of the lead dancer.

"Stay in bliss to your ignorance then, my lovely heathens." Jahangir laughed.

"When one feels a terrible, pounding ache in one's head, it's called a headache, sweet maidens," Nur Jahan expounded.

The Kashmiri girls merely laughed, further baffled by this explanation, for they had not ever suffered any headaches. Headaches were unknown in Kashmir, they would have confessed, if the emperor would have asked. But both the emperor and the empress were cantering past them, while they stood there in stunned silence.

"The emperor should take lessons from you, my lovely mentor." Jahangir flashed Nur Jahan a wistful glance. "How would you describe the Bubonic plague, except that the victims had buboes under the armpits, or in the groin, or below the throat?"

"Please, Your Majesty, let us forget about those terrible times. Those terrible deaths, people dying in droves," Nur Jahan pleaded softly. "All I can remember is people talking about mice. They had seen the foul creatures rushing out of their holes, striking themselves against the doors of the houses and falling dead at the very steps. Visiting deaths upon the occupants if they didn't vacate their own homes."

"Yes, sweet Nur, you are right," Jahangir murmured back. "This paradise on earth makes one almost forget the great misfortunes in the whole wide world. Kashmir is a garden of eternal spring, a delightful flowerbed, and a heart-expanding heritage for the dervishes. If one were to praise Kashmir, oceans of ink would run dry in writing paeans upon paeans..." His thoughts were swallowed by the panoramic wonder unfolding before his sight like the dream-clouds. He reined his horse at the edge of the plateau where Nur Jahan's newly built mosque stood lofty and picturesque.

Nur Jahan too had brought her steed to a slow halt beside the emperor, her gaze warm and brimming with admiration. The Pattar mosque with its scalloped doors and carved vaulting was welcoming the royal visitors with a silent grandeur. The Kashmiri girls were lost in the valleys down below. They were merely obeying the emperor's earlier command that they were free to leave as soon as the emperor and the empress rode ahead of them. Now the lover and the beloved were left alone to explore their own altars of love. Both were quiet, both astride their mounts like the miracles of nature caught on the canvas of time. Both were cherishing the luxury of silence and solitude. Jahangir was admiring the front facade of nine arches, from where the portico down below was still under construction. The shallow, decorative cusped arches, further enclosed in rectangular frames, appeared to be suspended in the air. Jahangir's gaze was abandoning this piece of great architecture, and turning to the sublime rider beside him.

"How much did it cost you, my Nur, to have this great monument erected in such a short time?" Jahangir asked capriciously.

"As much as that, Your Majesty." Nur Jahan pointed at her shoes in red velvet, studded with cluster of rubies and diamonds.

"If my court ulemas heard your response, my beloved, they would be horrified." Jahangir smiled. "Sullying the name of this mosque, they would say. For mentioning your precious shoes in connection with the mosque is an act of heresy itself, in their estimation." His eyes were gathering the mists of gloom and sadness.

"The ghosts of the dead are with you once again, Your Majesty," Nur Jahan commented. "Sadness weighs heavy on you, especially today! I was wrong in assuming that the beauty of Kashmir has melted away all your sorrows. Is it so very difficult to caste away the burden of grief? Come, Your Majesty, let us pray in this mosque. To pray for the peace of the dead souls, and for the peace in your heart."

"Pray for Man Singh first, I presume." Jahangir laughed suddenly. "Prayers for my old uncle! That doting imbecile, who probably took poison and surrendered his soul to the lords of hell!" he declared, no mirth shining in his eyes.

"Your Majesty!" Nur Jahan exclaimed. "Now that smoldering remark, Your Majesty, if I may be as bold as to say, reeks of bigotry. The entire Moghul court would be scandalized, if they heard such a remark from the emperor?"

"Scandal and tragedy have become worthy portions of pain in emperor's life, my Nur," was Jahangir's heedless response.

"You keep your griefs and tragedies of the past locked inside your soul, Your Majesty, as some precious gifts, not to be shared or abandoned," Nur Jahan sang with a dint of irony. "Pray, Your Majesty, absolve the grief for your son, with kind thoughts and sweet remembrances. This burden is too heavy for your delicate constitution. Your health, Your Majesty, how I pray and suffer."

"If Prince Jahandar was your son, my lovely Nur, you would have wept all the way from Agra to Kashmir, without ever relinquishing your grief," was Jahangir's thoughtless response.

"And if I had more sons like Prince Perwiz, Prince Shahriyar and Prince Shah Jahan, I would have kneeled before God in utter gratitude, thanking Him for His mercy for the healths of the other three. Everything belongs to God, His to give, and His to take, if we can only practice our own wills to surrender to one Supreme Will." Nur Jahan's eyes were flashing mirth and profundities.

"Prince Shahriyar is going to be your own son, my love, since he is to be betrothed to Princess Ladli. And pray, my sweet, that he stays in good health," Jahangir murmured. "You are right once again, love. Let us forget about our griefs, and fly to our beloved gardens to drink deep of health and beauty." He urged his horse to fly.

The fanciful flight in Jahangir's thoughts itself was leading him down into the valleys cool and slumbering. Nur Jahan riding behind him was merely letting her steed guide, and follow. The grand vistas in splendid contours were rising and dipping before their eyes in a splash of colors as they rode down the paths, dreamy and meandering. Jahangir, with the enthusiasm of a tour guide, was pointing out various sites to Nur Jahan. It was her first visit to Kashmir, and she had already turned quite a few of the pine-valleys into garden-retreats during her brief stay of more than half a year. Jahangir had bestowed upon her the palace of Hari Parbat at Dal Lake, as soon as they had reached Kashmir. This palace was built by Akbar during his frequent visits to Kashmir. But after his death, it was left in sore neglect. Its gardens, wild and unkempt, were a living testimony of utter neglect, though the faded splendor of the past was still intact behind the palace walls. But under Nur Jahan's guidance, the entire palace had emerged forth like a polished jewel. Its gardens were restored to their original beauty in design and neatness, its lakes boasting lotuses and its fountains flanked by colorful flowers.

The empress had paid thirty thousand rupees to an architect by the name of Haider Malik to discipline Dal Lake into some semblance of order and conformity. Haider Malik, with his skill and devotion, had managed to carve a canal from the very mouth of Lar Valley into the heart of this garden to nurture lawns and flowers. The wealth of the empress and the dedication of Haider Malik had wrought wonders in this much neglected garden of Dal Lake. The flowers had sprouted forth so quickly and in such abundance that even the old gardeners were awed and surprised. Jahangir was so delighted by Nur Jahan's artful restoration of this garden that he had named it Nur Afza. Not only had he named this garden after the name of his beloved empress, but the whole village, changing the name of Chardara Valley to Nurpur.

The Chardara Valley, now Nurpur, was welcoming the royal riders with the joy of a dream beautiful and awesome. The Dal Lake with its clear, blue waters was mirroring chenars and willows. Hari Parbat in the distance was a gleaming enormity, rising above the majestic heights of the planes and cypresses. The sun in the west was lowering its ribbons of gold on the orchards on each side of the garden. The cherry, guava, apricot and pomegranate trees were motionless against the hush of the falling dusk. A small bridge over the meads and cascades was coming into view as the emperor and the empress rode along, awed and humbled. The apple and orange trees down yonder were just a rippling silhouette. Their eyes were turning to the colorful tapestry in flowers, and absorbing the glory of nature all around with a sense of wonder and humility.

The roses in hues pink, yellow and crimson were as big as the sun disks. French marigolds were an ocean of sunshine. Irises, lilies and tulips were gathering sunshine in their own colorful goblets, large and luminous. The soft breeze itself was humming the tunes of the wind-chimes, lulling the crocuses and narcissi to sleep. Lilac, dahlia and jasmine appeared to be swooning in their own jars of color and fragrance. Nur Jahan was inhaling the scent of pine and lavender from the very womb of earth, while Jahangir, astride his mount, appeared to be drinking wine from the cups of beauty in nature.

"You have done wonders with this garden, the pearl of my harem." The dreamy languor in Jahangir's gaze was spilling compliments. "I would order our court painter, Mansur, to paint each bloom, each scene, if possible."

"And you, Your Majesty, said you preferred Damascus roses over the Indian, scented ones." Nur Jahan laughed with the sheer abandon of a young girl.

"Damascus roses are excellent, my love, silken and sweet-scented! Yet, one is entitled to prefer the scents of Indian roses over those of the other scented ones, and the emperor has the prerogative to shift his preferences." Jahangir laughed, watching one hoopoe who was sailing up and swooping down under the shade of the willows.

"If I had my gun with me, Your Majesty, I would have shot that bird." One ripple of mirth escaped Nur Jahan's lips.

"No shooting in this valley of love and enchantment, my love," Jahangir chided tenderly. "In Ajmer, you have had your fill of shooting the birds. Remember the one which weighed two hundred grams? And the like of it in size, color and beauty has never been seen before or after. What did I name it, oh yes, Qrisha," he reminisced fondly.

"Who can remember shooting the birds, when one can boast of being a tiger-slayer, Your Majesty? I hope you have not forgotten," Nur Jahan chanted happily.

"How can I, love?" Jahangir boomed quickly. "When court poets pen verses in praise of the empress, and neglect the emperor altogether?"

"You are jealous, Your Majesty," Nur Jahan teased. "Could we rest here, Your Majesty, and explore more charming wonders of this garden?" she murmured.

"No, my love," Jahangir murmured back. "The emperor's jealous heart yearns for the garden of Verang, our lone retreat of bliss and solitude! Where streams gurgle with the promise of love, and where nightingales serenade the buds of roses yet to be awakened to the sense of their own beauty." He raced ahead.

"Your Majesty, how I wish I had gardens like these in all the cities of Hind, especially in Agra and Delhi." Nur Jahan spurred her own horse.

"In Agra, you do have gardens vast and magnificent, my Nur," Jahangir commented merrily. "Nur Afshan, Nur Manzil, Moti bagh. You do need a few in Delhi and Lahore, though," he opined aloud.

"Not in Lahore, Your Majesty! Not in Lahore," was Nur Jahan's passionate response on a verge of poetic delirium. "We have purchased Lahore with our soul. We have given our life and bought another paradise."

"Your poetry, my Nur, gathers the moss of politics," Jahangir commented.

"When I pass through this garden with such beauty and perfection, a cry blessed arises from the very souls of the nightingales." Another poetic refrain broke forth on Nur Jahan's lips. "Can't you hear it, Your Majesty?"

"Be careful, my lovely poetess, your poetry may slay the beauty of Kashmir." Jahangir laughed.

"Look, Your Majesty, the deer with the silver ring in its nose!" Nur Jahan exclaimed, espying her pet deer in the orchard down below. "The same one who let me bore a hole in his nose and slip the silver ring. It has come from the garden of Verang to greet us here."

"Yes, the gifts of our love to the lovely beasts of Kashmir." Jahangir guided his horse, leaping over the small bridge. "And now, let us return to our paradisiacal Verang to put gold and silver rings into the noses of our goldfish." His heart was racing along with his mount to reach Verang.

The garden of Verang was half open to the sky and half concealed by the mountains. Jahangir and Nur Jahan were seated at the imperial pool, its clear waters catching reflections from the trees overhead in its mirror-like deeps. Nur Jahan had had her legs tucked under her over the Bokhara rug, and was luxuriating in the sense of a carefree abandon. Jahangir was in absolute bliss, his legs dangling knee-deep in the water, and his bare feet tingling with the sense of joy and freedom. Both the emperor and the empress were absorbed in slipping gold and silver rings into the noses of the fish which they had just caught in their gold net. Right below the pool was a terraced garden of most exquisite form and contour. Here, the blue Kashmiri irises were dreamy like the night sky, lolling against the bower of white tuberoses. The jafari flowers in molten clusters were drinking sunshine from the half empty cups of dusk, it seemed. Poppies were as crimson as the dark sunsets, and carnations as white as the pearly dawns. The graceful poplars over the streams were guarding a grand palace not far beyond. This palace could not be seen from any spot in this secluded garden, not until one had crossed the narrow path edged with planes and cedars.

Nur Jahan was lowering her golden net into the pool with the wistfulness of a mother who wished to hug her tender babes, not hurt them. Jahangir was securing one silver ring on the gill of a rather big fish, then releasing it back into its own liquid freedom. His gaze was wandering away to the terraced gardens down below with a savoring intensity. The pale dusk with all its wealth of gold and haze was vivifying the flowers into a rare tapestry not ever to be captured by mortal sight in word and color. Some sort of pain was stabbing his heart, while it knelt in throes of agony before some altar unknown. Silent, reverent. He could hear himself murmuring.

"It is a page that the painter of destiny has drawn with the pencil of creation." Jahangir was not even aware of his own poetic reverie as he looked at Nur Jahan.

"Our little, beautiful garden has turned the emperor to a poet." Nur Jahan smiled.

"You hide the stars of poetry in your eyes and in your head, my love, and the charms of your beauty alone have turned the emperor into a toad. Look, how he is perched!" Jahangir declared happily.

"If a rosebud can be opened by the breeze in the meadow, the key to our heart's lock is the smile of a beloved," Nur Jahan sang, as if drunk by the poetry in nature.

"Can a prisoner of beauty ever smile?" Jahangir gazed into her eyes. "I am a prisoner of your beauty, love. And a prisoner to the beauty of the flowers. And of course, to the fragrant nature in this bliss of a paradise."

"The heart of one held prisoner by beauty sees nothing, no rose, no color, inhaling only the scent of love," Nur Jahan teased, her white, oval face transfigured with joy.

"Sightless my eyes then would steal color from my heart, lovely Nur, kneading it into a rose of love to quench the hungers of your soul." Jahangir claimed her hand.

"My soul knows no hungers, Your Majesty," Nur Jahan protested happily. "It is sated with joy. Content and blissful it is, right now, that is. Little things, little endearments make it dance with pleasure, Your Majesty." She bubbled forth with joy. "The measure of my happiness, Your Majesty, if you must know, is that I have more fish with gold rings in this pool than yours."

"How can you tell, love?" Jahangir kissed her hand.

"Because, even under water, I can read my own inscriptions on the gold rings." Nur Jahan's heart was swooning.

"Is that true, my pearl?" Jahangir looked deep into the mirror-length of the pool. "Yes, I should think. A grain of poppy seed can be seen in the bottom of this pool. And if a pea fell into it, even a bird could see it." His gaze was shooting up to the half open sky, where one sliver of a moon could be seen cutting through the poplars like a blade of ice. "The crescent of the feast is apparent at the apex of the celestial sphere." He pulled his feet up from the pool, and sat hugging his knees.

"The key to the tavern was lost, but is now found." The poetic gleam alone in Nur Jahan's eyes was teasing the emperor.

"Your poetry alone, my Nur, would drive the emperor insane with desire, if not your beauty." Jahangir pressed her to him in one eager embrace. "Your beauty, too, shatters my bliss! Robs me of peace and serenity." He was murmuring against the violence of his kisses hungry and scalding. "And all I wish is to stay in bliss, with you." He was cupping her face into his hands and kissing her small nose. "Yes, to stay in bliss. I can sit here till eternity, talking with you, to be with you! Sharing even the hush and the silence with you. You would get tired, I know, but I would stay in the everlasting spring of joy and bliss." His gaze was returning to the terraced gardens. "I have never seen such exquisite blooms in my entire life, though I have been to Kashmir several times. A wondrous miracle wrought by your mind and heart, Nur, how did you do it?"

"My witchcraft is to blame entirely, Your Majesty." Nur Jahan could barely murmur, her cheeks flushed and her eyes shining.

"Besides that, my Nur?" Jahangir's gaze was ardent and dreamy. "The purity and innocence of your heart, perhaps? Yes, such a heart as yours can achieve wonders. These blooms, this time of the evening, are reminding me of a story I heard eons ago."

"Would you share that story with me, Your Majesty?" Nur Jahan murmured.

"With such an eager audience, how can the emperor decline?" Jahangir began hastily, lest he forget. "One king after his hunting expedition had straggled into a beautiful garden. Feeling thirsty, he asked the gardener to fetch him pomegranate juice. The gardener went inside and sent his daughter with a glass of juice. Finding the glass covered with leaves, the king asked the girl why she had covered the glass thus. The girl replied that the leaves were there to prevent one from drinking too fast, for when one is thirsty, one tends to drink too fast, and it is not good for anyone's health. The king was impressed by the wisdom of this young girl, and his thoughts were murmuring that he should make her his bride. Meanwhile, the gardener returned, and the king asked him about his income and about the quality of his fruit trees. Also, how much tax he paid to the diwan. The gardener complied truthfully that he didn't pay anything to the diwan. But he did pay tenth part of his earnings to the state, further admitting that he earned three hundred dinars a year. While the gardener was talking, the king was thinking to himself that in his dominions there were many such fruit trees, and that if he charged the revenue of a tenth of earnings, he would collect a great deal of money. The king was still thirsty and asked the girl to fetch him another glass of pomegranate juice. This time the girl was long in coming, and brought only half a cup. The king could not help asking about the delay and about the small portion in his cup. The girl replied that the first time one pomegranate was enough to fill the whole cup. But this time she had to squeeze several, and the cup would not fill. The gardener was quick to add that the quality of his fruit was entirely dependent upon the good disposition of the sovereign. The king was astonished to discover truth behind the casual comment of the gardener, thinking to himself that he would not levy any taxes on the fruit trees. Immediately, the king requested another cup of pomegranate juice. This time the girl returned quickly with a cup brimming with pomegranate juice. The king was convinced that the produce and abundance of the crops in his kingdom depended entirely on the justice and goodwill of the sovereign. Then the king divulged his thoughts and his identity to the gardener, requesting the hand of his daughter in marriage," he concluded rather sadly.

"I like such folk tales with happy endings, Your Majesty. Most of them are so very tragic!" Nur Jahan commented brightly. "If one had faith in such stories with such beautiful thoughts, maybe one could walk into the valleys of past, communing with the dead and seeking their blessings for peace in the present," she ruminated aloud.

"Surely, if one could raise the dead to life, one could commune with the dead in living," Jahangir murmured evasively, his look intense and ponderous.

"How do you mean, Your Majesty?" Nur Jahan's eyes were lit up with curiosity.

"To explain that, I would have to tell another story," Jahangir murmured.

"It would be sheer delight! I am your perfect audience, as you know, I love stories." Nur Jahan elicited more interest than she could feel.

"The emperor is in everlasting bliss just by being with you, my love. So close, so adorable, so bewitching," was Jahangir's ardent response. "And to tell stories is the only way the emperor can keep you beside him, or you would be fluttering in the gardens like a butterfly, leaving the emperor alone and desolate."

"If and when, depending upon the truth and sincerity of your wishes, Your Majesty, I can fall right into your arms like a moth attracted to one burning flame." Nur Jahan laughed.

"Then come close, my pretty moth, and stay in eternal embrace, inside the very heart of the emperor." Jahangir slipped his arm around her waist, kissing her on the lips. "Do you still wish to hear the story, love?" Ardor and mischief were shining in his eyes.

"Yes, yes, Your Majesty! If you hold me close like this, and keep your arms around me forever and forever," Nur Jahan murmured under some spell of joy and pain.

"Keeping you pressed close to me, and into my arms, is no favor to you, my pearl. My delight and privilege alone, entirely mine." Jahangir was gazing into her eyes adoringly. "You don't want to hear this story, my Nur? Say no! The emperor's soul is hungering for love. Can we, Nur...can we make love right here, since neither of us wish to return to the palace as yet?"

"Your Majesty!" Nur Jahan was appalled, her eyes flashing giddy reproof. "What if someone straggles into the...what impropriety! I want to hear that story, Your Majesty, truly, I do. We need to stay in this garden a little longer; it is most conducive to your health. Please, Your Majesty, I am dying to hear that story."

"So far, this garden has offered no cure to the malady of my soul." Jahangir heaved a mock sigh. "Fortunately, this story is not long. And this is a true story, my Nur, as far as the stories go. I presume." He paused, his look distant. "Shah Alam was a revered saint who used to raise the dead to life. After he raised several dead men to life, his father got incensed that this practice was contrary to the Will of God. So the father banished his son from his house. The saint was a widower and had a son of tender years by his late wife, so they both retired to a secluded hermitage. This saint had a female servant who had no children and was later blessed by a son by the prayers of this saint. She was the only one to visit him occasionally. Years had passed and her son had grown to be a young man of twenty-seven, when he died suddenly. So stricken was she with grief that she went lamenting to the hermitage of Shah Alam, pleading for the boon of her son's life. Shah Alam had ceased the practice of raising the dead for many a long years, so he told his servant that he had lost his powers. Since Shah Alam could not be persuaded, his son told the servant to wait outside till he himself pleaded with his father on her behalf. Shah Alam was confronted with utmost despair when he heard his son that he was willing to exchange his own life with the son of the servant so that the dead man could be raised to life. Shah Alam had no choice but to give in to the pleas of his son, and after making him lay down on his cot, he prayed earnestly, *God, take my own son in the place of my servant's.* His son's soul left his body immediately after this prayer, and the saint plodded out to face the grief-stricken mother. He told her to return home, informing her that she would find her son in good health. True to the saint's bidding, the mother hurried home, and was greeted by her son as if no shadow of death had touched his young body," he concluded rather tonelessly.

Nur Jahan had fallen into a reverie of her own, luxuriating in the sense of closeness rather than heeding the words which sounded remote and receding. She seemed fascinated by the emperor's bracelet of pearls and rubies, and was not even aware that the story had ended. The emperor's own attention was caught by the tapestry of colors in this garden, so tenderly vibrant against the haze of dusk and serenity. Each fiber in his soul was becoming aware of the hush and the quietude all around, longing for the presence of his beloved. She was nowhere to be found but deep down the valleys of death, he was thinking. His living beloved was with him! She was bending over and kissing his arm, her lips feeling the pearls and rubies on his bracelet.

"That bracelet has a story too, my Nur, and you know that story," Jahangir murmured tenderly. "Besides, the emperor is wearied of stories…and of life." He murmured the last part to himself. "Promise me, Nur, you would bury me in this eternal spring of a garden when I die."

"Your Majesty!" Nur Jahan's exclamation was choked by the sudden stab of pain inside her heart. "You would not die, not before me. You would have a long, long life. A thousand lives, I pray. Spending at least half with me, and half with…" She could not utter the name of the emperor's dead beloved.

"Death is as real as the air we breathe in and out, my love, and its course cannot be averted, much less diverted." Jahangir heard the unvoiced pang in Nur Jahan's heart, his own shuddering. "Let us make promises, love, while we live. Hoping, they would be fulfilled in the passage of time. If I die first, you bring me to Kashmir to bury me in this beloved garden of ours. And if you die before…I would carry you into my arms to this very spot consecrated by our love. A great monument would rise above your shrine, loaded with the loveliest of flowers from the very gardens you yourself have created."

"I am selfish, Your Majesty. I would keep you with me wherever I live. If it is Kashmir, your hope would be fulfilled." Nur Jahan's eyes were glinting poetry.

"Let there be neither light, nor a flower
On the grave of this humble person
Nor the wings of the moth burn in flames of love
Nor the nightingale send out his wailing cry," she recited without pain or sadness.

"My love!" Jahangir pressed her closer, rather clinging to her desperately. "Let us bathe in this pool with our goldfish. They are our children, and we their guardian angels. Our griefs and nightmares would be purged...right now, this very evening."

"Your Majesty." Nur Jahan's very thoughts were swooning. "What if..." Her unvoiced fears were surfacing before Jahangir's very sight.

Prince Shah Jahan was seen emerging from the shadows like a shining knight.

"You are right, love," Jahangir confessed quickly, his arms falling limp to his sides. "Next time, the emperor would issue edicts before leaving his palace, that he is not to be disturbed in this sweet bliss of a paradise."

"Your Majesty. Padishah Begum." Prince Shah Jahan greeted with one gallant bow of his head. "May I crave your audience, Your Majesty?" he asked somberly.

"What urgency makes your brow cloud thus, Shah Jahan?" Jahangir was heaving himself up thoughtfully.

"Grievous news from Deccan, Your Majesty." Prince Shah Jahan attempted a smile, his look dreamy.

"Join me in a stroll, my austere messenger." Jahangir slipped on his shoes, tossing a comment over his shoulders. "Would you like to join us, my Nur?"

"If you would excuse me, Your Majesty, I would rather sit here and contemplate." Nur Jahan smiled. "The view from here is serene and delightful."

"Then the emperor must balance the burden of calamities over his own shoulders alone." Jahangir turned to his heels.

"Padishah Begum." Prince Shah Jahan bowed with one flourish of his arm, before following the emperor.

The terraced garden down below was absorbing shadows from dusk as Nur Jahan sat watching the prince and the emperor strolling side-by-side. Her own thoughts were heavy with the weight of joys and pains she could neither recount nor abandon. So drowned was she in her lone contemplations that she didn't even notice the Kashmiri girls decking the terraces and pavilions of this garden with lamps and candles. She was aware of the prince and the emperor though, two glittering shadows in their own world scented with flowers. They too were oblivious of the lovely intruders, who were quick to breathe light into the garden and then vanish behind the shadows.

"The Deccanis have broken their peace treaty, Your Majesty," Prince Shah Jahan was saying. "Ambar Malik has formed a league with Bijapur and Golconda. He has called up the Maratha bands and have mustered sixty thousand troops. The rebellions are sprouting in all parts of Bengal. Mandu, Berar, Kangra, Balapur, just to name a few of the cities where the danger of rebellions is most imminent." He paused as if making sure that the emperor was absorbing all details.

"Then you must repair to Deccan at the head of a large force, my valorous prince." Jahangir snatched that pause to issue a quick command. "Yes, to fight those mites of rebellion, and to burn the roots of their seditions in the entire land of Bengal." Rage was brewing inside him with the violence of a volcano.

"I must, Your Majesty." Prince Shah Jahan gloated inwardly "But first, may I journey to Lahore, Your Majesty? To gather all the forces…and to take Prince Khusrau with me?" His latter request was one suave murmur.

"Prince Khusrau! Why must you take the unfortunate prince with you?" Jahangir declared impatiently. "Isn't it enough that he has been left into your custody entirely? Didn't you yourself leave him with Asaf Khan, who obeys each and every command of yours, keeping strict vigilance over Prince Khusrau? My first-born son, misfortunes have made him the victim of intrigues…the emperor rarely gets to see him." His heart was waving the reeds of premonitions. "Prince Khusrau, why my unfortunate prince? Why not take Prince Perwiz or Prince Shahriyar?"

"Prince Khusrau is prone to seditions, Your Majesty," was Prince Shah Jahan's winsome response. "Prince Perwiz and Prince Shahriyar, they are not as devious as Prince Khusrau, Your Majesty. Prince Khusrau, your prince incarnate? The other princes, my brothers, they have never raised the banners of rebellion against you, Your Majesty. Nor are they capable of even harboring seditious thoughts."

"Yes, my crafty prince, you are probably correct in judging your other brothers with kindness," Jahangir began thoughtfully. "But you have other motives behind your insistence in taking Prince Khusrau with you. He is best loved by the people of Hind and he is my first-born. Are those not a couple of valid reasons to prompt you to such an action?" he demurred aloud.

"What if I may decline, Your Majesty, to lead the Deccani campaign? I mean…under the weight of a genuine excuse that my wife, whom I love beyond any kingdoms on this earth, needs rest from journeys long?" Prince Shah Jahan began ruminatively. "She has blessed me with two daughters and three sons. Such an angel, never complaining about the hardships of the childbirths in alien lands, or about the discomforts on the battlefields."

"You are declining this honor, my prince?" Jahangir exclaimed, his eyes flashing. "I will tell you a story, Khurram Baba, which might seduce your own seditious thoughts to calm obedience." His tone was softening "The emperor is in a mood to tell stories this evening, rather needs to! Where does this strange need come from? Don't ask." He paused, words spilling down his lips will-lessly. "Paradoxically, this story originates from the very heart of Mandu. A raja by the name of Jai Singh ruled Mandu justly and happily. One day when one of his faithful servants was cutting grass, his sickle was turned to gold. He took the sickle to a goldsmith by the name of Madan, who told the astonished servant that an alchemist's stone might have transmuted this sickle to gold. Then both the servant and the blacksmith rushed to the site, and discovered the stone. They presented this stone to the raja. Jai Singh was glad to receive such a treasure, used it wisely to produce gold, and made his kingdom more prosperous than ever. He reigned twelve more years after this stone was found, and built a great fort. He was growing old, and losing interest in the world and its worldly treasures, and decided to retire. Before retiring, he held an assembly on the banks of the river Narbada, bestowing gifts upon his viziers and grandees. One Brahmin was his closest of friends, so he bestowed upon him the stone. This Brahmin was offended, thinking this gift as a worthless pebble, and was quick to toss it into the river. After learning about its worth, his sorrow was great. All his life was spent in searching this stone, but he never found it."

"A fantastic tale of delusion and enchantment, Your Majesty," Prince Shah Jahan commented cheerfully. "But what has this to do with my going to Deccan, or declining?"

"My imbecile prince, do you willfully refuse to glean the moral out of this story?" Jahangir chided genially. "The cities of Deccan are like the pearls presented to you by the emperor. And if you toss them away like the unworthy pebbles, you might lose all the kingdoms of Hind. Styled by me as Shah Jahan, Ruler of the World, do you think you can rule the emperor?"

"Under the burden of such threats, Your Majesty, must I march to Deccan?" Prince Shah Jahan murmured assiduously.

"And you think, my wise prince, that emperor can't snatch your own threats from the throne of your presumptions?" Jahangir murmured sadly. "A subject's duty, *first and foremost*, is toward his sovereign, against all the rest of the burdens he might have to share or endure. "

"Without Prince Khusrau as the mastermind of mischief, I dare not leave, Your Majesty." Prince Shah Jahan breathed tenaciously.

"Then take him with you, my heedless prince." Jahangir waved impatiently. "Yes, take him, if you can endure the laments of the harem ladies when they hear about it." His gaze was intense and piercing. "I feign would talk with my unfortunate son. The few times that I have seen him, he looked morose and dejected. And yet I love him as much as…" His heart was unveiling the portrait of Anarkali. "Yes, the emperor loves him. Take care of Prince Khusrau, Khurram Baba. Let no harm ever come to him by your hands," he commanded with an impatient wave of his arm.

"Your Majesty, you are wearing the gift of my pearl on your arm!" Prince Shah Jahan exclaimed evasively. "I can even tell which one is my pearl, though they both look the same." He smiled charmingly.

"The twin pearls, another story!" Jahangir caught and held the smile in his son's eyes with a profound fascination. "You are a genius in finding and discovering rare gems, my prince. When you gave me this pearl, you nurtured in me a longing to get another pearl of the same size, shape and beauty, so that they can complement each other on a bracelet of rubies." His thoughts were accosting memories warm and painful. "When I despaired of finding a matching pearl, Khurram Baba, you were the one who came to the emperor's rescue. Lending me hope that you had seen a similar pearl in the turban of your grandfather. And this is the product of your remarkable memory as far as jewels are concerned." He looked at his bracelet as if reading fortunes. "I can't tell which pearl is yours, and which one from the turban of my beloved father. How can you, my ingenious scholar? How can you remember such details about jewels as to when they were worn, who wore them, and where they were stored?" His eyes were kindling disbelief.

"Because my second love is jewels, Your Majesty." Prince Shah Jahan laughed. "I acquire jewels from all continents in the world. They even come to me of their own accord, it seems, Your Majesty. Though I dare steal some from the beautiful eyes of my Arjumand," he added wistfully.

"You are in love! Still in love?" Jahangir was awed, rather humbled by the flood of love and tenderness in his son's eyes. "This great love of yours is tragic somehow. All great loves are tragic. Take good care of Arjumand Banu, Khurram Baba. Never let her out of your sight," he murmured.

"Do I need reminding, Your Majesty?" Prince Shah Jahan laughed again. "She is wedded to my soul as well as to my heart; we cannot be separated. My soul-companion in wars and campaigns too, that's how our royal babes come squalling into this world of warfare and rebellion."

"May God keep you in His shadow, and may happiness go with you to Deccan," Jahangir murmured, retracing his steps toward the pool where Nur Jahan sat waiting.

"Your Majesty. I hope you will not stay in Kashmir for long," was Prince Shah Jahan's vague comment. "I hear the plague is headed this way."

"Plagues follow the emperor wherever he goes," Jahangir murmured over his shoulders. "And the emperor is not afraid, either of death or treason." He waved dismissal. "Inform the begums, prince charming, not to venture out near the pool this evening. The emperor will return shortly, and then we will picnic in the garden of Achabal."

Nur Jahan had not stirred from the spot where the emperor had left her, as if painted alive on the tapestry of this garden. Her silks and jewels were chasing the shadows and in return shimmering rather gleeful. Her heart was gathering no such glee, but pain against the haze of memories wild and passionate. Her own love for the emperor was tragic, though she had not caught his utterance in conformity with her thoughts mute and turbulent. Her love for him was like a river, deep and profound, she had been thinking inside the oceans of her own poetic reveries. She could not help loving this emperor, her aesthetic genius as she called him, and a mystic. A mystic who was foundering forever inside the whirlwinds of his own agonies indescribable. He was as much in love with his own agony and torment as with her wit and beauty. Living and dying in some tempest of sun-baked sufferings and wind-swept longings. Dying at the altar of his dead beloved each day, and reviving himself with the soma of pain in life from the bottomless depths of her own love and understanding.

The curse! This sea of inebriation!

Nur Jahan was suspended in her own thoughts like a marionette, buffeted by the storm-clouds of laughing fates. But she was not heeding the fates, rather defying their onslaught. The ocean of love inside her was swollen and brimming. She loved her joys as well as her pains. Welcomed her serenity as well as the chaos from within and without. Her heart was too warm and passionate to permit the nurturing of pain. It was eager to celebrate, not mourn. Always serenading joy, always lulling the pain to sleep. Right now, while sinking deeper and deeper into the realms of her subconscious, she was at peace with herself. Neither sad nor wistful, just inert and brooding.

Suddenly, Nur Jahan's senses were catching a signal of warning from the very silence of her subconscious. Her senses were alert, as if inhaling the reek of deceit and treason. Shah Jahan, whom she loved the best, was chilled in her awareness under a glacier of suspicion. Her intuition was revealing something corrupt and malefic, as if a jungle of schemes was sprouting inside the head of Prince Shah Jahan. Her heart had begun to throb, thundering with the pulse of presage. Even now, she was cutting this presage to shreds, rather exploring the nuances of joy and gaiety which could always be captured and vivified. Her thoughts were floating toward Prince Shahriyar, who was to be her son-in-law. This thought too was absorbed into the calm waters of her chill and inertia. Something inside her were coiling, awakening, expanding. She was lonesome.

Nur Jahan could see into the vault of her own heart and beyond the heavens. The tomb of Anarkali was unfolding, not inside her, but suspended from the heavens, pervading the very soul of the emperor. Her thoughts were marching into neat files as soldiers valiant and vengeful, trooping onward to demolish this tomb, carrying on their shoulders an altar pure and noble. This altar, her own altar of love, was to be erected inside the very colonnades of the emperor's heart and soul. So immersed she was into this cosmic surrender of her senses that she didn't notice the emperor's approach.

"Laden with burdens, the emperor always comes back to you, my Nur." Jahangir smiled, his arms held out to assist the empress to her feet.

"Your Majesty." Nur Jahan was startled to her feet. "What new burdens weigh heavy on your shoulders?" She claimed the emperor's hands and stood facing him.

"Bengal is on fire and burning away, while the cool-warmth in these pine-valleys is serene and comforting!" Jahangir declared.

"The Deccani treaty is broken then," was Nur Jahan's rueful response.

"This news is not that tragic, my love! The emperor has absolute trust in God. He will grant the emperor victory." Jahangir slipped his arm around her waist, diverting her attention to the blue patch of a sky, where a sickle moon serenaded the stars. "What do you see up there, my pearl?"

"One curved dagger of ice, aiming to slash the very heart of the sky." Nur Jahan's wit was returning, along with her awareness to pain and tragedy.

"What strange depiction of the ermine crescent, my love?" Jahangir pressed her closer to him. "Your comments, rather thoughts, were more inspiring when I had shown you a meteor on the horizon." His mood as well as his tone were ardent.

"I forget how inspired I was, Your Majesty." Nur Jahan smiled.

"'No star has ever raised its head so far,' you had said, my Nur." Warmth and tenderness in Jahangir's gaze were cutting right through her soul. "And what poetic élan? 'It is the celestial sphere, lions girded in service to the emperor,' didn't you say that, my pearl?" He grazed his lips against her cheek.

"Now I feel ashamed of ever singing such flattery to the emperor." A tremor of mirth escaped Nur Jahan's lips.

Jahangir was kissing her eyes, lips, throat, his heart longing to absorb her very soul inside him.

"When do we leave Kashmir, Your Majesty?" Nur Jahan could barely murmur against the shower of kisses.

"Not yet, dear love," Jahangir murmured back. "A couple of months from hence. Prince Shah Jahan is to lead the march to Deccan. When the emperor has worthy sons, he needs not worry." He was exploring the snow-valley in her bosom, and unrobing her.

The Bokhara carpet was the imperial bed of the royal couple under the canopy of stars, cold and glittering, the sky and the mountains singing, expanding.

Chapter Eight

Another balmy day in Kashmir, a new year, a new summer day! One large chamber in Kashmir palace was exposed to the brightness of such a day with its damask curtains tied back in gold tassels. The chamber walls were adorned with Persian calligraphy, which the emperor could not admire as he lay senseless on his gilded bed. He had had an asthma attack a day before this very afternoon, and had suffered shortness of breath. Today, while lying couchant against a heap of pillow, he had lost consciousness. Two hours had elapsed since then, and he was surrounded by his wives, princes, princesses and royal physicians. This was not the emperor's first asthma attack since his visit to Kashmir. He had had several within the last four months amidst his excesses of drinking and excursion. Prince Perwiz, upon learning of the emperor's illness, had journeyed from Burhanpur, hoping to be of some assistance in cheering the emperor. But his cheerful arrival was slashed with fears and doubts by finding the emperor in this comatose state, from where he could not return to greet his son. The royal physicians were trying desperately to revive the emperor, but of no avail.

Nur Jahan, seated beside the emperor's bed, was gazing at the emperor's hands as if they were the most dearest of objects she could not take her eyes off. Prince Perwiz was seated next to Nur Jahan, despair and dejection shining in his eyes. At the foot the bed, Prince Shahriyar was almost sunk deep into his chair, his expression rather solemn than stunned. Hakim Sadra and Hakim Rukna were standing by the window, whispering and consulting, now and then examining a few vials on the marble chest. The emperor's other wives were scattered here and there, glued to their chairs, numb and chilled. Amongst them, Nurunnisa, Khairunnisa, Salihah Banu, Malika Jahan and Sahiba Jamali, the most solemn ones as if sinking deeper into the pits of grief and silence. Nur Jahan herself had lost the roses on her cheeks, which once the purity of Kashmir had bestowed upon her to complement her beauty. The ribbons of sunshine were flooding into this room, as if reaching out to fill the hearts of the royal occupants with hope, but no one seemed to notice the warmth of nature from the very heart of sky, bright and generous. Only the physicians standing by the window could catch the shafts of sunshine, beholding the majesty of domed arches and galleries with stone pillars, all polished by gold from sunlight. They were more aware of the hush outside than of the inside gloom, wondering why the candles were lit in broad daylight on the terraces and balconies where brass planters stood blazing with a profusion of red geraniums.

Even before the onslaught of asthma, Kashmir had become the valley of ruin for the emperor. It was visited by plague right after Prince Shah Jahan's departure to Lahore, from where he was to commence his Deccani campaign. Almost half a year had sailed past since then, the beautiful spring settling into the bosom of the summer with sighs profound. These sighs were unnoticed by the emperor; he had thrown himself into a whirlwind of activity to aid the families of the plague victims. The food and medicine supplies were to be ordered, and the emperor had personally attended to those demands, lest dalliance cause more damage than ordained. He was supervising all supplies most diligently, and sending a flurry of messengers to the neighboring cities for constant flow of provisions for the families suffered and bereaved. And just before the plague had relinquished its hold on Kashmir, the emperor himself had fallen victim to asthma. So frequent were these attacks that he seemed to wade into the waters of recovery and illness with a desperate struggle to reach the shore of health. The shore of health could be a mirage, for he could not abstain from drinking, rather seeking the waters of oblivion.

Now as the emperor lay unconscious, the royal physicians were in utter despair, their own pleas to the emperor choked in their thoughts. Since the past few weeks, they had pleaded with the emperor not to drink or at least to cut down on his consumption of wine until he could gain back a few ounces of strength. The emperor had not heeded their pleas, and they had surrendered themselves to a sense of helplessness.

Prince Perwiz was rising to his feet as if stung by the arrows of divination and revelation. He had begun to pace around the emperor's bed in circles, as if caught under a spell of madness and delirium. Paradoxically, his thoughts were quite sober, reviving the ritual of his great, great grandfather, who had saved the life of his son by immolating his own to God. All eyes were turned to the prince, though he seemed oblivious even to his own pacing and silent prayers. The blue, feverish flames in Nur Jahan's eyes could only see his jeweled turban in red and green, but she was closing her eyes. Behind the closed shutters of pain and fever in her gaze, she could see nothing but the cold, emaciated hands of the emperor. Her anguished thoughts were kneading a string of prayers.

Look, Your Majesty, your son Prince Perwiz is here, ready to sacrifice his life to save yours. Nur Jahan's thoughts were reaching out to the emperor. *All the begums are here, your wives, your sons, your daughter.* Her hand was seeking the emperor's, guided by her soul. *My mamma, my papa, all are here, Your Majesty. And your grandchildren, two little adorable sons of your most beloved prince. All calling you, all praying for you. Come back to us, Your Majesty, speak to us...merciful God.* The string of her prayers was broken at the subtle tremor in the emperor's hand.

Nur Jahan's eyes were shot open, unlidding the veil of sorrow, gathering a mist of tears. Jahangir's own eyes were fixed to her in some daze of recognition. Prince Perwiz's feet were chilled at the foot of the bed in an act of pacing. Sighs of relief were suspended in the room. Ripples of joy were kindling all eyes with the warmth of joy and hope. The physicians were standing there like carved statues, only their eyes burning with awe and disbelief. No one could speak, the hush so profound that the emperor's voice, when it found its way, sounded ethereal.

"Why! What is this?" Jahangir's gaze was gathering all in its feverish intensity. "Why is everyone gathered here like the shining ants? Surely, the emperor has not contracted plague, or you all would be running miles away from him." His gaze was returning to Nur Jahan after lingering briefly on Prince Perwiz at the foot of the bed. "No, the emperor may be a victim of hallucination, but certainly not of plague." He was pressing his temples. "No fever, no headache, no bleeding of the nose."

"No, Your Majesty, no." Joyful protests were breaking forth on the lips of the begums.

"Come, my prince of Burhanpur. Come, embrace the emperor." Jahangir's eyes were gathering humor and perception. "You are a loving and dutiful son. May you prosper and succeed in life, always." His psyche, not sight, was piercing the veil of this tearful gathering.

Prince Perwiz obeyed with the speed of a gymnast, dropping his head on the emperor's chest, and forcing back his tears.

"And you all thought that the emperor was dying." Jahangir laughed suddenly.

"No, Your Majesty, no!" Another chorus of protests met the emperor's mirth.

"Then, begone, all of you. The emperor commands." Jahangir waved his arms. The splinter of finality in his tone brooking no disobedience.

A sea of silks was parting and dissolving, the jeweled gowns and colorful turbans disappearing behind the gilded doors into the vestibule yonder. Nur Jahan herself was heaving herself up as if weighed down by the tempests of dreams and dream-enchantments. Not even knowing that the emperor's gaze was devouring her with the intensity of a dream-lover.

"Not you, my Nur, not you! All, but you. You are the empress, remember," Jahangir murmured, his gaze sailing out of the window to the balcony yonder. "Why are these diyas and candles lit on my balcony on the very face of this bright day?" His eyes were shining with astonishment as he returned his gaze to his beloved.

"Tonight will be the night of Shab-i-barat, Your Majesty." Nur Jahan sank back into her seat with a sigh of relief. "Since you love to celebrate all festivals, Your Majesty, begums and I thought that these early marks of celebrations would bring you back to celebrate…back to consciousness."

"So, the emperor was unconscious, not sleeping as he presumed." Jahangir's look was dreamy. "Now I remember…I had a headache…it is coming back, not the…" He was looking at the profusion of bracelets on his arms which he didn't remember wearing before. "What are these?"

"Today is also the Hindu festival of Rakhi, Your Majesty," Nur Jahan offered quickly. "Remember, Your Majesty, this beautiful festival when the ladies adorn the arms of men with flower bracelets. But your Hindu wives have fashioned these gold ones with gems as the tokens of their love and devotion. In this case, it may sound absurd though, since sisters tie bracelets on the arms of their brothers for the gifts of cash." She reached out to claim the porcelain cup from the bedside table. "Drink this, Your Majesty, it would cure your headache." She held out the cup to the emperor.

"Plague!" Jahangir exclaimed. "You all thought I was dying?"

"Not me, Your Majesty, not for a moment!" Nur Jahan blew a kiss into the cup, offering it again. "My intuition tells me, Your Majesty, that you cannot betray my love so suddenly." Her eyes were holding out their own cups of wit and mirth.

"Your wit would kill me soon, if not your beauty, my pearl." Jahangir smiled. "What do you have in there? Camel's milk?"

"No, Your Majesty, goat's," Nur Jahan chirped coaxingly.

"Toss a few grapes in there, my Nur, and the emperor would drink. Chased by a flagon of wine, of course." Jahangir's own wit was returning.

"You promised, Your Majesty!" Nur Jahan feigned shock and disbelief. "You will not even get one cup, Your Majesty, until your health is restored. Besides, all the grapevines in Kashmir are burnt to cinders."

"And when did you learn to lie to the emperor, my lovely physician?" Jahangir mocked.

"If you drink this, Your Majesty, you would be gratified with a tale right out of the bowels of plague. It would be a mystical feast to your curiosity and intellect, I assure you," Nur Jahan coaxed.

"I will be moved to joy, mystically, if the plague has vanished completely." Jahangir claimed the cup reluctantly.

"It has, Your Majesty, it has." Nur Jahan stood propping pillows behind the emperor's back.

"This is no ambrosia for the mortal gods." Jahangir drank obediently.

"And wine turns to hemlock even for the immortal gods, if taken in excess." Nur Jahan returned to her seat thoughtfully.

"And where is that mystical feast, my lovely Nur? Let it pour from your lips which are the color of pomegranates, and the emperor would be healed." Jahangir's gaze was a blaze of curiosity.

"Just to whet your appetite, Your Majesty, let me comment that the things had come to such a pass during the epidemic that from fear of death fathers approached not their sons, and sons were afraid to go near their fathers," Nur Jahan began sweetly. "Now, the mystical feast. A strange thing happened in the town where the plague began. First, a huge fire broke out without any visible cause, and burnt down three thousand houses. Then the people of the city whose houses were intact spotted large circles on their front doors. Inside the big circles were two middle size circles and one small one. All the houses in this vicinity had such circles, some white and the other pale in hue closer to yellow. The mosques of this city were etched with the same circles appearing from nowhere. Right after the conflagration and the appearance of the circles, the plague had diminished, almost vanished."

"Many strange things I have heard about magic and miracles, but these occurrences supersede all cannons of reason." Jahangir was feeling drowsy all of a sudden. "All wisdom is with God! I trust the Almighty will have mercy on His sinful slaves, and will free them from such a calamity as plague." His subconscious appeared to be speaking, not his thoughts. "The emperor has been swimming inside the murky pools of illness, I gather. All the royal burdens falling on you, my Nur. Any important matters which the emperor must know and digest?"

"Beside the murrains, fading fortunately; peace and prosperity reign in your empire, Your Majesty," Nur Jahan soothed quickly. "One sad news from Agra. Muhammad Riza, the Persian ambassador of Shah Abbas, died of diarrhea," she offered reluctantly.

"May God rest his soul in peace," Jahangir prayed aloud. "Dispatch swift orders to Muhammad Qasim, my Nur, to convey the goods and chattels of the late ambassador to Shah Abbas. The Persian monarch, in his own good judgment, will reward the heirs of the deceased with all those material wealths, the emperor hopes." His thoughts were exploring one dream out of the very fabric of his subconscious. "How are Prince Shah Jahan's campaigns faring in Deccan?" he asked abruptly.

"Prince Shah Jahan is gracing his youth with the laurels of victories, Your Majesty." Nur Jahan was quick to feign joy for the victories of the prince, her intuition warning her against this proud victor. "The Marathas in Mandu had no recourse left but to flee against the onslaught of the Turkish musketeers. Of course, they would have fled anyway before the valor of Prince Shah Jahan. All foes and rebels are fleeing pell-mell. Ujjain has ceded, and the fort of Daulatabad is captured. The town of Kharki is fallen, and Ambar Malik has submitted."

"Yes, Prince Shah Jahan, my handsome and valorous son," Jahangir murmured dreamily. "I must send him gifts when I return to Lahore. In our treasury we have a precious plume with a ruby in the middle, which Shah of Persia sent me as a gift. That would be an appropriate gift for his valor and wisdom. Also, my horse named Rum Ratan, which the prince admires the best. That horse too, my Nur, if you know, was a gift from my brother Shah Abbas." Fatigue and weariness were making him opiate.

"You need rest, Your Majesty." Nur Jahan smiled, though her heart was gathering premonitions. "Just close your eyes, Your Majesty, and don't think of anything. I myself will fetch fruits and viands, garnished with Kashmiri almonds."

"No, my Nur, no! The emperor is not hungry," Jahangir protested with a sudden vehemence. "Hold my hand, love, and stay close to me," he appealed with the urgency of a frightened child. "I need your beauty…and your wisdom to guide me inside the jungles of my dreams."

"My wisdom, Your Majesty, tells me that Prince Shah Jahan doesn't deserve the gifts you propose to send him," was Nur Jahan's involuntary comment. "And I don't mean the value of those gifts, but the sentimental worth with which they were sent."

"Passing strange, my love. Strange indeed! Your comment about Prince Shah Jahan, not deserving." Jahangir's thoughts were choking his own dream. "Has he acted in some unmannerly fashion lately? What prompted you to say that?"

"No, Your Majesty. He is valorous and courteous, rather debonair. Perfectly at ease with himself, and in command of every task which he undertakes. Fortunes themselves smile upon him, and herald him to the steps of victories," Nur Jahan began cheerfully. "Only the tongue of my intuition is rude and clamoring these days, Your Majesty. Warning me that Prince Shah Jahan's every move needs to be supervised…about what, I don't know."

"A woman's intuition? If the emperor may resort to such a mundane utterance." Jahangir smiled, that illusive dream invading his very eyes.

"Not just a woman's intuition, Your Majesty, but the intuition of the empress, guided by the wisdom of the seers," Nur Jahan quipped.

"Then, my lovely seer, would you interpret this dream of the emperor?" Jahangir's heart was one throb of exhilaration. "While you thought the emperor was dying, my pearl, he was living the nightmares not ever lived before in the waking, sleeping hours of his entire life."

"Please, Your Majesty, don't relive that nightmare if it is sprinkled with ill omens," Nur Jahan pleaded quickly. "The seers themselves say that nightmares should be left unvoiced to ward off ill fortunes." Her own heart was throbbing ominously.

"You share all the burdens of the empire, my Nur, and shrink from sharing the emperor's dream or nightmare?" Jahangir chided.

"And how can I help not sharing it, when my heart is dying to snatch it from the very cups of your eyes, Your Majesty?" was Nur Jahan's effusive protest. "I would absolve its ill affects with my witchcraft if need be."

"If your witchcraft can reach that banyan tree," Jahangir began with all haste, as if afraid to lose his dream, "that banyan tree in Shaikhupur where we enjoyed hunting, and then journeyed to Daulatabad. Do you remember, my Nur?"

"How can I forget, Your Majesty, I killed a rather sleek tiger over there." Nur Jahan pressed the emperor's hand to her cheek. "And that banyan tree on which you carved the impression of your hand above the impression of Prince Shah Jahan's hand. Then those impressions were transferred on a tile of marble, if I recall correctly, and that piece of marble was fastened to the trunk of the same tree."

"Yes, the same one, my Nur," Jahangir began exigently. "Yes, in my dream, I was sitting under the shade of that banyan tree. Around me were heaps upon heaps of gold coins, all scattered. I was feeling a few on the palm of my hands, especially the ones with the Zodiac signs. One Nur-Jahani gold mohur was attracting my attention, the one struck in your name. I was searching for more gold mohurs minted in your name with other constellations, the one with the ram and the other with a bull. I had all those before me, turned over, so that I could read the inscriptions on the back. *Fate's pen wrote on the coin in letters of light.* I was reading the inscription penned by Asaf Khan, right under it the inscribed Kalima which seemed to be on fire, below which my name was inscribed. One gold heap before me was stirring. Prince Shah Jahan was materializing from under its glittering depths. He was carrying a severed head in his hand. Another form was emerging from the gold heap next to him. It was Mahabat Khan's. Prince Shah Jahan was tossing the severed head to Mahabat Khan, and exclaiming, 'Tell the emperor that his first-born is dead.' I could see Prince Khusrau's head, still bleeding, tossed at my feet in return. Mahabat Khan and Prince Shah Jahan were rolling in laughter, and disappearing under the mounds of gold." He closed his eyes.

"Mahabat Khan is another viper in disguise, Your Majesty," Nur Jahan murmured inaudibly. "The Kalima on your gold mohur is going to protect us all from any adversities which may lie in ambush."

"The emperor wishes to visit that clear pool in the garden of Verang, my Nur, before we journey to Lahore," Jahangir murmured opiately.

"We will, Your Majesty, we will." Nur Jahan was murmuring back, trying to lull the emperor to sleep with the sweetness of her voice and touch.

"Have you visited those caves behind our sacred pool, my Nur?" Jahangir was trying to keep his eyes open, as if afraid to sleep.

"No, Your Majesty." Nur Jahan was cupping the emperor's hand into both hers.

"Do you know what Verang means, my Nur?" Jahangir was persistent.

"Yes, Your Majesty. It means a snake," Nur Jahan breathed tenderly.

"A large snake, my Nur." Jahangir's eyelids were getting heavy, and his voice heavier still. "In those caves there is an altar for that snake, a retreat for the Hindus and the recluses to pray and meditate. Yes, I must take you there before we journey to Lahore. We must leave in a week's time at the most…look to the preparations of the journey, my Nur." He could barely keep his eyes open.

"Yes, Your Majesty. Now I must go and fetch your favorite dishes." Nur Jahan was willing him rest and sleep.

"No, beloved, stay. Never leave me. Not ever leave me." Jahangir's eyes were falling shut. He had seen the face of Anarkali in the eyes of Nur Jahan.

Chapter Nine

The spring in Agra had donned the palace gardens in the loveliest of blooms upon Jahangir's return from Lahore. The long journey from Kashmir to Lahore had not much improved the emperor's health, but Agra had greeted him with the hopes of salubrity, offering him garlands from the very hands of nature. This particular afternoon, sunshine itself was pouring joy into the flagons of celebrations for the wedding of Prince Shahriyar with Princess Ladli. The guests were pouring into the garden, anticipating a grand feast amidst the fanfare of grand ceremonies. Jugglers too were there, practicing their skills to entertain, and the young girls were whirling on their toes in accompaniment with the beat of the tablas. The bride and bridegroom were imprisoned in their own garlanded chambers. They had to go through a regiment of rituals in toiletry and dressing before they could journey on the path to a succession of ceremonies.

The Agra palace, from pillared verandahs to four gates in red sandstone, was decked with vines and garlands of flowers. One large chamber with damasked walls was the comfortable abode where Jahangir and Nur Jahan sat talking and laughing. Nur Jahan's parents had joined the royal couple, and they were all immersed in the luxury of their own merriment before joining the guests in the palace garden. The emperor was appareled most exquisitely in the finest of silks, the color of sapphires. One large diamond in his mauve turban was accentuating his pallor. This diamond was presented to him by Khwaja Jahan, the governor of Agra, and the emperor had found matching diamonds to adorn his ears. Right now, he was bathed in sparkle and glitter from the wealth of jewels on his royal person, and seated on his gold throne presented to him by a European goldsmith by the name of Hanarmand. The emperor was so pleased with this gift that he had installed it in his chamber.

Nur Jahan' gown of Chinese silk was lending her fair cheeks the tinge of rose and ivory. A tiara of rubies and diamonds was matching the jeweled sash at her tiny waist. She was nibbling on sweets from the silver bowl resting on an alabaster stand beside her. This bowl itself was exquisite in design, carved in the semblance of a fish and encrusted with jewels.

Asmat Begum and Itmadudaula Khan too were richly appareled, seated on gilt chairs dripping with red velvets. Asmat Begum was feeding her husband the delicious morsels of court gossip, and laughing. Nur Jahan was listening and smiling to herself. Jahangir was rapt in admiring the painting in his lap, which he had just received as a gift of his own aesthetic observations caught on the canvas by his court painters.

This work of art was vivid in each little detail, and throbbing with the colors of life. A pair of saras painted with bright blue wings were feeding their young ones with locusts and grasshoppers. One peafowl was visible from under the shade of the tamarinds, as if watching this whole scene with a great interest. Wild geese were soaring overhead into the blue bowl of a sky. Jahangir could relate with this scene most profoundly, for he himself had watched these saras in the process of hatching and feeding their young ones. He sat contemplating the painting with utmost absorption.

"Look, Itmadudaula, how my court painters have captured that entire scene with the brush of inspiration." Jahangir held out the painting to his father-in-law.

"Yes, Your Majesty. These young ones are still chirping in your garden somewhere, I can attest." Itmadudaula Khan claimed the painting, smiling. "Had I not known that Your Majesty observed the hatching and feeding of these saras, I would have thought that the painter had drawn this entire scene out of his own imagination."

"How patiently you observed, Your Majesty." Asmat Begum was leaning over to have a better view of the painting. "One young one was hatched after thirty-four days, and the other one after thirty-six, didn't you tell us?"

"I prefer the paintings of Farrukh Beg, of dancing girls and of royal ladies at their toilette." Nur Jahan's eyes were flashing this comment at her parents.

"A week ago, precisely, my Nur! Didn't you confess that all paintings are worthless as compared to the gold mohurs on which the emperor's picture is engraved? And in that picture the emperor is holding a wine cup, mind you?" Jahangir laughed.

"Just because mine is engraved the same way, and on the precious gold mohurs too, Your Majesty!" Nur Jahan teased happily. "You do look handsome on the gold coin, Your Majesty, I confess. But my own pulsates with the life of youth and beauty."

"Don't you believe her, Your Majesty!" Itmadudaula Khan exclaimed.

"All the paintings on her chamber walls rising up to the ceiling belie her artistic preferences."

"Oh, those awful scenes with the splashes of court splendor!" Asmat Begum chided, trying to stifle the sudden flaring of pain in her stomach.

"And wouldn't you be happy, my Nur, if the emperor bestowed upon you the paintings which he is wont to hide in the gold caskets layered with the softest of silks?" Jahangir's eyes were brimming with mischief, if not with adoration.

"Of course, Your Majesty," Nur Jahan sang sprightfully. "But I would be happier still if my beautiful pearl is found. Alas, I broke my necklace and lost that gem."

"Does the emperor not bestow enough pearls and diamonds on you, my Nur, that you should mourn the loss of such a paltry gift?" Jahangir consoled.

"A paltry gift, Your Majesty!" Nur Jahan declared. "That one pearl is worth fifteen thousand rupees, Your Majesty. Besides, you gave me that necklace on my birthday…" She could not say another word, noticing the gleam of amusement in the emperor's eyes.

"Didn't Jotik Ray, that diviner and astrologer, predict that this pearl would be found soon?" Asmat Begum was asking her husband.

"No dearth of diviners in the Moghul courts, Asmat? Another soothsayer divining that a fair damsel would bring this pearl to the empress in a state of ecstasy?" Itmadudaula Khan shifted his attention to the emperor. "What need you have of pearls and jewels, Your Majesty? Indeed, that is true. You are the world conqueror. Mighty of the mightiest in power and justice, where no treasures of the world are needed to rule and subjugate." His eyes were holding the lamps of flattery and inspiration. "You are the lord over all Hind, now that Prince Shah Jahan has subjugated all the lords of Deccan. Winning their hearts too, with his own charm and generosity!"

"Ah, my fortunate son! How the emperor sang praises of his victories with wine and rejoicing, and received him with all due honors," Jahangir murmured happily. "Alas, that he can't be here to attend the wedding of his brother." A shadow of pain was splintering his joy. "Didn't the emperor greet him with the ardor of a poet…Thy time is happy in that thou hast made me happy," he recited. "And as to your flattery, Itmadudaula, this verse which I penned on my birthday will suit your mood.

"Thou art the mighty One, O Lord
Thou art the cherisher of rich and poor
I'm not a world-conqueror or law-giver

I'm one of the beggars at this gate
Help me in what is good and right
Else what good comes from me to anyone
I'm master to my servants
To the Lord, I'm a loyal servant."

He picked one pallet of opium from the porcelain bowl, and tossed it into his mouth.

"Such humble verse with the breath of greatness, Your Majesty!" Nur Jahan applauded. "If Prince Shah Jahan has his own way, the emperor may become his servant, not the Lord's." Her warning was sweet and explicit.

"What makes you say that, Nur?" Jahangir's heart was probing its own sadness. "Is my favorite son harboring any designs of treachery?"

"No, Your Majesty. He is the pillar of devotion and obedience, as ever," Nur Jahan intoned charmingly. "Only that he is asserting too much authority in Deccan. Winning friends and alliances…men who can't be trusted as to remain faithful to the empire. He is gathering more forces than he needs against the Deccani contingent, I hear." A subtle warning was concealed behind the sweetness in her voice.

"The empress sounds very jealous, I presume." Jahangir laughed, shifting his attention toward his father-in-law. "Are the titles and favors making my beloved son proud and presumptuous, Itmadudaula? Is he becoming the victim of indiscretion?"

"The prince has an independent nature, Your Majesty," Itmadudaula Khan began discreetly. "No indiscretion on his part, as far as I know. I haven't heard anything except that his ward…" His reluctance was snatched by Asmat Begum.

"All base canards, Your Majesty," Asmat Begum began quickly. "Prince Khusrau is surrounded by all princely comforts. Living in utmost luxury, and evil tongues are filling Prince Shah Jahan's coffers with the soot of calumnies, that's all!"

"Ah, my unfortunate son. Khusrau, Khusrau." Jahangir let out a string of sighs. "I wish he was here too, to celebrate his brother's wedding." He got to his feet absently.

Jahangir stood facing the portrait on the wall as if he was all alone. This could have been true for no one spoke, with the exception that all were there and all immersed in absolute hush. Nur Jahan was watching the emperor, being watched by her parents in return. The emperor seemed to be gazing right through the canvas, as if divining the thoughts of the emperor of

Constantinople, who had sent this to him as a gift. The picture was hanging low in a gilded frame. The silk on the canvas was yellowed by age, but through its faded colors the masterful strokes of the artist could not be mistaken. This artist, with his ingenious skill, had succeeded in depicting the semblance of Tamelane on a man as common as any tourist walking on the streets of Tabriz. The man on this silk painting wore a plumed turban and a colorful robe. He was seated on a throne as regal as Tamerlane, but had no resemblance to this tyrant lord feared by the ages past. With the exception of that unmistakable aura of power and wisdom around his very features, which, to the naked eye, were presenting him in the semblance Tamerlane, but to the discerning eye of the emperor, nothing was concealed. Jahangir was always drawn to this portrait whenever he had a chance to sit in this room. He was wont to find solace in this portrait as some wide-open avenue of ideation and diversion, often unmasking it with his thoughts, and pronouncing this portrait-man as an impostor feigning to be Tamerlane. Right now as he stood watching the portrait with his back toward all, his heart was bleeding for Prince Khusrau. And in that red rivulet of pain and sorrow, his thoughts were painting the portrait of Anarkali.

"This portrait has no resemblance even to the immediate descendants of Tamerlane." Jahangir was half turning, when he espied Mehr Harwi.

Mehr Harwi was standing by the gilded doors, her eyes alone seeking the emperor's permission to enter this chamber. Jahangir granted his consent with a mere wave of his arm, and ambled toward the chest with koftgari design. Mehr Harwi curtsied low and fled toward the empress. Jahangir's attention was absorbed by a copy of the Quran on the polished surface of the chest, and he seemed lost in his own solitary contemplations. This copy of the Quran was bound in a gold cover with two jeweled roses in the middle. He had received this gift from Muzaffar Khan, and had decided to bestow it on Shahriyar and his bride as one of the wedding gifts. He picked up this copy of the Quran and stood flitting its pages.

Meanwhile, Mehr Harwi had fallen into a lengthy curtsy at the feet of the empress. She was gasping for breath, trying to find her voice. Finally, she had recovered, and was disclosing a large pearl on the palm of her hand.

"Padishah Begum. One of the Turkish girls found it in the oratory." Mehr Harwi was collapsing into a curtsy once again.

"Oh, my dream-pearl! My own gift from the astrologers and soothsayers." Nur Jahan was fondling the pearl on the palm of her own hand with a childish glee.

"A good omen to commence the wedding ceremonies of my granddaughter." Asmat Begum was rising to her feet, the pain in the pit of her stomach returning.

"This good omen would herald us all into the garden where our guests are waiting." Jahangir held out the copy of the Quran to his father-in-law. "Here, Itmadudaula, carry this with you. This is one of the emperor's gifts to the bridal couple."

"I feel honored to carry it, Your Majesty. They would be honored to receive it, I can…" Itmadudaula's speech was checked by an exclamation from the lips of Nur Jahan.

"Are you ill, Mamma? Here, drink this." Nur Jahan was snatching a porcelain cup from the table beside her.

Both Jahangir and Itmadudaula Khan were by Asmat Begum's side in a flash. Jahangir, becoming aware of the beads of perspiration on the brow of Asmat Begum, was offering her his silk kerchief. Itmadudaula Khan was assisting his wife to the chair.

"I am fine. Just one of those giddy spells." Asmat Begum was waving away all attempts at ministration. "Go, join the wedding celebrations. I would be sailing behind in a few minutes. Don't keep the emperor waiting."

"Mamma." Nur Jahan could barely murmur.

"Despite your protests, Asmat Begum, you would be besieged by our royal physicians," Jahangir muttered, turning toward Nur Jahan. "Come, my Nur, your mother's edict must be obeyed. The wedding celebrations are longing for the company of the emperor and the empress." He offered her his arm.

The emperor was looking into the eyes of Anarkali where Nur Jahan was dissolved into the mists unclearing. The dead beloved had risen from her bright sepulcher, bruised and unweeping. And his heart was chilled by this reflection frozen in time. Nur Jahan could not miss that look of agony in the emperor's eyes, and now her own heart was throbbing in torments everlasting. Her velvet shoes were digging deep into the Bokhara rugs down the vast, garlanded staircase, but she seemed not aware of the yielding steps beneath her against the poundings inside her heart. Jahangir, on the contrary, was banishing his pains and agonies, and awakening to the pathos of awareness. They had both landed down the hall of forty pillars as if drifting in a dream, but Jahangir was the first one to notice Hushiyar Khan, the eunuch of Nur Jahan. Commanding this devoted eunuch to his presence, the emperor was quick to dispatch him with the orders of summoning Hakim Ruhullah, who would then attend to the needs of Asmat Begum.

The emperor was now leading Nur Jahan into the tapestried hallway with a maze of doors to the left and right, which seemed to be expanding endlessly into more chambers and corridors. Nur Jahan was becoming aware of the chamber of mirrors with mosaic floors, to her right. This chamber was equipped with marble fountains in the middle, and a large tank the size of a swimming pool. She was so profoundly absorbed in recalling the details of this chamber, that she didn't notice they were stepping out into the open on the turreted gazebo.

This large gazebo was occupied mainly by the poets and the younger princes, and they were surging toward the royal couple with smiles and greetings. The musicians by the marble fountains were striking beautiful melodies, sweet and intoxicating. Shauqi, the mandolin player was oblivious to all but to the wild notes of his wedding songs. Nayi, the flute player, was vying with him with the loveliest of tunes ever evoked on a royal wedding. Prince Perwiz was seen surfing on the scene.

"Your Majesty. Padishah Begum." Prince Perwiz swayed and curtsied. "All the gardens in Hind are stripped bare to deck this wedding!"

"Not this garden, my prince, not Nur Manzil." Nur Jahan smiled. "This Nur Manzil of mine has everlasting blooms, and no one dare pluck one without my permission."

"Yes, my happy prince, our empress with everlasting youth has the power to keep her gardens in eternal bloom! Not only Nur Manzil, but Nur Afshan and Moti Bagh too. And don't forget the gardens in Kashmir." Jahangir's gaze was piercing. "You should plant gardens too, my inebriated scholar! Bhang grows wild in the village of Panj Bara which the emperor bestowed upon you, replace it with flowers," he chided.

"Bhang doesn't suit the tastes of our royal prince, Your Majesty. Though abundance of wine keeps him fit and merry." Asaf Khan, emerging from behind, seemed to be patronizing the giddy prince.

"Ah, my diwan of Gujrat, you are neglecting your duties." Jahangir flashed Asaf Khan a warm look. "Feasting and gormandizing, Asaf, while you should be attending to the affairs in Gujrat?"

"Padishah Begum ordered me to join these festivities, Your Majesty, instead of sending me a gentle invitation," Asaf Khan rejoined brightly.

"Oh, my dear, dear brothers! Do they ever obey the empress?" Nur Jahan teased. "And did you, Asaf, heed my other commands? Where is our dear brother Itaqid Khan? Our sisters, where are they? Manija and her husband Qasim Khan? Our little Khadija and her husband Hakim Beg?"

"The imperial orders didn't suit their temperaments, Padishah Begum," was Asaf Khan's mirthful response. "Besides, how could I disobey the emperor? His commands were to leave these happy kin in their unhappy kingdoms, where they could keep a check on the intrigues and rebellions of their subjects."

"Before this feasting could turn into a dish of warring territories, Your Majesty, may I present Sayyid Hasan, the ambassador from Persia?" Motamid Khan edged closer. He had just left the circle of the poets, Sayyid Hasan trailing behind him.

"If my brother Shah Abbas is not coveting Kandahar for his Persian domains." Jahangir laughed, granting consent with a quick wave of his arm.

"Shah Abbas, the king of Persia, sends this gift to the emperor of Hindustan, Your Majesty." Sayyid Hasan procured one crystal goblet encrusted with rubies.

"A most charming gift." Jahangir was eager to claim the goblet. "With the permission of the empress, it would be put to test." He flashed a smile at Nur Jahan.

Before Nur Jahan could protest, the wine-bearer was at hand to obey the emperor. Jahangir was quick to drain his cup thirstily, holding it out for replenishing.

"This goblet is too beautiful to be poisoned with wine, Your Majesty," Nur Jahan murmured, her eyes flashing daggers at the wine-bearer.

"This is the nectar of love, my empress, though you may choose to name it poison." Jahangir smiled, turning his attention to Sayyid Hasan. "For this rare gift, Sayyid, the emperor is going to send Shah Abbas his own jeweled jug fashioned like a cock. And that will hold more wine than this dainty crystal cup." He stood contemplating the rubies on the gold rim of this goblet. "And another rare gift! A wild ass exceedingly strange in appearance. Shah Abbas would be pleased beyond measure. This ass looks like a lion, exactly, without exaggeration. From the tip of its nose to the end of its tail, and from two points of its ears to the top of its hoof, there are black markings. And fine, black lines around its eyes. One might say the painter of fate, with a strange brush, has left this wild ass on the page of this world." His gaze was returning to Nur Jahan. "What would the empress bestow upon the ambassador from Persia?"

"My own gold mohur, Your Majesty, the one which is called the Star of Destiny." Nur Jahan smiled.

"Ah, the Star of Destiny." Jahangir's gaze was straying down the courtyard below where an elephant parade was just commencing.

These elephants being paraded before the guests were causing quite a din of cheer and applause. More than one dozen in a group, all these were the favorite elephants of the emperor. They were decked with coverings of fine brocade, beside being garlanded and painted with bright colors. He stood admiring the richly appareled elephants, but his thoughts were running a backward course, and holding Mahabat Khan captive on the way. The emperor had entrusted Mahabat Khan with all the expenditure for this wedding. Now noticing the precious brocades on the backs of his elephants as some needless expense, his gaze was searching Mahabat Khan where he had seen him earlier amongst the group of the poets. Mahabat Khan was still glued to that giddy circle, and enjoying the recitations of couplets wild and lurid.

"Mahabat Khan, come hither, and lay open the accounts of expenditure for this wedding," Jahangir commanded. "Particularly, how much did it cost to don the elephants thus in rich brocades?"

"Your Majesty." Mahabat Khan was leaving the happy circle of the poets, and stumbling into the snare of the emperor's inquisition. "I know nothing about it, Your Majesty." He was bowing and murmuring. "These brocades were prepared in the harem. Her Majesty, the Empress, had sent them to me."

"Then, may I put the same question to you, my empress?" Jahangir asked.

"Practically nothing, Your Majesty," Nur Jahan sang happily. "These coverings have been made by the palace tailors from the bags in which the letters and petitions of the nobles and the ambassadors are received. Nothing was purchased, so no funds from the royal treasury were pilfered."

"You are the paragon of thrift, my empress," Jahangir complimented.

The terraces were teeming with guests in waves upon waves of silks and jewels. But the emperor's gaze was arrested to the courtyard, where the chess game with beautiful girls dressed as pawns, knights, soldiers, viziers, kings and queens, were luring the male guests to a stalemate of awe and silence. The alfresco Parcheesi floor of the courtyard was divided into sixty-four squares with vermilion lines to create a life-size chessboard. A few girls as pawns and soldiers were banished from their squares, though they stood there laughing amongst themselves. They were dead, metaphorically, killed by their willful lords who were determined to trample over the lives of their subjects.

"And don't tell the emperor, Mahabat, that this chess game is not one of your brilliant schemes to turn these wedding festivities into a battleground of mirth and delirium?" Jahangir's gaze was returning to Mahabat Khan with the stars of inquisition.

"A great entertainment for the royal ladies, Your Majesty," was Mahabat Khan's delirious response. "This charming spectacle works to their benefit to rule, govern and displace their own lords." He averted his gaze.

"Most beneficial for the lords, I must say," was Nur Jahan's sweet comment, concealing one dagger of a threat. "For it improves their skills to shuffle and replace their ladies without a pang of remorse or contrition."

Jahangir began to laugh, greatly amused, more so by Nur Jahan's wit, than by Mahabat Khan's dull-witted insinuation. Overwhelmed by his own mirth, his gaze was frolicking once again, this time gathering the circle of poets in its ocean billowing with caprice and commands. He could see Talib Amuli in there, upon whom he had bestowed the title of Malikush Shuara, meaning the King of Poets.

"Leave that witless circle, my king of poets. Come, delight the emperor with your poetry where it is appreciated the most," Jahangir commanded. He was waving dismissal at the rest of the courtiers, who had flocked around him uninvited.

All were dispersing like the giddy waves, caught in their own mindless currents. Talib Amuli was sprinting past all, and edging closer to the royal couple with the speed of a comet. In his hand he was holding a large rose the size and color of a morning sun.

"Your flattering title itself, Your Majesty, has garbed my poetry into rags of silence." Talib Amuli curtsied. "But I do wish to present this rose to you, Your Majesty, as a gift of my mute inspiration." He held out the rose.

"A rare gift such as this should have been left breathing on its stem for all to cherish and admire. " Jahangir claimed the rose, inhaling its fragrance.

"Without the consent of Padishah Begum, I would not have dared pluck it, Your Majesty." Talib Amuli smiled, stealing a look of gratitude at the empress. "This is a gift of Her Majesty's graciousness, and I have taken the liberty to present it to the emperor."

"A faithless poet! Exchanging his own gift for a favor from the emperor." Nur Jahan's eyes were shining with mirth.

"You must garnish this gift with a rich verse of yours, Talib, or the emperor's ungraciousness would visit you soon," Jahangir commanded.

"Yes, Your Majesty." Talib Amuli bowed his head.

"Spring longs to riffle thy parterre
For the flowers in thy hand are fresher than those on his branch
I've closed my lips from speech that you'd say
His mouth is but a scar on his face." He glued his lips together in the imitation of a crescent.

"If the court poets made it a habit of acting and writing in this refrain, the emperor might strip them off their titles." Jahangir's own eyes were gathering poetic stars. "The verse of Anwari suits better on this occasion than any impromptu verses ever sung by the Moghul poets." He smiled before reciting the cherished verse.

"'Tis a day of mirth and jollity
A daily market of flowers and odors
The earth-heaps are suffused with ambergris
The zephyr sheds rose-water from his skirt
From contact with the morning breeze the pool
Is roughened and pointed like the edge of a file."

He was turning toward Nur Jahan with a whimsical smile. "The gardens of delight need exploring, my empress. Let the poets sing hymns of praises to the bridal couple, while we court the bride of nature."

The bridal couple had just emerged out into the garden, floating ahead of the musicians, as if carried on the strings of melodies from the wedding songs. A canopied stage smothered with velvets and brocades was welcoming them to its royal bosom. The servants with gold and silver trays balanced on their arms, had begun to serve hors d'oeuvres to the guests. Jahangir and Nur Jahan, caught in a flurry of greetings here and there, were straying farther from the jubilant sea of music and dancing. The terraces and marble fountains were left behind, and they were entering a grove where poplars stood tall and mighty. They could see the purple irises in the distance, the ones which Nur Jahan had insisted on importing from Kashmir. The feet of both the emperor and the empress were coming to a slow, involuntary halt before one jets d'eau. It was bubbling with the rhythm of a cataract, and gathering music in its own pool of marble and sunshine.

Jahangir and Nur Jahan were suspended there as if transported into some valley of peace. Both were quiet, both content to be alone, together. Both were welcoming the silence, both exiled from the fever of feasting and celebration. Nur Jahan's senses were in abeyance, still drugged with the wine of perfume and beauty in Nur Manzil. Jahangir too had drunk deep of the beauty of this garden, and his aesthetic senses were swooning. He had feasted on scent and color with the ardor of a lover, but much like a true lover, his thoughts were gathering doubts and sadness. Something alien and nameless was simmering inside him. A kind of sadness, which he had not ever felt before. It were strange and mysterious, as if his heart would choke with grief and despair. *Grief and despair?* They were no closer to him than song and music, which were reaching him on the strings of breeze in faded ripples. Something inside him was bleeding and cankerous, some enormous rent which could not be mended or healed.

"My heart is burdened with nameless grief, Nur. Stay close to me, always. Not ever leave me. Not even for a moment, all this evening," Jahangir murmured.

Nur Jahan was startled out of her own reverie of peace and serenity. She could not speak, her gaze alone searching the cause of the emperor's malady. His pale, sharp features were attaining the glow of ivory against the intensity in her wild, searching gaze. Actually, the feeling of sadness in Jahangir's thoughts and mirrored into his eyes was dissolving, leaving behind only the sparkle of awe, as if he had just discovered the beauty of his beloved. The white rose in crimson silks. The gleam of pearls framed over her oval face. Her lake-blue eyes. The dream-boat oceans. Her poppy-red lips.

*A goddess molded in ivory. The purity of pearls and rubies in her complexion. A goddess, whose worth I can never imagine. A goddess, whose youth I have tarnished with my own canker of love and despair…*Jahangir was thinking.

"Why so, Your Majesty?" Nur Jahan's murmur of a plea was carving a big ripple in this pool of silence. "The wedding of my daughter and of your beloved son, and you talk of grief?"

"Don't you hear the cry of a nightingale, my Nur? It is drowning all the festive songs in its loud laments. Also, pouring grief into the emperor's heart." Jahangir's gaze was arrested to the nightingale, who was ransacking a crow's nest up on the chenar.

"Not lamenting, Your Majesty, but serenading hope in life, as you yourself remind me year after year." Nur Jahan followed the emperor's gaze. "Look, Your Majesty, how it has emptied out the crow's nest of all its eggs! Now it would lay its own in its empty lair. How well I remember since last year! The crow mistaking the nightingale's eggs as its own, and hatching and tending the young ones till…" Her heart was fluttering all of a sudden.

"Ah, the crow! Black as the night with black, beady eyes," Jahangir demurred aloud. "In all aspects, the nightingale resembles the crow with the exception of its red eyes."

"With the exception of white spots, as on this female, Your Majesty." Nur Jahan tried to still the fluttering in her heart. "These lovely colors in spring are playing tricks on your sight and senses." She laughed.

"Yes, love, I can see…" Jahangir could see Anarkali in nature as well as in the lovely eyes of Nur Jahan. "Yes, I can see only love! Love in nature, and love in your beautiful eyes. The spring of love is bubbling inside my heart, and all around us." He slipped his arm around her waist. "Let us stroll down the grove yonder. Maybe we will meet a tiger in love, and the emperor will vie his love for you with vows much nobler than the animal passion?"

"Tiger in love, Your Majesty? I have only encountered the ferocious ones, the victims of my shooting." Nur Jahan could not help boasting.

"How did I ever forget to tell you about this, my Nur?" Jahangir began reminiscently. "I was in Lahore and you stayed in Agra, one of your cruel edicts which carve rents of separation." He laughed. "Well, in Lahore, Dewar Bakhsh presented me with a tiger who had an affection for a goat. Since this was strange, I tried an experiment. The goat was taken away from the tiger. The tiger was disconsolate after being separated from the goat. I ordered another goat to be brought to his cage. The tiger smelled this goat, and then broke its back in a fit of rage. A sheep was then brought to his cage, and he devoured it mercilessly. Finally, I ordered the old goat to be brought back to his cage. At once, he took the goat to its breast and licked its face. Never before I had seen such love by animals tame or wild!"

"And how do you propose to vie with that love, Your Majesty?" was Nur Jahan's bright challenge.

"By caging you inside a glass palace, so that no one could take you away from me," Jahangir retorted mirthfully.

"Not even death?" was Nur Jahan's sing-song rejoinder.

"Especially death!" Jahangir's feet came to a sudden halt under the canopy of cypresses. "I will stand guard at the door, fighting death till my last breath."

"Death fights no duels, not even with an emperor, Your Majesty. It strikes its victims in absolute stealth without a grain of mercy." Mirth and mockery were shining in Nur Jahan's eyes. "But you may paint my beauty with the pen of destiny, and keep it as a specimen for your experiments."

"What cruel jests, Nur?" Jahangir chided intensely. "Your wit tastes bitter to the emperor, wonder why?" He snatched her hand, kissing it reverently. "Let us return to the garden of festivity where songs breathe life, and banish death to its rightful abode of silence, behind the very gates of Hades." He drifted ahead of her.

"What made you say that, beloved?"

"Forgive me, Your Majesty," Nur Jahan murmured contritely. "Strange as it may seem, I was thinking about the time when you had had that old man brought to the palace, the one who was dying, and you ordered the court painters to paint a fresh picture each day to the very end of his life." The wedding songs were reaching her awareness.

"And not in the least strange that the emperor was thinking about love!" Jahangir's gaze was reaching out to the sea of colors in the distance. "Love of one beast to another? Love of a man for a woman…" He paused, smothering his thoughts, alive or dead, unvoiced. "Love of a father to his children. Love of a mother to her babes who stay eternally young in her loving thoughts. Yes, the love of a mother! Another story, the Great Truth, not a parable! Did I ever tell you that story, Nur? You can never fathom such love, Nur…in that story." His eyes were kindling a bright challenge.

"I know such love, Your Majesty," was Nur Jahan's tremulous response.

"Such a one which could make you sacrifice your own life for your child, Nur?" Jahangir's thoughts were inhaling the scent of that story.

"If it needs sacrificing, Your Majesty," Nur Jahan murmured.

"Not the need, my love, but immolating one's life without rhyme or reason," Jahangir thought aloud.

"Then, may I know the reason of its greatness, Your Majesty?" Nur Jahan could sense the emperor's need to tell this story.

"This greatness must be named love, if not aberration," Jahangir ruminated intensely. "And yet, it is neither sacrifice nor immolation on the part of that woman who took her life, but sheer devotion. Her son was addicted to opium, and she was used to feed him with her own hands. When her son died at the age of sixty, she took large quantities of opium herself and ended her life."

"Love, devotion, sacrifice, and many more, much noble passions breed inside the hearts of women, Your Majesty, but not in men's." Nur Jahan smiled to herself. "Would any husband think of killing himself after the death of his wife?"

"A lover, perhaps? And the emperor for sure, if you were ever snatched away from him by the cruel hands of fate." Jahangir laughed. "Do you remember Kalyan who tempted the fates? That life-immolating lover who gave up his life with joy and regarded death as a trifle?" Laughter was fading from his eyes.

"How can I forget, Your Majesty?" Nur Jahan chanted rather doubtfully.

"You sound unconvincing, Nur. If you remember, refresh the emperor's memory," Jahangir challenged, his gaze flying to the tapestry of colors in his garden.

"Oh, that blacksmith, Your Majesty." Nur Jahan's memory was clearing the fogs of doubts. "Yes, that Kalyan who was in love with a widow. Boasting that he would fling himself down from the balcony of Shahburj, if the widow would consent to marry him. When brought before you, Your Majesty, you had promised him that you yourself would convince that widow to marry him if he was brave enough to jump down from the window of your palace. How, literally, he accepted your challenge, and died of head injuries?" Her gaze was following the Carnatic jugglers coming into view.

"It was a sad passing, sad! Catching the emperor's jest as an ill-fated command?" Jahangir intoned sadly. "The emperor must present his gifts to the bride and the bridegroom before this day is drowned into its own waters of mirth and gaiety."

The emperor and the empress were caught amidst a throng of merry guests, exchanging amenities and felicitations, and drifting closer toward the garlanded stage. Mutamid Khan had joined the royal couple, carrying the gifts intended for the bride and the bridegroom. Prince Shahriyar and Princess Ladli, seated under the canopy of gold, were already surrounded by heaps of gifts from the guests. To these were added the emperor's gifts bestowed upon his son and daughter-in-law by his own royal hands. A chest of jewels and a set of exquisite paintings were presented to the bride. The bridegroom had received a jeweled coat with a matching turban and cummerbund. In addition, he had received two gold saddles, one for the Iraqi horse and the other for the Turkish steed. Both these horses were from the emperor's own royal stables.

The emperor was showering gold and silver coins over the heads of the bridal couple as the final ritual to bless this wedlock. Saida, the poet and goldsmith, favored both by the emperor and Prince Shah Jahan, had begun to sing a panegyric verse.

"O thou, of whose threshold the nine spheres are an exemplar
Aged Time hath grown young in thy reign
Thy heart is bounteous as the sun, and like it needs no cause for bounty
All lives are devoted to thy gracious heart
Heaven is but a bright orange from the garden of Power
Tossed by the gardener into the atmosphere
O God, Thy essence has shown from eternity
The souls of all the saints receive light from Thee
O King, may the world ever be at thy beck
May thy Shah Jahan ever rejoice in thy shade
O Shadow of God, may the world be filled with thy light
May the Light of God ever be thy canopy."

Saida's voice was trilling after the emperor as he scattered his last handful of gold and silver coins. Nur Jahan was right beside the emperor, her eyes gleaming with joy and pride. The emperor's other wives had joined too, a mist of happy tears clouding their eyes. A few were roasting in flames of jealousy though, amongst them, Nurunnisa, Khairunnisa, Salihah Banu, Malika Jahan and Sahiba Jamali. Jahangir's own eyes were shining, but with the light of premonition. His heart had begun to thunder suddenly. Some sort of cosmic violence was brewing inside his breast as if all the furies of hell were let loose. He had not ever experienced such violence before, not even inside the anguished deeps of his soul, and he staggered. Before he could arrest this rising storm inside his body and mind, his attention was caught by Banarasi. Actually, this express runner, Banarasi, was attracting attention from all by the sheer desperation of his haste to reach the emperor. He was like a gust of wind, carrying woe and despair into his eyes.

"What hideous demon of madness is pressing you to corrupt the joy of these wedding celebrations?" Jahangir demanded as Banarasi fell prostrate at his feet.

"Your Majesty." Banarasi gasped for words, but could not speak. He heaved himself up, but was shrinking with terror by the flashing of rage in the emperor's eyes.

"Untie this knot of delay, o' crumbling wretch, and answer the emperor," Jahangir thundered, as if trying to banish the thundering inside his own heart.

"Your Majesty...Prince Shah Jahan...a letter from him. Prince Khusrau...died of colic," Banarasi murmured incoherently, standing there dazed and stultified.

"From the valleys of ruin to the..." Jahangir's voice was one distant murmur of a thunder. His soul was listening to the drums of death, which were sounding the beat of treachery than the trumpets of misfortunes. "My son, my first-born son! A traveler on the road to nonexistence." He was drifting away, dazed and stricken.

The emperor was journeying on the road to silence, chased by grief and despair. Rocked by waves upon waves of agony, he knew not wither he journeyed, or when the walls of his own palace came tumbling down to lull his pain into a blanket of hush, stark and funereal. The wedding songs themselves were some mournful tunes, following him at his heels. Nur Jahan was beside him, the other wives frozen somewhere on the canvas of time.

"Your Majesty, the face of death is not alien to you. You have seen it many times before. Have repelled it with strength and courage! Don't let this grief overwhelm you now, for the sake of the ones whom you love and who still live," Nur Jahan pleaded.

"Tablets of death are swimming before my sight, Nur. And the emperor can read murder on the very rags of deceit and treachery," Jahangir murmured, the bright and glazed look in his eyes keeping the flood of agony inside him chilled and forsaken.

"Your Majesty!" Nur Jahan could barely suppress an exclamation. "Do you then, Your Majesty, suspect Prince Shah Jahan of..." Her thoughts were choked by this sudden assault of pain and elation. The pain was for the grief of the emperor, and elation at the sudden prospect of winning the coveted throne of Hind for Prince Shahriyar. She was becoming aware of her elation and shuddering inside. Her beloved Ladli would be the next empress of Hind; she could taste the poison of ambition within her thoughts, her soul whimpering inside throes of agony. Suddenly, the emperor's pallor was etched before her like a mask of death, and her heart was breaking under the weight of grief and shame.

"Yes, Prince Shah Jahan, my Nur, if you already didn't know, is becoming the victim of his own barbaric corruption." Jahangir murmured tonelessly. "Baidaulat." His lips uncurled to spew out the ill-fated curse baidaulat, meaning fallen from grace. "He has killed his brother...the Cain of the Moghuls." He was storming through the palace doors as if possessed by rage and madness.

"This sudden shock, Your Majesty. This grief cannot be mitigated by laying blame on someone...Prince Shah Jahan couldn't..." Nur Jahan strove to appease the grieving emperor.

"How often did you warn me about Baidaulat, Nur, but did I heed?" Jahangir's pallor was replaced by a sudden flush, as he ordered a flagon of wine to be brought to his chamber.

Chapter Ten

The spring, cremated inside the bowers of summer, was now chilled into the grave of winter. Still Jahangir's grief had found no balm of healing or consolation. The wine squeezed from wounds within had corrupted his health more than the wine from the gold flagons. Even Nur Jahan had despaired. Her wit and pleas were of no avail, sullied by the power of denial to grief by the emperor, and by his need for oblivion. When her despair was at its culmination, her own mother had passed away, leaving her grief-stricken and disconsolate. So deep and profound was her grief after the death of her mother, that even the inebriated emperor could not help but notice the canyons of sorrow in her beautiful eyes. This great tragedy had become Nur Jahan's great boon from the mysterious bounties of God's own mercy and benevolence, hurling the emperor back from the sea of drunkenness to the shore of sobriety. This one reed of sobriety which she had incapable of winning with her wit and pleas, was now bending toward her to console and to be consoled. She herself was like a reed, not even knowing that her grief had reduced her to such extremity. This knowledge had come to her when she had found herself clinging to this boon with all the purity of her former innocence in living, loving, and hoping, almost scraping the balm of healing from the canker of the emperor's love bruised and love incomprehensible. Alas, her own pure, undying love for the emperor had failed to crucify even one wound inside the bleeding ocean of his own heart and soul.

The emperor was ailing, and was pretending to climb the rungs of health. Sober and ill-fitted to carry the burden of love, Jahangir was to taste the bitter, bitter potions of more betrayals and tragedies. He had tried to exile his bitterness against Prince Shah Jahan in an effort to convince himself that his son was guiltless, but had not succeeded.

Prince Khusrau, it was believed, was murdered by the orders of Prince Shah Jahan. Though Prince Shah Jahan, at the time of his brother's murder, was on a hunting expedition in Burhanpur. Several canards were afloat, contradicting one story with another plausible one. But the popular story was that Raza Bahadur had entered Prince Khusrau's chamber late one night, and had strangled the prince. Prince Khusrau's bedcovers had been arranged in such a fashion as to portray that he had died a natural death. The morning after this murder, Prince Khusrau's wife had found her husband cold and dead on his bed. Her cries and laments had awakened the servants and the palace guards. A couple of messengers were dispatched hastily to inform Prince Shah Jahan, who had gone hunting in Burhanpur. Prince Shah Jahan had returned immediately, and had confirmed his brother's death, sending a letter to the emperor with several seals from his viziers who could serve as witnesses that the prince had died a natural death.

Jahangir had swallowed each story in some stupor of grief. The cankerous rage inside him had remained unappeased, though he had drugged his senses with the rivers of wine. Nur Jahan had become his bride of delusion. Anarkali was his beloved dream inside the silence of his oblivion. After Asmat Begum's death, Nur Jahan's own grief had jolted him out of his oblivion. He had found himself staggering toward her in some sort of hope and delirium, gathering warmth and strength from the fire of her grief, which his own cold torment had denied him so fiercely. The death of Asmat Begum had served the emperor as an antidote to his own grief. But the same death had become an everlasting draught of grief to Itmadudaula Khan. The grieving husband was plunged deep into the ocean of misery and disconsolation. His despair was so alive and palpitating that no shock, not even a miracle, boding fortunes or misfortunes, could wrench him out of his grief. While the emperor was awakened to the pain in living, Itmadudaula Khan was lowered into the pit of despair and darkness.

Darkness had become Jahangir's portion too, before the light of his awareness. Prince Shah Jahan was rumored to be plotting treason, if not defying the emperor's orders most craftily and deceitfully, feigning ignorance to all charges, and sending a siege of letters with honeyed protestations. Shah Abbas of Persia, taking advantage of this unfortunate events in the imperial household, was heard gathering his forces at the borders of Kandahar. Prince Shahriyar, the newly wedded bridegroom, lacking skills in warfare, was unfit to be sent on an expedition to defend Kandahar. Prince Perwiz, the victim of his own moods and drunkenness, was no worthy candidate to lead an army against the great forces of Shah Abbas. Itmadudaula Khan, mentally and physically rendered weak by grief and despair, was incapable of offering any sound council to the emperor in saving

Kandahar from the power-hungry designs of Persia. Nur Jahan, recently wading out of the mire of grief, was freshly caught into the currents of alarm by her father's failing health. Much too stricken by the blows of evil fates, the empress had ceased to be the emperor's advisor.

Jahangir himself had sought no advice in matters, small or great, from his beloved amidst this sea of grief and tragedy, postponing his decisions till he could recover his equanimity amidst the pine-valleys in Kashmir. This was the only decision Jahangir was prompt to put into practice by ordering preparations for this journey. He was hoping to revive his strength and the spirits of his household before embarking on any lengthy campaigns. One small campaign was on the way to Kashmir though, which could not be avoided. Jahangir had sent forces ahead to conquer the fort of Kangra, where the rebellions were rampant.

This very evening, the imperial cavalcade was to leave Agra toward the fragrant valleys of Kashmir. Jahangir was seated at his rosewood desk, filling his journal with entries bleak and laborious. Many a rueful months had elapsed since Prince Khusrau's death, and the emperor had not had a chance to refresh his journal. Now his pen was shaping memories no more rife or conflicting, but buried deep into seasons under the clods of earth. Prince Shah Jahan, in his presumptuous haste, had buried Prince Khusrau in his palace garden at Burhanpur. Then the emperor had ordered Prince Khusrau's body to be exhumed and sent to Agra. Here, he was buried close to his mother in the garden of Allahabad. Jahangir had further ordered a complete renovation of the garden, where marble terraces were to be built flanked by a variety of mango trees. The emperor had named this garden, Khuldabad. It was enclosed by a wall in red sandstone with four gothic gateways matching the facade of the fort at Allahabad.

The tomb of Prince Khusrau was richly carved, with a large dome painted in gold from within. Fair arches and galleries were to embellish the tomb in a shrine-like magnificence. A frescoed summer house was erected close to it, with a deep well to quench the thirsts of the visitors, and boasting one hundred and twenty steps. Prince Shah Jahan was ordered to send the widow of the late prince and their son Balaqi to the palace at Lahore.

Such chilling misfortunes with vain consolations for the bereaved and the bereaving, were melting in bold strokes from the jeweled pen of Jahangir, his journal dark and glowering. His thoughts were unwilling to carry the burdens of glaciers in time and memories. Donned in citron silks with a large opal in his turban, his pallor was deep and luminous. His features were not gaunt, but bloated. They were rather swollen as if the ravages of grief, neglect and drunkenness had made a permanent abode in the sinews of his body and soul. Anarkali was landing on his awareness with the swiftness of a wildfire. The glaciers in his mind were melting, but he was becoming more aware of his living beloved than the one risen afresh from the cold tomb of his past.

Nur Jahan was lounging on a velvety couch from where she could see the emperor's back and the great paintings on the damasked walls. She was immersed in reading Bostan and Gulistan, simultaneously, as if trying to follow the thoughts of the Persian bard, Shaikh Saadi. But her thoughts were blazing, rather smoldering inside the cinders of hope and hopelessness. She had picked the book of Ramayana to start with, then had switched to Mahabharata without knowing her haste or indecision. The next book to attract her attention was *Nal Daman* by Faizi, which was slipped back to its shelf most gently. Then she had discovered a brief repose in the tales of the Arabian Nights. Now Gulistan was her lone companion, while the emperor was laboring through the task of recording a plethora of events in his journal.

Nur Jahan's thoughts were getting restless again, fluttering aimlessly, and exchanging secrets with his ailing father, then bouncing down the valleys in Kashmir for hope and sustenance. Her gaze was straying from the book on her lap, and searching the paintings on the damasked walls. The portraits in gilded frames were staring back at her, and mocking her intense scrutiny. The court ladies at their toilette painted in bright colors were revealing some subtle spark of life, as if they would leap to their feet at the slightest commands from their lords or husbands. The English damsels fanning away their lovers under the bower of roses appeared more congenial to stay in their gilded frames. Nur Jahan's gaze was wandering again. She was looking into the blue, orange hearts of the flames under the hearth. The blaze of intensity in her eyes was shifting to the back of the emperor, as if lending him the warmth of her own love and hope. Before she could think of any excuse to break the emperor's concentration, he himself was turning abruptly.

"This task of writing is too burdensome for the emperor." Jahangir pushed his chair back and sprang to his feet. "I should make Mutamid Khan the master of this royal labor, all this editing and recording. He would prove to be a better scribe than the emperor." He stood by the hearth, warming his hands absently.

"If he stays honest, he will not become the author of lies, Your Majesty." The night-blue in Nur Jahan's eyes was revealing its own volumes of trials and tribulations.

She was watching the emperor's hands with utmost fascination. The flames crackling under the hearth were spraying gold on his white palms, and lending them the glow of sunsets. Jahangir's attention was shifted to the Persian carpet under his feet, where its pattern of rosettes appeared to shudder against the shafts of sunlight. The cold, cold shafts of December chill were settling into his own heart, as he lifted his gaze to meet Nur Jahan's. He could see the dance of ice and fire in her eyes.

"You yourself are one great patron, for the authors of lies, my empress," Jahangir commented, reading volumes from her beautiful eyes.

"If you are alluding to Prince Shah Jahan, then cast your worries away, Your Majesty. He is much too smart to cloak his weakness in the shroud of lies." Nur Jahan chose to defend the prince whose downfall she could not help but plot.

"Do you still believe, my Nur, that he did not murder Prince Khusrau?" Jahangir appeared to question his own doubts.

"What motive did he have..." Nur Jahan left a pause, which was intended to reveal her sense of uncertainty. Her hatred for this proud prince whose ambition she alone knew well was concealed hermetically inside her heart. "If he had intended murder, he would have not gone hunting knowing that he would be the prime suspect if Prince Khusrau died in his absence. Surely, he could have chosen poison..." She left another pause, as if demurring.

"Only glorious God knows what secrets are hidden inside the hearts of all! That's what Salim Chishti used to say...the saint, at whose hermitage I was born." Jahangir snatched that pause to voice his own strange course of thoughts. He had begun to pace, thinking aloud to himself. "Once my father asked Salim Chishti if he knew the hour of his own death since he was a saint. The saint, after much thought, replied that when Prince Salim, meaning me, would commit one verse to his memory and would recite before him, that's when he would die. Then my father forbade everyone to teach me any prose or verse. But one lady of the harem, ignorant of the emperor's injunction, taught me a couplet. I was almost two when I visited Salim Chishti with my father. No sooner had my father left to attend to some matters, that I was reciting this couplet to the saint. 'O God, open the rosebud of hope. Display a flower from the everlasting garden.'

"The saint was greatly agitated after hearing this couplet. He requested our court singer to sing sweet songs to him. When my father returned, he took the turban from his head and placed it on mine, saying, 'We have made Sultan Salim our successor, and have made him over to God, the protector and preserver.' Then he breathed his last. I heard my father exclaiming, that Salim Chishti has attained union with his true beloved. What strange, mysterious forces work in our heads. I am recalling this now that I am over fifty." He stopped near the hearth, his back toward Nur Jahan.

"You were not the murderer, Your Majesty. God's own mysterious ways and His grace summoned the saint to His presence," Nur Jahan murmured low.

"Not a murderer, but an accessory to the murder. An innocent child, just the same," Jahangir murmured back. He was stroking the fire to a vigorous blaze. "All the innocence of childhood and youth is gone. Prince Salim is now the Emperor Jahangir, fleeing sorrows and betrayals, seeking the sanctuary of bliss in Kashmir, leaving Kandahar to the tyranny of the Persians."

"Why not send Prince Shah Jahan on this campaign against the Persians, Your Majesty?" Nur Jahan commented softly.

"Send Shah Jahan! Send *baidaulat* to fight the wicked Persians?" Jahangir whirled around to face her. "He will carve valleys of ruin wherever he goes."

"Unpredictable as your health is, Your Majesty, it won't permit you to lead a campaign on your own. Kangra is close, but Kandahar?" Nur Jahan sighed.

"Ah, the ailing emperor and the grieving empress." Jahangir smiled. "Yes, the emperor might send him, so that he can prove himself the traitor that he is! And the emperor loves him? And still..." His heart was too ardent to spill words.

"There is no dearth of traitors in Sirhind, Your Majesty, if you wish to test their mettle," Nur Jahan challenged, her heart fluttering.

"Not any of our kin, the emperor hopes?" Jahangir flung himself beside her laughingly.

"No, Your Majesty. Only a Sayyid by the name of Shaikh Ahamd, calling himself Mahdi. Which means the second coming of the Prophet, if I understand it right."

"Then he is an impostor, not a traitor, my innocent Nur." Jahangir claimed her hands, kissing them wistfully.

"A preacher and a wise man, Your Majesty. A holy man, as far as my innocence can judge," Nur Jahan teased, her eyes shining.

"And what does this holy, wise man say, my pearl?" Jahangir asked intensely.

"'In the course of my travels,' he says," Nur Jahan began with a quick animation. 'I came to the dwelling of two lights, the sun and the moon. Then

I saw a very lofty and splendid building. From there I passed to the abode of discrimination, and then to the abode of truth. From there I reached the abode of love, and I beheld a brilliant dwelling. It had divers colors and lights and reflected glories. I passed from the abode of the vicergents and attained the highest rank.'" She began to laugh as if judging this man presumptuous, whom she had just called a holy and wise man.

"God forgive us!" Jahangir exclaimed. "This man is walking on the net of deceit and hypocrisy. And dragging his followers, which he must have gathered by the bushel, into the waters of impiety and infidelity. Hypocrisy attracts men like moths to a flame. This man must be imprisoned till his madness and confusion gain some semblance of sanity." He slipped his arm around her waist. "But that is when we return from Kashmir. Right now, the emperor must appease the hungers of his soul." He was kissing her hands.

"I am afraid, Your Majesty." Nur Jahan's passionate heart was courting fear more than love. "How my ailing father is going to make through this long journey?"

"The haven of Kashmir will wash away his sorrow and restore his health," Jahangir murmured a bit hoarsely. "Besides, we would journey at leisure. Our first stop is at Kangra" His lips were seeking hers.

They were locked into a tight embrace, their hearts mating passionately, even before their bodies were caught into the bliss-paradise of union and accolade.

The royal encampment on the banks of the river Banganga was swathed in silence, the mournful dusk bathing the colorful city of tents in its own haze and pallor. The impending darkness was just a burial shroud to lay the groaning day to rest, it seemed. All were hush, and the quiet mists a palpitating reality. Appearing to be more so, for the emperor had gone to inspect the siege at the fort of Kangra. A few of the royal guards who were left behind had completed their usual rounds. Now, they were enjoying their evening repast in utmost silence. Fatigue and lack of sleep had made their senses numb and their wits dull. Roasted mutton garnished with carrots was not enough to satisfy their hungering, thirsting spirits. They were hungering and thirsting for great feasts and great jubilations. Their allotted portion of wine, one goblet each, was ritually drained down their throats even before the evening meal began, and now they themselves were feeling drained and exhausted. Without song and entertainment to whet their appetites, they were not too keen to explore the morsels of dry roasted mutton. Besides, they were feeling rather dull-witted by the news of Itmadudaula Khan's sudden illness. Their strong, healthy spirits rebelling against the clouds of sadness or tragedies. They had formed a spacious circle where they sat sulking and languishing. Some of them were gazing at the sky, as if tracing the stars scattered here and there in the blue bowl of a sky. A few of the men had stirred themselves to activity, playing cards and gambling. These few were too intensely absorbed in their game to notice even the dark shadows which were plunging this rich bivouac into a silhouette of mists, gray and violet.

Farther down the banks of Banganga were the opulent tents of the harem ladies, furnished with carpets and gilded comforts. The emperor's wives had gathered in one large tent and were playing their own favorite card games, Chaupar and Chandal Mandal. They were nibbling on fruits and dainty sweets from the silver bowls. Their glass goblets were brimming with wine, for the emperor's wives were never to know the dearth of wine or food, even on journeys long or campaigns arduous. They were duly informed of Itmadudaula Khan's illness, but nothing could dampen their spirits. They had their jewels and fineries, and the dancing girls to entertain them. Even after learning that a devoted courier was dispatched to fetch the emperor due to Itmadudaula Khan's worsening condition, their attentions were not diverted from their games or entertainments. The illness of Nur Jahan's father didn't concern them, nor were they worried about the siege at the fort of Kangra. To them, wars were the domains of the emperor, and intrigues the privileges of Nur Jahan, whom they hated and envied. They were devoted to the emperor though, also holding dear the lives of the princes and princesses.

The death of Prince Khusrau had caused them much anguish and suffering. They had mourned the prince with great sorrow and laments. But now their sufferings were abated and their sorrows banished in anticipation of this grand journey to Kashmir. Prince Shah Jahan was their favorite concern now, and they were devoted to him heart and soul. His acts of defiance and insurrection they chose to ignore, though fearing the grief of the emperor. The minds of all the emperor's wives were molded into one cosmic whole, laying entire blame on Nur Jahan for any kind of rebellions or misfortunes. They were not afraid to protest that the intrigues of Nur Jahan alone had alienated the prince from the emperor. Right now, as they sat luxuriating inside the comfort of this large tent with dancing girls to entertain them, they had forgotten all about Nur Jahan's intrigues.

In her own crimson tent, leagues away from the happy brides of the emperor, Nur Jahan knew no intrigue, but her father's agony on his deathbed.

The candles burning low in silver candelabrum were a pallid dance of mists, hovering around the dying man swathed in woolen blankets and velvet coverlets. Itmadudaula Khan's face was flushed with fever, his breathing loud and laborious, the only sound splintering the hush in the night. He lay there unconscious, moaning occasionally. His haggard features, at times, could be seen convulsing between spasms of hot flashes, and beads of sweat trickling down his neck. Nur Jahan was sunk deep on a brocaded cushion right beside her father. Her small hands, white as snow, were clasped into her lap in the semblance of a prayer. The shadow of death was upon her too, it seemed, as she sat there with her eyes closed and uttering no sound. Only the diamonds in her ears and around her throat were breathing life of their own, vivid and glittering over the swath of her pale silks. She was not alone; two royal physicians with watchful eyes were standing alert to attend to the needs of the ailing vizier. Also, three ladies-in-waiting were huddled near the tent door, ready to leap to their feet at the mere whisper from the empress. Yet the empress was chilled inside her own pool of sorrow and immobility. The loss of her mother was too rife in her memory to entertain more grief. She was not prepared to let go of her father. Each fiber in her body and soul was willing him back to life with all the purity of her love and anguish unvoiced.

Nur Jahan's mute pleas had reached the emperor through the hasty import of the messenger near the fort of Kangra. This impregnable fort with seven imposing gates and twenty-three bastions was on the verge of capitulation when the messenger had reached the emperor. But Jahangir was so moved by the urgent pleas of the empress that, without delay, he had jumped on his horse, and was on his way to console his beloved. Arrayed in his chain mail and gold helmet, he was more of a gallant knight than a warring lord. Accompanied by a few of his royal guards, the emperor's Arabian steed was racing down the hilly slopes toward the bivouac across from the river Banganga. He had banished the warring scene from his sight and senses. The thunder from the cannons was left behind too, no more explosions to violate his sense of peace and freedom. And the Durga shrine at the foot of the Kangra fort, which he had glimpsed but in one flash of curiosity, was vanishing into the very mists of his contemplations. Soon, the emperor's white steed was leaping alongside the banks of the river Banganga. The haze from early dusk was gilding the waves to molten gold, and they appeared to shudder and expand. The imperial encampment down below was wearing a shroud of silence, stark and mournful.

Itmadudaula Khan had begun to moan and murmur once again. Nur Jahan's eyes were shot open, her hands reaching out to comfort her father, snatching his hand and pressing it to her bosom. One physician stood feeding the vizier a concoction of honey and borage. The ladies-in-waiting had bounced to their feet, noticing the emperor's stormy entrance. An invisible current of hope had slipped into the very silence of the tent, as the emperor rushed closer to the bed of his father-in-law. Even Itmadudaula Khan's eyes were unlidded, revealing a spontaneous glow of light, hope and anticipation. He appeared to be hurled back to a spasm of consciousness.

"Papa!" One anguished plea escaped Nur Jahan's lips. She indicated the emperor at the foot of the bed. "Papa, do you recognize him?" she murmured.

"Yes, my princess, yes." The feverish glow in Itmadudaula Khan's eyes was now falling on the emperor.

"Was a mother-born blind man present

He'd recognize Majesty in the World Adorner." An impromptu couplet trembled down his lips.

"Had you graced your talents with the pen, Itmadudaula, than with the sword, the emperor would have bestowed upon you the title, King of the Poets." Jahangir smiled. "You are yet to see our victory over the fort of Kangra," he murmured.

"The final victory…" Itmadudaula Khan could barely breathe. Light had left his eyes. "…is death." This throb of a prophecy was mirrored in his blank gaze.

"By the reckoning of the eye, there is one frame less

By wisdom's reckoning, the lessening is more than thousands." Jahangir lent voice his own couplet.

Hakim Qasim was bending over Itmadudaula Khan, trying to feel the pulse on his listless arm. His gaze, when lifted to the emperor and the empress, was revealing the tragedy of death. Even before he could pronounce the word *died*, Nur Jahan's head had slumped over the silent breast of her father. She was weeping and sobbing as if her heart would break. Her grief was lowering the mantle of darkness over her eyes and deep down her heart. Jahangir had flown to her side in some daze of fever and anguish. He was literally carrying her out into the mournful night toward his own luxuriant tent.

The Shalamar garden near the valley of Phak in Kashmir was efflorescent in such abundance that its canals and fountains were reflecting no shades in greenery, only the rich colors in blooms. One black marble throne on the white terrace where the emperor sat enjoying this spring day, was flanked by crystal-clear ponds. These ponds were edged with yellow, scented jafari flowers, swaying in the wind gently and happily. The emperor's health was failing again, though revived a little by the promise of life and renewal in spring. The long, dismal journey from Kangra to Kashmir and the harsh winter had taken their toll on the emperor's mood and health. Asthma and rheumatism had become his close companions, much closer than wine and opium, plunging him further into the pits of despair and depression. Nur Jahan, though freshly stricken with grief at the death of her father, had tried to check the emperor's excesses in wine and opium, but in vain. Her attempts in showing the emperor fair plans for a bright future had succeeded only in gaining one fraction of his attention amidst his bouts of euphoria.

Since the past few days, Jahangir had been spurred by one of his euphoric moods, visiting the beautiful shrines and gardens, and gallivanting in the pine-valleys without heeding Nur Jahan's advice to restraint and moderation concerning such pleasant excursions. This particular day, though feeling the stress of fatigue and weakness, his mood was still euphoric. He was seated in utmost comfort, several velvety pillows heaped behind his back and a colorful blanket of lamb's wool hugging his legs. He was watching a pair of saras under one chenar tree, hoping that that this spring day would be conducive for their mating, so that he could observe this miracle in nature— the miracle of a lifetime? Almost a month had elapsed since he had begun watching this pair of saras with a religious fervor. A feast to his aesthetic senses! He had named them Laila and Majnun, after the lovers of a folktale whose profound love for each other was still alive in ballads sung by the bards and troubadours. This pair of saras were oblivious to the world all around them, not even aware of the emperor's scrutiny, as if he was one of the inanimate objects in the garden. Nur Jahan, seated at the terrace steps, was adorning her goldfish with gold rings, and tossing them back into the blue pool under her feet.

Though the emperor and the empress seemed worlds apart, immersed in their own individual pleasures, they were together, and a part of this garden and scenery. Their spirits, merging and exchanging silences as well as the anecdotes, were the profound interludes, right out of the gardens of their thoughts and recollections. The anecdotes were of the past. Those words and voices were holding on to the glory of the present. They had shared and exchanged all, burying past into the graves of future, yet knowing that they had the power to unlid the casket of memories, if need be, at their own discretion and convenience.

Before departing from Kangra, Itmadudaula Khan's body was sent to Agra under the care of his son Itaqid Khan. The emperor had entrusted the son with special instructions that the body of his father was to be interned in the garden across from Jamna. Since Nur Jahan was the victim of her own grief, Jahangir had tried his best to revive her spirits before resuming his journey to Kashmir, acting more in affinity to the wishes of his heart than to the dictates of reason. Bypassing the inheritance of the brothers, the emperor had assigned all the lands and wealth of late Itmadudaula Khan to the empress. The empress was further showered with titles and honors which no other Moghul woman could ever dream of attaining and possessing. The drums and orchestra which were played before the emperor as his sole right and privilege, were now to be trumpeted before her wherever she went or appeared. She had also the choice and the privilege of sitting in the balcony, receiving nobles and courtiers alike, who were to prostrate before the empress and to receive robes of honor from her.

The grief of the empress was mollified by such diversions, as Jahangir had anticipated, and the journey to Kashmir was less doleful than expected. Nur Jahan had recovered enough to be able to talk about the tomb of her father which she was going to design and build. The emperor had taken great interest in her plans for such a tomb, and had encouraged her wholeheartedly, thinking that he had made Anarkali the empress of the world, realizing only later in Kashmir that Anarkali was not of this world, and that his death alone would unite him with his beloved. And he was courting it much too eagerly, rather welcoming it in oblivion and drunkenness.

Nur Jahan was planning a great tomb, and yet, a greater mausoleum for her father. Of pure silver, she was dreaming! Wishing to lavish all her wealth on this monument, and the emperor's too, if it required more. But the emperor, in one of his sober moods, had dissuaded her from the use of silver, presenting a genuine argument that it would be a temptation for the plunderers if the tomb was built of pure silver. The design of the tomb was met with the emperor's approval with slight changes or suggestions as to the structure and adornment.

The mausoleum of Itmadudaula Khan was to be erected on the left side of Jamna with a great wall enclosing the sprawling gardens. The tomb itself would be two storeys high with octagonal towers, surrounded by open pavilions. It would be hewn out of white marble, with the inlay of pietra dura. Nur Jahan's grief had found consolation in designing this tomb, and she was longing for the execution of her plans, rather possessed by her ideas and inspirations, while the emperor was seeking oblivion in drunkenness to appease the wounds of everlasting memories in his soul. He was much too painfully aware of his malady. *His curse*, as he called it, for being incapable of forgetting the unforgettable. Amidst the flashes of his euphoria and sobriety, he had begun to wonder why he couldn't forget Anarkali. Several decades were a giant wall of separation between him and her since her tragic death, and yet she had the power to dissolve that wall and be with him always. He was in his fifties, wedded to both his loves, Anarkali and Nur Jahan.

Paradoxically, the emperor was too much in love, in love with Nur Jahan, possessed by some sort of delirium in loving and suffering. He was wont to lay bare his mind and soul at her feet, hoping to absolve his sufferings in the deepest deeps of her own love boundless. Strewing her path with the gifts of kingdoms to attain the kingdom of peace inside his heart. Even in his need for oblivion and drunkenness, he could not endure to be separated from Nur Jahan, wanting her beside him always, and worshiping her through the very mists of his senses bruised and anguished.

Nur Jahan's love and perception could not miss seeing the waves of turbulence inside the rivulets of emperor's heart and soul. She would try to calm those waves as often as she could, but most of the time she would feel powerless against the storms and the tempests simmering and overflowing inside him like the floods of ruin and devastation. She had learned to surrender herself to the violence of his passions, neither despising his excesses nor rejecting his madness. Endowed with the bounties of her great passion, she could love him as he was, accepting his moods and weaknesses with as much ardor as his tenderness and generosities. At times, she was jealous of the emperor's dead beloved, but that sprig of jealousy too was conquered by the abundance of her love. She had become more of a mother to the emperor than his beloved, she would think, tending to his needs as to her own child's, who might have suffered the blight of grief and illness. Her warm, bright disposition was taking its toll though, against the burden of her own sufferings—and tragedies countless. Along with those, one canker of a fear had taken root in her heart that she would lose the emperor, if she could not separate him from his cup.

This canker was now swollen inside Nur Jahan's heart like a wound, for she had failed to check the emperor's excesses in drinking. No sooner had he reached Kashmir than wine had become his cup companion. The snow-capped valleys, offering him no diversion in the outdoor splendor of the gardens, had arrested him in his own small world of inebriation. Then illness had struck him like the rod of chastisement. The merciless attacks of fever and asthma had imprisoned him in his gilded chamber. He would lay there gasping for breath, while holding on to the string of life by the sheer will of Nur Jahan. Then he was visited by rheumatism, and each joint in his body was racked with pain. He was unable to sit up, or even hold a pen in his fingers to fill his journal with entries dark or pain-loving. Nur Jahan's love alone, beside her strict vigilance and tender ministrations, had driven the demons of his illness away. He had felt such relief and gratitude that he had surrendered himself, body and soul, to her advice and judgment. That was when he had entrusted Mutamid Khan with the task of writing his memoirs.

During the emperor's illness, the ill reports from the quarters of Deccan and Kandahar were kept secret from him by the explicit commands of Nur Jahan. Recently, now that the emperor's health had improved, Nur Jahan had dared reveal a portion of ill reports, considering the urgency of their import which demanded action. She had succeeded in concealing Prince Shah Jahan's overt acts of disobedience in euphemistic veils of comments and suggestions. The advance of Persian armies over the borders of Kandahar was also muffled inside the gentle folds of hope and encouragement.

Since Prince Shah Jahan was reluctant to lead an expedition to Kandahar, the emperor had no choice but to think about his other sons who would be willing to fight the Persians. Prince Perwiz was his first choice, but he had dismissed that idea, knowing that the prince was guarding the province of Bihar. Besides, he would prove to be more like a drunken knight on the field of combat than a valorous commander, Jahangir had thought. Prince Shahriyar was the only choice left to be sent on this campaign to Kandahar, and he had voiced his decision to Nur Jahan. Nur Jahan was ecstatic to hear the emperor's decision, but then had wavered, recalling the inexperience of Prince Shahriyar in matters of intrigue and warfare. Besides, she had just received the happy news of her daughter being enceinte, and wished Prince Shahriyar to remain with his bride till the birth of her grandchild. She could not afford to take any chances, considering the unpredictability of lengthy and arduous campaigns which could last for years, if not for months. Adroit in such matters of politics and decision-making, she was quick to devise a plan of her own, which could release Kandahar from the yoke of the Persians without involving any royal princes in such warring commands.

Nur Jahan was quick to suggest to the emperor that Mahabat Khan should be recalled from Kabul, and dispatched on this campaign to Kandahar. She admired Mahabat Khan's skills in warfare, that much she was willing to admit to the emperor, but that she distrusted him entirely was her secret confession to herself alone. In fact, she hated Mahabat Khan, whom she judged devious and deceitful, though devoted to the emperor. She was faultless in her judgments, rightfully so, for Mahabat Khan had his own idiosyncrasies of prides and prejudices which could not stay concealed. She could not forgive him for his audacity in sending covert warnings to the emperor that the emperor was delivering too much power into the hands of the empress. She too was left with no choices, considering the worthless sons of the emperor. Prince Perwiz as a drunken lout and Prince Shah Jahan was the patrician rebel, two unlikely choices to lead a campaign against the Persians. Prince Shahriyar, she was preparing as an heir apparent to the throne of Hind. So Mahabat Khan was a worthy choice to be thrown into the cannons of warfare, in Nur Jahan's estimation.

Mahabat Khan was dispatched to Kandahar, as the master of his own decisions, and furnished with a large army at his sole command. The emperor was pleased with this choice, and his spirit as well as his health had begun to improve. This improvement was brought about not by restraining his need for wine, but by exorcising his pain in loving and hating his rebel of a son, Prince Shah Jahan. Moreover, a great burden had been lifted off his shoulders with the knowledge that Mahabat Khan was on his way to defend Kandahar. The emperor was fond of Mahabat Khan and trusted his devotion and prowess in warring and subjugating.

Nur Jahan shared no such trust and devotion on the part of Mahabat Khan. Even now, as she sat veiled in the aura of peace and serenity, her thoughts were hovering over Kandahar. Her thoughts were a riot of revelations. With her perspicacity as her weapon of warfare, she could glean deceit and ambition from the very armor of Mahabat Khan's resolve to excel and conquer. So profound were the wild journeys in her head, that she was startled by the emperor's sudden exclamation.

"A miracle, Nur!" Jahangir's outburst was awakening the whole garden to its own sense of beauty and perfume. "The emperor is to observe the mating of the saras! Quite different from mating of the cranes, I hope. The view is delightful from here." His gaze was fixed to the amorous pair, Laila and Majnun.

"The mating of spring with the beauty of our gardens is enough to make me swoon, Your Majesty. This wondrous miracle itself, which has brought color to your cheeks." Nur Jahan laughed.

Bouncing off the gleaming steps with the agility of a young girl, Nur Jahan floated toward the emperor. She sank down to the Persian rug at the emperor's feet in one rustling heap. Hugging her knees with a delicious squeeze, she had abandoned her head on the emperor's lap. Her eyes were exploring the intimate courtship of the saras. The sunshine itself was kissing her flaxen curls, against which Jahangir's fingers could be seen stroking and fondling absently. His eyes were kindling poetic dreams, though he was oblivious to the poetic dream at his feet in crimson silks studded with diamonds, as if all the stars from heaven had fallen on her gown in twinkling clusters.

"Look, my love, how Laila straightens her legs, though bending so coyly." Jahangir had begun to run a commentary. "And Majnun, how tenderly he lifts his one foot, then the other? How passionately he sits on her back! How blissful they look. Pairing and loving! So beautifully, so naturally..." His comments had come to an abrupt end, as abruptly as the separation of the amorous couple.

Majnun was stretching his neck and digging his beak into the ground. Then he was walking around Laila, who was sitting motionless and wide-eyed.

"It is possible they may have an egg and produce a young one?" Jahangir was watching the post-courtship syndrome of the saras with much interest.

"Possible too, Your Majesty, that she may die during the labor-pains of childbirth," Nur Jahan teased, her first visit to Kashmir drifting closer to her awareness. "Then Majnun would sit grieving all his life on Laila's back," she continued ruminatively. "Remember, Your Majesty, when Qiyam Khan espied one sara sitting possessively on a nest. As he approached cautiously, that sara plodded away as if in great pain. What had appeared a nest to Qiyam Khan, was nothing but the remains of a dead bird. Discolored feathers, no flesh underneath, but bones and a host of maggots. And when Qiyam Khan moved away, hiding himself behind a tree, the sara returned, hugging the pitiful remains of bones and feathers, as if trying to breathe life into them. Didn't you conclude then, Your Majesty, that the sara's mate had died and he had been sitting on it since then, grieving and wishing death?"

"An eternal lover in every bird and beast." Jahangir laughed. "Not too old to be forgotten, not too young to be cherished." His eyes were gathering stars of adoration.

"An avid naturalist, Your Majesty, the emperor, my husband...can't help but crossbreed their love with strange species?" Nur Jahan quipped, hoping that the emperor would recall the time when he had ordered Markhur goats from Ahmedabad to be paired with the Barbary goats from Arabia.

"And what fantastic results did the emperor achieve!" Jahangir beamed, divining her thoughts. "What charming issues, the result of that crossbreeding? Not like the bleating, wailing ones of the regular goats, but the pleasant little ones, and quite peace-loving. They were comely too, especially the ones with the black stripes, and the ones with the glow of cherries. Pity that our court painters didn't arrest those colors on silk canvases." He kissed her hand.

"Pity that they painted those Carnatic goats," Nur Jahan murmured with implicit distaste. "Such grotesque forms, and such atrocious colors, Your Majesty. True artists are loathe to touch such colors, or to depict such enormities."

"Oh, those fat ones?" Jahangir lumbered to his feet slowly. "Were they not killed, and four pazahar stones recovered from their bellies? Hakim Rukna told me that such stones are an antidote against poison." He smiled, feigning vigor and energy, though feeling none. "Had I kept those stones, they might have served me as a cure for the poison in my heart against my own son and against all malefactors, who leave not the emperor in peace. As it stands, my love, let us explore the beauty of our Shalamar, before it absorbs ugliness in wars and treacheries. Ah, my beautiful Eden in Kashmir!" He appeared to steal warmth and strength from the blue lakes in her shining eyes.

"The air is rather chilly, Your Majesty." Nur Jahan held out the blanket. "Wear it over your shoulders, Your Majesty. This blanket woven from the wool of Carnatic goats would keep you warm," she breathed apprehensively.

"No, my empress, the emperor refuses to cover his shoulders with anything which is made out of the wool of Carnatic goats," Jahangir mocked.

"From the wool of Barbary goats, then," Nur Jahan coaxed.

"From the wool of both Markhur and Barbary goats." Jahangir claimed the blanket and his beloved into his arms, kissing her with the hunger of a famished lover.

"Your Majesty!" Nur Jahan protested even before he released her. "What if some eunuch straggles down here…some urgent message which can't be delayed?" A sea of violence was raging inside her heart, knowing that this kiss was meant for Anarkali.

"Then he would be beheaded, my love, but not before he had delivered his message." Jahangir turned away laughingly.

The lover and the beloved were strolling side-by-side. The emperor was wearing a subtle and whimsical smile, and the empress a wraith of serenity and self-surrender. The marble terraces with fountains splashing and gurgling were left behind. Farther down the sprawling lawns were the orchards of peach and almond trees. The yellow jafari flowers were waving at the royal couple, intoxicated by their own scented sweetness. A few notes from flutes, harp and dulcimer were escaping the palace walls. Nur Jahan appeared to be catching those tunes, her gaze admiring the clusters of white jasmine in oval flowerbeds. Jahangir could hear nothing, not even his thoughts, only feasting his eyes on colors vivid and shimmering. His feet were coming to a slow halt before one mulberry tree. An exotic vine-creeper was entwined around its trunk in seductive contours, which was alluring him to have a closer view. He stood gazing, his eyes penetrating the very sap of the tree-trunk.

"This amorous tree has no precious secrets to reveal, Your Majesty. You are searching for something which can't be found here," was Nur Jahan's dreamy comment.

"The amorous silkworms, my Nur," Jahangir murmured to himself. "Where are the eggs of the silkworms which I had ordered to be brought from Tibet and Gilgit? The leaves of these trees are great feasts for the silkworms, while its mulberries are not fit for human consumption." His eyes were still searching for silkworms.

"How you forget, Your Majesty!" Nur Jahan declared sweetly. "Those eggs were taken to the orchard of a silk dealer, by your own orders. That same silk dealer who sired twins. Two tiny girls with mouths full of teeth, and their backs joined together as far as their waists; how strange."

"Oh, those Kashmiri twins, now I remember!" Jahangir smiled, gazing at her. "Didn't I command my surgeons to operate on those unfortunate babes to release them from that bondage of deformity? How did I forget to inquire about that? Whatever happened to them?"

"You didn't forget, Your Majesty," Nur Jahan murmured. "You were taken ill. And the twins died even before the surgeons could get to the house of that silk dealer."

"Well, the mysteries of God and nature! They confound our senses to awe and surrender, if not to fear and stupefaction." Jahangir slipped his arm around Nur Jahan's waist, a sprig of inspiration trembling down his lips.

"From head to foot, wherever I look
A glance plucks at the heart's skirt, saying
This is the place, to stop at."

"Your Majesty!" exclaimed Nur Jahan, her eyes shining with sad-happy recollections. "This is the verse you composed in the garden at Kangra, right after you entered the victorious city, scattering gold coins from the fort to the gardens." Her eyes were attaining the sparkle of mischief. "Do you think,

Your Majesty, that the gardens of Kangra are more beautiful than the gardens of Kashmir?"

"Each garden has its own beauty, my love, incomparable in each season, each season which paints and redesigns this earth with the strokes of nature's own paintbrush," Jahangir murmured. "Though I wonder if the perfumes of paradise waft such sweet scents as they do here in Shalamar, in our own garden? And yet, Shalamar is the grandest in the fall. We will stay here till fall, then journey back to Lahore. We must stop at Kangra though, to see the construction of the mosque which I ordered to be built."

"Such a dismal and dreary journey in the fall, Your Majesty," Nur Jahan protested sweetly. "The beauty of spring we must enjoy in Kashmir, but can't we start from here in the summer, Your Majesty? How exhilarating to watch the colorless, decaying leaves on the way!" she teased.

"There is no exhilaration in decay, but to the eye
The glory of autumn is more brilliant than the spring." The eternal poet in Jahangir sang with a dint of sarcasm.

Nur Jahan could hear the music of pain and poetry inside the heart of the emperor, it seemed. She was drifting along with him, half swooning, half praying, swooning with pleasure at the very hearth of her perspicacity which was announcing that the shadow of Anarkali had left the emperor at this particular moment, and praying for the emperor's health with a sense of delicious relief that he had been able to stroll for this long without having any difficulty in breathing. The royal couple were leaving the grove of the lofty planes and graceful poplars. Another grove of only the chenars was welcoming them. In the center of this ancient grove was erected a white terrace, flanked by the fountains. A blaze of red, red roses could be seen swaying at the foot of these fountains.

"Much wine should be poured on rose." Jahangir's thoughts could not voice the couplet in his head, for a violent fit of coughing had taken hold of him.

"Let us return to your favorite throne, Your Majesty, where sun pours warmth, even from behind the veil of clouds," Nur Jahan pleaded.

The onslaught of coughing had subsided as abruptly as it had begun. And now the emperor and the empress were retracing their steps toward the black marble throne on their favorite terrace. Jahangir was trying to regain the rhythm of his breathing, and Nur Jahan striving to pave the way for her thoughts on the road to equanimity. Halfway to the throne, they were becoming aware of a courier in his livery of royal insignia. This courier was no other than the swift runner, Banarasi, himself. He was hovering closer to the throne, his eyes darting in all directions in search of the emperor. He had espied the royal couple even before they had caught sight of him, and was now hastening toward them with the speed of an arrow.

"Your Majesty. Padishah Begum." Banarasi fell into a lengthy curtsy.

"Don't water this garden with your tears, Banarasi. Shalamar is sacred to us." Jahangir stole a warm look at Nur Jahan. "Such a beautiful spring day…and what woe is written all over your face?" he asked kindly.

"Your Majesty." Banarasi gasped for breath. "Khan Jahan of Multan…a messenger from him just arrived. The troops of Shah Abbas have laid siege on Kandahar."

"Is that all?" Jahangir smiled. "Abul Aziz, the young governor over there, has enough forces to crush those mighty foes into insignificant lumps of blood and gore. Besides, Mahabat Khan's contingent must be close at hand, since Prince Shah Jahan is disinclined to take charge of this campaign," he added intensely.

"Prince Shah Jahan is not only disinclined, Your Majesty, but…" Banarasi stopped, catching a mute warning from Nur Jahan's flashing eyes.

"But what, you impudent colt?" Jahangir demanded with a sudden kindling of rage and impatience. His breathing was labored.

"Prince Shah Jahan has obeyed your command, Your Majesty," was Barnarsi's befuddled response. "He has marched as far as north to Mandu…"

"And then what, my truant sage? Speak up, or your tongue will be fed to the mulberry trees. A great feast for the silkworms!" was Jahangir's incensed command.

"Shah Jahan, the prince, Your Majesty. He is demanding the command of the Moghul armies, the governorship of the Punjab, the ownership of the fort at Ranthambor…and then, he says, he will march to Kandahar. And that too, after the rainy season, if all his demands are met," Banarasi offered quickly.

"Baidaulat, he dares?" Jahangir's breathing was heavy and difficult.

"Summon Hakim Qasim, Banarasi," Nur Jahan commanded.

"No need for a physician, Nur." Jahangir was flying toward the palace.

"You need rest, then, Your Majesty," Nur Jahan pleaded. She was keeping pace with the emperor, and praying for his health.

"Send orders to Baidaulat, my Nur, to return to Agra with all his troops. He is yet to be deprived of all his jagirs." Jahangir was trying to control his breathing and was succeeding. "And we must journey to Multan at once. All princes and viziers would be ordered to meet us there. Prince Perwiz and Asaf

THE MOGHUL HEDONIST

Khan…Multan is to be our stronghold, to dispatch forces…to Kandahar…"
The wooden steps of his palace were spinning under his feet.

The emperor was smiling to himself, a swift haze slipping before his sight in the likeness of a splendid dream. The smile on his face was shrinking to one painful convulsion. His features were flushed, then attaining pallor as white as the shroud of death.

Hakim Qasim, assisted by a coterie of servants, were relieving the empress of her royal burden. Nur Jahan herself was in a daze, no prayers escaping her thundering heart. The emperor had fainted into the arms of bliss. He was in oblivion, seeking love of his beloved, not the agony of his empress.

Chapter Eleven

The Lahore fort with all its bastions and gardens was an imposing city in itself. It appeared to be looming over the palace gardens like a giant rock, cradling the stables, pavilions and colonnades in its impregnable arms. Jahangir was standing across one shapeless moat, facing an arena of stables where all sorts of beasts were kept for his sole pleasure-indulgence in breeding and entertainment. Appareled in silks of green and purple, he was a part of the scenic splendor, beyond which the palace gates could be seen hosting the loveliest of blooms. The emperor had just abandoned the luxury of his palace after being informed by his chief fowler, Abul Latif, that one of the female elephants was in labor and about to deliver. He himself had instructed Abul Latif for the delivery of such news, and had hurried to the scene with the exhilaration of a father-to-be. Nur Jahan and other ladies of the harem, uninterested in such matters, had stayed inside the palace with no intention of venturing out to watch this miracle of a birth. They were playing cards, and unrolling the parchments of intrigues in their minds and hearts. But Jahangir, as a born naturalist and with his penchant to unfold nature in every aspect, would not have missed this opportunity, not even for all the kingdoms of the world. And this intensity of his need and aesthetic pleasure were visible in his eyes as he stood there all agog, surrounded by a coterie of his royal attendants.

Since his journey from Kashmir, Jahangir's health had improved, but there was little to no hope of total recovery against the bouts of his excesses, which could not be restrained. Moreover, he was besieged by a string of misfortunes which could not lend him the opportunity to nurture his body and mind with strength. The first stop in his journey from Kashmir was on the outskirts of Rawalpindi. Then the royal cavalcade had halted at Multan. The city of Multan was their stronghold to dispatch reenforcements to Kandahar. Jahangir was still ailing and weighed down with grief by the tenacity of Prince Shah Jahan's disobedience, as he had reached Lahore. Prince Shah

Jahan was hurling a succession of embassies down the emperor's way, protesting his devotion to the emperor, and cloaking his disobediences in the mantle of misunderstanding between him and the emperor. Tearing this mantle of misunderstanding to rags, the emperor could not be dissuaded from sending orders from his sick bed, forbidding his once beloved son to ever set foot inside the courts of Agra or Lahore. No sooner had he recovered a little, that another vicious blow from fate had clamped him down to bed. The emperor's mother, Miryam Uzzmanni, had died suddenly in her palace at Agra. Though crushed by the burdens of grief and illness, he had summoned enough strength to journey to Agra. Miryam Uzzmanni was buried in a tomb at Sikandara next to her husband, the late Emperor Akbar, and Jahangir had returned to Lahore, utterly crushed by the weight of his own grief, and of his mental and physical sufferings.

Nur Jahan was always beside him, consoling and soothing the ailing emperor. She was his anchor of love and light in the darkest of times. But he was wooing his bride of wine more intensely than ever, approaching closer to Anarkali in oblivion, and neglecting to court joy from the one and only love of his life, Nur Jahan. Amidst his rare moods of sobriety, he had begun to entertain remorse, if not the imponderables, thinking to himself that he was wedded to Nur Jahan in the eternal damnation of his own guilt.

Paradoxically, Nur Jahan herself had begun to suffer the guilt of her own passion, wild and tempestuous. Her great, great passion which had failed to heal the canker of loss and grief inside the ever-turbulent soul of the emperor. All her wedded life she had tried, but in vain. The dead beloved was alluring him to the abode of darkness, while she herself could not entice him to the sanctuary of light. Her own lighthearted gaiety, always clinging toward hope, was now suffering the blight of hopelessness. For the first time in her life, she was truly and madly jealous of the emperor's dead beloved. Her very soul was stricken by the rods of misery and disconsolation.

The goddess of death and doom! Nur Jahan's very thoughts had stabbed Anarkali with accusations mute and heartrending. She had begun to curse her own love and beauty, which could not save the emperor from drowning into the pit of misery and sorrow. Her heart and soul had uttered such loud laments that they had penetrated the emperor's oblivion, even when he could not be awakened from the stupor of his drunkenness. Finally, he could be seen surfacing on the shores of sobriety to heed the pleas of his living beloved. Both were swept together into the currents of awareness, both seeking refuge and anchor inside the tormented souls of one another.

The emperor had cut down on his consumption of wine more so to please Nur Jahan than to improve his health. And the sea nymph of jealousy in Nur Jahan's heart was swallowed by the tides of love inside her heart.

The ill-fated news at home and from abroad had not changed much during the several bleak months of the emperor's convalescence. Those months were not always bleak, interspersed with feasting and entertainment, when black fates slept. But nothing could rub off the tarnish of deaths and rebellions which could be seen looming over the courts at Agra and Lahore. This particular September morning, Jahangir had awakened with a sense of hope and promise. Somewhere in this jungle of misfortunes were joy and peace not far behind, he had thought. Now sunshine, warming his heart, was polishing his thoughts too as dearest of his companions, as he stood watching the birth of the baby elephants.

Nur Jahan too had shared the same sense of optimism as of the emperor's, this bright, peace-loving morning. She was awaiting the birth of her grandchild with a longing akin to the mingling of joy and pain. Her beloved Ladli was about to pour blessings into this household with a royal babe, and Nur Jahan was wishing to hasten this moment with dreams and prayers. Her efforts to keep Prince Shahriyar at her daughter's side had proven unsuccessful, but she was not unhappy. Prince Shahriyar had to play the part of an heir apparent, and was dispatched to Dohlpur to settle some accounts which needed urgent attention.

Nur Jahan had sat with the harem ladies, listening to the royal gossip, her restless thoughts bouncing back and forth eternally to gain entry into the chamber of her daughter. It was not long after the emperor had left, that she herself had slipped away to see her daughter confined in her own gilded chamber. Ladli Begum's confinement was self-imposed, for she had grown much too heavy to carry her burden around without panting, or scolding her ladies-in-waiting for comfort and assistance. Nur Jahan, unsuspecting the hour of birth, had entered her daughter's chamber when the pangs of childbirth were choking her breath and voice. While Nur Jahan was witnessing the miracle of a birth in her daughter's room, the emperor was witnessing the same miracle from the womb of his favorite elephant named, Bansi-badan.

"Miracles happen every day, Your Majesty, God's own miracles," Abul Latif was murmuring. "Your favorite Bansi-badan, Your Majesty. You have treated her like a princess all these years, and now she is going to be a mother."

"How long has been the gestation period? Eighteen months, is it?" Jahangir was thinking aloud, his lips tasting the soma of exhilaration.

"Nineteen months, Your Majesty," Abul Latif offered happily.

"Then the child will be male. If it were eighteen months, then the baby would surely be female." Jahangir's thoughts themselves were murmuring.

"Look, Your Majesty, you can see the baby's feet," Abul Latif chimed excitedly.

"Yes, the baby elephants are born with their feet first. What mysteries lurk behind the designs of nature…" Jahangir's eyes were a beacon of light.

The baby was born, and the mother was scattering dust upon it with the slow, rhythmic movements of her feet. The baby elephant could neither cry nor stir, while the mother reached down to pet it with her trunk. Suddenly, the baby elephant was lumbering to its feet, and dashing straight toward its mother's breasts.

"What tenderness, how enchanting!" Jahangir's exclamation was swallowed by a whirlwind of noise from behind.

Hushiyar Khan, in the livery of gold and crimson, with the speed of a hurricane, was whirling closer to the emperor. In a flash, he was at the emperor's feet in one breezy curtsy, and announcing gustily.

"Your Majesty, Ladli Begum has given birth to a beautiful daughter. Padishah Begum is requesting your company." Hushiyar Khan's eyes shone with excitement.

"And Bansi-badan has given birth to a handsome male elephant." Jahangir laughed, retracing his steps toward the palace gates.

The narrow path sprinkled with red dust was heralding the emperor closer to the palace. The willows with swooping arms were admiring their reflections in the crystal-clear lakes. Jahangir had halted briefly to admire the lotuses floating so blissfully by the grand steps of the palace in their own serene pools. The arches and the cupolas of the facade were fading against an array of pavilions, as Jahangir mounted the vast staircase to reach the palace doors. The emeralds in his ears and a large amethyst in his turban were caught in a blaze of sunshine, before they were concealed behind the imposing doors in gilt and ebony.

Nur Jahan was in raptures beyond imagination. She had swathed her granddaughter in the softest of silks with her own hands, before leaving her into the care of the royal ayahs. Fluttering down the damasked hallway, she had shared her joyful news with the other ladies of the harem, not minding in the least their joyless murmurs of felicitations. Then she had flown to her own chamber, as if whipped by the mists of her own delirium and giddiness. Abandoning herself to the comforts of her chamber, she had summoned the dancing girls, more so to retain the abundance of joy inside her than to banish the affectations of the harem ladies from her thoughts. She was settling herself to the rhythms of serenity, the dancing girls before her some mist-illusions.

While luxuriating thus in her own sense of peace and solitude, Nur Jahan was barely aware of the girls in shimmering whirlwinds. Since her thoughts were seeking the pools in reveries, the studs in the noses of the dancers and tilaks on their foreheads were reflected in her mind's sight alone. She was becoming aware though, that these two dancers were performing Bharata Natyam with the mythological representation of gods and the goddesses. Their intense, spiritual movements were filling her thoughts with awe and bliss, making her float somewhere in realms alien and nameless.

Nur Jahan was transported to some magical world of her own, where repose and silence reigned supreme. Her thoughts were wandering away from the dancers to the gilded furnishings in this room, the figurative angels and nymphs in the large, gilt frames, the large painting on the mantel depicting men on horseback, riding close to the arena of the lions and the elephants, a pair of hoopoes flying overhead. The gilded painting next to it was of the peacocks with their plumes fanned out, standing by the reed-infested canal brimming with lotuses. Her gaze was wandering no more, a beatific smile alighting on her lips and in her eyes. She herself was painted in the flash of time, her face wreathed in a subtle glow from the sparkle of diamonds on her royal person.

This was the scene upon which Jahangir materialized, finding his beloved in a halo of light and repose. He was holding out his arms, joy flooding from his eyes. Unmindful of the dancing girls, Nur Jahan sank into the emperor's arms. Her heart was thundering, and her eyes warm and radiant. Jahangir was quick to dismiss the dancers, before installing his beloved on the velvety davenport.

"I can't contain this joy, Your Majesty. How painful joy is at times...my own little granddaughter," Nur Jahan muttered effusively.

"More joy if you can contain it, my Nur! The emperor himself has sired a male elephant, metaphorically." Jahangir pressed her hands into his own.

"Very propitious signs, Your Majesty. These beloved births, this blessed day!" Nur Jahan exclaimed.

"I hope, Nur, these births, especially the birth of our granddaughter, prove propitious to our home and state," Jahangir ruminated wistfully.

"Imagine, Your Majesty, me, a grandmother! Does that mean I am getting old?" Nur Jahan chirped brightly.

"Grand, and beautiful, yes." The stars of adoration in Jahangir's eyes were caressing her youthful features. "And a young mother to the entire royal brood in our empire, including the emperor," he teased. "Though the emperor is getting old, really old. A grandfather many times over. What is your secret, Nur? You never age. How do you stay so young and beautiful?"

"The draughts of jealousy, Your Majesty, that's my secret." Nur Jahan laughed. "My secret to youth and beauty…I am fated to drink those draughts so religiously that age is shamed into exile." Her ruby-red lips were drinking their own wine of mirth.

"Then soon you would grow old, my love. Much too long have you been deprived of those draughts of jealousy! Several months now?" Jahangir kissed her hands. "Anarkali is banished inside the caskets of time, inside my very soul, never to escape into this reality of a delusion. She has aged along with the emperor, and has grown wrinkled, while your love and beauty keep me alive, if not youthful." His heart was gathering the throbs of a presage.

"The old emperor has yet to suggest a name for our granddaughter, Your Majesty," Nur Jahan sang evasively.

"The old emperor's memory is failing too, my Nur. He has forgotten all the beautiful names," Jahangir quipped.

"I have been thinking, Your Majesty, Princess Wali, or Princess Ladali? Do they appeal to you?" Nur Jahan suggested charmingly.

"How could you even think of such atrocious names, Nur?" Jahangir exclaimed with a sudden passion. "Your fine taste in building gardens and monuments must defy even the shadow of ugliness in such names. Arzani, yes, Princess Arzani, sounds much better, if not beautiful."

"I knew, Your Majesty, your old memory would resurrect at least one beautiful name!" Nur Jahan smiled to herself.

"Your guile, Nur, and your bewitching charm confound the emperor each hour of the day." He slipped his arm around her waist. "Nothing beautiful could ever be born from the ugliness in the emperor's head or heart! But from your heart pure and mind beautiful, all that I see or hear is beauty. I have yet to visit the tomb of your father. How much wealth and genius have you lavished on that monument?" he asked abruptly.

"The purse of the poor empress dares not flaunt its poverty, Your Majesty," Nur Jahan quipped with the spontaneity of a skilled politician. "And the genius belongs to the architects, Your Majesty."

"The emperor has heard otherwise." Jahangir got to his feet, stealthy presage inside him surfacing again as he began pacing. "It boasts of your wealth and genius alone, the emperor has heard, my love. You are its sole architect."

"Since you dissuaded me to built it with pure silver, Your Majesty, it displays the rags of my riches." Nur Jahan's eyes were polished with the jewels of her wit.

"You should be proud to flaunt those rags with jeweled expressions before the emperor's eyes, my Nur, since he is bound to see them sometime." Jahangir flashed her an enigmatic look. "More jewels are shining on your father's tomb than in the emperor's treasury, I have heard."

"I would be stealing a heap of jewels from your treasury, Your Majesty, if I dared embellish this tomb with words. Your treasury, Your Majesty, can fashion a hundred such tombs with jewels precious, and never see the dearth of any pilfering." Nur Jahan was becoming aware of the emperor's dark mood.

"Won't you delight the emperor with your sweet expressions, my Nur?" Jahangir murmured, his feet coming to a slow halt before the window, and he stood looking out at the terraces down below.

"With great pleasure, Your Majesty," Nur Jahan began quickly. "To begin with, the floor is all sandalwood, in hues tan, gold and brown. My own design for the floor is farshi-chandani, overlaid in the patterns of stems, flowers and tendrils. The mausoleum itself stands in the middle of the garden on a decorated platform. This platform is surrounded by fountains and walkways. The arches and turrets of this mausoleum are softened by a domed kiosk. This kiosk cascades down gracefully over both the tombs of papa and mamma, both resting in peace, side-by-side, their tombs flanked by latticed railings." She paused, her thoughts transporting her to the actual site in Agra, cradled by the banks of Jamna. "Yes, the tombs are like the brilliant caskets, inlaid with semiprecious stones. Pietra dura of the marble tombs is exquisite. Onyx, topaz, jasper and carnelian fit perfectly, like a jeweled tapestry. Carved and inlaid archways in marble seem to be the handiwork of the angels themselves. The facade is carved with the designs of a cypress, the sprinkler, and a cup and saucer..." She paused, as if on the verge of revealing something which she wished the emperor to discover with his own eyes.

"I should have made you the architect of Prince Khusrau's tomb." Jahangir turned slowly. "My unfortunate prince, he rests under a canopy wrought in mother-of-pearl."

"It would be wrought in pure silver, Your Majesty, if you leave it to me. But that you would not permit," was Nur Jahan's subtle comment.

"No embellishments of any sort on other tombs could ever compare with the ones on Itmadudaula's tomb, as I gather from your description, Nur." Jahangir drifted toward her, eliciting a bright smile. "I have this sudden longing, Nur, to visit your father's tomb. A week's journey at the most if we start right away, in a leisurely pace, that is."

"Right away, Your Majesty!" Nur Jahan exclaimed incredulously.

"And why not?" Jahangir commented with the repose of a dreamer.

"Your Majesty! You promised your viziers that you would stay here till the embassies from Kandahar and from…" Nur Jahan's very thoughts were choking against the ardor and intensity in his gaze.

"You know, Nur, the emperor's whims. If he decides on something, no embassies in the world can ever detain him." Jahangir's eyes were gathering a passionate storm against their facade of repose. "Unless, your ingenuity, my pearl, can unroll that tapestry in marble right here in this chamber?" he challenged.

"The last beautiful stitch, which I was concealing from you, Your Majesty?" Nur Jahan began sweetly. "I will show it to you, Your Majesty, if you promise not to leave Lahore until all unruly affairs have fallen into some semblance of discipline."

"Your ingenuity is working, already." Jahangir smiled. "The emperor was wondering why your description sounded incomplete."

"Then you promise, Your Majesty?" A soft flush crept over Nur Jahan's cheeks.

"My spirit, right now, is too ardent to make any promises," Jahangir murmured, his very gaze devouring her.

"At the very entrance of the mausoleum, Your Majesty, the cypresses are now encircled by the twining creepers." Nur Jahan could barely murmur this great secret of their own mutual love.

"Ah, the emblem of our love into the very arms of nature." Jahangir pressed her to him, kissing her wildly.

At the very inception of whetting his appetite, a loud knock jolted him out of his passionate frenzy. In a flash, he had stumbled to his feet, thundering with the rage and impatience of a warring lord.

"Come in at the peril of your own life. If this intrusion is not worth a kingdom, you will forfeit your head." Jahangir waved his arm at the stunned eunuch by the door.

"Your Majesty!" Hushiyar Khan inched closer, and fell at the emperor's feet. "The Persian ambassador, Haider Beg, craves your audience, Your Majesty. Kandahar has fallen…" He could not breathe, feeling the emperor's rage looming over him.

Nur Jahan stifled one painful lament, while the emperor stood there glowering. The serpent of rage inside him was uncoiling, and spewing venom into the very throbs of his anguished heart.

"The blight of fortunes," Jahangir murmured under his breath. "Go, grant admission to the messenger of woe, and stand guard at the door," he commanded.

"Yes, Your Majesty." Hushiyar Khan bounced back to his feet, and fled.

Jahangir and Nur Jahan's eyes were locked together after the dazed eunuch had fled. The eyes of the empress were shining with torment, while rage and anguish were smoldering vivid in the emperor's. Both were mute, both arrested under some spell, abysmal and profound. Haider Beg was announced, and they seemed oblivious, chained to their own world of silence, noticing his presence only when he lumbered closer, offering curtsies. He was standing there humbly, waiting to be addressed.

"What evil news you bring, Haider Beg?" Jahangir demanded intensely.

"No evil news, Your Majesty. The king of Persia sends his greetings, and hopes that the relationship of brotherhood between him and Your Majesty will prosper." Haider Beg lowered his eyes as well as his head.

"Is this the purport of your embassy, Haider Beg, and nothing else?" Jahangir's eyes were shooting commands.

"The king of Persia also informs you, Your Majesty, that he has taken Kandahar in accordance with the wishes of your late father and grandfather," Haider Beg began smoothly. "And the king of Persia further states that since Kandahar rightfully belonged to the Persians, he hopes that this possession will cause no rift between the two mighty empires, Hind and Persia."

"That petty kingdom as Shah Abbas called Kandahar? Writing to me respectfully that this petty kingdom is not worth losing our friendship and brotherhood…" Jahangir paused before giving vent to his rage. "And now he takes that petty kingdom with the sword of treachery. What besotted worm of an ambassador you are! Tell my brother Shah Abbas that Kandahar belongs to the Moghuls, not to the Persians. And we will take it back not by the sword of treachery, but by the sheer brutal force of our mighty wills and arms. Begone, begone. And never dare convey such an evil report concealed inside the raiments of deceit and ambition." He waved dismissal.

Bowing impeccably and without a word, Haider Beg vanished behind the doors. Before the emperor could contemplate his anguish, another messenger entered breezily. This rude messenger was Itibar Khan, the governor of Agra, almost colliding with Haider Beg on his way out. He was followed by Hushiyar Khan, whose attempts in impeding the governor's approach were proving unsuccessful. Both were bowing before the emperor, but Jahangir's eyes were flashing rage at Hushiyar Khan alone.

"Didn't the emperor command you to keep guard at the door?" Jahangir demanded.

"Your Majesty..." was Hushiyar Khan's choked response.

"Begone, begone." Jahangir waved dismissal. "And don't let anyone enter, even if you have to use a whip to restrain their impudence." He turned to Itibar Khan. "And what do you have to say in your defense, my knight of Agra?" he demanded.

"Your Majesty, pardon me. I bring grievous news which can't be delayed," Itibar Khan pleaded, wearing a shroud of ominous silence.

"More grievous than the fall of Kandahar? All the kingdoms melting in their own pools of insidious plots?" Jahangir lamented aloud. "Evil times and rude fates, Itibar Khan? Let the rivers of misfortunes run free, and the emperor will not hold you prisoner to his rage."

"Your Majesty, Prince Shah Jahan had a little skirmish with Prince Shahriyar in Dholpur. Prince Shah Jahan sent his vizier Darya Khan with a small contingent of troops to seize Dholpur from Prince Shahriyar. Prince Shahriyar gathered his own troops to counter the attack, and many men from both parties were killed."

"Oh, *baidaulat*! Unworthy of all the favors which I bestowed upon him." Jahangir's attention was shifting to Nur Jahan. "Didn't the emperor bestow the pargana of Dholpur on you and Prince Shahriyar, my empress?"

"Yes, Your Majesty," Nur Jahan murmured, striving to pacify the emperor lest his anger make him ill. "But Prince Shah Jahan had petitioned you for the ownership of Dholpur, Your Majesty, if you recall."

"Petitioned!" Jahangir exclaimed. "That royal wretch has torn off the veil of respect, and has turned his face toward the valley of ruin." His rage was landing on Itibar Khan. "Tell *baidaulat* that he is deprived of all his jagirs in the north, including Hissar. And that he is not permitted to set foot in Agra or Lahore."

Itibar Khan stood there chilled, his lips moving without sounds or words.

"Depart posthaste, Itibar Khan, and deliver this message. This is the emperor's farman to baidaulat. The prince is not to plead with the emperor, or to approach him without summons." Jahangir waved dismissal, his anger mounting as Itibar stood there chilled. "Begone, I say, begone. Don't stand there like some mighty oak. You will be chopped down to insignificant timber by the emperor's very wrath, if you don't flee." His gaze itself was issuing this farman.

"There is more, Your Majesty…" Itibar Khan suppressed a sigh. "Prince Shah Jahan has unfurled the banners of revolt, and is marching toward Agra."

"Oh, that insolent, ill-starred rebel! My own son? Now that Kandahar is fallen, this inauspicious son of the emperor is out there to strike an ax at the foot of his own dominions." Jahangir's anger was replaced by anguish. "Must the emperor now abandon the cause of Kandahar and fight with his own son? Yes, Itibar Khan, yes. This open rebellion must be quelled, even if the emperor has to gather forces from all quarters of his empire. Dispatch urgent summons to Mahabat Khan in Kabul. He is to return to Agra with all his forces. Summon all, Afzal Khan from Kandahar, Prince Perwiz from Allahabad, Prince Shahriyar from Behar. Another urgent message to Asaf Khan to transfer the imperial treasury from Agra to Lahore. And you yourself repair to Agra to guard the citadel. Begone, begone. No more, no more."

Itibar Khan retraced his steps slowly and heavily. His thoughts were burdened by the loads of sufferings on the emperor's shoulders and inside his heart. Besides, his own bitter judgment against the undutiful son of the emperor was weighing heavy on his own shoulders. Jahangir's eyes were flashing after the retreating vizier, but no more commands were escaping his lips. His heart was constricting with rage and anguish. His arms too were shooting up in one hopeless gesture, and his gaze returning to Nur Jahan.

"Pain and weakness are still my companions. And I must ride and fight my own son on the dusty roads unsuitable to my health!" Jahangir exclaimed histrionically.

"Must you, Your Majesty?" Nur Jahan demurred aloud, presage and anguish stabbing her own heart.

"Must the emperor? When his son has drunk the wine of error!" Another exclamation escaped Jahangir's lips. "Wine! The emperor needs flagons of wine to drown his sorrow."

"A stroll in the garden perhaps, Your Majesty. Wine? In such a state that you are, will…" Nur Jahan's appeal was torn asunder by the bolt of lightning in Jahangir's eyes.

"A meager stroll is no substitute for wine, Nur! The emperor will go hunting, drinking wine from the bruised lips of nature and from the eyes of the hunted beasts," Jahangir announced.

"Hunting, Your Majesty!" declared Nur Jahan. "You would break your vow of nonviolence?" Her eyes were shining with disbelief.

"That vow, my Nur, was taken when baidaulat was the constellation of my affections," Jahangir mocked. "That was when my grandson Prince Shuja was ill, and I had vowed that I would not again sport with a gun or inflict any injury on a living thing with my own hands. Wasn't that the solemn vow of the emperor at the tomb of Muinuddin Chishti?" His anger was abating all of a sudden. "And now that Prince Shuja is not ill, and that Prince Shah Jahan is drowning into the ocean of his own hideous follies, the emperor is absolved of all his vows. Forbidden by your lovely eyes, my Nur, the emperor can neither crave a drink nor a hunting expedition. Do you have a quick remedy to appease the emperor's sufferings? Yes, I know…" He drifted toward her in some dream-haze of desire and torment.

In a flash, Nur Jahan was caught into a wild embrace, her lips and cheeks burning against the violence of kisses from the lips of the emperor. Both were foundering into a deluge of passion, the violence itself mitigating the pain and suffering in their hearts and souls. Both had surrendered their minds and bodies to the naked lust of the desires unsated and insatiable. Both were intertwined like the cypress and the creeper, where injuries of the soul could not hurt the emblem of love.

The royal encampment southward of Delhi was swathed in hush and quiet of the evening. The colorful tents were keeping the ladies of the harem in utmost comfort. Another such luxuriant tent was Nur Jahan's comforting abode with Bokhara rugs and gold awnings. The guards and sentries outside were keeping watch over this silk city of tents, vigilant at all times to gratify each little need or whim of the royal ladies. Though surrounded by all imaginable luxuries, Nur Jahan's thoughts were trooping down the rough paths on the field of Baluchpur. Baluchpur was the warring field where the emperor, along with a contingent of great army, was encamped to fight against the forces of Prince Shah Jahan. The mind of the empress was at peace though, entertaining no fears or tragedies. Her intuition alone was witness that the emperor would return wearing the laurels of victory, while the royal rebel would be forced to retreat in disgrace. Actually, her thoughts were leaving the battlefield and accosting the pine-valleys of Kashmir, where they were sure to journey after this decisive battle. She was recalling the emperor's promise of such a journey with a sense of joy splintered with pains and sadness. Her thoughts were digging down the passion-fields of ardent nights and suffered days, unearthing sweet and bitter memories where the emperor's caprice and passion could be seen rising on the heights of absurdity when the oceans of his grief were fresh and churning. Then Anarkali was forgotten amidst the fever of his warring thoughts and thoughtful strategies. And the emperor's anger was consumed by the breeze of passion, where Nur Jahan alone was the queen of love and intrigue.

Before their march from Lahore, the empress herself had secured swift alliances for the emperor. Her network of spies had informed her that Prince Shah Jahan was supported by most of the great amirs stationed in Malwa, Deccan and Gujrat. Also, swift couriers were feeding her with news from all quarters of the empire. Abdur Rahim and his son Darab Khan had defected, swearing allegiance with the rebel prince, Prince Shah Jahan. Prince Shah Jahan had gathered the forces of twenty-seven thousand armed men, and Sharza Khan, Himmat Khan, Rustam Khan, Darya Khan, Mansur Khan, Bairam Beg and Sarbuland Khan were his most prominent generals. To match the forces of the rebel prince, Nur Jahan had summoned the Rajput feudatories to the support of the throne. The princes of Bundi, Kotah, Amber and Marwar had genially responded to the urgent request-commands of the empress. Bir Singh Deo was the foremost among them to embrace the cause of the emperor and the empress. The emperor's own summons to his princes and viziers were quickly heeded, all willing to join in this campaign against Prince Shah Jahan. Prince Perwiz, Prince Shahriyar, Asaf Khan and Mahabat Khan were given the command of mighty contingents to fight and succeed. Many, many more allies of power and eminence had joined the royal troops to chastise this rebel prince.

Then the imperial cavalcade, equipped with a mighty will to win, had marched forth from Lahore in a jubilant flood of hope and adventure. Jahangir and Nur Jahan had reposed briefly at Nur Sarai before commencing this feverish journey to Agra and Delhi. There, in their favorite rest-house with the paintings of lotuses, peacocks and dueling elephants, they were lovers, not warriors, knowing only the bliss of nearness and togetherness, and forgetting about the warring world in the realms of reality and illusion.

This sarai was erected by Nur Jahan Begum.

Jahangir had ordered this inscription to be carved on one marble slab before leaving that paradisiacal rest-house. Nur Jahan was smiling inside the pool of her calm introspection at the thought of this sweet remembrance. A sad, happy smile was surfacing in her eyes too, but she was not aware, only vaguely conscious of her thoughts and recollections. Inside the folds of her joy; pain was awakening, wide-eyed and turbulent.

On the vast field of Baluchpur, Jahangir in his chain-mail and gold helmet, was shooting orders like the poisoned arrows. His heart and soul were poisoned too, with rage and hatred for his son who had dared rise against the emperor in open rebellion. Though Prince Shah Jahan, afraid of direct confrontation with his father, had retired himself below the hills, letting his generals assume full command of the battle. The battle was raging furiously as anticipated. The imperialists were pounding the unskilled forces of the prince with a shower of arrows and a battery of insults. Jahangir himself, astride his Arabian steed, was commanding his generals to launch a succession of assaults. Mahabat Khan was ahead of the cavalry. Asaf Khan, with eight thousand troops under his command, was stationed to the right flank of the emperor. Behind the emperor's own contingent of troops was Abul Hasan with horse and soldier in equal number to Asaf Khan's, for a possible assault or reinforcement. Abdullah Khan, with his troops of ten thousand, was covering the left flank of the emperor. Prince Perwiz, Prince Shahriyar, Itibar Khan and Nawazish Khan were scattered on all sides at the head of their own disciplined ranks. From the vantage point of his own position, Jahangir could see that Prince Shah Jahan's troops were being routed besides being disheartened.

Suddenly, Prince Shah Jahan's general, Bikramajit, was seen brandishing his sword to meet the challenge of the imperialists. He was shot in the temple by Nawazish Khan. The proud Bikramajit was unhorsed, and trampled by the riderless horses from the band of his own undisciplined army who had lost their heads from their shoulders in this fierce melee. Witnessing the fall of this mighty general, there were chaos and confusion in the ranks of Prince Shah Jahan's troops. All were fleeing, hounded by the imperialists. Such a pandemonium of flight had ensued, that the soldiers of the rebel prince were being crushed under the feet of their own warring elephants. Even the princes of Merwar, known for their valor, were fleeing for their lives. Kunwar Bahim himself was seen galloping down the slope to inform Prince Shah Jahan of this woeful defeat.

Jahangir, astride his snow-white horse, was exultant and beaming. He had expected a long, grueling battle, and this whiffa of swift victory was making him drunk with joy and exhilaration. He could see one of his soldiers carrying the severed head of Bikramajit, and riding toward him posthaste. A spurt of laughter was escaping Jahangir's lips, as he watched his soldier flaunt this trophy of war as a lesson and warning for all who dared challenge the emperor.

"Now this head is worth nothing until it is fashioned into a drinking cup!" Jahangir declared. "Bikramajit! Isn't he the one who raided the walled city of Agra? Robbing all the jewels and treasures which rightfully belonged to the noblemen of our court? Stealing nine hundred thousand rupees from Lashkar Khan alone, though the gates of Fatehpur Sikri were barred against him and baidaulat?" His eyes were flashing queries at the viziers who had joined him.

"Yes, Your Majesty. The very same rebel, this mighty Bikramajit," Mahabat Khan murmured without much enthusiasm. "Do you wish us to pursue Prince Shah Jahan, Your Majesty?" he asked enigmatically.

"Yes, pursue him to the very end of the world! And bring him before the emperor alive or dead," Jahangir commanded under some spell of pain and delirium.

Mahabat Khan galloped away, without even waiting for further instructions from the emperor. He seemed oblivious, even of Itibar Khan, who was hurrying past him to seek the emperor's attention.

"Your Majesty, Prince Shah Jahan was seen fleeing toward Mandu," Itibar Khan announced, his eyes shining with excitement and apprehension. "Prince Perwiz and Prince Shahriyar are already in swift pursuit after the fleeing prince. Do you wish me to join them, Your Majesty?" he appealed.

"No, Itibar Khan, no," Jahangir chanted happily. "The affairs at Agra demand your presence. You must return to Agra and guard this city against any horde of future rebels." His tone was heavy and his breath labored. "Mahabat Khan is already on his way…you must look to the preparations of our journey to Ajmer before you leave." He was struggling against the shortness of breath, and fearing an asthma attack. "And then to the pine-valleys of Kashmir…for health, for health." He spurred his horse in the direction of the silk city where Nur Jahan sat awaiting the news of victory.

Chapter Twelve

Kashmir, with all its glory of peace and perfume, had failed to pour strength into the ailing body of the emperor, though several months of rest and respite had slipped past since his return to Kashmir after the victory of Baluchpur. He had fallen ill shortly after he had shared the news of victory with Nur Jahan. Asthma and arthritis had become his most evil of foes, following him at his heels to the very shrine of Ajmer. The journey to Kashmir had been long and cumbersome, and he had made the beautiful palace of Achabal his home and retreat. Nur Jahan was his constant companion, loving and caring with utmost devotion, but his health was not improving, as if he was destined to founder inside the pools of his own gloom and depression. He was courting Anarkali once again, his spirit broken and despairing. His thoughts, it seemed, were longing for liberty from the agony of flesh, and release from the fetters of their own mental anguish. Such morbid, yet frolicsome thoughts of his could inhale the scent of Anarkali from each lovely bloom in his garden, and from each bright wound within his heart.

Evenings were the most saddest of times for the emperor. During those hours of silence and inactivity, his thoughts could catch the solitary murmur of trees, which appeared to be lamenting some loss or weeping inconsolably. Paradoxically, his own aching soul was the author of such laments in league with his effort to efface the memory of his fugitive son Shah Jahan.

By the sheer stroke of luck, or by the clemency of early summer, Jahangir's condition was improving slowly since the past two weeks of rest and restful contemplations. So, this particular evening, he had ventured out on the terrace in his favorite garden of Achabal. To Jahangir, this was the most delightful of all the gardens in Kashmir, and he was wont to delight in this one the most. It was lush and resplendent, cradled in between the great hills rising above the palace grounds, and down below the valleys of Kashmir dipping in lovely contours. Nur Jahan, delighted by the emperor's willingness to sit on the terrace, had ordered clay lamps to be lighted at the pools and fountains. The white terrace where Jahangir sat on his gilded chair was a perfect spot much favored by him. From here he could see even the distant chenars and white poplars, peering from behind the hills, lofty and invulnerable. The mirror-like lakes farther down the sleepy pavilions were reflecting verdure in hues silver and emerald, filling the emperor's sight and senses with awe and wonder.

The Persian rug at the emperor's feet was lending Nur Jahan warmth and comfort, where she had abandoned herself to dreams and languor. Her head too was abandoned on the emperor's lap, and she was gazing at the jafari blooms down the terrace steps under some spell of dreamy abeyance. No glittering jewels were adorning her royal person this evening, but soft, creamy pearls. Her blue velvet dress stitched with pearls was accentuating the white purity of her small, oval face. The fountain of her youth was still brimming with the glow of passion, and not corrupted by the ripples of age.

Jahangir, on the contrary, had aged quickly. The small ridges around his lips and at his temples had carved deep trenches on his gaunt, pallid features. His eyes had attained a feverish brightness, as if ready to kindle the flames of agony at the slightest of provocations, especially if the provocations came from the arena of rebellions concerning his rebel of a son, Shah Jahan. The emperor was wearing purple silks this evening, the blue-purplish bags under his eyes soft and swollen. The large amethyst in his turban was casting gloom over his pale and sunken cheeks. His gaze was taking flight with the hoopoes and the golden orioles. Though the silence within him was touching the hem of reality. The storm within him also, underneath that sheet of silence, was yawning and awakening. His thoughts were rising in defense to avoid, not challenge, the fury and stealth of this inner storm. So, they were escaping the gates of his eyes to find the balm of healing from the coffers of peace and loveliness in nature. Paradoxically, his gaze was reaching out to court not peace, but violence. It was arrested to one small spring at the foot of the sloping lawn. This spring was gurgling and spluttering fury all of a sudden, its violence disrupting the hush and peace in this garden.

"Look at that spring, Nur!" Jahangir declared intensely. "Did it always gush out with such violence without rhyme or reason? It seems to be sitting at the mouth of a volcanic eruption?" He was fascinated by the fury of this small spring.

"Yes, Your Majesty. And several similar ones down the valley, they too court violence at times," Nur Jahan responded dreamily, without lifting her head.

"How could it be otherwise, now I remember," Jahangir murmured to himself. "This Achabal of yours, my love, is designed over a powerful mountain spring which rises out of the Sosanwar hill," he demurred aloud.

"This was also the site of worship for the Hindus, who named this place Akshanala. Didn't you yourself enlighten me on this subject, Your Majesty?" Nur Jahan murmured.

"A sight of worship, yes, my pearl, where a Muslim emperor can sit and worship you till eternity." Jahangir was stroking her hair absently.

"The garden of paradise for me, Your Majesty, if I may borrow your expression. And this could be ours till eternity if we don't have to return to Agra, Delhi or Lahore." Nur Jahan pressed the emperor's hand to her cheek quite wistfully.

"I have to leave this paradise, only to check the rebellions of my own son, baidaulat!" Jahangir sighed.

The emperor was quiet again, holding and cherishing this summer evening in all its peace and stillness. One more glorious day was gone, leaving behind haze and swoon, and hush and pulchritude. The gold, blue flames from the clay lamps were still struggling to melt the pallor of the dusk and to reveal their own beacons of light. Jahangir's gaze was sailing over the chenars and poplars, discovering a patch of gold sky where dusk had splattered it with crimson streaks. *Just like the molten anguish inside my own heart*, Jahangir was thinking against some surge of awe and wonder. His thoughts were tracing the paths of baidaulat's rebellions and carving wounds down the very sunsets amidst their journeys long and aimless.

Prince Shah Jahan, after his defeat at Baluchpur, had retreated to Mandu in the province of Malwa. Upon learning of Prince Perwiz and Mahabat Khan's advance, he had decided to confront them, but was stalled by a sudden blister of rift and confusion amongst his own companions. His generals had begun to defect, seeking alliances from the imperialists. So disheartened had he grown by the infidelity of his supporters, that he had no choice but to cross the Narmada River and seek sanctuary at the fort of Asir. Since Prince Perwiz and Mahabat Khan were still following at his heels, he had decided to capture the fort of Asir and to make it as his stronghold. This fort was in possession of Mir Husamuddin, the husband of one of the cousins of Nur Jahan. Nur Jahan, adroitly aware of all the moves of this rebel prince, had dispatched a missive to her cousin, instructing him not to let this prince enter the fort of Asir.

Jahangir, while journeying thus in his thoughts on those bruised paths, was trying to recall the import of Nur Jahan's missive. But his thoughts themselves were the masters of their journeys, entering the terrains of treachery, where more rebellions could be seen shining in the eyes of Prince Shah Jahan. In obedience to Nur Jahan's instructions, Mir Husamuddin had strengthened his fort against the imminent assault of Prince Shah Jahan. But Prince Shah Jahan, through the unerring deceit of his chief plotter Sharifa, had succeeded in seducing the ruler into submission by means of great promises, behind which lurked great threats. Soon after, Prince Shah Jahan had left Gopal Das in charge of the Asir fort, and he himself had found refuge in Burhanpur. He was still being pursued by Prince Perwiz and Mahabat Khan, and was getting wearied of flights and indecisions. Since his plans to retire to Deccan were foiled as he was quick to judge, he was willing to sue for peace from Mahabat Khan. Mahabat Khan had no intention of granting any sanction of peace to this rebel prince until he showed some signs of contrition. And the first sign of contrition which he demanded was to hand over Abdur Rahim, who had defected and was greatly favored by the prince. Prince Shah Jahan, though gaining time for further escape, was left with no choice but to comply. Before delivering Abdur Rahim into the custody of Mahabat Khan, he had made him swear an oath of loyalty to him. Abdur Rahim, despite his pledge to Prince Shah Jahan, had turned to be a staunch supporter of Mahabat Khan, pledging his allegiance to the imperialists once again.

Prince Shah Jahan was duly informed of Abdur Rahim's implicit desertion, and had no time to lose to fly toward Deccan. He was to suffer more desertions from his generals; Bairam Khan was the last one to defect before his anticipated flight toward Deccan. Now in total despair, Prince Shah Jahan was reported to be crossing the Tapti River, still pursued by Prince Perwiz and Mahabat Khan, but had succeeded in escaping once again, this time into the foreign territory of Golconda, which was outside the purview of the Moghul rule. That was the last the emperor had heard about his son's swift flight before embarking on his journey toward Kashmir. Prince Perwiz and Mahabat Khan were instructed to continue their pursuit. Prince Shahriyar was constrained to cut short his endeavor of capturing the fugitive prince, since his own health was failing.

Jahangir's thoughts were turning toward Prince Shahriyar, but some obscure portrait of the long past loss was replacing this dimly lit recollection of the present. The vast chamber in his mind was dark and imposing. He could see the ghost of Prince Khusrau. Prince Khusrau's son Balaqi was there too, whom the emperor had recently appointed the governor of Gujrat. This dark chamber in Jahangir's mind was shuddering and expanding, exploring all nooks and crevices, carving rivulets of memories on the very shores of Bengal where Asaf Khan was assigned the post of governorship. More shadows were imposing their presence inside the darkness of his mind. Anarkali was but the emblem of Nur Jahan, whose presence he could feel with all the agony of love and illusion. The dark waves in his thoughts were charged with the currents of anguish and implacability. Narmada river was coming into view, its waters lashing at the fort of Asir. Nur Jahan was imprisoned inside the fort of Asir, her missive floating into a pool of water around her, all words blotched and muddied. What had made Mir Husamuddin wear the chains of submission?

"What did you write to Mir Husamuddin, my Nur, when baidaulat was on his way to Asir?" Jahangir asked abruptly.

"Your Majesty!" Nur Jahan was startled out of her reveries. "Such a long time, Your Majesty. You should not think about those sad events," she murmured softly.

"Those sadnesses will be forgotten, if the emperor's curiosity is satisfied." Jahangir's eyes were shooting a plea-command which could not be denied.

"A gist of that letter then, if it appeases your sadness." Nur Jahan heaved herself up, sailing toward the edge of the terrace. "What did I write? Nothing escapes my memory…yes, it's coming back to me. This is what I wrote, Your Majesty, 'beware a thousand times, beware, not to allow Prince Shah Jahan and his men to come near the fort. But strengthen the gates and towers. Do your duty! And do not act in such a manner that the stain of a curse and ingratitude for favors should fall on the honor or the forehead of a Sayyid.'" She stood gazing into the pool of limestone below.

"To think of that, Nur, I too rebelled against my father," Jahangir ruminated aloud, his gaze admiring the red Himalayan tulips.

"All children rebel against their fathers at some point in their lives. And the sons of the emperors, or the sons of the future emperors, are no exceptions," Nur Jahan commented without turning.

"By the virtue of being born as emperors, the emperors first and foremost, they tend to rule, not to be ruled? So, they become a rule to the exception," Jahangir intoned rather cheerfully. "Carrying the burdens of kingdoms on their shoulders, the emperors demand obedience from their sons." His gaze was caressing the back of his beloved. "The beauty of Kashmir has cradled the emperor into the mists of inertia, and he has ceased to think about the affairs of his empire. Any news of baidaulat, Nur, or from any other quarters, which might interest me?" he asked disinterestedly.

"Prince Shah Jahan is in Deccan, the last I heard about him, Your Majesty," Nur Jahan murmured. "He is seeking alliances with the Golconda government, I have heard, and with the English merchants of the south. Jagat Singh and his allies in the north are seeking protection and patronage from us. To that request, I have already sent an answer, offering them assistance and complete protection from any intrigue or plotting by any prince or vizier." Her senses were surrendering to the peace in this garden.

"Your goldfish with gold rings need a better abode than this pool of limestone, Nur," Jahangir commented. "They should have a pool of all marble. The emperor would order another pool built, of marble, with the inlay of mother-of-pearl."

"They are happy in their humble abode, Your Majesty." One tinkling of mirth escaped Nur Jahan's lips. "Besides, the gold in their noses would clash with the white in marble." She half turned.

"Come and sit by me, Nur. The emperor's heart is sinking." Jahangir smiled, as if gathering strength from her lovely eyes.

"Your Majesty, you do look pale and tired." Nur Jahan floated toward him, her look apprehensive. "The air is rather chilly; we better go back to the palace before…" She was stalled in an act of sitting at the emperor's feet.

"No, my love, no. Sit in your own gold chair. Your blue velvets clash with the maroon rug." Jahangir smiled again. "The emperor is not talking about some physical ailment, but the disease of the soul." He was gazing into her eyes. "The emperor has failed in many things, my pearl. Where did he miss? How far has he stumbled into the abyss of follies?" His gaze was smoldering all of a sudden.

"Where indeed, Your Majesty, if you think you have failed?" Nur Jahan sank into the chair beside him. "By loving too profoundly the one who could not be present to requite your love?" she murmured.

"And loving not enough the one whose boundless love has sustained me this long," Jahangir breathed profoundly.

"We all wade and founder into this ocean of life without guidance, Your Majesty, knowing not where and whither. But by the law and virtue of our natures we could do no more or less in what we strive to do." Nur Jahan's own eyes were spilling profundities. "You have loved me enough to keep me close to the shore of safety."

"Not enough, my love, not enough! And now the emperor has only one wish, to live and to die in this paradise, with you beside him." One kindling of a presage in Jahangir's heart had uttered this cry, not his lips.

"To live, yes, Your Majesty. This paradise forbids..." Nur Jahan's thoughts were shattered by one bolt of an exclamation from Jahangir's lips.

"And who is this rude intruder? Woebegone and unattended?" Jahangir's gaze was attacking one lonely figure on the forked path serenaded by the fountains.

A light of recognition was alighting in the emperor's eyes. Nur Jahan too had recognized the old, forlorn man approaching close to the terrace.

"Abdur Rahim, Your Majesty. Your own vizier who defected to Prince Shah Jahan, and now has pledged his allegiance to the imperialists," Nur Jahan murmured low.

"Your Majesty. Padishah Begum." Abdur Rahim prostrated himself at the feet of both the emperor and the empress.

"Raise your head, Abdur Rahim, and let the emperor see some sparks of loyalty in your eyes," Jahangir commanded.

"Too ashamed to raise my head, Your Majesty, lest you see the ravages of disloyalties on my wrinkled brow." Abdur Rahim could barely murmur.

"Such times, Abdur Rahim, such trying times." Jahangir's tone was softening. "Let us blame the follies of all men on the decrees of fate. And no man need be ashamed of his errors or eccentricities. You have suffered enough, and your faults are forgiven. What news you bring from the bosom of the warring kingdoms?" he asked kindly.

"More than my heart and tongue can contain, Your Majesty." Abdur Rahim raised his head, sitting there crouched on the Persian rug.

"Let this sadness wait, Abdur Rahim, until the emperor has rested," Nur Jahan commanded, her heart thundering.

"Padishah Begum," Abdur Rahim muttered, as if in great misery.

"No, my Nur, no." Jahangir waved her request away with one impatient gesture. "The emperor needs not postpone the burden of sadness"

"All pain and suffering, Your Majesty, all laden with ill import, if you wish to wait till tomorrow?" Abdur Rahim implored.

"Right this moment, Abdur Rahim, if you wish to escape the gallows of the emperor's wrath," Jahangir commanded.

"Your obedient servant, Your Majesty." Abdur Rahim bowed his head. "Prince Shah Jahan didn't stay idle in Golconda, the news must have reached you. But his own troubles multiplied along with his intrigues to conquer and subdue, wherever he could lay his claim to authority. Even the sovereign of Golconda didn't offer him much assistance, only sending him paltry amounts of cash or goods whenever the prince requested. Mirza Muhammed of

Bijapur, who, along with his family, had followed Prince Shah Jahan to Golconda, also absconded without any reason. Prince Shah Jahan was furious. He sent Jafar Beg with a body of troops to arrest Mirza Muhammed. The battle was fought in a dense jungle across from the big canal. Prince Shah Jahan's own men were caught in a swamp, and Sayyid Jafar was wounded. Khan Quli and several of the prince's men were slain. Mirza Muhammed fought bravely, but was overcome by wounds and died. His head was cut off and sent to Prince Shah Jahan. After this terrible skirmish, more desertions followed in the camp of Prince Shah Jahan, but he decided to move on to the town of Masulipatan. Half of the town was emptied for the fear of sacking, even before Prince Shah Jahan reached there. He then turned his attention to the northeast, and crossing Chhatar Diwar Pass, entered the Moghul territory of Orissa. Ahmed Beg, the governor of Orissa, and Ibrahim Khan, the governor of Bengal, were taken unawares by Prince Shah Jahan's sudden intention of conquering their territories. Prince Shah Jahan quickly appointed Abdullah Khan to lay the siege, and Orissa capitulated. The victorious prince then marched boldly to Ahmadnagar to fight Ibrahim Khan. The governor fought valiantly, but was killed. His severed head was presented to Prince Shah Jahan as a trophy of victory. Unfortunately, Prince Perwiz and Mahabat Khan, at this time, were in Burhanpur, settling the affairs in Deccan. Prince Shah Jahan, after the conquest of Orissa and Bengal, rewarded his generals with riches and homes. Raja Bahim, Darya Khan, Abdullah Khan and Shujaat Khan were the most favored ones, getting the largest of the shares from the loot.

"And my own son Darab Khan too, if he only knew the worth of the material wealths, and if God had guided him to the right path.

"Back to Prince Shah Jahan, he marched to Bihar, and the strong fort of the Rhotas was submitted to him. Then he continued his march to Allahabad, now pursued by Prince Perwiz and Mahabat Khan who had left Burhanpur far behind in their haste to capture the prince. By this time Prince Shah Jahan had taken full possession of Jaunpur and had encamped in the forests of Kampat, laying siege to the fort of Allahabad. Despite the monsoon rains, Prince Perwiz and Mahabat Khan had managed to reach Allahabad. Even before the fighting had began, quite a few of Prince Shah Jahan's generals had deserted the prince and had joined Mahabat Khan. Though the forces of Prince Shah Jahan had fought to the last, till their general Raja Bahim was killed, Prince Perwiz and Mahabat Khan had won the battle. Prince Shah Jahan's horse was wounded, but he had succeeded in escaping once again. He had retreated to the fort of the Rhotas, where his wife gave birth to another son..." He paused. But before he could continue, one anguished inquiry trembled on Jahangir's lips.

"And what did he name his unfortunate son; do you know?" Jahangir asked, his eyes shining with pain and delirium.

"Prince Murad Bakhsh, the newborn prince, Your Majesty," was Abdur Rahim's befuddled response.

"And baidaulat, where is he now? Still a rebel? Still a fugitive?" Jahangir's thoughts were foundering inside the ocean of love-hate.

"No more, Your Majesty, no more. Let another day share the burden of tragedies?" Nur Jahan pleaded, alarmed by the emperor's feverish gaze.

"Go on, Abdur Rahim," Jahangir commanded again. "Time is swift in its flight, neither sharing the burden of tragedies nor gathering fortunes in its empty bosom."

"Prince Shah Jahan escaped to Golconda once again, Your Majesty," was Abdur Rahim's laconic response, woe written all over his face.

"Leave no account of the hideous misfortunes concealed, Abdur Rahim." Jahangir's eyes were flashing rage.

"Prince Shah Jahan stayed in the fort of the Rhotas only three days, Your Majesty. Before leaving toward Ghuree, the prince commanded Darab Khan to follow him. But Darab Khan, my unfortunate son, was getting tired of Prince Shah Jahan's fighting and fleeing escapades, and didn't want to follow the fugitive prince. He and his son were taken hostage by Prince Shah Jahan's orders, but the prince advised Abdullah Khan not to harm them. After Prince Shah Jahan left, Abdullah Khan put my grandson to death. Darab Khan, my son, was seized by Mahabat Khan, and executed...my son and grandson, both gone..." He could not speak, overwhelmed with grief and despair.

"All your jagirs would be reinstated, Abdur Rahim. And you would reclaim the title of Khan Khanan, though no such rewards bring any consolation to the victim of loss and grief." Jahangir eased himself up slowly and thoughtfully.

"By the help of God, the kingdoms of Emperor Jahangir
Have twice given me life and twice the Khan Khani." An impromptu couplet broke forth on Abdur Rahim's grieving lips.

"Ill and tormented, the emperor must leave this valley of peace, and fly to the dale of fire and unrest." Jahangir didn't acknowledge Abdur Rahim's couplet of a response, his gaze unseeing. "To Lahore, to Lahore! Come, Padishah Begum, let us take one last stroll in our garden, before we are expelled from this paradise," he murmured without looking at her.

"Your Majesty." Nur Jahan was forcing back her tears with all the will of her passionate heart. "We would always return to this paradise…" She could not continue, numbed by shock as the emperor collapsed on the floor in one silken heap.

The grand room in the palace at Lahore was lit by a myriad of candles in the gold candelabrum. Jahangir was seated in his jeweled chair, attended by his physician, Muqarab Khan. From where he sat, he could view the trellised courtyard and the gardens dipping closer to the palace gates beyond. This room was all gilt and ivory, and furnished with the murals of court scenes from wall-to-wall. The ceiling too was all gilt, and painted with the Zodiac signs. Nur Jahan was lounging by the marble hearth in her own chair of carved rosewood. She was reading the works of Rumi with an intensity akin to oblivion and self-surrender. The porcelain vases over the mantel behind were brimming with fresh tuberoses, wafting forth the scent of peace and serenity. Nur Jahan herself had arranged some of these floral arrangements, but now as she sat there reading, she seemed oblivious to all but to her own intensity in self-surrender.

Jahangir was donned in pale silks, the large emerald in his turban sparkling. Though ill and suffering, he had gained a considerable amount of weight, his paunch and a double chin quite prominent. His face was full and bloated, his eyes heavy and swollen. He had begun to drink heavily and religiously. Even now as he sat listening to his physician's advice, he was drinking from his gold cup quite contentedly and heedlessly. Concerning his health, the emperor had thrown all caution to the winds, as long as his mental and physical sufferings could be appeased inside the pools of oblivion and drunkenness. He could not endure even the thought of his beloved son turned to an inveterate rebel, defying the emperor's love, and disobeying his commands.

The emperor was accepting no solace from Nur Jahan's own rivers of love and entreaties. The long journey from Kashmir to Lahore was a turbulent one, since he was once again the victim of asthma and violent headaches. His condition had not much improved after returning to Lahore, but despite his infirmities, his presence alone had brought peace in the neighboring cities of his empire. Prince Shah Jahan was self-exiled in Golconda. Prince Perwiz and Mahabat Khan were gaining new alliances in anticipation of capturing the rebel prince if he dared emerge from his safe lair with the intention of seizing the Moghul territories. Muqarab Khan had worked wonders in improving the health of Prince Shahriyar, though Indian fever had quite a damaging affect on his eyesight. After Muqarab Khan's ministrations, the prince was now able to read for a couple of hours at one stretch without experiencing any fatigue or headache. Ladli Begum was happy to have her husband's health restored, and gathering more happiness by the presence of her mother in Lahore.

Nur Jahan too was happy in a sense that she was finding solace and delight in the company of her granddaughter. Princess Ladali was almost two years old, and endowed with the disposition of love and laughter inherited from her grandmother. Another sanctuary of solace or distraction for Nur Jahan was her brother Asaf Khan, whom she had begun to respect and suspect concurrently. Respecting him for his wisdom, and suspecting him for his duplicity in keeping both the emperor and the prince happy, where no deceit could be suspected on either side. Only Jahangir was dissatisfied to stay in Lahore, yearning to be back into the pine-valleys of Kashmir. Besides, he was dreading the onslaught of heat which was sure to visit Lahore in a couple of months, if not before. Wine and heat were the worst of his enemies, but he could not banish either by the virtue of his needs and circumstances. The former one, he was compelled to keep in order to drown his sufferings. And the latter one, he was trying to abandon in the hope of feeling refreshed. He had begun to plan another trip to Kashmir, regardless of the fact that urgent matters needed his attention at Lahore. He was convincing himself that his illnesses were the result of caprice in seasons than of his own addiction to wine.

"It's not even summer, and the emperor feels stifled in this gilded tomb of a palace." Jahangir interrupted the litany of Muqarab Khan's advice after drinking deep from his gold cup. "The only remedy to the emperor's suffering is to inhale the scent of spring in the pine-valleys of Kashmir."

"The wine of beauty in nature's cup, for sure, Your Majesty, is beneficial to your health, not the wine in your cup. If I may propose, Your Majesty, that you cut down on your consumption of wine?" Muqarab Khan entreated.

"The wine soothes my senses, my besotted physician," Jahangir commented, stealing a glance at Nur Jahan. "And the wine I drink from the beautiful eyes of my empress, heals my soul. And yet, I thirst for the wine of beauty from the nature's cup too, my good physician, as you suggest," he murmured wistfully.

"Kashmir with all its charm and beauty cannot heal you, Your Majesty, if you do not curb your passion for drinking," Nur Jahan commented softly.

"It heals me in a way, my empress, that it makes me forget about all the bloody intrigues of my own kindred. Prince Khusrau, first! Now Prince Shah Jahan, baidaulat! In the guise of Cain, first murdering his brother, now usurping the kingdoms of his father?" was Jahangir's giddy comment.

"You have become so skilled in avoiding the subject of drinking, Your Majesty, that no one can approach the door of your excesses." One crescent of a smile was arrested on Nur Jahan's lips. "How can an emperor, who is ailing, rule this vast empire, Your Majesty? The welfare of your subjects depends upon your health."

"You should worry more about Prince Shahriyar's health, my empress, than the emperor's. The emperor suffers no impairment of vision or hearing," Jahangir proposed congenially. "Ask Muqarab Khan how the prince's sight fails as well as his memory."

"Prince Shahriyar is strong and healthy, Your Majesty, if you only knew." Nur Jahan's gaze was shifting from the emperor to the physician. "Tell the emperor, Muqarab Khan, how well the prince fares."

"Prince Shahriyar is enjoying good health, Your Majesty. His eyesight too is restored, completely."

"Yes, his eyes," Jahangir contemplated aloud. "They will no doubt continue quite well, if they be not deprived of light by his brothers. The Moghul Cain, I mean! Leave us, Muqarab Khan. The emperor might need your services in Kashmir, though he would be busy hunting and exploring his own gardens." He waved dismissal.

"Your humble servant, Your Majesty." Muqarab Khan turned to his heels.

Before Muqarab Khan could reach the gilded portals, Asaf Khan sailed in with the ease of a royal relative, much favored by the emperor. Nur Jahan flashed him a searching look, but he rewarded her mute curiosity with only a smile. Approaching closer to the emperor, he bowed slightly, his expression one of devotion and urgency. The emperor was replenishing his cup from the gold flagon beside him and turned to Asaf Khan beamishly, now that his cup was brimming with wine.

"Your Majesty, Mahabat Khan is craving your audience," Asaf Khan announced.

"Let him wait, Asaf. Share a cup of wine with the emperor." Jahangir indicated the gold flagon, where more jeweled goblets were waiting to be claimed.

"Share from the emperor's own cup, Asaf, if you wish to drink to His Majesty's health. He needs not drain this poison all by himself," Nur Jahan suggested sweetly.

"The empress commands, Asaf, and the emperor heeds not, as my Nur would tell you." Jahangir sipped his wine. "Yes, he stays disobedient to her royal wishes, just like baidaulat!" His gaze was reaching out to Nur Jahan again.

"May I sit, Your Majesty?" Asaf Khan murmured, his enthusiasm depleting by the half drunk, half mocking gaze of the emperor.

"Not for long, Asaf, not for long. The emperor wishes to commune with the spirits of Kashmir, with his own empress," Jahangir intoned evasively.

"You should admit Mahabat Khan, Your Majesty. He might have some dire news to confound our sense of peace," Nur Jahan implored, rather suggested.

"What does Mahabat have to say which appears to be of utmost urgency, Asaf?" Jahangir commanded suddenly.

"He mentioned Ambar Malik, Your Majesty, and something about his march toward Kandahar," Asaf Khan professed reluctantly.

"Then, you may summon the evil messenger, Asaf. And you may stay to witness the inquisition." Jahangir issued another command.

Asaf Khan retraced his steps obediently in order to summon Mahabat Khan to the emperor's presence. After he was gone, Jahangir and Nur Jahan's eyes met, and were arrested to each other briefly, communing in silence. Nur Jahan's eyes were shining with a mute plea, which he knew so well and condoned. His own eyes were returning to the abandoned cup on the table with the inlay of mother-of-pearl. An overwhelming sense of weariness was alighting in his eyes as well as into his soul, as he got to his feet. His gaze was turning to Mahabat Khan, whose presence was announced by Asaf Khan.

"Your Majesty. Padishah Begum." Mahabat Khan fell into two consecutive curtsies, then stood waiting to be addressed.

"Be concise in what you have to say, Mahabat. The name of Ambar Malik itself saps my strength and patience," Jahangir commanded.

"Ambar Malik, Your Majesty, has left Khirki," Mahabat Khan began with the ease of a born diplomat. "He has sent his family to the fortress of Daulatabad, and is marching toward Kandahar on the borders of Golconda. This is a friendly visit, he says, but he is pretending. Actually, he is hoping to conclude an offensive and defensive alliance with Qutbulmulk."

"And why didn't you accept Qutbulmulk's alliance yourself, Mahabat, when he was offering it to you with all the humility of a slave?" Jahangir inquired, as he began to pace absently, rather thoughtfully.

"He was seeking alliances from us both at the same time, Your Majesty.

From Prince Shah Jahan and from the imperialists." Mahabat Khan's gaze was fixed to Asaf Khan, not following the emperor in his pacing.

"Didn't Qutbulmulk send Sher Ali to you as his ambassador, Mahabat Khan?" Nur Jahan interposed quickly. "At least, that was what I understood. He was personally willing to wait on you at Dewalgaon to enlist his eldest son in the imperial service, and to profess his fidelity to the emperor." She exchanged a quick glance with Asaf Khan before returning her gaze to Mahabat Khan.

"Padishah Begum," Mahabat Khan's attempt in explaining was silenced by Jahangir's abrupt exclamation, though he kept pacing.

"Oh, that black-hearted slave! Ambar Malik, my own Abyssinian slave. Striving to win kingdoms for himself, and thwarting the will of the emperor." Jahangir's slow, deliberate pacing had nothing in common with his aimless thoughts.

"Padishah Begum..." Mahabat Khan attempted again. "That was when Adil Shah of Bijapur was seeking our alliance too. We had to choose between the two."

"Asaf! You didn't inform me about that alliance." Nur Jahan's eyes were flashing accusations at her brother, as if he was an accomplice to some devious plot.

"I did, Padishah Begum," Asaf Khan began doubtfully. "By express letter, informing you that Adil Shah is offering homage. And that he is promising a contingent of five thousand cavalry under the command of Mulla Lari for a permanent imperial service as a price for Moghul support."

"You forget, Asaf, that sealed missive was handed to me." Jahangir drifted toward his seat thoughtfully. "Another missive informing me that you sent Lashkar Khan as an emissary to Adil Khan, who was received by the king with the profoundest of respects...well." He made a wearied gesture, his gaze resting on Mahabat Khan. "So, my prudent vizier, you have left Prince Perwiz in Burhanpur, exposed to the claws of baidaulat, which he is wont to bare whenever a chance affords him."

"Prince Perwiz is surrounded by able viziers and valorous soldiers, Your Majesty," Mahabat Khan intoned confidently. "Besides, Your Majesty, I promised Mulla Muhammad to meet him at Shahpur. He is bringing a heavy contingent of horse and cavalry. Then both of us will wait upon Prince Perwiz, who is camping at Lal Bagh close to Burhanpur."

"Baidaulat is not going to swoop over Burhanpur, Mahabat, but will move toward Bengal and Allahabad first; the emperor can read his mind." Jahangir's gaze was profound, some sort of prophecy smoldering in his eyes.

"We are planning to march in that direction, Your Majesty, even before Prince Shah Jahan could think of stirring," Mahabat Khan was quick to inform.

"And does he?" was Jahangir's explosive inquiry.

"Not for a long, long time, Your Majesty. He has made Golconda his home," Mahabat Khan murmured reluctantly. "A string of desertions are gnawing at the heart of Prince Shah Jahan, Your Majesty, and he will not stake the safety of Golconda till he has gathered enough alliances to challenge the imperialists."

"Then the emperor can journey to Kashmir without the fear of his kingdoms dissolving into the mists of wars." Jahangir's thoughts were straining to catch a beam of light which could lend him comfort, if not peace.

"We would guard your kingdoms with our lives, Your Majesty," Mahabat Khan vowed with a sudden burst of passion.

"With this sincere note of a promise, Mahabat, leave us." Jahangir waved dismissal, his gaze shifting to Asaf Khan. "Asaf, look to the preparations of our journey to Kashmir." His hand was reaching out for the flagon of wine.

"And who is to check the intrigues of Ambar Malik?" Nur Jahan shot this inquiry at no one in particular.

"Your forgetful brother, Padishah Begum," Asaf Khan murmured over his shoulders. He was leaving, followed by Mahabat Khan.

"Your Majesty, don't you think you have had enough wine for one day? What's the sense in drugging your senses?" Nur Jahan pleaded.

"You have another antidote for my sufferings, love?" Jahangir sang painfully.

The emperor had filled his goblet to the brim, but his eyes were drinking pain from the pools of sorrow from the eyes of his beloved. He abandoned his goblet as if stung by the arrows of awareness. Nur Jahan's heart was pounding, as if pleading with the emperor. Both were drifting toward each other under some spell of daze and anguish. Jahangir was kneeling before her, and kissing the hem of her dress, his lips leaving a trail of kisses on her pale silks as he heaved himself up slowly and deliriously. He was kissing her bosom, throat, lips, the tip of her nose and her hair.

"Your slave, my pearl." Jahangir's very heart was murmuring endearments. "I love to kiss your skirt, your nose, each little strand of hair on your head." He folded her into one tender embrace, his barren soul searching for that loss of love, upon whose mercy its hungers could not be fed, but with the promises in dreams.

Chapter Thirteen

The emperor's palace in Kashmir, on the hill of Hari Prabat, was shining like an unpolished jewel hewn out of the very bosom of the rocks. Its wooden structure was painted in hues dark and maroon, which were shimmering under the bright haze of the sun. A myriad of windows with green awnings were almost kissing the tall cedars, as if feeling the very heart of nature with a wild abandon. Inside the palace were palatial halls, and the chambers furnished with Bokhara carpets to vie with the paintings in gilded frames. Jahangir, this afternoon, had chosen one large chamber with Persian carpets to indulge in the luxury of spending a few hours with his wives.

The emperor's health had improved since his visit to Kashmir, lending him much joy to admire the beauty of spring in his gardens. With the renewal of vigor and strength in his body and mind, he was nurturing his former tastes in being an artist and a naturalist, happily and deliciously, forgetting about his son's schemes and rebellions, and luxuriating in the sense of hope and freedom. In fact, he was possessed by a need to arrest each grain of beauty in Kashmir on the shimmering canvases which he could carry along with him on all his journeys. Some sort of fanaticism had settled upon him to cultivate this need, since the moments of his salubrity were numbered few as compared to the onslaught of mental and physical sufferings.

Since the past two weeks, the emperor's need had become paramount in his actions and thoughts. He had commanded Mansur to paint flowers, valleys, and even the deepest of ravines with rugged terrains. Mansur had become a part of the royal household. Even this particular day, he was summoned by the emperor to add finishing touches to a variety of his paintings under the close scrutiny of the emperor. A privilege, which Mansur himself so desired and cherished, Jahangir could tell by the intensity of his brushstrokes as the artist sat refining his masterworks. Jahangir was exceptionally buoyant this afternoon, attentive to the comments of his other wives, though Nur Jahan was still the cynosure of his attention. An astonishing sense of peace had visited him this time in Kashmir, as if Anarkali had come back to him, guiding his spirit toward joy and healing, even leading him toward the path of love where Nur Jahan alone stood greeting him. He was drugged by the sweetness of this gentle presence, in return, bestowing this sweetness on Nur Jahan and on all his other wives.

In conformity with his mood, Jahangir was opulently dressed. A heron plume in his red turban was further enhanced by the clusters of rubies and diamonds. Rubies in his ears, and the ropes of pearls from his neck down to his waist, were adding a smooth glow to his features, which had sloughed off their bloating and swelling.

Nur Jahan too, infected by the vivacity of this spring day, was donned in red silks the color of the Himalayan tulips. Her oval face, haloed by the sparkle of rubies and diamonds, appeared to glow with the luminescence of a white flame. A tiara of diamonds in her hair was shooting its own blue flames into her lovely eyes. Her wit too was shining along with her beauty this particular afternoon, as if infected by the buoyancy in nature with all its spring scents and colors. The large floral arrangements in jade and alabaster bowls had transported the glory of the garden into this royal chamber brimming with life and laughter. Nur Jahan was swooning with pleasure by the scented blooms all around her, barely aware of the scent of the attar of roses so munificently sprinkled on her silks. Nurunnisa, Khairunnisa, Salih Banu, Malika Jahan, Sahiba Jamali and Karamasi, among many more wives adorned with precious jewels, too, were drugged by the scented blooms of Kashmir, their spirits light and frolicking. They were luxuriating against the gold and brocaded pillows, and enjoying their favorite game of cards, Chandal Mandal. Karamasi, with a subtle laughter brimming in her eyes, was watching Sahiba Jamali's concentration and reluctance in playing the next hand. But suddenly, her attention was turned to the emperor.

"Is Prince Shahriyar coming to Kashmir, Your Majesty?" Karamasi Begum's light-brown eyes were sparkling like the agates.

"How can he, my love, when baidaulat keeps testing his prowess at war," was Jahangir's light-hearted response.

"Prince Perwiz alone can thwart the schemes of Prince Shah Jahan, Your Majesty, if you wish Prince Shahriyar's presence here in Kashmir," Sahiba Jamali murmured, her almond-shaped eyes glowing with pride at the mere thought of her valorous son.

"The prince and the emperor, then, would think of nothing but sport and hunting," Nur Jahan commented more to herself than to all the other wives so besottedly immersed in their game of cards. "Then, surely, the emperor's wives would be neglected and cast into the dungeons of silence and inactivity."

This great chamber was filled with the music of mirth from the lips of all ladies, who could not resist Nur Jahan's wit, though they could feel the fires of envy and jealousy rippling through their veins by the sheer power of her charm and beauty. Even Mansur could not restrain his smile, rather giggling to himself while adding finishing touches to the portrait of Jahangir in which the emperor was holding a glass of wine. Jahangir met the mischief in Nur Jahan's eyes, and exploded with a mirth of his own.

"The emperor would rather keep company with the rishis than with his own sons and wives!" Jahangir exclaimed. "Your wit shines less than your beauty, my Nur. It is quite dull as compared to the sparkle of mischief in your eyes."

The waves of mirth from the lips of the other wives were fading and dissolving. They were drawn into the enchanting circle of their own game and concentration. But Nur Jahan's mirth and mischief were settling into the luminous glow of her eyes.

"If you keep company with the rishis, Your Majesty, you might succumb to painful austerities. Hoping to attain the rank of a Brahman?" Nur Jahan quipped.

"Are you reading Ramayana again, Nur? The Rig Veda of your thoughts runs parallel to the holy texts splintered with a thousand avatars," Jahangir teased profoundly. "What was the name of that avatar, Nur, the one leading the life of great austerities?"

"Visvamitra, Your Majesty," Nur Jahan intoned happily. "He is the one who became the champion of Ramachandra. Sakuntala was his daughter by the nymph Meanka whom the gods, jealous of his increasing powers, sent to seduce him from his passionless life," she expounded with the passion of an avid scholar.

"You not only retain your youth and beauty, my Nur, but depths of knowledge which you gain and continue to explore." Jahangir's eyes were shining with admiration. "By now you must have concluded that knowledge and austerity purify the soul?"

"What of the body, Your Majesty, which hungers for food, defiling the altars of its soul with unsavory viands? Especially with the meat from the cows which are sacred to the Hindus?" Nur Jahan shot a challenge, as if anticipating an intellectual feast.

"That's why Moghuls don't eat beef," was Jahangir's blithering response without the least hint of ideation. "Anything that is forbidden, is either sanctified to be worshipped, or abhorred to be shunned as some evil plague." His blithe was gathering the rags of profundity. "Before the time of Bharat, the meat of cows was permitted. And cows were even killed at certain sacrifices. The reason of their prohibition is ascribed to their unwholesomeness as food. In the hot climate of Hind, the inner parts of the cow's body stay cold. The natural warmth is feeble, and the digestion weak. And cow's meat is unhealthy for anyone who lives in Hind. That's why the Indians invented *pan* filled with lime and betel-nut. A curious concoction as an appetizer, good for digestion. The betel leaf of pan inflames the body heat. The lime in the betel leaf dries up everything wet. And the betel-nut acts as an astringent on the gums, teeth and stomach."

"An emperor, who could have been a physician, Your Majesty?" Nur Jahan smiled sadly, catching the familiar look in the eyes of the emperor where Anarkali reigned supreme.

"A physician, who could never heal the ailments of his own body and soul." Jahangir smiled back. He too could not help noticing her sadness, and averted his gaze.

The emperor's heart was aflutter all of a sudden, foundering inside some vacuums of loneliness and longings. His gaze, searching the faces and forms of his wives, and wandering aimlessly, was landing on Mansur.

"Show the emperor your great works of art, Mansur, and be rewarded if your pains are worth the prize," was Jahangir's abrupt command.

"Your Majesty!" was Mansur's startled response, his brushstrokes on the canvas obeying not his fingers. Abandoning his brush on the pallet, he snatched one canvas and straggled to his feet. "This one, Your Majesty, has been touched and retouched several times in a season, and needs no improvement, unless your aesthetic tastes detect some flaws." He held out the canvas humbly.

"The glass of wine in there needs a ruby tint in its sparkling crystal." Jahangir elicited one snort of a laughter.

He was holding the canvas before him with the intensity of a connoisseur, his look at once subtle and exploring. His own portrait was gazing back at him, revealing volumes of memories sweet and tormenting. The wine glass on the canvas poised so lovingly in his hand could be seen spinning in his head like a time-clock, marking the hours of his death. But he could see no dark shadows looming against his thoughts, and he delivered this masterpiece into the hands of Nur Jahan.

"Look, Nur, isn't this a fine work of art, living and breathing? Do you think that the emperor's soul can be seen naked bleeding through these colors?" Jahangir murmured as if to himself.

"The shades in your robe, Your Majesty, match the red, red wounds in your heart, not the scars in your soul," Nur Jahan breathed intensely. "A true resemblance to your true self, no swollen eyes and no bloated features. The portrait of an emperor in good health with the stamp of regal stature and royal bearing. These ruby earrings pale before the color of your lips…this one I like better than the one with Zodiac signs in the background." Her attention was turning to Mansur, who stood there holding his breath, his gaze bright and smoldering. "An exquisite work of art, Mansur! You are a genius," she complimented profusely, returning the portrait to him.

"Show us some more, my genius artist," Jahangir commanded. "You will be rewarded with kingdoms if the emperor can yield to the wishes of the empress. And the emperor can see those wishes brimming with gifts in her eyes." His gaze was following Mansur, who was hurrying to claim and flaunt another canvas.

"It would be a blessed relief, Your Majesty, if the portraits with Christian themes in our palaces could be replaced with the portraits of the Moghuls," Sahiba Jamali exclaimed with a sudden passion, shuffling the cards quite adroitly.

"You don't like those masterpieces, my mistress of beauty? Not even the ones in the palace halls at Lahore?" Jahangir asked with a tender indulgence.

"I rather prefer the one with the Venus and Satyr, Your Majesty," Sahiba Jamali admitted reluctantly.

"My favorite is the one with the Countess of Somerset, where she is seated listlessly at her boudoir," Nurunnisa opined dreamily.

"Just because that lady in the portrait is connected with the murder of Sir Thomas Overbury?" Jahangir reminded her genially. "You sure are the mistress of mystery and intrigue, my love! Loving the faces of evil, and cultivating not the love for sanctity."

"She was interested, Your Majesty, only after you had told us that this same countess was awaiting the trial of murder." Malika Jahan was laughing to herself.

"And that portrait of Shah Abbas, Your Majesty?" Khairunnisa could not restrain to parade her dislike for that portrait in this sea of criticism. "You sent Farrukh Beg, Your Majesty, all the way to Isfahan to draw and paint the face of that despotic Persian monarch. I still can't understand."

"That face is classic, my love." Jahangir laughed. "Portrayed thus, so that the noble deceits of the Persian monarch could stay frozen in time." His gaze was returning to Mansur, who was waiting for the emperor to applaud his next masterpiece.

"This one, Mansur, is the classic depiction of poetry in art." Jahangir's gaze was lured to the painting like a magnet. "The lion is strong and ferocious. And the lamb, much too small, to dare taste the salt of mighty kingdoms." He was lost in watching his own version of the Mercator's map.

One lion was sprawled on the canvas, right across from Persia and Turkey, pushing the poor Persian lamb into the Mediterranean.

"Another masterpiece, Nur. Should we take this one to Agra? Perhaps to Lahore?" Jahangir was parting with this one reluctantly.

"If Thomas Roe was to see this version of the Mercator's map, Your Majesty, he would jump right past the Atlantic, hoping for the Red Sea to part and swallow him." Nur Jahan smiled. "We should hang it on the very walls of ether between sky and earth."

Jahangir was lost to the charms of the next canvas, and was not even listening. A collage of colors was glaring at him with the daggers of challenges in its eyes. This scene was depicting a large throne of the emperor. He himself was seated regally on this jeweled throne. Four holy men were seated next to him. The Sultan of Turkey had his own humble seat below this jeweled throne. James 1 of England was standing farther down, quite insignificant in form and stature. The potentates of Spain and Portugal had no place on this canvas, as Jahangir had ordered their murky forms replaced by graceful horses. He was awed, rather moved, how his orders were portrayed so beautifully with the loyalty of a soldier in the Artist. *Sinewy, graceful steeds, more worthy than the kings and the sultans*, Jahangir was thinking, not even aware of a thin smile parting his lips. This canvas too was relinquished to the approbation of the empress, while he himself was eager to explore the mysteries in the next one.

"A soft halo should grace the head of the emperor too," Nur Jahan was murmuring to herself, admiring the shade of each nimbus over the heads of the four holy men. Her low comment was unheard by Jahangir, whose attention could not be torn away from the next canvas.

This great painting was revealing the emperor's great foe, Ambar Malik, his eyes dark and profound. The Abyssinian slave was crouched, rather crushed under the weight of the globe, his eyes uplifted and his face ghastly. The scene overhead this pitiful figure was somewhat bizarre. A giant globe was resting on the back of an ox, and the ox was standing on a goldfish half the size of the globe.

"You will draw the portrait of the emperor standing on this globe, Mansur, in an act of shooting the arrow at that cadaver of a foe." Jahangir sprang to his feet. His thoughts were lurching in the abyss of Deccan and falling on baidaulat with the force of the avalanches unpredictable. "A time to explore the garden in the very heart of Hari Prabat." He clapped his hands. His eyes were shining with anticipation, and his thoughts struggling to wrench themselves free from under the gliding avalanches.

"Your Majesty, Your Majesty…can't you wait…this game will be over…" Several protests were breaking forth on the lips of the emperor's wives. They did not wish to abandon their cherished game of Chandal Mandal.

"The emperor will have to wait till eternity, if he heeds the wishes of his wives." Jahangir turned to Nur Jahan, holding out his hands.

The ghost of Anarkali was present in this garden of Eden as the emperor and the empress promenaded side-by-side in utmost silence. The Dal Lake, shimmering white in the distance, was fringed with saffron from shore to shore. The wooden palace in the background could be seen looming like a fortress of fire, since it was smitten red and gold by the flood of sunshine. Nur Jahan seemed to be inhaling the scent of life from each bloom and scene with a sense of wild abandon. But her senses were too keen not to notice the scent of the dead beloved throbbing so achingly within the heart of the emperor. This particular afternoon, her eyes were shining with the intensity of the blue, Peruvian nights.

Nur Jahan, though accustomed to sharing the presence of Anarkali with the emperor, had grown quite defensive and protective in her thoughts. Right now, in an effort to still her pain, she was courting the mists of illusions where her reveries could be seen crystallized. Her heart was lonesome, and the longings in there chilled, yet smoldering. She was a part of this world, yet not belonging to it. In a cosmic sense, she had begun to experience the serenity of the vast oceans inside the very bowers of her reveries, absorbing the warmth and sunshine from without, and not knowing the turbulent depths from within. She was a part of this one great delusion where her wit and gaiety were the gifts of the subconscious, not the rewards of her labored intellect.

The only reality which could divert Nur Jahan's attention from the mists of illusion, was the living, throbbing entity of fear inside her. This fear had grown and had multiplied within her from one grain of sand to a desert of sand dunes. This desert of sand dunes had begotten many more fears of its own, since the emperor's own life was caught inside the grinding-wheel of ailments and recoveries. Her fears were many, but the more potent ones were the numbered few. Prince Shah Jahan's plethora of rebellions was one great fear, and Prince Shahriyar's shaky legacy was the other. Mahabat Khan's rise in power was another billowing fear. And yet the most terrible of them all was the fear to lose Jahangir into the shadows of death where ailments seemed to be hurling him closer to it, each hour of the day and season. She could share the emperor's dead beloved with him, but not the idea of his own death, where he would be no more. *His death will be my oblivion,* she was thinking. *The living, breathing lamp of my own life dying, yet knowing no death.* She could think no more.

Jahangir, unlike Nur Jahan, was not thinking at all. He was basking in the presence of the dead beloved, yet aware of the living beloved beside him. Both these beloveds had become one to him, yet his longings were not ever appeased. Though lately, he had discovered a subtle sense of peace, as if drifting toward his lost beloved on the wings of hope and anticipation. This hope alone had the power to hurl him back to his love for life with the ardor of pain and joy in loving and living. Against this facade of a reality, he had succeeded in erecting his own fortress of defense to ward off all pains, most of all, the pain of betrayals and the rebellions. As soon as he had stepped out into his garden, the avalanches in his head were silenced. The gates of his inner fortress were secured, keeping at bay all tides of tragedies and hopelessness. Swiftly and vaguely, his senses were getting drunk with the scents from love absent and love present. His very thoughts were seeking oblivion, cherishing more the scent of death than the odor of living. His sight itself was drinking wine from the goblets of the Himalayan tulips.

A gazebo of color and fragrance were the red, red roses on the white trellises. The lilacs in their profusion of purple were spraying their own perfume over the fountains and down the terraces. The planes and poplars were tracing their lace patterns on the lawns, borrowed from the glint and sparkle in sunshine. The red gravel paths and the marble terraces were a beautiful maze before the eyes of the royal couple, but their feet were coming to a slow halt by the lakes reflecting the glory of the mighty willows. They stood contemplating the willows, their eyes reaching down the very heart of the valley of Lar, where the cypresses stood lofty and shimmering. The cherry trees, donned in the white mists of their own early blooms, were attracting the emperor's attention.

Jahangir's feet, quite will-lessly, were straying toward the white terraces where vestal lilies in brass pots appeared to sing hymns to the very face of peace and serenity in nature. Here, it was all light and tranquility. The hush was so stark that not even a blade of grass could be heard stirring. The air, all perfumed, was holding its breath, as if afraid to taint the purity of this stillness. The entire landscape of silk and velvet, of color and perfume, was frozen, it seemed, in its own glory of freshness and pulchritude.

Jahangir had named this garden Nur Afza, meaning Light Increasing. And now, the light alone was accosting him as he waded toward the marble terraces. This light was shattering his sense of oblivion, and coiling around his awareness. Nur Jahan was his dearest of light-shadow, not lingering far behind him. From where he stood watching from the highest terrace, he could see the unrolling of tapestry in color with a fresh sense of awe and gratitude. Though his former sense of peace and emptiness was splintering, his heart was bubbling forth to embrace nature and beauty into the very arms of his soul. Another sense of peace and emptiness was awakening inside him, with which he was too familiar. Anarkali was with him, his heart longing to reach out and possess her in the body of Nur Jahan. His gaze was alighting on a pair of mainas perched on one branch of the mighty Chenar. These birds were engaged in some squabble of the worst domestic violence, it seemed. They had begun to chirp and lash their anger at one another with sharp beaks, and were breaking the hush of this lovely afternoon. The wind itself was unfurling its wings, caressive and frolicking. Jahangir was turning to Nur Jahan, the heron plume in his red turban swaying gleefully.

"Look at those mainas, Nur." Jahangir's tone was brimming with the enthusiasm of a naturalist. "Once my father saw the same kind here in Kashmir. The same kind of strident, implacable pair. My father asked one of the viziers what was the reason of their fighting. He answered that the male insisted on pairing, while the female wouldn't accede to his demands. The vizier proposed further that if their nest was to be searched, blood stains would be found to confirm his assertion. The nest was searched and his assertion was found true. Isn't is strange, Nur, how even the voices of the birds change in conformity with their moods?" His gaze was seeking answers.

"Not so strange, Your Majesty, if one is acquainted with the Hindu philosophy from their holy scriptures." Nur Jahan smiled.

"So, you assume that the emperor is not acquainted with the Hindu scriptures or their philosophy, my pearl!" Jahangir exclaimed. "A besotted knight in the wilderness of ignorance, that's how the emperor appears to you against the seat of your own wisdom?"

"You yourself enlightened me on this subject, Your Majesty, remember?" Nur Jahan's own light-hearted gaiety was returning. "The doctrine of the vital airs! How the abdomen is considered to be the seat of fire, and how it keeps the heat of the body intact? And how the same internal heat plays an important part in the production of voice."

"And how the emperor forgets, my Nur, blissfully forgets!" Jahangir waved his arms in mock despair. "How you possess and retain the knowledge of the worlds, created or uncreated? Pray, refresh the emperor's memory, what did I say?"

"I retain only fragments here and there, Your Majesty, that's all." Nur Jahan laughed. "You wouldn't like to feel those fragments, would you, Your Majesty?"

"I must, my Nur, if those fragments can patch my memory into some semblance of a pattern, which I seem to erase and reconstruct at times," Jahangir murmured.

"Well, Your Majesty, I will try to reconstruct it myself." Nur Jahan's eyes were gathering sadnesses, if not profundities. "What did you say, yes…when the animal soul wishes to speak, the man acts directly through the tongues of abdominal fire. This fire mixes quickly with the vital air pervading the ligament known as Brahma Granthi, below the navel. This mixture then journeys through the chest into the head, and escapes through the mouth. I can't recall the rest, with the exception that there are twenty-two *srutis*, or particles of sound, discernible to the ear." Her attention was drifted down the fretwork of ponds and canals where the goldfish floated freely.

"These fragments graze not even the hem of my recollections, my Nur." Jahangir watched her wistfully. "And yet my mind is unfolding a story about one Raja with all the intensity of a rude intrusion." He sighed to himself. "Come, love, let us make our pilgrimage to our favorite lake. We must visit our children, our goldfish with gold rings in their noses. Isn't it blissful not to have a care in the world?" He went past her and began dismounting the terrace steps.

"The bliss in life comes to those, Your Majesty, who mourn not for the losses in the past or present, and who cease to fear the misfortunes in the future," Nur Jahan murmured to herself. The path flanked by irises was absorbing her attention.

"Yes, such a brand of reality is engraved in the emperor's soul. And the emperor sees nothing but lies and illusions," Jahangir intoned rather cheerfully.

"Since vital airs have escaped my memory, Your Majesty, why don't you too practice their rhythm? Liberate your thoughts from the burden of that intrusive Raja, and delight this whole garden with your voice? The memories, the recollections?" Nur Jahan chanted effusively.

"He would be lost to the emperor forever then, and you alone would preserve him in the everlasting font of your memory-book." Jahangir laughed. "And yet, I might as well pour it into the treasure chest of your world, for you are my world," he continued with the urgency of a scholar who could not lay his hands on anything substantial. "In the country of Dravida, there was a Raja named Manu. Being ten hundred thousand years old, he had withdrawn himself from the worldly concerns, living simply and practicing great austerities. One day he was performing his ablutions on the banks of the river Kritamala when a fish came into his hand and said, 'Preserve me.' He kept it in his hand day and night. When it grew in size, he put it in a cup. It grew larger, and he transferred it into a pitcher. When the pitcher couldn't contain it, he preserved it in a well, then a lake, and finally into the Ganges. When it grew too large for the Ganges, he took it to the ocean. When the ocean was filled with its ever-increasing bulk, a revelation dawned upon him. He heard a loud, commanding voice. *I am the Supreme Being. I have assumed the form of this creature for thy salvation and that of a few of the elect. After seven days, the world will be destroyed and a flood shall cover the earth. Get thou into a certain ark with a few of the righteous together, and with the divine books and choice medicinal herbs. And fasten the ark to this horn which cometh out of me.* The deluge continued for one million, seven hundred and twenty-eight thousand years, after which it subsided..." He was seeking the comfort of the marble bench, while trying to quell the sudden tempest of mirth.

"All the fables and the mysteries, Your Majesty, which confound our senses." Nur Jahan joined the emperor in his mirth, claiming her seat next to him. "Another such apocalyptic vision sane or saintly comes to my mind." Her eyes were teasing the fish in the lake, their gold rings glittering in the waters. "In Kalkyavatara, it is written that a time will come when not even one just prince will be left upon this earth. Iniquity will abound, and the grain will become excessively dear. The age of men will be shortened, so they won't be able to live beyond the age of thirty. Death and devastation will reign supreme. To remedy this disorder, a prince will appear on a white horse, flashing a sword for the final destruction of the ones who love inequity. And that prince will re-establish righteousness." She was watching the cypresses sigh and tremble.

"And I am the Adam, and you my lovely Eve." Jahangir slipped his arm around her waist tenderly and possessively.

"Not true, Your Majesty, not true. Wrong place, wrong time," Nur Jahan quipped merrily. "The story I read says Adam, after his fall from the Paradise, was thrown on the island of Ceylon. His consort, in Jiddah on the Red Sea. Azrail, the angel of death, in Sistan. The serpent in Ispahan, and the peacock in Hindustan."

"And our fish-children tossed into Dal Lake in this Eden-valley of Kashmir," was Jahangir's hilarious response. He folded her into his arms, kissing her.

"Your Majesty." Nur Jahan gasped for breath. "The fish with the pearl rings are my children, Your Majesty, and the ones with the gold rings, yours," she muttered.

"Not ours, my love, you mean not ours, the whole lot of them?" Jahangir murmured profoundly. "Virgin conceptions, they are, and vestal heathens perhaps, the entire brood of them." He released her, abandoning his senses to the beauty of this Eden. "This sort of joy and peace comes once in a lifetime, Nur. Once," he murmured.

"Didn't I tell you, Your Majesty, we would always return to this paradise," Nur Jahan murmured back.

"Yes, this joy and peace, once in a lifetime," Jahangir repeated to himself, his gaze piercing the depth of this lake where the beauty of Kashmir lay slumbering. "This joy and peace, returning in dreams only. Hauntingly sweet! Murmuring and teasing that this dream will never be repeated. The dream itself murmuring and mocking that such joy and peace will not ever return. That this dream itself shall fade, not ever returning, not even in the promise of dreams." His gaze had discovered the ghost of Anarkali down yonder. She was wading toward him with the lamps of love shining in her eyes.

"Why this sudden sadness, Your Majesty?" Nur Jahan watched his taut profile with a sudden alarm.

"Not sadness, my Nur! The emperor is talking about joy and peace. One almost wishes to die, to arrest this essence of..." Jahangir intoned sadly. "Yet, sadness is not far behind. Soon, the news of fresh rebellions...baidaulat...the emperor has to return once again..." His gaze was returning to her slowly. "My love, my sweetest, profoundest of loves," his arms were tightening around her once again, "to consecrate our love, we must be one, in body and soul, right here."

"Your Majesty!" protested Nur Jahan. "What if someone..." She was swept into the currents of pain and joy, the wild, hungry kisses of the emperor scalding her lips.

Suddenly, the nature's own fury of lust and desire were whirling around Nur Jahan's senses like the mindless hurricanes. She was yielding and groaning, ashamed and delirious. The rape of Anarkali in this Eden of Kashmir was some searing violence in her own body and soul. The ripping of silks, exposing her breasts, was some liquid corruption down the very rivers of her misery and helplessness. She could feel the weight of male urgency stabbing at her lotus of awareness, and piercing it with a razor-sharp violence. The body of the emperor was crushing her under its burden of urgency and violence, but then it was caught into convulsions of fresh agony, not of the passionate spirit, but of the body shaking and crumbling. He was gasping for breath, trying to ward off the familiar assault of asthma. With a cry choked inside her, Nur Jahan was rocking the emperor into her arms. Her own senses were gathering mists dark and tormenting, and succumbing to prayers mute and lacerating.

The beauty of spring had lost its violence of youth, but the ailing emperor was reluctant to part with the memory of this eternal spring in its faded glory. More than two weeks had slipped past since his illness in the garden, and he was still lingering at the altar of bliss with Anarkali, who had become one, in body and soul, with Nur Jahan. This particular bright morning with the scent of spring filtering inside the parlor, Jahangir was feeling better and thinking of venturing out into the garden. Tenderly ministered by Nur Jahan during the assaults of his fever, asthma and delirium, he had regained enough strength to sit up and enjoy the luxury of a royal parlance. More than that, he had the energy and awareness to command his royal physicians, forbidding them to enter his chamber, and choosing Nur Jahan as his sole physician. Still drugged, rather deluded by the bliss of an accolade with Anarkali, he was courting the idle pleasure of staying in bed and dreaming. Besides, he was discovering his newly found sense of bliss-solitude and luxuriating in the sense of oneness with Nur Jahan. His thoughts were mired in some sort of spiritual swamp, daring not to accost the realm of the subconscious, lest he meet Anarkali once again and immolate his life at the ruins of desires terrible and unprofaned. A surreal sense of peace had become his companion, swaddling him into the sheets of bliss and comfort. He could lay in bed for hours without getting impatient, and would drift into dreams while talking with Nur Jahan, rarely touching the hem of unreality, and seeking the company of Anarkali only in his sleep.

Nur Jahan had no such luxury of pagan dreams, but irreverent nightmares. Right after the *rape of Anarkali*, as she called that passionate interlude, a messenger from Agra burdened with ill imports had arrived in Kashmir. Such news could not be unburdened before the ailing emperor, so Nur Jahan alone had withstood the first impact, without flinching or revealing the flood of her inner tribulations. She had succeeded in numbing her senses against fear and shock, heeding only the deepest of her fears concerning the emperor's health.

Prince Shah Jahan had assumed the guise of the Roman Antony in Bengal, though he had lost his power, and had succumbed to self-exile. But Mahabat Khan was attaining the power of Brutus, and coveting the Hind of the Moghul Caesars with the ambition as stealthy as the daggers of revolt concealed inside the robe of any corrupted rebel, Roman or Moghul. Nur Jahan, softening the import of such news in her mind, was waiting for a chance to release them when the emperor was fit to receive such a medley of evil reports.

The devoted messenger, Fadai Khan, was instructed by Nur Jahan herself what to say and when to reveal, only when commanded by her. Beside tending the emperor's needs, she had ordered preparations for their journey to Agra, hoping and praying for the emperor's health, and longing to be back in Agra to preserve the throne for Prince Shahriyar. Since Prince Shah Jahan had rendered himself impotent by his own acts of greed and rebellion, depriving himself of any claim to the throne, Nur Jahan was ready to subjugate his pride and ambition to any legacy of the Moghuls. The ambition of Mahabat Khan alone was cutting her wits to shreds, but she was equipped with enough ammunition against him to deflate his ego along with his treacherous designs. This bright morning, she too was feeling serene and optimistic. Her thoughts were shuffling the ill imports in a manner appropriate for the emperor's ears, where they could trickle down his awareness slowly and gently. Fadai Khan was to be summoned at the opportune moment, acting as a prudent messenger, obeying only the sole commands and the instructions of the empress. Prince Perwiz was another contender for the throne, Nur Jahan was thinking, while softening the blows of ill imports within her mind. This was another fresh obstacle on the battlefield of her gentle schemes; her thoughts were wandering as she sat at her chiffonier, attended by her lady-in-waiting, Mehr Harwi. Mehr Harwi was parading jewels and dresses before the empress for her approval and selection. Nur Jahan was not paying much attention, her thoughts murmuring that she would not confront that obstacle until it dared challenge her own royal patience.

Jahangir, oblivious to the combat of schemes and gentleness inside the mind of his absent empress, was comfortably installed in the parlor. He was dictating his memoirs to Mutamid Khan, who was the statue of obedience and discretion. Jahangir was seated on his gold throne, the velvets and brocades under him rippling in pools of sunshine which was streaming through the glass windows in sparkling shades. His complexion was rather sallow against the ripples of deep purple on his silk robe, the color of wild berries. His jeweled cummerbund was matching the glittering rings on his fingers, which were lending some warmth to his cold, white hands. Mutamid Khan, seated on the Persian carpet in colorful hues of rosettes and medallions, was awed by the aura of peace and serenity in this room. Even the gilt portraits and the gleaming tapestries were enveloped in some sort of hush, but he was barely aware of their beauty and design. He was further awed by the changing of colors in the emperor's eyes, from soft blue to liquid violet.

Jahangir sat contemplating the jade and crystal vases brimming with purple, saffron and white tuberoses. He had just finished dictating the details of the weighing ceremonies on his lunar and solar birthdays of this current year, and was now resigned to his own world of quiet reflections. His recollections were a mingling of incredulity and astonishment at the flight of years which were dissolved into a whirlwind of chaos and illusion. This year branded with the number 1625 was making a bold entry into his head. Time and timelessness, and the emperor was fifty-six years old, and had reigned for twenty-five years already. This thought alone was carving a rent in Jahangir's thoughts, blowing it into a bubble of illusion which would never burst. His gaze was alighting on the musician, Muhammed Nayi, who was evoking the loveliest of tunes on his flute. Seated next to him was Shauqi, equally in rapport with his mandolin. Jahangir's gaze was wandering again, and his thoughts entering the passionate realms where he could be seen trundling on the rungs of youth.

Still young... One mockery of a thought in Jahangir's head was kindling to a flaming absurdity. *Only of late...weak and suffering...the orgy of fever, asthma, delirium. No less virile or youthful, otherwise.* His thoughts were tangled somewhere into the marshland of Vedanta.

There's one lamp in this house, by whose rays. Wherever I look there is an assembly. This couplet by Baba Fighani was coming to Jahangir's mind. His thoughts were clinging to the pages of Vedanta where a Brahmin's life was sectioned into four stages.

"Mutamid Khan, what are the Hindi names for the four periods in a Brahmin's life, explicitly prescribed by the Vedanta? And what do they pertain to, do you recall?" Jahangir asked abruptly.

"All those names were recorded in the journal of your memoirs from the previous year, Your Majesty, and I remember them clearly," Mutamid Khan responded with the delight of a devoted chronicler. "The first period is called Brahmacharya, Your Majesty. When a Brahmin boy is only eight years old. At that time he is initiated into a stage of maturity, abstaining from bodily pleasures, living on alms and studying the Divine Scriptures. The second period is Grihast, when he marries at the age of sixteen and leads a family life till he is forty-eight. The third period is Banprasta, when he retires to a jungle with his wife for twelve years, communing with nature, and providing food for himself and his wife from the bounties of nature whatever they may offer. The fourth, Your Majesty..." He could not continue as Nur Jahan floated into the parlor as some apparition of light and beauty.

Nur Jahan was wearing white silks with billowing sleeves, all stitched with sapphires. Her oval face, wreathed in flaxen curls, was luminous by the sparkle of diamonds and sapphires in her hair. She indeed was a beautiful apparition haloed in light, gliding toward the emperor with the aura of a goddess right out of some heavenly mists. Mutamid Khan bowed his head, and the musicians fell to curtsying in the same manner. Jahangir simply smiled, indicating the gilt chair beside him, and returning his attention to Mutamid Khan.

"The fourth one, my prudent scholar, is called Sarvabiyas. The emperor's memory is favoring him this morning," Jahangir intoned cheerfully. "That is when a Brahmin leaves all his possessions, contemplating God for the rest of his life."

"Are you talking about some mendicant, Your Majesty, who might have been the son of a wealthy king?" Nur Jahan asked softly.

"If you are thinking about Buddha, then you are sadly mistaken, my empress." Jahangir flashed her an adoring look. "For some vague reason, my empress, the science of Vedanta was coming to the emperor's mind."

"The science of Vedanta better be studied at Agra, Your Majesty." Nur Jahan tossed a careless remark.

"Are you getting wearied of Kashmir, my empress?" Jahangir asked.

"No, Your Majesty," Nur Jahan murmured. "But the affairs at Hind must not be neglected for long, Your Majesty."

"They are secure in the hands of our skillful vizier, Mahabat Khan, are they not?" Jahangir murmured back, his gaze intense and searching.

"He is ambitious, Your Majesty." Nur Jahan smiled.

"All men are ambitious, my empress, I thought you knew that by now." Jahangir flashed her an enigmatic look. "With the exception of a pious few who have lost everything, even their sense of wit and reason."

"Piety should be applauded, Your Majesty, not condemned." The blue pools in Nur Jahan's eyes were unfolding ideation, if not mysteries.

"Only if their piety could benefit the world in some way, temporal and spiritual, my empress." Jahangir's own eyes were gathering profundities. "If all of us favored the concept of dispossession, thinking of feeding on spiritual gluttony alone, and hoping to live on alms proffered to us, then there would be no one left with any material possessions to distribute alms to the ones seeking."

"Spirituality does benefit, Your Majesty, in some subtle ways, if it is not caught into the swamp of greed and cruelty. Spirituality is not for the ambitious, for ambition can never reach the shores of spirituality, which rejects vice and corruption." Nur Jahan's gaze was smoldering with some inner fire of torment, which she could not voice.

"Ambition, mentioned by you twice in one sitting, my empress, means that you are concealing some important matters which the emperor should be aware of." Jahangir's gaze was holding her captive. "Has Mahabat Khan, by any chance, shown any signs of disloyalty? Or has he usurped some kingdoms?"

"No, Your Majesty. He is wise enough not to uncloak his disloyalties until he has gained enough power to act upon his spurious designs," Nur Jahan offered reluctantly.

"Then he has designs?" Jahangir murmured an inquiry.

"Not obvious ones, Your Majesty. He pretends to be devoted to you." Nur Jahan smiled.

"And what pretense on your part, my empress, is making you while away this time in riddles?" Jahangir asked intensely. "A messenger from Agra, perhaps? You are shielding the emperor from the pain of some details dark and unfortunate. Baidaulat, rising in defiance and rebellion once again, is that it?"

"True, Your Majesty, Fadai Khan is here from Agra. Fortunes are on our side, though…" Nur Jahan's measured toned were silenced by an abrupt command from the emperor.

"Mutamid Khan, summon that wretch of a messenger to our presence." Jahangir's eyes were gathering impatience, if not anger.

"Prince Shah Jahan is suing for reconciliation, Your Majesty, that's why we have to return to Agra." Nur Jahan's discretion itself was melting against the beacon of accusations in Jahangir's eyes. "You were ill, Your Majesty, and I didn't wish to burden you with something which carried no urgent threat."

"Always the gentle physician of time, concealing eternity in her eyes to heal the emperor," Jahangir mocked tenderly.

Fadai Khan, escorted by Mutamid Khan, was bowing before the emperor and the empress, his expression one of utter devotion and humility.

"What wars have been brewing inside the heart of Hind, Fadai Khan, while the emperor has been away? Be succinct in your report, yet leave no detail missing. The emperor has not visited his gardens for two whole weeks, and he is dying to take a stroll." Jahangir's tone was impatient and commanding.

"All the wars have been fought, Your Majesty, only the results are simmering and craving your attention." Fadai Khan complied promptly. "Since Mahabat Khan had made alliance with Adil Khan of Bijapur, Ambar Malik, in his alarm and confusion, retrieving his guns and ammunition from Daulatabad, had hastened to storm and besiege Sholapur. Prince Perwiz and Mahabat Khan were still in Bijapur, putting the affairs to order and gaining alliances, when Ambar Malik was left free to attack Sholapur, which being the bone of contention between Adil Khan and Nizamul Mulk. Prince Shah Jahan, being informed of these events, had left Orissa, and had hastened to Sholapur enroute to Teligana and Golconda. The prince was heartily welcomed by Ambar Malik, and the two had formed a close alliance to defeat the imperialists in Burhanpur before Prince Perwiz and Mahabat Khan could reach there. Ambar Malik was bent on conquering Sholapur, while Prince Shah Jahan had proceeded toward Burhanpur under a large contingent of reinforcements from Ambar Malik. The fort of Burhanpur was defended by Sarbuland Rai whom Mahabat Khan had posted to receive further reinforcements from Mulla Muhammad. Prince Shah Jahan was not slack in making attack on the fort of Burhanpur under the guidance of his skilled generals, Shah Quli and Abdullah Khan. Shah Quli had succeeded in seizing the citadel, but due to the want of further support, had capitulated. Then Prince Shah Jahan had made a second attack, but was defeated. He was still preparing for a third one when Prince Perwiz and Mahabat Khan had arrived at the head of large forces. Prince Shah Jahan was forced to retire to

Rohangarh in the Balaghat, where he suffered a severe attack of yellow fever. During the prince's illness, his general, Abdullah Khan, under the spell of some religious zeal, left his camp. This pious general has now renounced the world and is settled in Indore to meditate on God. And Prince Shah Jahan, under the spell of his own repentance for his unfilial conduct, as he says, is imploring pardon from you, Your Majesty."

"Is Baidaulat still ill?" was Jahangir's abrupt inquiry.

"Not in good health, Your Majesty. Still recovering," was Fadai Khan's abashed response, overwhelmed by this sudden revelation that the emperor still loved his son.

"Crossing through a sea of confusion, men attain liberty from chaos." Jahangir's eyes were gathering the clouds of pain and sadness. "A body which is bleating to fight with the arm of its strength achieves no gain when the arm of fortune has abandoned one's body and soul." His gaze was intense and profound. "And what bounties Mahabat Khan is adding to his laurels of victories?" This inquiry was torn out of his mute pain.

"Only the ones he wishes to claim from the wealth of your generosities, Your Majesty," Fadai Khan offered reluctantly.

"And if the emperor finds otherwise, he would hang you alive on the tallest cedar in Kashmir." Jahangir shot one missile of a command.

"He married his daughter to Khwaja Burkhudar, Your Majesty. The lucky groom is the son of Naksh Abandi," Fadai Khan blurted out in all consternation.

"And without the royal consent of the emperor?" Jahangir exclaimed. "And what else, Fadai Khan? You will be stripped naked and fed to the beasts in these pine-valleys if you dare conceal the treacheries of Mahabat Khan or of any of my undutiful subjects." His face was flushed and his eyes shining.

"It is rumored, Your Majesty, that he has collected large sums of money from the recent campaigns, sending no due payments to the royal treasuries," was Fadai Khan's flustered response. "He has accumulated quite a selection of the choicest elephants too, Your Majesty, and he has no intention of contributing any to the imperial forces at Agra," he added, as if trying to deflect the daggers of rage from the very eyes of the emperor.

"Oh, the ignorant beasts called men, who know not their appetites till they are choked with the morsels of their own greed and gluttony." Jahangir got to his feet, waving his arm in a gesture of dismissal. "Back to Agra, where treason sits high on the…" He slumped back on his throne, gasping for breath.

"Quick, summon Hakim Qasim." Nur Jahan was on her feet, her heart sinking against the edicts of dark fate.

Chapter Fourteen

The only dark fate which Nur Jahan had feared the most, was the illness of the emperor, following him to the very gates of Agra. This fateful journey from Kashmir to Agra was beset by a heap of challenges, which the emperor had to confront and overcome. The ailing emperor had grown intemperate, bemoaning eternally the loss of the pine-valleys where he could have stayed if left free from the burdens of his own royal duties. Nur Jahan's love had helped him regain some semblance of health, but not until he had found rest and comfort in his own palace at Agra.

Jahangir had forbidden all even to mention the name of Prince Shah Jahan in his presence, turning a deaf ear to his son's pleas at reconciliation. He was slowly and most willingly relinquishing all claims of sovereignty into the hands of Nur Jahan. During the period of the emperor's convalescence, the empress was given charge of all the state affairs. Her decisions were to be applauded and her commands obeyed, by the explicit instructions of the emperor's own wishes and commands. One whole month of rest and carefree abandon had worked wonders on the emperor's health and resilience. He was fit to share the burden of his royal duties, finally emerging forth as the emperor incarnate. Endowed with such bursts of energy at times, he could feel he was ready to mete out pardons or punishments according to the edicts of his own will and justice.

Nur Jahan had become the emperor's revered saint behind the veil of this astonishing transformation, his staff and his salvation! Paradoxically, this salvation was guarded by the vision of Anarkali, and he had begun to drink heavily once again, exceeding his portion of wine one cup each day, and adding more each succeeding day, falling into the welcoming arms of peace and serendipity.

This particular afternoon too, with a flagon of wine by his side, Jahangir was feeling a sense of power and liberty. He was the master of his own will and decisions. Donned in richly embroidered robe of Chinese silk, he was a paragon of royal glory too. He was seated on his gold throne in his favorite palace at Agra, yet sailing on white clouds over the lovely vistas in Kashmir, his mind transporting him there in a gold chariot harnessed by white steeds. A plethora of commands and decisions were escaping the fantastic visions in his reveries, which could hasten his journey to the Eden of his desire. This very day, he was to send a letter of pardon to Prince Shah Jahan, and to conclude the process of reconciliation without further delay. As to the fate of Mahabat Khan, he was to be transferred to Bengal. A farman was already sent to Mahabat Khan in Ranthambor that he was to repair to Bengal immediately. Mahabat Khan was staying with Prince Perwiz at the castle of Ranthambor, and quite content with his duties as the most amicable of the governors. Both he and the prince had formed some sort of coalition, and were expecting no such orders from the emperor. Mahabat Khan was to hand over the fort of Ranthambor to Baqar Khan, and to proceed to Bengal. Prince Perwiz was to stay there and accept Jahan Lodi as his new governor.

Nur Jahan, seated by the emperor, could not possibly divine the gold chariot harnessed in his mind, her own thoughts earthbound. She was contemplating the dancers and the musicians. The bodies of the young girls in ripples of chiffons were a whirlwind of colors in her wandering thoughts. She was awaiting the outcome of her own decisions through the lips of the emperor, the decisions and commands which she herself had inculcated into the emperor's head by the sheer witchcraft of her own will and desperation, her will to conquer her enemies and the enemies of the emperor, her desperation to share the emperor's love along with the ghost of Anarkali, and to defeat the mental and physical ailments of the emperor with the most potent brew of all time, the brew of her own love and hope, garnished with the will to succeed. She was molded in her chair like one portrait exquisite, where the brush strokes of the artist could be seen accentuating her very silks in patterns of gold and crimson flowers, a portrait which had succeeded (without the emperor doubting or detecting) in diluting the emperor's wine with water before it was brought to him.

Nur Jahan's wit, right this moment, was slashed with fears and doubts. Though with her practiced will, she could make water taste like wine to gratify the parched thirsts and hungers of the emperor, she had thought. Right now, she was praying, praying for the emperor's health, and praying that he wouldn't notice her ingenious concoction of less wine and more water. Her gaze was sweeping over the gilded portraits on the wall, more so to still her fears than to admire the works of art. Madonna and the Child. The Last

THE MOGHUL HEDONIST

Supper. The Christ on the Cross. Her gaze was lingering over the painting in oval frame, where the Virgin Mother stood haloed by the light of her own innocence and holiness. She was tearing her gaze away, shifting her attention toward the emperor.

"You look rested and jubilant this afternoon, Your Majesty." Nur Jahan smiled sweetly. "How delightful it is to feel at peace, and to know the blessings of good health."

"This joy is in anticipation of our journey to Kashmir, my Nur, my Light." Jahangir smiled in return. "The valleys of Kashmir are calling us, Nur. And our children, with gold and pearl rings in their noses! Joyfully, they await our return."

"They would rejoice more at our freedom, Your Majesty, if the affairs at Agra were peacefully settled." Nur Jahan's gaze was shifting to Mutamid Khan.

"They are, they are, in my mind and inside my heart, my empress." Jahangir drained his goblet thirstily. "And they will be committed to paper this very day, before we march to our Eden on the waves of bliss." He laughed.

Before Nur Jahan could respond, Asaf Khan was announced by Hushiyar Khan at the guarded portals. He appeared to sail on the waves of his own inner mirth, though he had no cause to rejoice. But his heart was giddy with some mysterious absurdity of its own, which he could neither dispel nor explore.

"Your Majesty. Padishah Begum." Asaf Khan bowed ceremoniously.

"Welcome, my kin and my friend." Jahangir indicated him a seat below the throne. "Feel free to receive the bounties of our love, for the emperor is happy today, and is favored by God's blessings in health and prosperity. What happy news you bring to add to our happiness?" he asked suddenly.

"The most propitious news, Your Majesty." Asaf Khan balanced his weight on the velvet seat with the delight of a favored courtier. "Under the grace of your favor, Your Majesty, the Dutch have established their first factory in Bengal in the town of Chinsura, a few miles off the Portuguese settlement of Hugli. More trade with the Dutch will check the influence of the Portuguese, Your Majesty, and more revenues from Bengal," he concluded rather vaguely.

"The emperor's generosity was extended to the English, also, granting them free trade throughout the Moghul empire, including Bengal," Jahangir ruminated thoughtfully. "Not long ago, two years from hence, the English were granted free trade with Surat. They are everywhere, at the ports of Golga, Sind, Surat, Bengal and Cambaya. And our gains are less as compared to the cost of their meddling and scheming proclivities. Should we expect the same from the Dutch, Asaf, or should we hope for great revenues?" he asked cheerfully.

"Great revenues, for sure, Your Majesty, for the Dutch treaty subjects them to the needs and demands of your empire," Asaf Khan began unconvincingly. "The English were given free rein to import and export without any prohibition, resulting in less gains for us. Besides, no limitations were set as to the quantity of the commodities imported or exported." His sense of buoyancy was fading as mysteriously as it had commenced.

"Then the treaties need to be improved or improvised." Jahangir helped himself to another goblet of wine from his gold flagon. "The empress knows about each treaty from its seed to its blossom, fair or cankerous." He turned toward Nur Jahan, capriciously. "What do the English covet the most in Hind, my empress?"

"Besides gold and jewels, Your Majesty, they seek the calicoes of Golconda," was Nur Jahan's merry response. "If one could divine the secrets in their hearts, they might be longing for the empire itself."

"And the emperor is concerned only in protecting his empire from the disloyalties of baidaulat." Jahangir's gaze was returning to Mutamid Khan, and back to Asaf Khan. "I wish to dictate my letter to Prince Shah Jahan in your presence, Asaf, and you will be the messenger of our reconciliation," he murmured as if to himself.

"I am much favored by your kindness, Your Majesty, and would be honored to bear such tidings of peace to my son-in-law," Asaf Khan murmured back.

"Be quick, Mutamid Khan. The emperor doesn't wish to dwell on this subject much longer than need be." Jahangir fixed his attention to his royal scribe, coaxing his thoughts with a draught of wine. "In response to Prince Shah Jahan's appeals, the emperor consents to forgive, depending upon his total obedience. He must never step foot in Agra, even with the intention of seeing the emperor, unless summoned. He is to surrender his claim on the forts of Asir and the Rhotas. He is commanded to send his sons, Prince Aurangzeb and Prince Dara Shikoh, to our palace at Agra. After all the conditions are met, he will receive the final pardon, and will be allotted the government of Balaghat as his own kingdom to rule and protect." He paused, his gaze feverish.

As the pause lengthened, Hushiyar Khan ventured to announce Fadai Khan. Jahangir drained his cup once more, the ridges around his lips deepening under his pencil-sharp mustache. Nur Jahan watched the emperor with bated breath, her eyes bright and shining. She was elated by the concise missive of a farman to Prince Shah Jahan. Asaf Khan was unhappy, barely concealing his misery against the mask of a thin smile. Fadai Khan was approaching the throne as if spurred by fate.

"Your Majesty." Fadai Khan offered a lengthy curtsy.

"What feat of bravado brings you to our court this early?" Jahangir's gaze was piercing. "You were not expected here till we were ready to leave for Kashmir."

"As commanded by you, Your Majesty, I was to report the imprisonment of Mahabat Khan's son-in-law as soon as he was brought to Agra," Fadai Khan confessed quickly, his look pleading and befuddled.

"Then was Khwaja Burkhudar, if that is the name of that wretched bridegroom, lashed and chastised as commanded?" Jahangir's gaze was sad and feverish.

"Yes, Your Majesty. His hands were tied behind his neck and he was taken to the prison under the care of our royal guards," Fadai Khan murmured hastily.

"Was the emperor's farman delivered into the hands of Mahabat Khan, stating that he is to leave for Bengal immediately?" Jahangir asked with the abruptness of an inquisition, as if he had seen the shadow of vile import in Fadai Khan's eyes.

"Yes, Your Majesty, he received your farman." Fadai Khan gasped for breath. "Another reason, Your Majesty, why I came early. Mahabat Khan craves your audience before he…" His words were choked by the kindling of rage in the emperor's eyes.

"That vile traitor! How dare he defy the emperor's orders? Was he not commanded explicitly to depart, and not to plead for an audience?" Jahangir's look was savage. "Has he quaffed the waters of immortality, that he dares cross the breach of etiquette, invoking the emperor's wrath? Is he not aware that he is charged with fraud and embezzlement during his campaigns against Prince Shah Jahan? Are the laurels of his victories not stained with greed and treachery? Is he not ashamed that he gave his daughter in marriage to Khwaja Burkhudar without the consent of the emperor?"

"He is, Your Majesty, he is," Fadai Khan murmured, the look in his eyes revealing more than he could voice.

"Then why, in God's name, Fadai Khan, he is seeking the emperor's audience at the peril of his own life?" Jahangir's anger was accosting the flames of impatience.

"He has the support, Your Majesty…another reason for such a request," was Fadai Khan's flustered response. "Prince Perwiz does not wish to part with Mahabat Khan, Your Majesty."

"Another rebel prince following in the footsteps of baidaulat?" Jahangir's eyes were flashing fury and impatience. "Jahan Lodi is already on his way to replace Mahabat Khan. Tell my charlatan of a prince that he must gird the mantle of obedience if he wishes not to share the fate of his rebellious brother," he commanded, dismissing all with a wave of his arm.

The emperor was getting to his feet, while this vast chamber was being vacated by all in a flurry of obedience. Jahangir was assisting Nur Jahan to her feet. His expression was changing from one of flashing anger to that of tenderness, as if no raging storm had ever alighted there to rule over his senses, gentle or capricious. Nur Jahan, accustomed to such stormy moods of the emperor, could not be mistaken that that rage was the child of his own anguished heart, and that this tenderness the bloom of his fantastic imagination fanned by the scent of a memory, greeting Anarkali. And for once, she was not sad to walk in the shadow of Anarkali. The dearest of her wishes was fulfilled by the emperor's farmans and commands, and she was grateful. Prince Perwiz, lately swollen with pride, was to be brought to his senses by these recent commands of the emperor, and her heart was comforted. Prince Shah Jahan, the paragon of pride and arrogance, had become the rightful heir of emperor's disfavor. Mahabat Khan would slough off his own load of ambition inside the jungles of Bengal. Prince Shahriyar was the uncontested victor to reach the throne of Moghul legacy!

The emperor was slipping his arm around the waist of his empress with a tenderness akin to reverence, murmuring endearments and leading her toward the bedroom in rose and ivory, where no court intrigues could ever reach them. They were entering their Eden, half Eden, if it could be compared with the Eden in Kashmir.

"Our Eden, Nur. The scent of Kashmir is in your hair." Jahangir could barely breathe. He was leading Anarkali into the nuptial chamber of his lost paradise. "Your lips, your eyes, my desire…love, must taste surfeit before this long, long journey to Kashmir. The cool, fragrant valley, your body, this scent of Kashmir, what witchcraft is seducing my heart…"

"I am wearing the attar of roses, Your Majesty, the only scent which I always wear." Nur Jahan was laughing, painfully, hysterically.

Chapter Fifteen

The attar of roses, floating in the bathtub like the limpid agates, was drugging Nur Jahan's senses to peace and oblivion. Her eyes were closed, smoothly and hermetically. She was immersed deep into the jade pool of a bathtub, luxuriating in the sense of bliss and solitude. The scent of Kashmir was in her body and soul. It was seething deeper and deeper into her psyche in swift, quicksilver waves, charged with the currents of beautiful memories. With her practiced skill in loving, she had learned to arrest life's treasures where the emperor's nearness alone could dissolve her pains and fears into the bubbles of time.

Nur Jahan, though holding on to the strings of bubbles in her mind, was aware of the beauty and serenity of this great bath. This spacious bathroom on the fourth storey of this palace in Kashmir was her haven and her sanctuary. Here, she could feel rested and absolved, resting from the fatigue and weariness of the royal burdens and intrigues, and feeling absolved from all anxieties of the royal household, which could never fail to hound her wherever she went. Her eyes were unlidding slowly and dreamily. The marble floor with blue and turquoise tiles was expanding before her sight like a vast ocean. The small recesses with the inlay of mother-of-pearl were furnished with candles, absorbing colors from the damasked walls and attaining the hues of sea-shells. The blue and gold canopy overhead was absorbing her attention, though her mind was still intent in watching the ebb and flow of the bubbles quaint and luminescent. She could see the bubbles bursting in her head, more following their lead in clear, floating mists.

Nur Jahan, in utmost repose of her body and mind, was letting go of all the bubbles. *I have the body of a Nereid;* her thoughts were murmuring compliments. With her flaxen hair hugging her breasts and a few gold strands tracing down her snow-valley, she seemed oblivious of her repose and beauty. Her one arm was poised on the curve of the jade tub, and the other languishing on her flat belly, artistically smooth and listless. She was foundering into the delicious deeps of the mad, mad hours spent with the emperor, where his passion knew no boundaries. He would not let go of her. The bubbles in her head were creating a riot, and swelling without bursting. She could feel the rapier of his maleness piercing her time after time, as if he was making up for the loss of love sublime and love unattainable after centuries of denial and suffering.

Indeed, I have learned to live in the shadow of Anarkali. The riot of bubbles in Nur Jahan's thoughts was seeking turbulent depths. *Can death ever be sundered apart from life? No, it lives, again and forever in us, in every cycle of life and death.* The orgy of bubbles in her head was swollen and menacing. *I am the beloved, and Anarkali, the unloved shadow. The emperor loves a shadow! Reaching out to her through me, and loving me instead. Can I kill this shadow? Mangle its beauty, sever its head from its pretty shoulders, reduce it to a lump of deformity? Where is my shadow? Is someone out there yearning to love—my shadow? To embrace it, to annihilate....* The bubbles in her thoughts were clashing with each other, swollen and undying.

Nur Jahan was squirming her back up against the slippery jade, feeling the mists in reveries inside her very limbs and thoughts. The bubbles inside her head were an entire universe by itself, reflecting beams upon beams of light, yet touching only the heart of banality and insignificance. This afternoon, rife with passionate bliss, was the foremost bubble of reality in her head, perched right on top of the other bubbles of equal passion and tenacity. All were caught into the mist-frame of three months where Kashmir alone could welcome and entertain them with the breath of reality.

Since their arrival in Kashmir, Jahangir himself was caught into the mists of longings, lavishing all his time and energies in exploring the heart of the valleys. Whether hunting or visiting his gardens, he would not rest until forced by the intrusions of his own illnesses, unwelcome and unpredictable. His illnesses had been few and sporadic, fortunately, during this whole span of one year, and even those could not deflate his ardor to hunt and explore. At times, he would venture out with only a handful of courtiers, and wander far and deep into the valleys rugged and dangerous. Then upon returning to the palace, he would entertain the ladies of his harem with anecdotes wild and astonishing.

Nur Jahan, while bathing, was not recalling those anecdotes, but the delightful afternoons sweetened with love and passion. She was sitting up in the bathtub, her thoughts floating upstream into the tunnel of her consciousness. Her very senses were tasting the wild abandon of more than a dozen afternoons under the canopy of three month sojourn in Kashmir, when the emperor's love were hers and hers alone. After his recovery from each illness, it had happened thus without fail, that Jahangir would retire to his own chamber and would sleep till late. Nur Jahan, of course, was his inseparable companion. In fact, both would wake up late in the afternoon with no fear of intrusion, for those were the emperor's strict orders before retiring to his chamber. Upon waking on such afternoons, the emperor, in return, would obey only the commands of his own desire. Such terrible hungers would goad his desire then, that he would not tire of making love or notice the shades of dusk welcoming another evening, wanting more and more till Nur Jahan's pleas and groans could whip him apart from his desire and implacability. She too would want more, clinging to this passion as much as he did, but always fearing for his health and sanity.

The bubbles in Nur Jahan's head were bursting now, and melting into the stream of her repose and awareness. They were lancing no wounds, and dissolving into nothingness. Prince Shah Jahan was in perpetual exile. Mahabat Khan was suffering disfavor and disgrace. Prince Perwiz was nursing his pride with the rivers of sweet-scented wines, and enjoying his drunkenness. Prince Shahriyar was healthy and affable, and hoping to be the only heir to the throne of Hind. Ladli Begum, the joy of Nur Jahan's heart; Princess Ladali, her granddaughter; and of course, Prince Shahriyar, all were in Kashmir, sharing the bounties of the emperor's favors, and of her own loving indulgences. An overpowering sense of fatigue was holding Nur Jahan's thoughts into pincers of awareness all of a sudden. She was not the youthful goddess of ageless time, but a lonesome woman only one year away from half a century, feeling frail and vulnerable, tasting the soot of age and time, utterly alone and forlorn, totally and absolutely lonesome. The age unutterable! The time unfathomable.

Jahangir, seated in his chamber adjoining this sumptuous bath, was feeling no such pangs of loneliness which were visiting Nur Jahan. He was seated in his gilt chair, reading *The Rose Garden* by Saadi, divinely content, and feeling a subtle presence inside the altar of his very soul, where no one could enter but Anarkali. More than half a century old himself, precisely six years over fifty, he was neither feeling the burden of those years, nor the weight of his illnesses. The mirror in his mind was reflecting only his youth, and his gluttony to pain and suffering. He was a young prince in love, in love with the only woman he could possibly love and worship, Anarkali herself. Anarkali had never died. How could she when she lived inside him?

Some sort of bliss-madness was shining in Jahangir's eyes, as he kept reading the works of Saadi. His thoughts were holding not the words but their cadences, deep and enigmatic. Slowly and thoughtfully, his sight was absorbing the words. One bold quatrain on the illumined page was arresting his attention.

"Of what use a dish of roses to thee
Take a leaf from my rose garden
A flower endures but five or six days
But this Rose Garden is always delightful."

This quatrain of Saadi was transporting Jahangir into his own palace garden overlooking the Mansabal Lake.

Lalla Rookh's garden, Dorogha Bagh! Why didn't I name it Nur Bagh, or Anar.... Jahangir's thoughts were frolicking all of a sudden. *A beautiful garden jutting out into the lake like some great high-decked galleon.* His thoughts were envisioning this garden where his wives were planning a farewell feast this evening.

A night of feasting with song, music and dancing, more for the entertainment of the ladies themselves, than for the pleasure of the emperor. Jahangir's thoughts were bidding another farewell to Kashmir, this time not pressed by the betrayals and rebellions of his family and friends but by his need to visit Kabul, the land of his ancestors. *Kabul, the home of the Moghuls!* Jahangir's thoughts were mocking his own decision to visit Kabul. But he could not help making such a decision, anticipating the scent of homecoming, longing for the welcoming arms of Kabul. *Kabul, the Jerusalem of Hind!* Was it prudent to visit this Jerusalem of his ancestors, when that time could be spent in the Eden of his desire, Kashmir, Kashmir?

Kabul, Kashmir! Are both not the reflection of one paradise, born one after the other, and many more such paradises sprouting elsewhere in lands remote and unexplored? Jahangir's thoughts were peering into darkness.

He abandoned the book on his rosewood desk, and got to his feet involuntarily. In conformity with his mood and nostalgia, he was wearing the old crown of his late father, given to him as a token of peace, stability, happiness. This gold crown had twelve points, each point balancing a large diamond on its head. The base of this exquisite crown was studded with pearls and rubies in clusters of ten each to vie with the diamonds at twelve points. The large diamonds were sparkling vividly against the shafts of sunshine, as he stood demurring by the window. His features were gaunt with the transparency of silk, matching the pale silks on his royal person. He was turning slowly and thoughtfully to absorb the essence of this room as if he had not ever seen it before.

The paintings in gilt frames were large and alluring. The high bed, with a canopy of lace and brocade, was hiding its satiny comforts under the coverlets of chintz and velvet. The jade and crystal vases on the mantel were holding a medley of jafari and hyacinth blooms. Jahangir's feet were digging deep into the silk-wool rug as he began to pace slowly and thoughtfully. Age had not marred his youthful features with wrinkles, though sadness was etched deep into his eyes. Both he and the empress were blessed with the amrita of youth in their veins, it seemed, keeping them young forever and everlastingly. The only times when the ravages of age could be seen visiting him, were the times when his eyes were puffed and his face bloated by the effects of drunkenness. Not that he had stopped drinking, but the wine seemed to have lost its potency. He was drinking as usual, now and forever, more heavily at times, and restraining only under the siege of his illnesses. The wine was diluted of course, but he was wont to drain it quickly without savoring its taste. The ocean-thirst need inside him demanded goblets of wine, and he had yet not discovered that it was diluted.

No such ocean-thirst was claiming Jahangir's attention at the moment, as he kept pacing. His slow, steady steps were barely making any sound on the Bokhara carpet, and the silence within him was dissolving into tides of memories, gentle and nostalgic. Anarkali was a heartbeat away from him, edging closer and closer with the rhythm in time. He could feel her presence. His senses were calm and slumbering. She was guiding his thoughts into realms tranquil and peace-loving. Her presence was one rose of a memory, each petal soothing the tides of time and timelessness.

Prince Shah Jahan had sent his sons, Prince Aurangzeb and Prince Dara Shikoh, to the palace at Lahore, along with the gifts of jewels, armor and elephants. He had obeyed the commands of the emperor, retiring to Nasik, repentant and remorseful. In obedience to the emperor's commands, he had written a letter to Muzaffar Khan, surrendering the fort of Rhotas to him and to the imperialists. He had dispatched a similar letter to Hayat Khan, relinquishing his claims on the fort of Asir. Mahabat Khan had also acted most prudently in obeying the emperor's commands without protests or entreaties. He had repaired to Bengal after depositing a large chunk of his embezzled cash into the royal treasury. Recently, another farman by the emperor was sent to Mahabat Khan through Arab Dost. This farman was stating explicitly that Mahabat Khan was to dispatch all the war elephants to

Lahore, the war elephants which he had accumulated in overwhelming numbers during his campaigns to quell the rebellions of Prince Shah Jahan. Prince Perwiz too was ruling wisely in Burhanpur after accepting Jahan Lodi as his advisor with utmost obedience to the emperor's wishes. *Prince Shahriyar is in Kashmir, devoted and sweet-tempered,* Jahangir was thinking, while pacing and breathing the scent of peace and silence.

These were the rose-petal thoughts on the silken trails of Jahangir's memories, as he plunged deeper and deeper into the rhythm of his contemplations. He could see these thoughts strewn like flowers in the lovely eyes of Anarkali, as she stood offering garlands upon garlands of peace to the silent altars inside his soul. This kind of worship and offering was alien to his senses, yet he was at peace within himself and with the world. His decision to visit Kabul, his whim or caprice, was surfacing in his mind as the products of not of his own thinking, but as the outcomes of some strange mixture of fate and destiny. Dream and nostalgia were his gifts of repose, bestowed upon him through the lips of his beloved. Nothing was a part of his thinking or existence!

His bliss, his health, his illness, nothing? Jahangir was thinking. All were strangers in his body, visiting and leaving at the discretion of their own wills and moods. Even the hungers and thirsts of his body and soul were not his own, but coming to him from some emptiness from within and without. And yet again, he was at peace with himself, comforted by this presence within him, trying to explore some strange void inside him which appeared light and abysmal. This void, this emptiness within him, was one gleaming ocean of strength and vitality he had not ever experienced before. He had become more observant and more passionate, loving Nur Jahan more than ever, and humbled by her wit and beauty.

Jahangir could catch the drift of his thoughts, parading in rhythm with his pacing, but even his thoughts were not his own. Something inside him was repeating this litany of a revelation. All thoughts were entering his mind like some nameless birds, and escaping into nothingness. Those bird-thoughts were constricting and expanding inside their own empty cages where no thoughts or memories could ever enter or escape. He could sense something inviolate and astonishing inside the very kernel of his being, a dark tunnel of life with only a chink of light escaping through the eye of a needle!

Yes, Anarkali is with me, granting me this respite of peace before I die. One chink of light was expanding in Jahangir's thoughts, his feet coming to a slow halt by the canopied bed. *She is summoning me to the bridal chamber of death. I will not live long. She is the one who has sealed my soul with the waters of surface-calm. It will not ever again feel its turbulent depths locked by the hands of time.* His very thoughts were suspended there in some void of timelessness. So deeply immersed he was in this sea of the imponderables that he did not notice the appearance of Nur Jahan.

Paradoxically, Nur Jahan was caught in abeyance by the statue-like immobility of the emperor's form and demeanor. She had stopped right in the middle of the room, her heart lurching, then somersaulting in great violence. She was watching him with utter fascination as if he was some stranger imprisoned in this room by the sheer caprice of her own imagination. Appareled in silks, the color of gold, she herself was a wraith of light and magic, where reality could not penetrate into the essence of dreams, fading and drifting. She was bathed in the nimbus of fire and light, her eyes shining with such brilliance that the emperor was not long in discovering her presence.

Jahangir was rather jolted out of his profound emptiness, unable to contain this vision of light and beauty in his awestricken gaze. He almost staggered in his act of reaching her, his feet coming to one stumbling halt. Their eyes were locked, his smoldering with bewilderment, while hers twinkling wonder and innocence.

"To be struck by the bolt of beauty, and to suffer a slow, lingering death is not the emperor's idea of a pleasant journey on the road to nonexistence," Jahangir murmured. "I would rather be hit by lightning than by the shafts of your beauty."

"Our cherished garden would be struck by the serpents of lightning through the very lips of the Begums, if we don't join them soon, Your Majesty." A fountain of mirth escaped Nur Jahan's lips, as she sailed toward the emperor.

"And you don't care, Nur, if the emperor dies." Jahangir claimed her hands, grazing his lips against them reverently.

"Why talk of death, Your Majesty, when life is young and beautiful?" Nur Jahan protested cheerfully. "Peace reigns in your empire, Your Majesty. And your health is improving! And the beauty of Kashmir is forever painted in your eyes."

"Yes, beautiful and heavenly, this garden, my pearl." Jahangir drifted back to the window overlooking his gardens and terraces.

Jahangir's gaze was lost into the heart of nature's own handiwork. In the distance, Dorogha Bagh sat cradled like a jewel above the shimmering waters of Mansabal Lake. This jewel of a garden was hosting the living, throbbing colors in silks and brocades this evening. The tunes from lutes and flutes were sailing on the wind and reaching his awareness. His gaze was peering into the ocean of festivity without seeing.

"I wish to stay in Kashmir, Nur." Jahangir was murmuring to himself. "Are we really leaving? I fear we will never return to this Eden again."

"We will return to our Eden again and again, Your Majesty, as I said before," Nur Jahan murmured, not heeding the sting of foreboding inside her. "Kabul is not far, Your Majesty. We will return soon after your pilgrimage to the tomb of your grandfather. Babur, he loved life, I have heard, pouring laughter into the hearts of everyone wherever he went. Now is the time, Your Majesty, when peace reigns in Hind, to link with the past and to hold future into the sparkling cup of hope."

"Past is not now, and future is not yet." Jahangir turned, smiling to himself.

"And yet you will be happy to visit the gardens and palaces of your great ancestors, Your Majesty." Nur Jahan was puzzled by the enigmatic gleam in the emperor's eyes. "You are happy in Kashmir, Your Majesty, I know, but a cloud of sadness never leaves you," she demurred. "You have been talking about Kabul for a whole week now. And a week before that…just before your illness, didn't you confess that what would please you the most would be to explore the heart of Kabul?"

"If the soul of Kashmir could let the emperor leave." Jahangir held her into his arms. "Light of my heart, you know what will please emperor the most?" He was gazing into her eyes most tenderly. "To unrobe you and to make love to you, till the eternity itself is left with no power to sunder us apart." He kissed her eyes. His own were closing in some holy ritual of a bliss to feel the presence within.

"Even that, Your Majesty, will it ever dissolve your sadness?" Nur Jahan slipped away with the gentleness of a dove taking its accustomed flight. "We must join the Begums, Your Majesty, or an eternity of rift in this royal household will follow us to the end of the world." Mirth and mockery were shining in her eyes.

"Yet, stay, beloved, stay. Stay with the emperor for a while. Our last evening in Kashmir. A moment of bliss. The emperor has no need for festivities." Jahangir lowered himself on the gilt chair, indicating the other to her. "Come, my pearl, the feasting will last till dawn. You are the empress, remember, and the emperor's other wives can't rise in sedition against you. And the emperor himself will obey you after he has drunk his fill with your beauty. Or, should I command you to supply me with a flagon of wine?" he challenged, as he noticed her reluctance to seat herself.

"The emperor knows only to command, Your Majesty, not to obey." Nur Jahan flashed a sweet reproof, sinking into her chair with a look of absolute surrender.

"Subservient to the commands of my heart, how can I not obey you, my love?" Jahangir smiled. "'God is witness that there is no repose for the crowned heads. There is no pain or anxiety equal to that which attends the possession of sovereign power, for the possessor there is not in this world a moment's rest,' that's what my father used to say," he contemplated aloud, his look profound and reminiscent.

"He said much more than what you or I could ever remember, Your Majesty." Nur Jahan's own eyes were gathering profundities. "If I recall correctly, you yourself told me what he said about care and anxiety. 'Care and anxiety must ever be the lot of kings. For, of an instant's inattention to the duties of their trust a thousand evils may be the result. Even sleep itself furnishes no repose for the monarchs, the adversary being ever at work for the accomplishment of his designs.'" Her heart was pounding with a sudden violence, as if some calamity lay in ambush on their way to Kabul.

"Do you suspect any treachery on the part of Mahabat Khan, my sibyl empress?" Jahangir asked abruptly.

"I suspect him, yes, Your Majesty. His profusion of loyalty and devotion toward you doesn't sound sincere." Nur Jahan smiled, trying to appease the violence in her heart. "The men who claim absolute surrender to the will of the emperor are not to be trusted. The buds of insurrection could be simmering deep under his mask of humility and subservience. His plotting, scheming mind needs only one whiff of an opportunity to don the mantle of sedition. Disgrace, I fear, doesn't sit well on his pride."

"Guilt, not surrender, is his ageless foe." Jahangir laughed. "Now that he has admitted his guilt of fraud and embezzlement, he is powerless to cultivate more deceits. Besides, the fate of Prince Shah Jahan is a lesson enough to keep him away from his own malefic designs, if he has any. He is wise, my Nur, knowing that the same fate will be his lot if he dares disobey the emperor's commands."

"In his wisdom, I truly hope, Your Majesty, that he abstains from the perils of intrigues," Nur Jahan commented cheerfully.

"And yet, it has indeed been said that the kings will find enemies in the very hair of their own bodies." One prophecy of a thought escaped Jahangir's lips.

"And that, Your Majesty, is true," Nur Jahan quipped, her eyes flashing mischief. "You indeed have been enemy to your own self, fighting not the foes of your dreams, and courting illnesses with wine as your inveterate foe." She laughed. "Let us not talk about enemies in this paradise, Your Majesty. Our paradise of a garden is calling us. Its delights should neither be shunned nor postponed."

"Those delights can wait, my Nur, till the emperor can drive away the demons of his indulgences with memories fresh and delicious, and can fill his cup of hungers and thirsts with the goblets of wine in your eyes brimming with wit and beauty." Jahangir's gaze was wistful, as if he was willing time to cease its march.

"What wit and beauty, Your Majesty, when Kashmir alone is the object of your desire?" Nur Jahan teased.

"Without you, my pearl, the lamps of this desire could never be kindled," Jahangir murmured effusively.

"And gallivanting without me, Your Majesty, into the very heart of the pine-valleys while I was left with the begums?" Nur Jahan smiled to herself. "And what about those hunting trips without me?"

"Foolish pride of the emperor, my love," Jahangir murmured beamishly. "If your hunting skills were not superior to the emperor's, he would have been delighted to have you as his charming companion without being slighted by the fact that his own hunting skills are inferior to yours. And as to my gallivanting, you yourself deserted the emperor. Were you not looking forward to an excursion planned by the begums? Regardless of this fact, the emperor wishes to take you to those treasure spots on our next visit, and the next, if you can divine such pleasures."

"You may share those treasures with me now, Your Majesty, so that I can look forward to possessing them completely on our next visit, and the next, and the next ever after," Nur Jahan requested, her eyes shining with a dreamy anticipation.

"Our first trip will be to the spring known as Kuthar, before it dries up," Jahangir began fervently. "It has remained dry for eleven years, I am told. The legend, now bordering on the verge of truth, is, when the planet Jupiter enters the sign of Leo, this spring starts to flow on the following Thursday. During the seven succeeding days, it dries again, filling once more on the next following Thursday, and continuing to flow for one whole year."

"And if it dries up by the time we return to Kashmir, Your Majesty, will you not take me to see this marvel of nature?" Nur Jahan asked eagerly.

"Probably not, my Nur, if you manage not to return within a year," Jahangir teased. "There are many more wondrous sights than this one rude spring! It is much too proud and regimental, asserting its right to stay dry for eleven years."

"Then I will succumb to the poverty of my thoughts in exploring those wonders which my eyes have not seen." Nur Jahan elicited one mock sigh.

"They are arrested in my eyes, love, if you can but see." Jahangir's eyes were shooting a subtle challenge.

"The eyes have no lips, Your Majesty, if you can but lend life to those wonders through the tongues of words," Nur Jahan retorted brightly.

"Then you must catch this bubbling wonder first, Nur!" Jahangir declared intensely. "It is a fountain close to the valley of Shukroh. Under this fountain is a low hill, looking like an exquisite dot of scenic splendor above the pine-valleys. On the summit of this hill sits this fountain, bubbling in eternal peace throughout the year. It has become a place of pilgrimage for the devout, who ascribe sanctity to this fountain as the very spring of life. Incredible as it may seem, the snow never falls on this spur."

"Like a large spring in the village of Biruwa, where the lepers bathe early on the first day of each week." Nur Jahan's fascination with Kashmir was running wild in her memories. "That too is the site of pilgrimage for the devout and the faithful who believe that by simply bathing in its waters, health could be restored..." She paused, catching the glint of amusement in the emperor's eyes, and holding it into her own dreamy ones. "You were there, Your Majesty. So enchanted were you by the peculiar shade of velvet in the grass and by the open pastures and sloping plateaus, that you didn't pay any attention to that spring, that incredible spring with pure, crystal waters! The hope of the afflicted!"

"Not as incredible as that quivering tree which you have not seen, my Nur!" Jahangir declared amusedly. "That tree stands tall and mighty in the village of Haltbal. Even if the smallest of its branches are shaken, the whole tree becomes tremulous."

"You have yet to take me to the valley of Lar, Your Majesty, which borders on the mountains of great Tibet. The most incredible of sites as you professed," Nur Jahan began wistfully. "The breathtaking vistas and the lofty mountains! At the foot of which two springs run parallel, as you told me. Can't believe that the waters of one are extremely cold, of the other exceedingly hot. Will only believe when I touch them."

"Your sweet fingers would get numb in the one, and scorched in the other, my sweet. The emperor will not allow it." Jahangir laughed. "Instead, he will take you to Kargon where a defile called Soyam gets so hot at the time of the conjunction of Leo and Jupiter that the trees catch fire. And if a vessel of water is left on the ground, it will boil. A great site, both of us would be melted together! Sated with life, united in love!"

"I would rather choose to be frozen on the snowy peaks of the Himalayas, Your Majesty," was Nur Jahan's response.

"If you don't want to be melted together with the emperor, my pearl, then I would rather perish in the golden wastes of Sahara, myself." Jahangir laughed.

"Let's not tempt the fates, Your Majesty, with the talk perishing." Nur Jahan's eyes were straying toward the portraits on the wall. "It's time we joined the feasting. The begums are waiting, and they will be disappointed if we delay any further."

"I would rather we stayed here and made love all evening," Jahangir murmured. He got to his feet as if stung by the novelty of his desire.

"Your Majesty!" Nur Jahan exclaimed, her eyes warm and pleading.

"Let us go, my love." Jahangir held out his hands. "Why is my heart so heavy, Nur? All this love and warmth in our paradise, our Kashmir, our Kashmir." He grazed his lips against her cheek most tenderly.

"Would it be light, Your Majesty, if we were to stay in Kashmir? Not leave tomorrow?" Nur Jahan asked softly.

"Who knows, my Nur? My heart, this temple of the imponderables," Jahangir declared cheerfully.

"Much like the temple of Bhutesar in Satpur, Your Majesty. The one dedicated to Mahadeva, where one hears the sounds of a ceremonial worship, and no one can tell where those sounds come from," Nur Jahan reflected aloud.

The emperor and the empress were approaching closer to the walled terraces of this enchanted garden called Dorogha Bagh. Behind them, the sun, crowned in golden red, was dipping farther down the chariots of the west. The music was in the air, and the terraces were throbbing with festive colors in gold and velvets, flaunting jeweled buntings. The begums and princesses were a shimmering sea of silks and brocades. And the princes with bright plumes in their colorful turbans could be seen laughing and feasting. The tall poplars shading the velvety lawns were sifting and scattering light from a myriad of candles so profusely lit by the fountains. The violets and red roses in their round flowerbeds were vivid and glowing, as if wreaths of sunsets had fallen on the ground. The large tables with damask tablecloths were laden with fruits and viands of countless varieties. The wine-bearers in liveries of red and gold were eager to drain their gold flagons into the sparkling cups. The emperor and the empress were floating freely, much like the singers and the musicians who were there to entertain the royal family in the semblance of troubadours.

Nur Jahan had caught sight of Princess Ladali deflowering a pot of tulips, and was quick to arrest her into her arms. Jahangir was distracted by a bevy of younger princesses who were trying to emulate the dancers by pirouetting on their toes. Nur Jahan was kissing and hugging her granddaughter. She was joined by Ladli Begum, who was arrayed in the finest of silks and jewels much like Nur Jahan's, with the exception of a diamond tiara on her head.

"Our beloved Ladali will turn out to be a flower thief, if you do not teach her to admire the precious blooms." Nur Jahan's eyes were cradling her daughter into the light of love, and lowering the bundle of velvets on the carpet.

Princess Ladali, barely three years old, was not only a bundle of velvets, but of pearls with a creamy net so craftily woven in the brown thatch of her curls. She was bouncing away in glee, not even acknowledging the presence of her mother. Nur Jahan was watching her granddaughter with a tender fascination, while Ladli Begum was exploding into a volley of mirth.

"You have spoiled her, Padishah Begum, and you expect me to teach her the virtues of beauty and aesthetics?" Ladli Begum chanted joyfully.

"An utter folly too, in neglecting to teach my own daughter the art of survival in this court of intrigues." A subtle rill of sadness was alighting in Nur Jahan's eyes.

"Intrigues dare not come near me, Padishah Begum, as long as I am favored by you," Ladli Begum chanted with all the purity of joy and innocence. "Favored by my own mother! The most powerful and the most benevolent of the empresses on the continent of this whole wide world? And the empress most beloved by the emperor!"

"And how long these favors are going to last, my sweet princess?" Nur Jahan's gaze was profound. "For how long, my love, how long? When the empress is dead…cold and powerless in her grave to rescue you form the tides of deceit and treachery?"

"Forever and forever, Padishah Begum, I hope and pray." Ladli Begum's happy disposition was not deflated by such sad musings. "You will live, Padishah Begum, to see our dear Ladali wedded and for many, many more years to pour your love on many more generations to come." She drank daintily out of her cup, laughing.

"Do you ever advise your husband, my heedless Ladli, to stay close to the emperor as much as possible? To win his favors as many as he can?" Nur Jahan began exigently, as if the tides of time were pressing upon her heart and mind. "Prince Shahriyar is to be the heir to the throne, and he must prove himself worthy. He has to pave his way toward this legacy and to learn how to rule, not to be ruled by his scheming, plotting brothers."

"You have, Padishah Begum, I mean, paved the way smooth for Prince Shahriyar," Ladli Begum acknowledged with a gleam of pride and gratitude. "Prince Shah Jahan, being in disgrace, and Prince Perwiz..." She could not betray the violence of her own dreams against the probing gaze of her mother.

"And Prince Perwiz, the king of ambition, though he has not rebelled as yet." Nur Jahan snatched the words out of her daughter's thoughts with a keen sense of perspicacity.

Their eyes were locked, as if they stood cementing the link of understanding without words, and sharing an infinity in love and hope, which could only be shared by two loving hearts. Their mutual trance was broken by the breezy approach of Prince Shahriyar. He was balancing two goblets of wine in his hands, and entering their world with the scent of hilarity.

"My charming prince, are you seeking oblivion in the cups of wine?" The stars of admonition trembled in Nur Jahan's eyes as she greeted the prince. "And the empress stands here neglected, not a drop to sweeten her palate or thoughts."

"The emperor himself sent you this goblet, Padishah Begum." Prince Shahriyar offered her the cup with a gallant curtsy of his head. 'The emperor's heart is floating there at the bottom of this cup,' that's what my father told me to say." He laughed, stealing a tender look at his wife.

"I can see his heart floating in a nimbus over the very heads of his wives," Nur Jahan quipped. Her own gaze was reaching out to the emperor where he stood drinking, and laughing. "Look, how he ogles the dancers over the shoulders of his wives, while claiming to be the most attentive of husbands! I have seen and intercepted that look before, but not his other wives, not them. They are too giddy to notice." She laughed. "You should be there with the emperor, my handsome prince. Suing for favors and wooing the bride of kingship, not wasting your time in courting your own bride." She stole a glance at her daughter. "She will be there, always," she murmured.

"And the throne too, Padishah Begum." Prince Shahriyar's mirth was bubbling in his eyes. "With one of my brothers turning a rebel and a traitor, I might inherit the throne." He drank deeply out of his cup.

"Keep an eye on Prince Perwiz, my imprudent prince. He has enough ambition to color your dreams with the blood of hatred and intrigue," Nur Jahan warned smoothly.

"Both my eyes are riveted on him, Padishah Begum." Prince Shahriyar chuckled deliciously. "He is bloated with pride and arrogance. Telling his viziers that he is the rightful heir. Marking me doomed as the son of a concubine, and Prince Shah Jahan as the vessel of treachery and perdition. His own words, Padishah Begum, not mine."

"Shahriyar!" Ladli Begum exclaimed, her eyes flashing.

"No concubine of the emperor is branded with shame or disgrace, unless she herself chooses to entertain such demeaning thoughts." Nur Jahan's eyes too were flashing. "Abstain from drinking in excess, my prince, lest your tongue lashes out disrespect, instead of respect, respect which you owe to your own self, to your wife and to your mother." She was turning away, her gaze suddenly warm and tender.

Ladli Begum and Prince Shahriyar stood watching the empress, as she glided past them swiftly and gracefully. Silence was their link to love and friendship, no words escaping their lips. The empress was lost beyond the profusion of French marigolds, before they turned to face each other. Their eyes met, resurrecting the blooms of scented memories. Ladli Begum's eyes were bright and glowing. Prince Shahriyar's were brimming with love, which he could not share with anyone but with his adored wife.

Nur Jahan, with her own lighthearted gaiety, was attracting admirers on her way to the low terrace, where the emperor stood conversing with his other wives. The younger princes and princesses were flocking around her. They could be seen vying with each other to claim her as their sole confidante in sharing their own little anecdotes. She in return was gratified to see the gleams of joy and gratitude in their eyes as her rewards of indulgence and kindness in caring and sharing. Even the dancers with bare shoulders and gossamer skirts were greeting her with palms joined and uplifted, and showering her with compliments. Barely had she escaped the charge of her own sisters and their husbands, when her gaze was arrested to the emperor's daughters. Princess Bihar Banu was standing there with her husband Tahmuras, radiant and mirthful. A few feet away from that happy couple was a circle of princes, entertaining Princess Sultanunissa, but she seemed forlorn and detached, molded alive in her own solitary world where no one could reach her. Nur Jahan could not help noticing the shadow of misery in the eyes of this older princess as she flitted past, and a stab of remorse lunged at her very sense of gaiety before she could advance further.

Why didn't I ever befriend Sultanunissa.... Nur Jahan's thoughts were creating a name and a face from the white mists of the past. A name was emerging, *Man Bai,* the mother of Princess Sultanunissa who had died even before Jahangir had acceded to his throne. *Why didn't I befriend any of the princesses....* Her thoughts were welcoming the too familiar face of Karamasi Begum, the mother of Prince Shahriyar and Princess Bihar Banu. *How could I? Did I have the time? A succession of intrigues and rebellions...Prince Shah Jahan, the warring lords, the perfidious wars...the emperor's illnesses...* Her thoughts were huddling against some warm refuge.

Nur Jahan was floating in some daze, her senses stealing the scents of purity from clusters upon clusters of white lilies. Her sprightly steps were leading her up to the terrace where the emperor stood drinking with the fervor of a hedonist. The gleaming marble under her feet felt smooth, yet unwelcoming. It seemed to be swimming in liquid colors from the reflections of silks and brocades adorning the royal ladies. Karamasi, Nurunnisa, Khairunnisa, Salihah Banu, Malika Jahan, Sahiba Jamali, and many, many more of the emperor's wives were feeding the emperor the delicious morsels of gossip. Sahiba Jamali was breaking through the circle of the other wives, edging closer to the emperor, not even noticing Nur Jahan, who was caught halfway between this circle of wives. She stood exchanging amenities with each one of them, and laughing with a wild abandon, more so to drown her regrets and sadness than to gratify the happy brides with her wit and gaiety.

"Your Majesty, Prince Perwiz is drinking much too heavily, I have been informed." Sahiba Jamali was murmuring low. "My son, my only son...even insensible to the needs of his royal household and of his little kingdoms." Her voice was drowning against the beat of the tablas.

Nur Jahan was closer to the emperor now, inside the intimate circle of the other wives. She had caught the spark of fear in Sahiba Jamali's voice, and was expecting some sort of soothing response from the emperor to still the fears of his wife. As the emperor stood there drinking without uttering a word, Nur Jahan's own attention was shifting to the emperor, demanding a response from her gaze alone. Her eyes were speaking more than she could voice, as if accusing him of drunken stupor and of neglecting to soothe the fears of his wives. Jahangir himself was watching her, the cup of wine poised before him in an act of taking another sip.

"The emperor has heard what his beloved wife just said, my Nur," Jahangir murmured, shifting his attention to Sahiba Jamali. "All the emperor can do, my love, is to send him a letter of reprimand, forbidding him to drink. So scarce are the grains of obedience inside the heads of my sons, that I wonder how they discipline their own children." He drained his cup greedily.

"Little kingdoms can be destroyed with little neglect. And large kingdoms crash on one's head with the weight of self-neglect if restraint is not practiced," Nur Jahan murmured to herself.

"An edict, Your Majesty, not just a reprimand! Yes, a strict farman should be dispatched, if he is to be saved from drowning himself into the rivers of wine." Sahiba Jamali's anguish itself had elicited this poetic plea.

"No edict of my father could ever restrain me from excessive drinking, my love." Jahangir laughed suddenly. "I will chastise him personally. That always worked for me, when my father came and imprisoned me under his strict commands." His eyes were glowing with some inner fire-need of liberty and surcease, all in one.

"Are we allowed to chastise you personally, Your Majesty?" Malika Jahan sang half earnestly, half teasingly.

"Only if you can usurp the emperor's empire, my sweet rebel." Jahangir laughed.

"That is simple, Your Majesty. We can all arrest you in your own palace at Kashmir, and rule Hind from behind the veils of treachery." Salihah Banu could not help jumping into this pool of mirth and mischief.

"If you wish to keep your pretty heads on your shoulders, my loves, you will not resort to such a treason." Jahangir could not help indulging his wives in this game of idle pleasure, though his heart was throbbing suddenly with a real sense of doom.

"You wouldn't behead your beautiful wives, Your Majesty. Your kind and forgiving heart would not permit it. It would break," was Nurunnisa's mirthful comment.

"My heart is accustomed to breaking so religiously, my love, that it feels not the splinters of grief anymore. Justice shall be done!" was Jahangir's jovial comment.

"We would be the power and justice both, Your Majesty, us together. Nothing could harm us!" Khairunnisa declared happily.

"The empress can smell treason from the very breath of air. In fact, from the fort of Agra to the very borders of Kabul." One prophecy of a comment escaped Nur Jahan's psyche. Drowned in her mirth, she could not unspool the mystery of this treason, which had nothing to do with the emperor's wives.

Asaf Khan had landed into this pool of mirth, and was now seeking the emperor's attention.

"It will be a treason not to enjoy the fruits of Kashmir, and the delectable feast which is longing to be consumed." Asaf Khan was tossing this plea into the sea of mirth and gaiety. "If I was not afraid of the breech of etiquettes, I would attack those viands even before the emperor could taste one morsel?"

"The emperor can't live on mirth alone." Jahangir was quick to escape this sea of mirth, commanding over his shoulders, "Come, Nur, join your brother in the gluttony of this feast."

The chenars, flanked by marble fountains, were hosting an array of tables with shimmering tablecloths in gold and damask. The large fruit and floral arrangements were gracing the tables laden with Moghul cuisine of the finest varieties. In the distance, the poppies and carnations were swaying in the wind, oblivious to the music of feasting and merrymaking. Jahangir and Nur Jahan were flitting from table to table, tasting all viands with their eyes alone, and claiming not a morsel from this bounteous feast. Asaf Khan, joined by other princes and princesses, was following them, eager to devour everything if the emperor could only hasten the ritual of feasting.

"This grape will be enough to announce the bacchanal feasting." Jahangir snatched one grape from the ruby-red cluster and tossed it into his mouth.

Asaf Khan was quick to attack the steaming dishes with a sigh of relief, now that the ritual of feasting was announced formally. The princes were heaping their gold plates with viands and vegetables, whatever appeared delectable and inviting. The princesses were more keen on the dainty fruits as the appetizers, the plums, apples, peaches, melons, apricots, all sliced in shapes of shells and flowers.

"The emperor is craving for some dish of a culinary excellence by the ingenuity of our royal cooks, my Nur." Jahangir turned to Nur Jahan. "I hope some such delights are awaiting the emperor this evening, depending if this feast was prepared under your skillful instructions, of course."

"Fish, rice and vegetables in a variety of flaming colors, Your Majesty," Nur Jahan teased.

"Half cooked rice, unflavored fish, tasteless vegetables! The emperor has partaken of such peasant feasts quite often while hunting." Jahangir's eyes were tearing the veil of her banter with the warmth of a smile. "The emperor is craving pheasants garnished with almonds. Hares cooked in wine. Legs of lambs stuffed with nuts. The tender chicken cutlets swimming in a sauce of poppy-seeds."

This evening of song and music, of dancing and feasting, had drifted past the hour of midnight, coming to a sated halt in the middle of the garden. The emperor was seated on his gold chair with a brocade canopy overhead. Nur Jahan and Asaf Khan were keeping him company and finalizing the plans of their journey to Kabul. The garden was still lit with candles and colorful oil lamps, though it was absorbing more light from the full moon with its own canopy of stars. The princes and princesses had retired early, longing for rest before their long, long journey to Kabul. The begums too had sought the comforts of the palace, abandoning the beauty of this garden with tender adieus. A coterie of servants were still hauling the carpets and furniture back to the palace, and restoring Dorogha Bagh to its neat, uncluttered serenity. The night air scented with the perfume from flowers was evoking some lone yearnings in Jahangir's heart. His heart was groping for something in the darkness which it could neither touch nor unveil. Some sort of peace and self-surrender was seething in the very fabric of his psyche, holding on to the glory of this year's bounteous spring. But he knew that he would not ever feel the same even if he was to visit a million such springs into the very heart of Kashmir. Nur Jahan's own thoughts were turning to the journey ahead, but she was content to listen to the exchange of views and ideas between her brother and the emperor. Actually, she had ceased to fondle any threads of conversation, since her own thoughts were awakening to one flame of a warning which she could neither catch nor extinguish. Asaf Khan was bubbling with enthusiasm, not in the least aware of the hush and enchantment in the bosom of this fragrant garden.

"A great entertainment of jugglers and magicians has been arranged for Your Majesty's pleasure in Jehlum, Your Majesty," Asaf Khan was saying. "Those jugglers are awesome, Your Majesty. They have honed their art and magic to such perfection, I hear, that one feels floating inside the mists astonishing and spellbound."

"A rope-dancer performs with his feet and hands, and a poet with his tongue, my father used to say," Jahangir ruminated aloud.

"Poets only weave the mists of lies, Your Majesty, but the jugglers and the magicians, they flash the mists of miracles before our sight, pouring wonder inside the very temples of our hearts," Asaf Khan intoned proudly, as if he himself was the magician.

"Miracles abound only within the temples of diverse creeds, Asaf. And wonders are only the products of our own mental deceptions, for who could dare ascertain the truth inside the fabric of lies?" Jahangir murmured profoundly. His sight as well his senses were cherishing the murmur of songs from the moonlit fountains.

"Then, should we close our eyes to the wonders of wisdom, Your Majesty, and abandon miracles in some dark pit of lies?" Asaf Khan protested.

"My father told me a story, Asaf, which might explain these imponderables," Jahangir began reminiscently. "One man named Hasan Sabbah was once on a journey by the sea in a company of other seafaring men. Suddenly, a storm overwhelmed them. They were all seized with great consternation, and fearing that they would be drowned. Hasan Sabbah, on the contrary, remained calm and cheerful. When questioned by others what kept him so cheerful, he answered simply, 'All of us will be saved.' On reaching the land safely, all his companions were assured that the edicts of future were revealed to him. Had they asked him, he would have told them that he was undisturbed through this assurance alone that the Will of God could not be altered. And that his announcement of the good tidings for their security was caused by that reflection, that if they were to drown, no one could have saved them. And that if he had voiced his reflections about drowning, they would have taken to vain supplications."

"Since my reason is confounded, Your Majesty, I better go and worship God in the secret chambers of my heart." Asaf Khan's eyes were shining like the feverish stars. "Praying that our journey to Lahore be safe, that the magicians in Jehlum will not allure us for long, and finally that the gardens of Kabul will not imprison us for life." His inward turmoil was surfacing in his eyes, his gaze bright and restless.

"Most worshippers of God are intent on the advancement of their own desires, not on His worship, that's my father's saying too," Jahangir quoted under the weight of a sudden weariness, which was constricting his heart.

"Strange, Your Majesty, that you have been quoting your father all evening," Nur Jahan commented abruptly. "I have never heard you talk about him so much, but lately."

"Yes, I feel his presence, and the…" Jahangir's thoughts dared not utter the name of Anarkali. Flashing a smile at Nur Jahan, he turned to Asaf Khan. "Leave us, Asaf. The emperor wishes to take a stroll in his garden, and to cast off the spell of beautiful memories before they arrest him here forever." He got to his feet slowly and thoughtfully.

Asaf Khan bowed his head and sauntered away most obediently, not another word escaping his lips. Jahangir assisted Nur Jahan to her feet, and stood gazing into her eyes. They were both suspended there, it seemed, against the haze of their own reveries. Much like lovers under the spell of ineffable silence, they began promenading.

"To bid farewell to this Eden is like parting from a beloved. Though, my beloved is leaving with me," Jahangir murmured.

"This is not the last farewell, Your Majesty," Nur Jahan murmured back.

"It seems like one, Nur, the last *one*." Jahangir's gaze was devouring the flowerbeds of poppies and carnations.

"And yet we will return again, Your Majesty," Nur Jahan breathed tenderly. "You always feel this way, Your Majesty, whenever we leave Kashmir. And yet you know we will always return. Again and again, and forever. A time will come when we will just stay, and never leave."

"Yes, my Nur, yes. I wish to die here…in these fragrant pine-valleys, buried deep under the beautiful tapestries of my own gardens." Jahangir's thoughts were throbbing with the will of their own, drunk by the hush and beauty of this garden.

"Why dwell on death and darkness, Your Majesty, when life is offering you joys and hopes from its own treasures bountiful? You have withstood the tests of tragedies and rebellions, and have never faltered. And now this…talk of death, why, Your Majesty?" Nur Jahan appeared to demure aloud as if expecting no answers.

"I don't know, Nur, my heart is heavy. I can feel its sadness. It is telling me something…some sort of foreboding, as if we will not even reach Kabul. Maybe my soul has seen the tablets of fate, which announce that we will not ever come back to our Eden." Jahangir was heeding the verdict of his thoughts.

"And the tablets in my soul repeat, Your Majesty, that we shall return." Nur Jahan's optimistic thoughts were coming to her rescue.

"Then, shall we heed the tablets of your soul, my pearl, and say goodnight to our children?" Jahangir elicited one snort of a laughter.

"Children!" exclaimed Nur Jahan, forgetting about the fish.

"How neglectful of you, my empress!" Jahangir declared with a sudden blithe. "Our dear little children with gold and pearls in their noses."

The moonlit lake under the canopy of stars was calm and smooth, yet rippling with lace-shadows from the cypresses and the willows. Jahangir and Nur Jahan were standing under one great willow by the pond, where the wild lilies in clusters of orange were wafting their own night scent. The night air was cool, and further scented by a myriad of blooms creeping wildly over the edges of this shell-like pond. The emperor and the empress were gazing wistfully into the clear depths of the pond where the goldfish with royal adornments in their noses floated freely and luxuriantly. Jahangir stirred, turning to face Nur Jahan, his expression suddenly rapt and incredulous.

Nur Jahan was molded pure by the very hands of moon-beams, sparkling like some apparition of gold and light. Her pale, ivory features were luminescent and glowing. The blue heavens and the glittering stars had landed into her very eyes. Jahangir's thoughts themselves were bowing in worship at her feet. He was standing before the goddess of love. Without her he could not live. Even the memory of Anarkali would fade into a vacuum, if she was to vanish like a dream. Something inside him was stabbing and lamenting. For a millionth times in his life he had fallen in love with this woman, this Nur, this light. He had wronged her as many countless times as the brilliant stars in a millennium. He had been unfaithful to her, by loving another.

"My Nur, my light." Jahangir could barely hear his own murmur of a plea. "Have I ever told you that I love you?"

"Not that I can recall hearing it, Your Majesty." Nur Jahan smiled sadly.

"Then you must never forget, my beloved, that the emperor loves you with all his heart and soul, infinitely and passionately." Jahangir claimed her hands, kissing them. "I have always this fear, my Nur, that I am going to lose you." His heart was aching tenderly, knowing not the violence of lust, but the bliss in love.

"You will never lose me, Your Majesty. I might…" Two big tears were glittering in Nur Jahan's eyes. "If you truly love me, Your Majesty, you will take care of your health, will stay healthy for me, for our great love." Tears were spilling down her cheeks.

"Beloved!" One agonized cry was arrested on Jahangir's lips, as he kissed her tears. "One holy kiss under the moon to seal our love. Come, beloved, the emperor will hold you close tonight, much like a devoted lover, without the animal lust of a man courting pain and oblivion, but a man striving to understand love and to nurture bliss in health and in loving." He slipped his arm around her waist, leading her toward the palace.

The moonbeams themselves were following the lovers to the palace doors. Their hearts were the streams of love, pure and gurgling, but such a love could not be desecrated with expressions. Nur Jahan was swooning with bliss, and the emperor was rapt in murmuring endearments.

"You are the light of my heart, Nur, the light of my soul, the light of my love…" Each fiber in Jahangir's body was consumed in love for Nur Jahan.

Chapter Sixteen

On the outskirts of Jehlum, the royal encampment by the river Behat was a splendid city in itself. A few elms and poplars scattered here and there could now boast of the splendid tents of the princes and the viziers with white and green awnings. In the middle of which was erected the most opulent one of the emperor's in gold and scarlet. Across from the river, separated by a low, wooden bridge, was another city of silken tents for the royal entourage. Those tents were for the guards and soldiers who were to keep account of the provisions necessary during this long journey. Since Asaf Khan was appointed to keep stock of these supplies, his own grand tent was pitched right amidst the lesser grand ones of the guards and the soldiers.

Barely a week since the royal cavalcade had arrived in Jehlum, and Asaf Khan was more involved in arranging entertainments for the emperor than heeding the reports of Mahabat Khan's unwelcome, yet planned journey toward the very banks of river Behat. The emperor, ignorant of such reports, had abandoned himself to the luxury of daily entertainments, which were conducive to his good health. Greatly pleased by the emperor's joyful spirits, Nur Jahan herself had neglected to delve into the rumors of Mahabat Khan's secret plans or meanderings. Besides, she was much too much in love, rather suspended on the wings of bliss by the emperor's own love for her. In such a state of bliss-rapture, she would have failed to notice even if the hurricanes struck, drowning all into the blue turquoise waters of the river Behat.

The entertainment on the banks of the river Behat, this particular afternoon, was more magical than wondrous. It was evoking gasps of delight from the lips of the royal ladies as well as from the younger princes and princesses. The emperor in his Persian robe of gold and a red turban studded with emeralds, sat entranced, unable to tear his gaze away from the whirlwind of magic and illusion, fascinated by the skill of dancers and magicians. He was seated on a throne of mother-of-pearl, the low dais under him smothered in lengths of velvets, soft and shimmering. Seated next to him was Nur Jahan, her own colorful silks broidered with gold and silver. At the foot of the throne were tiers upon tiers of seating arrangements strewn with rich Persian carpets and brocaded pillows. All these seats were occupied by the royal household, including the aunts and the uncles, and of course, the emperor's wives. Since Asaf Khan had seen the rehearsal of this entertainment the night before, he had excused himself on the grounds of much-needed rest, and had retired to his own encampment.

Just before leaving, Asaf Khan had invited Prince Shahriyar to his encampment, proposing rest, since the prince had been unwell for a few days, adding jokingly that the air on the other side of the river Behat might benefit the prince's health. Prince Shahriyar had accepted the invitation eagerly, for on the other side of the river there was an abundance of verdure in contrast to the scanty elms and poplars where the emperor had chosen to erect his own luxuriant tents. Besides, there were fields upon fields of wheat on the other side, and he had been thinking of solitary walks with his adored wife and Princess Ladali. So Asaf Khan's proposal had come to him as a God-send boon, and he had requested the emperor if he and his family could accompany Asaf Khan.

The sanction to such a whimsical request was granted by the emperor, but his own heart had pounded with such astounding violence that he had a mind to retract his decision. This nameless violence within Jahangir's heart had vanished swiftly while he had watched his son leave, returning his attention to the pillars of pomp and magic. Nur Jahan's heart too, for some strange and astonishing reason had fluttered at the very inception of the emperor's consent, her thoughts uttering a warning. It was rather a foreboding, but she was quick to dispel it, ascribing her fear to her sole concern for the health of Prince Shahriyar. Though Prince Shahriyar was suffering no major ailments. Only inertia and languor had kept him confined to his own tent, feeling or imagining little aches and pains in his limbs, and no traces of fever to justify his complaints.

Prince Shahriyar, along with his wife and daughter, had left long since, but now as Nur Jahan sat watching the jugglers and the magicians, her heart had begun to flutter once again. It was restless and shooting warnings, longing to cross the river to keep a watch over the emperor's troops, who, for sure, could be languishing in a carefree abandon. Before she could penetrate the truth of her inner warnings, her gaze as well as her thoughts were arrested to the magical performance of horror and disbelief.

One man was being dismembered limb by limb by the very hands of a magician, and each part of his body thrown into a basket. The last part of this body was his severed head. The magician was overturning the basket, and all limbs were attracted toward the head as if to a magnet, each part of the body whole and intact, as if this body was never torn apart. The man was walking away with his head held high, smiling and waving. The gasps of disbelief from the audience followed by a great applause were fading as the jugglers from Bengal appeared on the stage amidst the blaring of horns and trumpets. They were revealing the body of a decapitated man from under the sheet, and then restoring him to full stature by the swishing of wands over his head. The same man was producing a few coils of ropes, and tossing them into the air where they could be seen suspended without any support. One Pomeranian was tied to the lower extremity of the rope and left dangling. This frisky dog was quick to climb the rope, and had vanished into the thin air with the speed of a comet. In the same manner, one at a time, a hog, a lion, a tiger and a panther were tied to the end of the rope, all vanishing into some void which could not be discerned by a naked eye. The performers were gathering into a circle, curtsying and enjoying the thunderous applause.

"Never in my entire life I have experienced such witchcraft and disillusionment." Jahangir was laughing, his gaze shifting to Nur Jahan. "Now the emperor is ready for hunting, and I hope it turns out to be as delightful as this magic and mystery."

"Since I am not invited to hunt, Your Majesty, may I visit my brother's encampment which boasts of verdure and a few clusters of flowers? Besides, since our journey from Kashmir, I have rarely spent any time with my daughter and granddaughter, and my heart is longing for their company," Nur Jahan requested suddenly.

"You uninvited yourself this morning, my love, remember?" Jahangir smiled. "And your brother, and my son and his family uninvited themselves from the pleasure of this fantastic performance…strange. You are all conspiring against the emperor, I can feel it." His eyes were gathering the rills of amusement and tenderness.

"Yes, Your Majesty, we are going to abduct you into the jungles of our schemes. You will be our prisoner, shackled to our own commands to indulge in the pleasure of hunting and entertainment," Nur Jahan retorted, her heart still restless.

"The emperor is your lifetime captive, my love, not ever wishing to be released from the shackles of your beauty and witchcraft," Jahangir quipped. "Won't you come with me, to hunting, my Nur? I can't endure to be parted from you, not even for a moment," he murmured, trying to disperse the dark clouds in his thoughts.

"If you wish it, Your Majesty, I dare not decline," Nur Jahan murmured back.

"The emperor is a slave to your wishes, my pearl." Jahangir got to his feet slowly and thoughtfully. "No, you must go. For some vague, absurd reason, I feel that you need to get away from the emperor…for a while, at least."

"I can't fathom my own unrest, Your Majesty. I feel…can't explain what I feel. But something inside me is commanding me not to leave you, as if you will be left alone, and…"

"Alone, my love!" Jahangir was smiling, watching his other wives approaching closer. "You will go, my Nur. Just for this afternoon…until I return from my hunt." His low murmur was rather a command than a consent.

This early afternoon with its sepulchral haze was suspended into a vacuum, as if no wondrous acrobats and magicians had ever splintered its hush. The entertainers had retired to their own silken abodes, and the emperor was alone in his gilded tent. He was anticipating a great hunt, and was thinking about Nur Jahan's reluctance to leave, though both had donned the masks of cheerfulness while parting. He could still see her face wreathed in the saddest of smiles as she was being escorted over the bridge by the royal guards and by her lady-in-waiting. His own heart was sad…still sad. His thoughts somehow were turning to his other wives who could be indulging in the afternoon siesta, or playing cards in the comfort of their own luxuriant tents.

Jahangir's thoughts were straying and frolicking as he stood contemplating whether to summon his valet right this moment, or wait till he is done selecting his hunting gear and riding habit. Some sort of mad elation was thundering in his head, sounding nameless commands, the import of which he could neither catch nor decipher. A whirlwind of memories were craving the attention of his awareness, and approaching closer to him with a threat of the hurricanes. All memories were now seething and breaking into liquid mists. They were peering into the eyes of doom, and fogging the profounder depths of reality where light could never lift the veil of darkness. An ocean of love was throbbing inside his heart, calling Nur Jahan, repeating her name. Anarkali was outside this realm of madness. His mind and heart were on fire, leaping out of his body, and consumed by the wildfires of their own imaginations. Impatiently, he was turning toward the low desk in jade and ivory where his gold flagon lay gleaming. He filled his cup with ruby wine and stood sipping it absently. His thoughts were entering the tent-chamber next to his own where his royal servants kept guard, and into the next reserved for the soldiers, and into the last one where the imperial guards of the highest rank kept vigilance.

A sumptuous palace in the wilderness. One rude thought in Jahangir's mind was suspended against the sudden sprouting of noise.

The afternoon hush was broken, rather shattered. There were splitting and sundering of sounds, as if river Behat was gathering some tempests. The voices were rising and ebbing in his own head. Jahangir was thinking. He was turning slowly, espying Mutamid Khan, whose loud exclamation could not be missed as a rag of illusion.

"This temerity and presumption is beyond all rule." Mutamid Khan was protesting with someone only he could see. "If you will wait a minute, I will go in and make a report to His Majesty."

Jahangir's heart was a volcano of forebodings, something inside him stabbing and lacerating. He sought his chair and sank into it with a feeling of hopeless, helpless pain. His one hand was clenched into a fist on his lap, and the other poised before him with his wine cup held firmly. Jahu and Arab Dost had charged into the royal tent, falling at the emperor's feet in a succession of curtsies.

"Your Majesty," Jahu gasped. "Mahabat Khan…" He could not continue. Tears of shame and misery were glistening in his eyes.

"Your Majesty," Arab Dost attempted with a small ammunition of courage. "Mahabat Khan…he is here with a large body of Rajput soldiers. A coup, Your Majesty, the treason, the vilest of…" His confusion was truncated as Mahabat Khan himself stormed into the tent. He was attended by two of his sons, a wall of Rajputs following him. This solid wall of men was attaining the gleam of spears and shields, all raised high, all glinting threats.

"Your Majesty. I have assured myself that escape from the malice and implacable hatred of Asaf Khan is impossible, and that I shall be put to death in shame and ignominy!" Mahabat Khan declared with a dint of fear and courtesy. "I have therefore boldly and presumptuously thrown myself upon Your Majesty's protection. If I deserve death or punishment, give the order that I may suffer it in your presence." His look was feverish and challenging.

"And who are those unblinking idiots you have brought with you?" Jahangir's own eyes were gathering the daggers of rage and inquisition.

"They are the cannons of my protection, Your Majesty, if you do not comply with my wishes." Mahabat Khan grinned triumphantly.

"Your wishes, you demented fool!" Jahangir drained his cup and flung it down on the carpet. "How dare you approach the emperor when I have forbidden you! What does this all mean?" he demanded with one hopeless gesture of his arm.

"That means, Your Majesty, that you are my prisoner, and you will do as I command," was Mahabat Khan's delirious response.

"Command, you vile traitor?" Jahangir wiped the beads of perspiration from his brow in some daze of hopelessness. "I should have known. Begone, I say, before you crumble under the edict of death which you yourself have chosen to accept."

"Death stands between you and me, Your Majesty, and it will strike both ways, if you but move a finger to issue such an edict." Mahabat Khan's very eyes were murmuring the challenge of death and doom.

"Briny odors of the Dead Sea are escaping your very lips, Mahabat. Death is not between us, but behind you. Soon, the emperor's troops would be crossing the bridge, and nothing will save you from the pit of death and degradation." Jahangir tossed back a feeble challenge, his thoughts aghast and foundering.

"Two hundred Rajputs are guarding the bridge, Your Majesty, equipped with instructions to burn it, if anyone dares cross it on either side." Mahabat Khan appeared to be sketching fresh plans in his head.

"It is already burning, but sealed with the waters of Jordan. No harm will ever come to it," Jahangir murmured to himself, his gaze returning to the devoted subjects at his feet. A low command was escaping his lips. "Arab Dost, summon Mutamid Khan. Tell him to fetch my riding garments. The emperor is going hunting."

Arab Dost leaped to his feet, but was stalled in his act of obeying the emperor's orders. Mahabat Khan had unsheathed his sword and was forbidding him to leave. Jahangir's own hand was reaching to his jeweled hilt, but falling listless into his lap. The emperor's eyes were feverish, revealing the first blow of shock and bewilderment. Mutamid Khan had heard the emperor's command, and was breaking through the wall of the Rajputs with riding garments into his arms. He was offering them to the emperor with all due courtesy, and not minding the foul air charged with threat and danger.

"This works perfectly in conformity with my plans, Your Majesty." Mahabat Khan was heard bubbling with a fresh spurt of madness. "You would ride forth hunting, Your Majesty, as if it was your own free will, while you would be subject to a strict surveillance. A good chance to prove to your subjects that nothing has changed. For the sake of peace and harmony between our troops and your troops, we will keep the fact of your captivity concealed. You will seem to be commanding, while we command!"

"The emperor will go to his dressing chamber and change." Jahangir got to his feet as if drifting in a dream.

"No, Your Majesty, you cannot leave this chamber." Mahabat Khan blustered forward. "We will erect a screen right here. My Rajput soldiers will hold it for you, while Your Majesty changes."

Jahangir stood there unperturbed and demurring. The cold, tingling sensations in his head were holding him captive inside some clamps of shock. Jahu and Arab Dost were moving closer to the emperor like the shields of steel, claiming their positions on each side of him with the fierce devotion of the imperial guards. Mutamid Khan was facing Mahabat Khan, glaring and stomping his foot with the fury of a mute challenge.

"These Rajputs better not dare come near His Majesty. We ourselves will hold the brocade coverlet as a screen for our emperor. And order your dumb Rajputs to face the other way." Mutamid Khan was furious, towering above the traitors.

This chamber of intrigue was swallowed into a sudden hush, as the emperor changed in mute obedience to his own will and trepidation. Jahu and Arab Dost were holding the brocade coverlet as if turned to solid posts, only their eyes shooting daggers and threats. The Rajputs, instead of turning their backs, had closed their eyes, their faces flushed and inscrutable. Mutamid Khan was standing there ramrod, his eyes raining fire and brimstone. Mahabat Khan was pacing, as if he had lost the method to his madness and was searching this loss desperately. Jahangir was emerging forth in his riding habit like a dazed knight out of the very pages of the Arabian Nights, the sparkle of emeralds in his turban accentuating his pallor. Mahabat Khan's eyes were burning with the fire of madness, his feet coming to an abrupt halt, and he stood facing the emperor.

"Before we go hunting, Your Majesty, we will visit the empress in her own royal tent, and request her to accompany us." Mahabat Khan gloated inwardly.

"The empress is visiting her brother on the other side of the river, if you wish and dare cross the bridge and confront the imperialists." Jahangir's look was dazed, where his mute sufferings could be seen accosting the pain in living.

"It's not true, Your Majesty! I will conduct the search myself," was Mahabat Khan's flustered response. "Let us go, Your Majesty." The daggers of doom in his eyes were revealing his own blunder and confusion.

The emperor was walking ahead, accompanied by Jahu, Arab Dost and Mutamid Khan. Mahabat Khan was behind the emperor with his sons on either side of him. The Rajput soldiers were following at a respectable distance, as if the emperor himself had chosen to take a stroll in this silk city with his general and his troops. The emperor was the first one to enter the tent of the empress, followed by his own devoted companions. Mahabat Khan, the rebel and the traitor, was right behind them. Mahabat Khan, now facing the truth of the emperor's words, was courting despair and bewilderment. His mind and heart were on fire. He could hear his own thoughts cursing his stupidity in neglecting to capture the empress, who was sure to thwart his noble schemes. Madness and delirium were coursing in his blood, and chaos and desperation were goading his mind to action. He was rather distracted, not even knowing what he was doing or saying.

Since he had missed the opportunity of capturing the empress, Mahabat Khan's next aberrant plan was to visit the tent of Prince Shahriyar and hold him captive. He had not even heard the emperor that Prince Shahriyar too was on the other side of the river with the empress and her brother. Adamant in searching the tent of the prince, he was urging the emperor to lead, rather demanding answers to his blithering inquisition. Once again, this royal entourage, followed by the Rajput troops, was seen halting before the tent of Prince Shahriyar. Not finding the prince in his royal abode, Mahabat Khan was overwhelmed with such confusion that his fears and madness were multiplying. He was ordering the emperor to proceed toward the hunting grounds, and storming ahead of him as if ready to lead an army. Realizing too soon that Jahu had chosen to stay in the tent of the missing prince, Mahabat Khan was quick to retrace his steps. Suspecting Jahu of some foul conspiracy, Mahabat Khan had ordered his soldiers to slay him.

After this dark deed was done, Mahabat Khan was at the emperor's heels once again. He was offering the emperor his own horse, and insisting that the emperor should accept this offer and ride to the hunting grounds without further delay. The emperor, though dazed, was more in command of his senses where royal authority could be seen mounting higher and higher over the perils of life and tragedies. So, he was summoning his stirrup holder to fetch his own royal steed so impeccably chosen for hunting expeditions. Amidst this unsettling issue over the horses, the emperor's mahout Gajpat Khan and his son were appearing on the scene, riding the imperial elephant in obedience to the emperor's former command to accompany him to the hunt. Mahabat Khan. suspecting that these men were coming to rescue the emperor out of his captivity, was quick to command his soldiers to slay these men. After this brutal slaughter was perpetrated in broad daylight, Mahabat Khan's savage thoughts were returning to the issue of the empress.

"Your Majesty, before we proceed to this hunt, you are to send a note to the empress." Mahabat Khan's flustered command was escaping the tremor of his own rage and madness. "You are to write, Your Majesty, that your safety is insured under my command, and that any scheme of engaging in war with me would be a great mistake, resulting in dire consequences. And that a peaceful surrender on the part of the empress would benefit both her and the emperor."

Jahangir was more stunned than baffled by the incongruity of this scene, which was grazing only the surface-calm of his shocked awareness. His former rage was dissolved inside the absurdity of this living nightmare. Paradoxically, he was not even thinking about his empire being usurped by the hands of this lowly general, but about his pain in the unfathomable deeps of his loneliness where he longed for Nur Jahan beside him. The wound of long forgotten grief inside his heart was splintering open. It was accosting the poetry of love in dreams, and swallowing the wounds of reality. He had summoned Mir Mansur, ordering him to fetch his own horse, condoning the violence and brutality visited by the insanity of Mahabat Khan. Urged by this vile traitor, he had also commanded Mir Mansur to pen the missive to the empress as dictated by Mahabat Khan. While taking his signet ring off to be sent with the missive, one couplet had come tumbling down his lips, and he had commanded that to be added as a postscript.

To thee I have sent the scent of myself. That I may bring thee more quickly to myself.

Jahangir stood tasting the perfume of the couplet in his head, even after Mir Mansur had left with the missive and the signet ring. Mahabat Khan was seeking the emperor's attention most humbly, as if he had committed no murder or treachery which could be a cause of offence to the emperor.

"Your Majesty, now your slave will be in your attendance on this hunting trip." Mahabat Khan was assisting the emperor on his own royal steed. Then he was commanding his soldiers with a desperate wave of his arm.

Nur Jahan was feeling comforted by the warmth of her granddaughter sleeping in her lap, but her heart was still shooting rapiers of warnings and forebodings. Ladli Begum and Prince Shahriyar were lolling against the satiny pillows, oblivious to the stabbing fury in Nur Jahan's heart. They were whispering amongst themselves in the bliss-comfort of their own royal niche on the thick, Persian carpet. Asaf Khan was seated opposite Nur Jahan, more intent on talking than listening, and avoiding the inquisition from the empress most craftily. Actually, Nur Jahan had no intention of subjecting her brother to inquisition, but wanted to know about any covert intrigues which were to pose a threat to the empire of Hind. Not once did she suspect any threat from Mahabat Khan. Had she thought about this fallen general even once during her journey from Kashmir to Jehlum, perhaps a little suspicion would have entered her head that Mahabat Khan could rise in insurrection. But as it was, she had dwelt more on Prince Shah Jahan's acts of obedience, which had a false ring concealing the all-time alarm of danger and sedition. Right now, as she sat talking, rather listening to her brother, she was ascribing her sense of foreboding to the false sense of peace between the emperor and Prince Shah Jahan.

Asaf Khan himself had chosen to not talk about Mahabat Khan. He had been the author of ruin and degradation for this general, more so by his own malicious designs than through the deep-rooted hatred of Nur Jahan. He was satisfied on one account now, that this man of power and intrigue was thrown into a pit of eternal obscurity, from where he could never rise to contend against his beloved son-in-law, Prince Shah Jahan. Secretly, Asaf Khan's allegiance belonged to Prince Shah Jahan, though he appeared to favor the cause of the emperor at all times and under all circumstances. Even this afternoon, as he sat conversing with his sister, he was careful to guard his secret communications with Prince Shah Jahan, informing the prince about the emperor's illnesses and his royal itinerary. So engrossed was he in guarding these secrets, that he too could spare no thoughts concerning Mahabat Khan. Besides, he had no fear of treachery from this man who was banished to Bengal.

Amenable as ever, Asaf Khan was in great spirits this particular afternoon. He was joking and laughing, with the sole intention of entertaining the empress, as if her visit demanded entertainment. On the contrary, Nur Jahan didn't wish to be entertained, but informed about any stealthy intrigues or rebellions which might ensue during their journeys long and distant. She was rather disappointed in gleaning nothing from her brother's discursive account of peace and harmony in all quarters of the empire. She was succumbing to silence, rather than probing and prodding. Right at this moment, Asaf Khan was relating some mundane event which had touched some lives in the court at Agra a few months from hence. Nur Jahan was listening quietly, while watching the velvet bundle of a granddaughter in her lap with the warmth of love and tenderness. Her own thoughts were opiate and wandering aimlessly. A strange hush had settled into this tent of silk and damask. Asaf Khan's own voice was attaining the quality of a murmuring cataract, lulling this hush into further vacuum of silence.

In a flash, the murmuring cataract in Asaf Khan's throat was choked by the breezy intrusion of Mir Mansur. He had staggered into the tent with a woebegone look, the script of doom and tragedy written all over his face. He was gasping for breath, and falling at the feet of the empress in one heap of misery. Ladli Begum and Prince Shahriyar were startled to their feet. Asaf Khan was frozen in his act of speech and action. His thoughts were imputing this rudeness to the news of the emperor's sudden illness or death. He could not move, he could not think. Mehr Harwi, who had obliterated herself in one dark corner, flew to the empress' side, frightened and flustered. Nur Jahan commanded her lady-in-waiting to take the sleeping princess into the adjoining tent without a dint of fear or urgency. After Mehr Harwi had left, Nur Jahan's attention was reverted back to that heap of a messenger at her feet. Mir Munsur was lifting his head, and offering one sealed missive, along with the signet ring of the emperor.

The mistress of grace and serenity as ever, Nur Jahan was the only one not flustered by the unusual rudeness and abruptness of this messenger. Her features were still glowing with the warmth of love and tenderness for her granddaughter, whom she had just relinquished into the care of Mehr Harwi. She slipped the signet ring on her forefinger and unsealed the missive most carefully. A luminous pallor swept over her tender, glowing features as she deciphered the contents. Folding the missive back slowly and thoughtfully, she lifted her gaze to the messenger of doom.

"Mir Mansur, go and alert the troops for a possible attack," Nur Jahan commanded with that power of finality which brooked no disobedience.

After Mir Mansur retreated most obediently, Nur Jahan's eyes turned to Asaf Khan, flashing suddenly.

"Our emperor is in Mahabat Khan's custody," Nur Jahan murmured softly in wild contrast to the flashing intensity in her gaze. She stole a quick glance at her daughter who stood leaning against her husband, mute and stricken. "All this, Asaf, has happened through all your neglect and stupidity. How can you be so besotted as not to discover the advance of Mahabat Khan? What happened to the imperial spies who are scattered all over the empire in thick clusters?" The blue in her eyes was on fire.

"How could I know!" Asaf Khan murmured wretchedly. "The spies are more intent on tracing the footsteps of Prince Shah Jahan than peering into the hearts of the insignificant generals…by your own orders, Padishah Begum."

"I should have known!" Nur Jahan lamented aloud, wringing her hands. "What never entered into the imagination of anyone has come to pass. And now you, Asaf, should be stricken with shame for your negligence and for your inexcusable conduct before man and God. If there were enough guards to insure the safety of the emperor, this should not have happened." She got to her feet and began to pace.

"What did the emperor write?" Asaf Khan asked distractedly.

"The emperor writes, of course, that he is safe, that there is no need to engage into any kind of skirmish. That if we even attempted to fight a battle, it would result in dire consequences," Nur Jahan murmured. She appeared to be digesting the import of these words herself, than gratifying her brother's dull curiosity.

"The emperor is right, of course," Asaf Khan murmured to himself.

"Any child could see through this message, Asaf. That this missive was dictated by Mahabat Khan's own plotting, deceiving mind. The emperor was forced to write it." Nur Jahan's own anger was dissolving into a pool of torment.

The empress was pacing, and feeling the cold, cold blasts of pain and anguish. Her heart was somersaulting amidst the numb, chilling currents of grief and hopelessness. She was trying to escape this cold fury, so that she could materialize her plans in rescuing the emperor from this captivity.

"We will launch an attack right away, Padishah Begum, if you but command." Prince Shahriyar emerged out of his shock like a gallant knight.

"Here is my valorous prince." Nur Jahan stopped in her act of pacing. "While my own brother sits there craven and unconcerned." She flashed her brother a smoldering rebuke, her gaze returning to Prince Shahriyar. "We must plan, my wise prince. The attack has to be in the morning. Do summon Fadai Khan. We must get the reports straight, and then plan in accordance with that reptile Mahabat Khan's hissing moves."

Prince Shahriyar bowed his head, and left the tent in prompt obedience. Ladli Begum was about to sink back to her former seat, when Nur Jahan commanded her to look after the comfort of Princess Ladali in the adjoining tent. After Ladli Begum had left accompanied by shock and bewilderment, Nur Jahan's attention was turning to her brother.

"You must not succumb to despair and dejection, Asaf," Nur Jahan began without any trace of anger or bitterness. "This is not the time to plunge oneself into some pit of misery and hopelessness, but to awaken one's courage and wisdom to act and conquer. You must do your best to repair this evil. We need support and advice, your advice, as to what course to undertake."

"What kind of advice a wretched man can give accused by his own sister, of sloth and negligence, Padishah Begum," Asaf Khan protested, leaping to his feet suddenly.

"The words uttered in pain and anguish, Asaf! Demented times and demented thoughts. Why can't you forget all for one bleating moment, and rise above the heap of your simmering hurt and pride? Look into the eyes of this rife necessity, Asaf, and think only of rescuing the emperor!" Nur Jahan declared impatiently.

"If you take my advice, Padishah Begum, then plan craftily, devising some sort of peaceful negotiations with the vile traitor. He has committed a capital offense, and he is no fool as to understand that this treason will cost him his head if he persists in keeping the emperor prisoner," Asaf Khan opined fiercely. "War will cost many lives. Our own lives would be endangered, if we launch an attack. An unwise move, I should say."

"Our lives! What are our lives as compared to the emperor's? Do you know what would happen, my prudent brother, if any harm came to the emperor? All of us would be thrown into the waters of shame and ignominy…slaughtered like the beasts, if not banished like some stray cattle from the pastures rich and…" Nur Jahan's thoughts were truncated by the appearance of Prince Shahriyar followed by Fadai Khan.

"Are Mahabat Khan's troops in view? How many, do you know?" Nur Jahan queried Fadai Khan even before he could lift himself up from his curtsy.

"Two hundred Rajputs are posted on the bridge, Padishah Begum," Fadai Khan breathed ominously. "A large number are with him, and a great number encamped not far from the royal barges on the east side."

"And where is the emperor now? Have you heard?" Nur Jahan's gaze was intense.

"The emperor has gone hunting, Padishah Begum, as scheduled. Attended by Mahabat Khan and his body of Rajput soldiers," Fadai Khan murmured.

"What is the morale of our troops?" Nur Jahan asked intensely.

"Filled with shame and chagrin, Padishah Begum. They are longing to kill the Rajputs with their bare hands." Fadai Khan's eyes were sparkling with devotion.

"They don't have to wait for long, Fadai Khan," Nur Jahan assured unconvincingly. "Prepare them for a decisive battle which must commence early in the morning. Mahabat Khan's audacity must not tarnish the polish of our imperial strength."

"What hope do we have to win this fight with the Rajputs, when they are guarding the bridge with naked defiance to the imperial authority?" Asaf Khan declared abruptly.

"If Mahabat Khan doesn't repent of this evil, Asaf, he will be thrown into the waters of perdition, along with his horde of Rajputs, by the might and valor of our own troops. What are small bridges against hope and faith, which can conquer the mountains?" Nur Jahan flashed a quick reproof at her brother. "Go, Asaf, with Fadai Khan, and do your duty," she commanded sternly. "Instruct Abul Hasan and Iradat Khan to gather all the troops they are to lead and command. Early next morning, we must cross the bridge, and capture the captor."

Fadai Khan bowed his head with utmost obedience, his eyes bright with elation. As he turned to leave, Asaf Khan followed him reluctantly. Prince Shahriyar kept standing there mute and ponderous.

"What would become of the emperor if we rescue him not from this lizard of a traitor?" Nur Jahan stood wringing her hands, her gaze bouncing off the shoulders of Prince Shahriyar, feverish and sightless.

"I myself would lead the troops, Padishah Begum," Prince Shahriyar murmured consolingly. "No need to worry. The emperor is safe, and will be rescued from this farce of a captivity." He vanished outside the tent.

Finding herself alone, Nur Jahan flung herself in her chair and buried her face into her hands. Tears were stinging her eyes, pouring down her cheeks in torrents. Her heart was constricting in convulsions of pain and agony, and she was sobbing uncontrollably.

Chapter Seventeen

The sleepless dawn was awakening with a shudder as the imperial troops stood gazing at the cold, pearly sky. Suddenly, the sun's own eyes were lowering banners of molten gold as the soldiers stood waiting final orders from the empress. The night long preparations of the imperialists in neat files, and the advance of a few ranks closer to the bridge, could not be left unnoticed by Mahabat Khan. His fear and suspicion concerning an imminent attack by the imperialists were now confirmed. Before this attack could be materialized, he had ordered the bridge to be burnt. The emperor was imprisoned inside the vacant tent of Prince Shahriyar under the close vigilance of Mahabat Khan himself. He was heard barking orders all night long to his own soldiers who were shuffling back and forth to feed him with the morsels of the latest maneuvers by the imperialists.

The burning of one small bridge, or even the fires of hell, could not deter Nur Jahan from her desperate plan in launching the attack. She was wearing no jewels but the jewels of her resolve and implacability. Her commands were a shower of rapiers, arresting all in the haze-mist of awe and submission. Such were the powers of her beauty and courage that all men were implanted alive on the poles of obedience, subservient and spellbound. Before anyone knew, the entire regiment was plunged deep into the blue turquoise waters of the river Behat. The imperialists were seen gathering as one giant wave, and fording their way toward the other shore where the emperor sat captive under the mad tyranny of Mahabat Khan.

The calm waters of the river were turned into angry tides by the intrusion of the horses, the camels and the carriages. A flood of footmen was following in their wake too, wading after the horsemen in the liquid fury of its own. Amidst these violent currents was rising Nur Jahan seated on her noble elephant. She was cradling her granddaughter into her lap, and shooting commands, if not arrows. The imperialists, drugged with the waters of pride and courage, were approaching closer to the royal encampment to confront the traitors and the intruders. These traitors were a wall of eight hundred Rajputs astride their graceful steeds and warring elephants to crush the advancing imperialists with all their might and strength. Suddenly, the river was engulfed by a tempest of war cries. The warring elephants of the Rajputs were a raging storm. Another stealthy assault from the rear was a tidal wave, violent and billowing. A horde of horsemen was dashing headlong toward the imperialists, and plying their swords indiscriminately.

The spears and arrows were a sheet of angry clouds, as if raining God's own wrath from the very mirror of the sky. Pandemonium had visited the earth, the raging, maddening fury of the waters stabbing and consuming all who dared challenge the fates. Nothing could be discerned but quicksilver death and riderless horses. The blue waters were tinged with scarlet, the sun itself aghast at this shimmering sheet of red and gold. All was hazy and confused. Men were unhorsed, wounded and dying. Some were gasping for breath, others drowning inside the ripples of their own screams, wild and agonized. The carriages were pressing too close, the elephants jostling each other, the men and horses wading frantically.

The imperialists were caught unaware into a whirlpool of frenzy and assault. Their ranks were dispersed, their wills shattered. Panic and confusion had crushed their pride and valor, and they were fleeing for their lives. Pain and terror themselves were whipping them back to the refuge of their own encampments where they could be safe from the assaults of the fierce Rajputs. Some were still fighting, more in defense than to gain victory. The imperialists had become an undisciplined lot, courting despair and hopelessness. The men in command, too, were overwhelmed with shame and fatigue, knowing not whither they went, or which direction they were to lead their soldiers.

Nur Jahan herself was fighting desperately. She had emptied her fourth quiver of arrows, and was retrieving another one to blind the very eyes of fates, if not of the Rajputs. She was a woman possessed, neither knowing fear, not courting hopelessness. While shooting arrows at the enemy, her gaze was flashing daggers at her own soldiers in cowardly flight. Without turning, she was shooting another command at her eunuch, Nadim, who was intent on protecting the empress with his own unerring skills.

"Ask the valorous Moghuls, Nadim, is this the time for delay and irresolution? Tell them that the empress commands that they should strike boldly and with utmost confidence. If we keep advancing, the enemy will be repulsed. They will be the ones taking flight, not us." Nur Jahan's commands were as swift as her arrows.

Prince Shahriyar was right behind Nur Jahan, intrepid and reckless, and fighting valiantly. He seemed oblivious to the hungry, roaring waves which had swallowed the sanity of the few and were consuming the madness of the others. He was a part of this fury and violence, the waves themselves licking clean his bloody sword, while he contemplated another blow to strike his next foe, and the next. Fadai Khan was nearing the shore against a shower of arrows, but none reaching his swift, slippery movements. He seemed not aware of the men drowning right and left of him, his will alone carrying him on the currents of fates toward the gilded cage of the emperor. Mutamid Khan was following the lead of Fadai Khan's will and resilience. He had escaped Mahabat Khan's vigilance during the night, and had supplied the empress with the latest news from the camp of imprisonment. Now, he was eager to return to that prison, accompanied by Abul Hasan and other grandees. Asaf Khan with his son Abu Talib, along with Iradat Khan, was hemmed in by a group of desperate Rajputs. All these three men were fighting desperately, succeeding in breaking that terrible circle, and resorting to flight.

Meanwhile, undetected, Fadai Khan had succeeded in reaching the tent of Prince Shahriyar, where the emperor was held prisoner. While the Rajputs were engaged in driving away the rest of the imperial soldiers, Fadai Khan, with a handful of his followers, was besieging the Rajput guards with threats and arrows.

Mahabat Khan was not there to check Fadai Khan's siege and tenacity. He had just left the emperor with a few Rajput guards, venturing forth on the shore to confirm the news of victory. His heart was in ecstatic swoon, as he stood watching the flight of the imperialists, and his own men raising cries of victory and jubilations. Self-pride and self-gloating were the beacons of madness in his eyes as he beheld the elephant of the empress lumbering toward the shore. The warring beast was pierced in the back by a myriad of arrows, its trunk slashed with sword-cuts, but the empress was unscathed.

The elephant of the empress was leaving the bloody waters of Behat, plodding on to the wet sand with strides as small as the crawling of an ant. Suddenly, one stray arrow from somewhere landed into Nur Jahan's lap, piercing straight into the arm of her granddaughter. With the swiftness of a skilled physician, Nur Jahan plucked the arrow out, her hands and white silks splashed with blood.

Mahabat Khan, bloated with the wine of victory, cantered toward the howdah of the empress. Nur Jahan didn't even look up; she was absorbed in wrapping the wound of her granddaughter in her own pashmina shawl.

Mahabat Khan was met by the loud cries of Princess Ladali, and he stopped in his act of summoning his guards to make the formal arrest. Nur Jahan's pale, luminous features and scarlet lips with the silken warmth of tenderness, struck Mahabat Khan with a stab of remorse. His throat was dry and his heart trembling. He was rather smitten with the agonies of the damned by the aura of her sad beauty which could never fail to bewitch even the purest of the puritans. One diabolical urge was uncoiling inside him like the serpent of vengeance, to kill her before she could poison his heart and soul.

Nur Jahan was oblivious to the affect of her sad beauty on this wicked man. All her love and attention were devoted to her granddaughter. A few unruly curls had escaped her red scarf, these flaxen clusters gleaming on her shoulders like the treasures of gold from the sun's own bounteous wealth. The light and transparency in her features and the glow of ivory down her throat were molding her whole being into the unreality of a goddess, not of this earth. After bandaging her granddaughter, she was pressing her to her breast and murmuring endearments, as if she was all alone in this jungle of pain and tragedy. Princess Ladali was lulled to some semblance of comfort, whimpering as if in a dream. Nur Jahan's eyes were finally turning to Mahabat Khan, calm and serene as the dream-blue skies.

"No need to arrest the empress, Mahabat Khan. She submits to your tyranny voluntarily," Nur Jahan murmured, her eyes suddenly glittering. "No need to post the guards either. I will stay in my tent until commanded by you to see the emperor." She alighted from her howdah, assisted by her eunuch Nadim, and followed by her lady-in-waiting, Mehr Harwi.

Mahabat Khan stood there rapt and awed, unable to move or speak, even oblivious to the presence of Prince Shahriyar and Ladli Begum who had just reached the shore. The empress was sailing gracefully toward her own tent without another word or glance at the impudent traitor. She was followed by her daughter and son-in-law, who were floating after her in some stupor of fatigue and torment. While Nur Jahan was drifting along, a few of the emperor's own soldiers had begun to beat the drums, as was customary to announce the arrival of the empress. Mahabat Khan would have stood there stricken till eternity, had not his son Bihroz rushed to him with the news that Fadai Khan was about to capture the Rajput guards and to gain entry into the emperor's tent.

Mahabat Khan was startled to action with the instinct of a wild beast. He was waving his arms and shouting orders. His commands and instructions were quick as lightning to gather the scattered Rajputs and to capture Fadai

Khan. He himself was flying toward the emperor's tent with the fury of a hurricane. Fadai Khan, catching this uproar, had abandoned his post and was fleeing toward the shores of safety.

Mahabat Khan, brandishing his sword and dashing through the files of his Rajput guards, was met by a scene most placid inside the gilded prison of the emperor. This scene was rather comical in contrast to the uproar and confusion outside. The emperor was comfortably seated on his throne, his devoted servants Hushiyar Khan and Mukhlis Khan standing before him like a wall of defense. They were the statues of immobility, their eyes riveted to the scattered sheet of arrows at their feet, which had neither harmed them nor the emperor. The emperor was protected by the aura of his own serenity which could not be disrupted, as was obvious to any discerning eye which could behold this astonishing scene. Even the wall of defense by his two devoted servants was unnoticed by the emperor, and he seemed not aware of the stormy return of Mahabat Khan.

Jahangir was reading the verses of Rumi, his one hand still holding the jeweled pen. A few couplets scribbled by his own hand on the gold-sprinkled paper were the only witness that they had claimed his attention for a while. Mahabat Khan, after storming into the tent, had shattered this wall of immobility by a furious wave of his own arm. He had begun to pace like a madman, unable to utter any more commands or inanities. Hushiyar Khan and Mukhlis Khan were now standing on either side of the emperor's throne, still clothed in dignity and silence. Jahangir kept reading as if oblivious to the incongruity of this scene, where his authority itself was ruled by the whims and insanity of this traitor, wild and unpredictable.

Actually, after the first shock of his captivity, Jahangir had donned a mask of amenity and friendship. His fertile mind was plotting as it had not ever before in all the tragedies during his entire life. In fact, his own aesthetic senses, a mixture of whim and caprice, were challenged by the novelty of this strange coup, challenged rather by the absurdity of his own captivity, where Mahabat Khan respected his authority, and yet commanded with the stupidity of an absolute fool. Jahangir was not long to discover this fact, which had amused him, after he had recovered from the initial shock of this unavoidable tragedy. While hunting, Jahangir had succeeded in banishing all his fears inside the deepest chambers of his heart, where all his past secrets and tragedies lay buried. He had rather enjoyed the hunt, heeding the voice of wisdom for once, as if it was reaching him through the mysterious voids in his soul and psyche.

This madman is dangerous, and the emperor needs to win his trust and friendship before he can subjugate this traitor to his own imperial will. One sliver of an inspiration like this and many more kindled by the lamps of revelations were befriending the emperor after his hunt and his journey back to the gilded prison inside the tent of Prince Shahriyar. Mahabat Khan was greatly respectful of the emperor's needs, almost subservient in fulfilling those needs, and brimming with devotion and solicitude. Jahangir too had summoned his spirit of buoyancy, especially after the hunt. Besides carrying inspirations and revelations in his head, he was quick to melt his anger and bitterness inside the pools of hopes which would assist him in conquering one demented rebel worth many kingdoms.

Jahangir's thoughts were lit by the fire of challenges. *He has conquered many a kingdoms,* Jahangir's thoughts expounded, *but they were the dull, soulless challenges, nurturing no joy or fulfillment inside the laurels of victories. To defeat this living, throbbing temple of animal kingdom in Mahabat Khan's heart is a unique challenge, which the emperor has not ever encountered or undertaken,* He was avidly and astonishingly elated by this prospect, to conquer the demoniacal kingdom inside the mind and heart of this traitor. Jahangir's own body and soul had begun to pulsate with the sense of adventure, all the griefs and illnesses of the past dissolving into the bubbles of delusion and delirium.

Paradoxically, the griefs and illnesses were gathering inside the realms of Jahangir's psyche with the stealth of inevitability, but he himself was not aware of their concealed violence. He was the man pressed by fate, donning the mantle of self-deception, and mounting the rungs of liberty and surcease, while defying reason with the whip of insane reasonings. His thoughts had begun to weave a tapestry of intrigue, welcoming the blind, churning depths of mysteries in his own soul suffered and suffering. His heart was a cauldron of fire and implacability, longing to be united with his beloved, this time, Nur Jahan, his true beloved. He could not endure to be parted from Nur Jahan, could not placate the stabbing fury inside his heart. One night of separation, and the truth had dawned upon him like a bolt of lightning, that his soul was linked with that of Nur Jahan's inside the cosmic mists of time and age. His longings to be near her were so wild and terrible, that they had made him the master of intrigues overnight.

During the night-long repast and conversation with Mahabat Khan, Jahangir had discovered that this lunatic of a general not only hated Asaf Khan but the empress too. After discovering this fact, all his thoughts were centered on one point, and that point was to insure the safety of his beloved at all costs. Mahabat Khan had urged the emperor to deprive the empress of all power, and Jahangir had granted his consent. Encouraged by the emperor's air of sympathy and understanding, this madman was dissolved into tears of humility and gratitude. To win his absolute trust, Jahangir had assured him that he himself distrusted the empress.

Jahangir was counting on Nur Jahan's disposition to anger and implacability in situations dire and uncontrollable. He was sure that she would launch an attack, but he had assured Mahabat Khan otherwise, telling the besotted lunatic that since he had sent the missive along with his signet ring, she would not dare disobey the emperor's command. Jahangir's mind was miles ahead of Mahabat Khan's in plots and intrigues, since his beloved's safety was paramount in his thoughts and since Mahabat Khan's hatred for the empress could not be melted with gifts or threats. Jahangir had no hope that Nur Jahan would win, but was convinced that her attack would cause rifts amongst the Rajputs, thus weakening their strength and resolve. His head was brimming with plans to win further trust of Mahabat Khan. Since Nur Jahan would attack, and would probably be unsuccessful, the emperor would issue an edict of punishment to chastise the empress for defying the emperor's orders. This plan was brewing in Jahangir's head like the gunpowder from a cannon, and he could not help exploring more possibilities. This edict of punishment would be followed by an edict of pardon, as if Mahabat Khan himself was the author of both the edicts. In the aftermath of his plans and schemes, Jahangir was not exactly sure what he was going to say, but he was positive that he would shape the flow of the events with the inexorability of his own will and prudence.

Wearing the mantle of surface-calm, Jahangir had already disillusioned the mad traitor. Mahabat Khan had begun to act and think that the emperor was resigned to his fate of captivity, and was favoring his cause in forcing the empress to relinquish all power and grandeur. The mantle of surface-calm, strange as it might seem, was also the result of a sudden transformation in Jahangir's mind, soul and spirit. He had begun to view things as the mists evanescent, embracing the beat of realities and delusions into the rhythm of time. Some cosmic puzzle, vague and pre-ordained, he had thought, which would complete its course, and reveal its completion as if it was mounted on the wheels of fortunes and misfortunes, scrambled and unscrambled by a million minds in its own core since eons. He didn't know, but a kernel of spirituality was sprouting inside him, rather awakening somewhere inside the ocean of his soul and psyche. He was sucked into the tunnel of light, yet groping for something inside the pool of darkness.

This blind, terrible search for something inside the silence of Jahangir's heart was kindled by the fires of a longing to live, while witnessing the cinders of death, hot and glowing. His body and mind were gathering the sparks of vitality and renewal, but something inside him was on the verge of atrophy and surcease. And yet again, he could feel his thoughts riding on the currents of euphoria, reaching out for the clouds of delirium, as if they contained in their little hearts the waters of sanity, if not the promise of hope and mercy.

Mahabat Khan, in return, was so befuddled by the emperor's outward show of self-surrender, that he had begun to doubt his own will and authority in keeping this royal prisoner under constant vigilance. Guided by the flood of his own inner turbulence, Mahabat Khan had begun to cling to the trust and the friendship of the emperor. Before that night of candor and camaraderie was over, he was so deliciously bewitched that he had presented a valuable gift to the emperor. This gift was an old coin with the picture of the king-philosopher of India by the name of Menander carved on one side, and the other side depicting the bust of Pallas Athene. After receiving this gift, Jahangir had bestowed upon him his own gold coin with the zodiacal bull, adding that this was a token of his trust and friendship for Mahabat Khan. With this great note of trust and friendship, both the emperor and the general had agreed on taking some rest. Before leaving, Mahabat Khan had set his own gift beside the emperor's, declaring that he was leaving his own trust and friendship with the emperor. Now as Mahabat Khan kept pacing, he could not help seeing those two coins glittering beside the inkstand, where the emperor's jeweled cup lay abandoned.

"Your Majesty, now the empress is in my custody too. Your royal granddaughter got injured in the fray…" Mahabat Khan began feverishly.

At the mention of his granddaughter's injury, an imperceptible shadow of pain swept over Jahangir's features, but no pain was surfacing in his eyes as he lifted his gaze. He was wearing purple silks with a matching turban. The large amethyst in his turban was accentuating his pallor, as if no blood was coursing in his veins but light and ether. His gaze was intense and profound, flickering suddenly with a gleam of inspiration, as if the lake-blue depths of a lonely stream had come alive.

Jahangir's hand was reaching out for the goblet of wine, his gaze never leaving Mahabat Khan. Mahabat Khan was wading inside the currents of his own soliloquy and self-absorption, not even aware of the emperor's close scrutiny. While sipping his wine, Jahangir had claimed his pen and had scribbled a brief note on the gold-sprinkled paper. With utmost calm and without haste, he folded the note into a small square, and slipped it into the hands of his eunuch, Hushiyar Khan.

Stealing a look at the raging lunatic in his feverish pacing, Jahangir whispered to Hushiyar Khan, "You are to deliver this note into the hands of the empress in a swath of bandages which I will send." Jahangir's lips were parted in one crescent of a smile.

"So much needless panic and bloodshed." Mahabat Khan's pace was dwindling, and the look in his eyes dark and smoldering. "How could Padishah Begum disobey the emperor? How could she think that her forces of five hundred against my five thousand would ever win, or did she know? How many imperialists are slain and how many Rajputs lost? What grievous tragedy! I am working on your behalf, Your Majesty, you must understand that. The power is slipping from your hands..." His feet were coming to a stumbling halt near the emperor's throne. "You have given too much power to Padishah Begum, Your Majesty. The drums and orchestra beat before her wherever she goes. As if, as if she could rule and crush the empire of Hind in her tiny fists if she wished, and with her charm and witchcraft alone. She has cast a spell over you, Your Majesty, wielding power and disobeying your commands. Padishah Begum, yes, she is carving her way to the throne with Prince Shahriyar as her pawn. Prince Perwiz should be the rightful heir to the throne, as the matters stand. Yes, Your Majesty, I am here to save you from the scheming influence of Padishah Begum. To insure your safety, and to proclaim you as the sole sovereign of the whole empire. Your kingdoms have been usurped by Padishah Begum for so long, for so long."

"Your prudence, Mahabat, is lifting the veil of darkness from the emperor's eyes." Jahangir drained his cup, replacing it on the table wrought in gold and ivory. "The emperor is much grieved by this tragic warfare, much more even than the fact that his own granddaughter has suffered an injury. The emperor wishes to send her the bandages and to inquire about her health. That account settled, we will discuss other matters."

"Yes, Your Majesty," Mahabat Khan murmured doubtfully. "I myself will command your royal physician to..." His thoughts were disrupted by one impatient wave of the emperor's arm.

"No, my good friend, no. No need to alarm the emperor's physicians." Jahangir turned his attention to his eunuch. "Hushiyar Khan, fetch that roll of bandages from the emperor's hunting chest and take it to the tent of the empress. And return posthaste. The emperor wishes to know how the little princess fares."

Mahabat Khan stood there demurring, but when Hushiyar Khan proceeded to leave, he balked his way with the alacrity of a panther. Jahangir sat there watching unperturbed, as if there was nothing unusual in the manner of his corrupt general. Mahabat Khan was summoning his guards to escort Hushiyar Khan, also instructing them to stay alert and note every word which passes between him and the empress. After the eunuch had left with his escort, Mahabat Khan turned haughtily toward the emperor.

"Padishah Begum has submitted voluntarily, Your Majesty, but she can't be trusted," Mahabat Khan gloated shamelessly. "She has disobeyed you, Your Majesty. If your justice still prevails, she deserves strict punishment. Now is the time, Your Majesty, to free yourself from the yolk of her power. You should have believed me when I told you that she would attack." He appeared to be gasping for breath.

"Not disobedience, but treason!" Jahangir muttered ominously. He was summoning the daggers of steel in his eyes to play the part of a tyrant.

"Treason!" Mahabat Khan was taken aback, as if stunned by the impact of this accusation. His cup of vengeance was brimming, yet the beauty of the empress was scorching his soul with the tortures of the damned. He didn't wish her death, only subjugation, with a dash of humiliation. "Treason, Your Majesty, calls for death, if not exile," he murmured.

"On the scale of the emperor's justice, only death is the answer to treason." Jahangir's gaze was bright and intense.

"You will not sentence the empress to death, Your Majesty, will you?" was Mahabat Khan's flustered plea-inquiry.

"Yes, death sentence, a just edict the emperor will write himself," Jahangir intoned firmly. His inspiration to deal with this madman with a little madness of his own was working wonders, Jahangir was quick to notice. "Yes, treason earns no favor from the emperor for anyone, be they kin, foe or friend."

"If you write that edict, Your Majesty, I myself will carry it to Padishah Begum." One cry of fear and ecstasy escaped Mahabat Khan's madness.

"Summon Mutamid Khan, Mahabat; the emperor feels rather week." Jahangir pressed his temples and closed his eyes.

Mahabat Khan obeyed the emperor with the speed of a falcon. He was soaring out of this tent on his own, and leaving his own guards abashed. Jahangir kept his eyes closed, the wisps of inspirations, garnished with wild schemes inside his head, now a great conflagration. Even his heart was a jungle of wildfire, caught inside the convulsions of agony and longings. His whole body was burning with the fever-agony of separation from his beloved. The emperor's own safety and the safety of his beloved were staked against the pillars of power and madness. And Mahabat Khan alone was the guardian over both, remaining in utmost command despite the mental strategies concocted by the emperor's despair and ingenuity.

Such thoughts, and many more savage ones about his beloved's absence and captivity, were whirling in Jahangir's head as he sat listening to the thundering within his heart. Though the master of his own decisions and strategies, his thoughts were walking on red, hot coals to be united with his beloved, and to breathe the air of freedom in her presence. He was aware of Mahabat Khan's power resting mighty over his subservient soldiers, the Rajputs. Besides, the Rajputs outnumbered the imperialists five to one, and were ruled by a madman. Perspicacious as the emperor was, his senses were honed more acute during those past few hours of his captivity. And he had guessed quite accurately that Mahabat Khan would not permit Nur Jahan to see the emperor unless he could win his trust by professing his own mistrust and indifference toward the empress. His thoughts dancing on red hot coals could now behold the result of his strategy and inspiration, where Mahabat Khan's shrewdness was confounded. He could envision Nur Jahan receiving his note in a swath of bandages, and her candor in perceiving all. Her wit and wisdom, he knew, would unravel the puzzling events which could commence their march as soon as Mahabat Khan would return with Mutamid Khan.

Mutamid Khan, too eager to see the emperor, obeyed Mahabat Khan most sincerely and willingly. Meanwhile, Jahangir had succeeded in bringing order to the chaos within him, and when Mutamid Khan arrived, his expression was calm and contemplative. He had donned the mask of sadness and relentlessness, while dictating the edict of death for Nur Jahan. Entrusting this sealed edict into the hands of Mahabat Khan, Jahangir smiled into his eyes as if he was grateful to this mad traitor for opening his eyes to the invincibility of Nur Jahan's power over the emperor. Mahabat Khan, in return, drunk with the wine of trust and friendship from the emperor, was grateful to deliver this edict into the hands of the proud empress. He had floated out of this tent in demented glee, though his heart was courting fears and forebodings. He could feel his heart constricting, longing only for a glimpse of the sad beauty of the empress.

Mutamid Khan was sitting at the feet of the emperor, pale as a corpse. His look was glazed, and he was unable to voice his horror at such a shocking edict. His hands, which had trembled while penning the words, were now listless and white as the glaciers of ice. After Mahabat Khan's exit, Jahangir whispered quickly, his eyes glued to the guards who were standing within a hearing distance, alert and tireless.

"A ruse, Mutamid. Gird your courage. Believe not a word of what the emperor says. He is carving his way to meet the empress and to gain liberty."

The empress, surrounded by the guards outside her tent, was preparing herself for a shock after shock inside the misery of her own captivity. The emperor's little note, swathed in bandages, had enveloped her into mists of despair and hopelessness. Hushiyar Khan had left with his escort, and she had not deigned to share the import of this note with her daughter or son-in-law, who had watched her read it with a gasp of incredulity. She had devoured each word with a profound, enigmatic gleam which could not be concealed behind the facade of serenity in her expression.

Nur Jahan's eyes were feverish and sparkling now, as she continued pacing, much like a caged tigress, it was obvious. Her thoughts were communing with the emperor's inside some dark tunnel of magic and mystery. Her wit and wisdom, right this tragic moment, were sharp as the naked blade of a dagger, poised for stabbing. They were cutting the heart of this dark tunnel within her, where unvoiced thoughts could embrace the cult of love and longings. Her thoughts were gathering such wordless rapport with the emperor's own thoughts that she had not even noticed the abrupt intrusion of Mahabat Khan. Only Prince Shahriyar had leapt to his feet, and the moaning princess in Ladli Begum's lap was sucked into silence.

Noticing Mahabat Khan inside the tent, Nur Jahan was suspended in her act of pacing. The feverish sparkle in her eyes was kindled to a burning intensity. Mahabat Khan too was suspended, stricken dumb by the shafts of her beauty and sadness. His heart was lurching down to some Scythian deeps, where tortures of the body and soul were abysmal and everlasting. He was holding out the edict, awed, stricken.

"The emperor wishes you to read this edict, Padishah Begum." One hoarse challenge escaped Mahabat Khan's pain and exultance.

Nur Jahan claimed the note with silent grace and dignity. Her features were pale and luminescent from the fire of tragedy and misfortune smoldering inside her. She unsealed the note most reverently, and was lost in its contents as if no one existed in the world for her but this note of hope and tragedy. A shadow of pain swept across her features, but her demeanor was calm and graceful as she stood searching the meaning behind that brutal expression.

She was a sculpture of ice and fire, of gold and ivory. She was not aware of her own charm and beauty, which her sadness had carved and sculpted. Neither was she aware of the ugliness of passion in the eyes of Mahabat Khan, which were feasting on her sadness with a mingling of desire and reverence. She had closed her eyes for one brief moment, as if praying for wisdom and fortitude. Her eyes, when she opened them, were like the clear, blue lakes, revealing nothing but their own polished depths of serenity. She had snatched one mystery of a thought from the emperor's own lips, her own thoughts were confirming, and she was ready to voice it without fear.

"My last request, Mahabat. May I see the emperor before I…" Nur Jahan left the pause for a dramatic affect, as if her heart was breaking. "May I hope to bathe with my tears the hand which affixed this seal to my death warrant," she murmured.

"I will plead with the emperor, Padishah Begum." Mahabat Khan fled, as if his very eyes were gouged with the brands of iron, hot and searing.

Mahabat Khan's heart was racked with pain and grief, as he returned to the emperor's gilded prison. But his thoughts were clearing, sloughing off the burdens of pains and griefs, and getting more demented and tyrannous in their search for peace and sanity. A million imponderables were surfacing in his head, as he entered the gilded prison of his own will and dementia. He found the emperor contemplating his favorite coins, and he stood watching without saying a word. Actually, he needed time to decipher his own thoughts, and to glean some sort of truth out of the emperor's moods. Hushiyar Khan and Mukhlis Khan were lolling against the gold pillows at the foot of the emperor's throne, as if resting in utmost comfort. Mutamid Khan, seated across from them, was spilling entries into the royal journal with swift, bold strokes in Persian.

Jahangir's lips were taut and his pallor gleaming, as he sat contemplating his gold coin with zodiacal bull. He was abandoning it whimsically, and picking up the other one from the table in gold and ivory. This coin was the gift from Mahabat Khan on the night of his captivity, when both had drunk deep of wine from the goblets and from the cups of friendship. Only the Rajput guards posted right outside the tent were a harsh reminder that no such amity existed between the general and the emperor. Jahangir seemed fascinated by this antique coin, as if looking into the very eyes of Menander, the Bactrian Greek philosopher-king of northwest India. He was turning the coin over, watching the Pallas Athene on the reverse side, his expression rapt and pensive.

Pride and self-gratification were leaping out of Mahabat Khan's very eyes, as he watched the emperor admiring his gift with such affectionate intensity. He inched closer, first peering over Mutamid Khan's shoulders to assess the import of his liquid entries. Discovering that the royal scribe was delineating the history of his own antique coin, he was further bloated with a sense of euphoria. He was forgetting, completely and absolutely, his own aching, searing torment, and edging closer to the emperor.

"Your Majesty, I have another gift to present to you when we reach Lahore. Another gold coin with the engraving of Chandra Gupta with his queen!" Mahabat Khan declared with the pride of a connoisseur. "Also a coin struck by Alexander to celebrate his victory. On this is the engraving of Alexander himself on horseback, attacking the Indian King Porus on his war-elephant," he added proudly.

"And the emperor will show you the portrait of his father holding the globe of dominion." Jahangir lifted his gaze slowly and thoughtfully. Such poise and warmth were in his eyes that not even a seasoned prude could detect the rivers of pain simmering behind them. With one flash of a smile, he asked nonchalantly, "And how did the empress receive her edict of death?"

"Padishah Begum craves Your Majesty's permission to see you before..." Mahabat Khan blurted out, unable to deflect the stab of pain and remorse in his delirious thoughts. "This is the last wish of the empress, Your Majesty, as Padishah Begum said."

"What's the use, you tell me, Mahabat?" Jahangir murmured.

"I don't know, Your Majesty," Mahabat Khan muttered distractedly. "The wishes of the dying are to be honored, as far as I know." Pain and hopelessness were tearing his own heart to bleeding shreds.

"Are they? My edict can't be altered. Should I grant the empress her last wish?" Jahangir appeared to question the air itself.

"I am here to serve you, Your Majesty. If you decide to grant the empress her last wish, I am your obedient slave. I will fetch Padishah Begum myself," Mahabat Khan murmured with half relief, half dread. His thoughts were entangled in chasing the fleeing nobility.

"Then summon the empress to the presence of the emperor, Mahabat. This day is going to be long and wearisome, it seems." Jahangir sighed, as if he was surrendering to the wishes of Mahabat Khan, not to his own.

Mahabat Khan departed quickly without any advice or protest, this time urged by his duty as a captor, which was hanging around his neck like one giant millstone. The burden of this edict was heavy on his shoulders, and the arms of fate were coiling around his own neck like the noose of death. His thoughts were finding diversion in racing after the royal rebels on the other side of the river. He was afraid of losing control, and falling into the same pit of misfortune which awaited the empress.

Mahabat Khan had escorted the empress in some stupor of fog and delirium. Astonishingly and inexplicably, he was feeling both drained and humbled by her sad beauty. The empress was bowing before the emperor as a lowly suppliant, and Mahabat Khan was quick to announce that he was going out to instruct his troops to follow the fleeing rebels.

Mahabat Khan had left the tent, but he was heard posting more Rajput guards, and barking instructions. He had doubled the number of guards, it seemed, but soon his voice was fading, his hurried steps too growing faint and distant. Jahangir had kept his attention fixed on Mahabat Khan, neither acknowledging Nur Jahan's curtsy, nor granting her the permission to speak. He had maintained his poise of authority, his gaze harsh and forbidding. Now that Mahabat Khan had left, he sat contemplating his hands, suffering not to lift his eyes, lest he break the bonds of propriety in snatching her to himself, endangering the life of his beloved along with his own. He was waiting for the command of his honed perspicacity to announce the ultimate departure of Mahabat Khan. He could barely keep his gaze averted, his hands themselves aching to confirm the nearness of his beloved. A sea of agony was churning inside him, kneeling in gratitude before some presence omniscient. God Almighty had spared him the anxiety of a mental combat in winning this opportunity, and he was humbled, even amidst this great torture in not being able to snatch his beloved into one eager embrace. As soon as his honed perception confirmed that Mahabat Khan had finally left and would not be back for a while, he clapped his hands without raising his eyes.

"Leave us, my devoted friends. And stay friendly with the guards." Jahangir swept his gaze over the three men, who sat with their heads bowed and their lips sealed.

Mukhlis Khan and Hushiyar Khan scrambled to their feet, and Mutamid Khan followed their lead. They were quick to offer hasty curtsies to both the emperor and the empress, before escaping the charged silence of this strange abode. No sooner had they left, that Nur Jahan fell into the emperor's arms sobbing like a child. All the restraints of her misery and anguish were broken loose, flowing through her eyes in a flood of tears.

"Your Majesty!" Nur Jahan groaned. All her pain, all her love, all her grief were embodied in this one tremulous expression. Her heart was breaking under the weight of shame, humiliation, hopelessness.

"Hush, dearest, hush. The light of my heart, hush." Jahangir's own anguished pleas were spilling endearments. "You have no idea how terribly disconsolate I have been without you. Had I been blind, lame, or twisted in limb, or deformed of body and soul, I would have not been more grieved than I was in being separated from you. You are my life, my soul, my staff, my refuge. How could I then survive without you? Now that we are together, we will plan. The emperor has a plan. Have patience, my pearl, have patience. We are fighting evil and madness. This is no fair war, of pride or honor, but a hideous game of deceit and dementia. Hush, my best and the dearest, hush." He grazed his lips against her hair. "My profoundest of loves, no more tears and sorrow. We will not ever be separated, not ever again. If the emperor is not already drowned in this sea of captivity, my love, you will drown him into the flood of your tears." He cupped her tear-streaked face into her hands, and smiled into her eyes.

"Your Majesty." Nur Jahan smiled back, trying her best to dispel the torrent of her joy and tears.

"My sweetest of loves." Jahangir dried away her tears with kisses. "Come, sweet, sit by me." He gasped for breath. "This chair I have kept beside me all this time, imagining you in there. Telling Mahabat that it is for him, but never offering him to be seated near me. He has not defiled its sanctity, not as yet, and nor will he."

Nur Jahan drifted toward the chair beside him, dazed yet pacified. Her tide of grief was abating, and she was mastering her will to conquer all the misfortunes which lay sprawled before them like the locusts foul and poisonous. No more tears were clouding her eyes, and she was deliciously content to be with the emperor.

"These terrible fates, Your Majesty, we will conquer them together." Nur Jahan's calm and optimism were returning.

"Master of our own fates we tremble like the salves, when fates confront us with the superiority of their own invincible powers." One feeble epigram escaped Jahangir's suffered anguish, his gaze profound and wistful.

"The grains of adversity and uncertainty are the salts of life, Your Majesty, without which life would have no taste or flavor." Nur Jahan's mind was sketching a string of plans to gain release. "Is Mahabat Khan's madness as unpredictable as his plots, Your Majesty?" she asked abruptly.

"Each one of us has a tendency to be raving mad or unpredictable at times, my Nur," Jahangir began quickly, his thoughts still mired inside the pools of profundities. "Saints and sinners both, all tormented by the fires of evil and good in their souls. The only difference between a saint and sinner is that the former absolves his fire of evil through penance and austerity, and retains the flame of goodness. The latter, of course, corrupts the flame of goodness by the virtue of his own need and desire, and nurtures the fire of evil. Goodness is like ether, pure and mysterious, with a tendency to soar towards heights lofty and noble, when awakened by the rod of consciousness. I am beginning to understand my own moods…more so the fits of madness attacking Mahabat Khan's. Future will reveal more as to who is the captor and who the captive. I hold him in check under the sway of my mental powers." He sighed.

"Why waste time looking into the eyes of the future, Your Majesty, when the face of present demands living?" Nur Jahan urged softly. "We must plan, Your Majesty. What is to be done? Why that edict? What is to become of me—you?" she murmured.

"An illusion, my love, all is illusion," Jahangir murmured back, unable to expound the complexity of his plan which depended upon the whims of Mahabat Khan, not upon his own will and prudence. "Hold on to this illusion, my pearl, the only reality worth possessing. Illusion has many a capricious veils, and each veil, when lifted, reveals the caprice of many doubts." His eyes were shining with a poetic gleam.

"Are we going to wander in captivity, Your Majesty? Distraught and homeless, while our empire and sovereignty are being usurped by the evil designs of this madman?" Nur Jahan hummed her concerns.

"Are we all not homeless—and wandering?" Jahangir's poetic reverie was donning the mantle of ideation and mysticism. "Yes, wandering on the face of this earth in misery and wretchedness, bent double by the burden of greed and ambition. Fear clawing at our hearts, and false courage cutting open the wounds of ego…" He paused, noticing Nur Jahan's pained expression. "I have been writing couplets, my love, rather quatrains. Centuries upon centuries of wait has driven the emperor quite mad, stark mad with pangs of separation and longings indescribable…" He paused, before reciting, "My burning heart hath melted my body with separation's pang. A soul-consuming sigh burnt me, as t'were a lamp. The day of my joy became black like the night of grief. Separation from thee hath made my day like this."

"Your Majesty!" Nur Jahan was too overwhelmed to trust her voice. "I too wrote, or rewrote a quatrain, Your Majesty. Pressing the edict of death to my breast, while suspended on the gallows of wait. An eternity lingered before the summons came." Her grief too was entering the sanctuary of poetic comfort.

"Let there be neither a light nor a flower. On the grave of this humble person. Nor the wings of the moth burn in flames of love. Nor the nightingale send out his wailing cry."

The saddest-blue in her eyes was sparkling all of a sudden. "You must inscribe this verse on my cold tomb, Your Majesty, promise."

"Haven't I heard this before, in another world, in another century?" Jahangir murmured chokingly. "Yes, my love, with the pen of my bleeding heart I might inscribe this verse till my own heart will cease to throb." He was trying to ward off the blows of agony. "On judgment day, my dearest recluse, you will see my wounded heart, if its wounds bleed not to death right this moment in fear of losing you."

"Recluse!" declared Nur Jahan. The mingling of poetry and mischief in her eyes were kindling them to midnight-blue.

"Oh, Recluse! Do not create terror in my heart about the Day of Judgment. I am aware of the extreme suffering which results from the separation from beloved."

"Your wit alone, my Nur, has the power to break the shackles of captivity." Jahangir laughed low, as if he had forgotten how to laugh.

"Your Majesty, what's to be done? Please tell me before Mahabat Khan returns. How are we going to..." Her frenzied plea was stifled by the sudden impact of Mahabat Khan's blistering tones outside the tent.

"Your Majesty." Mahabat Khan charged into the tent like a stray animal. His nostrils were flared, and his lips hanging loose under the bushel of his dark mustache. "Great losses on both sides, I have learnt. Several of my Rajput soldiers are dead. Fadai Khan has fled toward the Rohtas to join his sons. Asaf Khan with his son Abu Talib, and Balaqi, the son of late Prince Khusrau, all have fled toward the fort of Atok." He was blathering under the strain of rage and urgency. "We must march to Atok, Your Majesty, to catch those royal rebels who have been the cause of such havoc." Panic and frenzy were glowing in his eyes as he gasped for breath. He seemed to have forgotten about the edict of death, not even noticing the empress seated beside the emperor.

"Your judgment is faultless, Mahabat Khan. Asaf Khan is the sole cause of this needless havoc and warfare." Jahangir appeared to commiserate with the mad traitor.

"I have already dispatched my son Bihroz, Your Majesty, along with a contingent of Rajputs to invest the fort of Atok." Mahabat Khan was quick to catch his breath, and to dole out his bulletin of news and decisions. "Abul

Hasan has submitted without any trace of provocation, and has sworn his fidelity to me. Now with your permission, Your Majesty, permit me to capture Asaf Khan and his followers, so that I could parade them before you in chains of disgrace and humiliation. The fort of Atok is best suited for this purpose." His rage was spent, his look wild and feverish.

"You have the absolute consent of the emperor to punish the offenders as you may deem proper." Jahangir assumed the look of utter resignation. "I have listened to the pleas of the empress. It took me long to discover that I have been mistaken in my judgment. Asaf Khan is the one who instigated this attack. The empress was too distraught and frightened to think about anything. She was merely obeying her brother in whatever he proposed. She herself has vowed complete submission, pleading mercy and forgiveness from the emperor. I have acted hastily, neglecting to discover the truth against the veil of my own blind rage. If I could recant my edict, the most merciful God Himself might forgive me for almost committing this injustice. With your full support, of course, if you too believe in the innocence of the empress," he concluded, feigning detachment, as if he was surrendering his will to the will of this traitor.

"Forever your slave, Your Majesty. Your will and your justice I embrace most warmly!" Mahabat Khan exclaimed with the vehemence of a devotee who knew nothing about the edict of death. "The most merciful God, may He save us all from the tyranny of foes and cutthroats," he murmured deliriously, his eyes shining.

"The emperor's justice is the mercy and justice of God's own will," Jahangir breathed sadly. "The empress will stay with us." His gaze was thoughtful and searching, as if diving straight into the method of his madness.

"We march toward the fort of Atok this very evening, Your Majesty. Our Rajput forces would be our shields of protection. Asaf Khan and his followers must be captured," Mahabat Khan announced with a sudden glint of authority. "We will march as if nothing has changed. Your imperial forces would stay with us, but they would be subject to my command. I would look to the preparations of the journey myself." He waved his arms as if already commanding some invisible battalions. "And now, Your Majesty, I myself would conduct Padishah Begum to her own royal tent." A sudden fire of victory and elation was blinding his sight.

"Leave the empress with the emperor, Mahabat. She has no more troops to command." Jahangir waved his own arm in firm dismissal.

"Yes, Your Majesty." Mahabat Khan stood there demurring. "Rajput guards will be announcing the hour of our journey." He sprinted out of the tent.

Jahangir's gaze was turning to Nur Jahan in worshipful silence. His pallor was accentuated by the bellows of his own inner torment, which he was trying to empty inside the tides of his stoicism. Mists of tears were gathering into the eyes of Nur Jahan, but she too was forcing her pain and tears back inside the rivers of her mute sufferings.

"This Babylonian sadness, my love. It too will cease as well as the Babylonian corruption," Jahangir murmured soothingly.

"Yes, Your Majesty. We would break the chains of captivity, I assure you." Nur Jahan was smiling through the mists of her tears.

"It's an illusion, love, not the curse of inevitability, just remember that. Just an illusion." Jahangir claimed her hand, pressing his lips to this treasure of loveliness.

Chapter Eighteen

The fort of Atok with its bastions and ramparts was gleaming under the sun. It was being besieged by a battalion of the Rajputs. Mahabat Khan himself was at the head of his forces, bloated with pride and confidence that soon he would capture Asaf Khan and parade him before the emperor in chains of humiliation. Not far from the fort was the silk city of royal encampments, woven in false colors of peace and harmony. The imperialists were idle and languishing against the strict vigilance of the Rajput troops. They were seething with rage and bitterness, and waiting for an opportunity to roast these heathens into the fires of the damned.

The journey from Jehlum to Atok was a parade of pomp and pageantry floating ahead of the emperor's cavalcade, as if he was in total command, though he was not heard issuing any orders. Mahabat Khan was always visible on the scene, barking orders and shooting decisions with the mad genius of a ruthless general. The emperor was permitted hunting, even presiding over his court in the usual manner of power and authority, both of which he couldn't claim. Mahabat Khan was the sole arbiter, master of the state affairs, and executioner of all commands. Even today, he had ordered the emperor's throne to be erected in the open at the foot of a verdant hillock. He was anticipating victory, and was voicing his commands that the emperor would mount his throne to receive the royal prisoners namely Asaf Khan and his followers.

The emperor's throne with gold latticework was splashed with velvets, and furnished with a brocade canopy in shimmering folds. This throne was unoccupied for the time being, and its gold chair encrusted with jewels appeared to bemoan the absence of the royal occupant. Jahangir had chosen to stay with Nur Jahan in the luxury of his own tent, while the traitor was away on his own siege. The royal encampment itself was brimming with colorful tents reserved for the princes, begums and for the entire cavalcade, but the emperor had alienated himself from them all with the aloofness of a hermit.

There was a great lake at the foot of these hills where the elephants could bathe and bask under the sun. Jahangir's only indulgence or diversion was to ride up to this lake and watch the happy beasts till they were clean of all grime, and could be heard snorting with pleasure. The meadows too at the edge of the lake had become Jahangir's favorite retreat for solitary contemplations, where he was wont to retire, condoning the strings of guards following him. Just five days since the royal tents were pitched here close to the fort of Atok, and the emperor had a feeling that he had been living here for the past five centuries.

The courtiers were hovering near the gold throne, waiting for the emperor, but the emperor was leaving not the comfort of his own private abode. Besides, he was loathe to abandon the delightful company of his beloved, which was most favorable to his own whims and pleasures. Dressed impeccably in citron robes, he was looking more like a sun-god than a captive emperor, whose ransom for life was his kingdoms which he could neither claim nor barter for freedom. The empress was dressed like the moon-goddess, in pale silks and soft, glowing pearls. Her cheeks had grown pale, rather luminescent than before. The blue lakes in her eyes were vivid and blazing, as if the wild storms from within would escape her very gaze in bolts of lightning. One flash of a lightning was escaping her eyes this very moment, as she sat molding the emperor's indecisions into sprigs of resolves.

"My faithful eunuch, Hushiyar Khan, Your Majesty, would obey my orders to slit the throat of this vile traitor, if you but command," Nur Jahan whispered.

"And our royal throats would be slit by the hands of the merciless Rajputs," Jahangir whispered back. "Though I am worried about you, not me. Upon my life and honor, my Nur, I dare not lose you."

"What a farce this is, Your Majesty?" Nur Jahan's eyes were gathering bullets of intrigues. Her gun named Qarisha laying beside her so harmlessly, was arresting her attention. "Take me to hunting with you, Your Majesty. Qarisha has been faithful to me. It has shot many a beasts, and this beast is no match against my hunting skills. I would kill him, and our faithful imperialists would spread the rumor that the traitor died while hunting. Even the Rujputs won't suspect you, Your Majesty, since they watch you like the hawks. Oh, this is ridiculously simple!" She sighed, noticing a gleam of amusement in the emperor's eyes.

"Even the emperor's Sandoz is faithful enough, my pearl, to slit his throat with its unerring aim." Jahangir's gaze reached down to caress his own jeweled sword in its hilt. "But this is no solution. Thousands of Rajputs loom mighty over our heads. His farce and madness alone are our shield and protection. As long as he claims to respect and uphold the emperor's sense of inviolability, with the assurance that he has no treasonable designs, the unrest and rebellion amongst our troops and kingdoms could be kept at bay. We will catch him unawares when the opportunity affords us such a challenge."

"When, Your Majesty? So far we have not availed of any opportunity," Nur Jahan murmured hopelessly.

"Before action, a set moment of time and place is planned, a proper niche, waiting for the hour to strike its own trumpet of right action, if one is to achieve success. One has to hone one's senses to hear that call, to work in conformity with its command, devising means to collect all pieces of the puzzle, of time, as an analogy, if you will, so that success can be viewed as a whole, not draining through the hourglass of mistakes. If we act hastily without waiting for that call, the puzzle of time will confound our efforts. We will confront chaos, not conformity." Jahangir's very eyes were spilling profundities. "My plan is to gain absolute trust of Mahabat Khan, and then strike when he is least suspecting," he added with the clairvoyance of a diviner.

"If Prince Shah Jahan gets wind of our captivity, Your Majesty, he is sure to rise in rebellion once again." Nur Jahan was trying to infuse a sense of urgency into the plans of freedom, yet to be tested. "Looting treasuries on the way, and filling his own coffers with gold and jewels,"

"How strange and pitiful, my love, that it takes one a lifetime, if ever at all, to discover the follies of one's youth," Jahangir began heedlessly. "One's mindless indulgence to the pleasures of the world, however sweet to the palate, turn most bitter when aged, especially, when they manifest afresh in the characters of one's own children. Alas, for the jewels of this world, which have been poured in such profusion upon my head, bear no longer value in my sight. Neither do I any longer feel the slightest inclination to possess them."

"This state of captivity has altered you considerably, Your Majesty," Nur Jahan thought aloud, her own wit succumbing to despair. "You are resigned to it, floating in some sort of dream, which may vanish when you awaken. We mustn't despair, Your Majesty. Hope is our only seed of joy, which can bloom into the flower of liberty if we try to nurture it with action." Her gaze was catching and holding the poetic gleam in the emperor's eyes into her own. "Gold and jewels can still buy friends and fidelities. I have a little left, from the hands of this bandit of a traitor who plundered most of them." Her voice was one tremor of regret. "And I would use those few to purchase alliances, who would be willing to cause rift and dissension amongst the Rajputs themselves."

"Hush, my love, hush. Be comforted. We would gain liberty, all in time, all in time." Jahangir's eyes were gathering warmth and tenderness. "This captivity has been a blessing in disguise. It has given me time to think, to be with you, totally and absolutely to be with you, in mind and body, in soul and spirit, my spirit wandering no more in realms unforgotten. That was a dream, the life which I had spent in utter ignorance of my own self, all those years. Yearning for love which was no more, and neglecting the one which danced before my eyes in a whirlwind of illusions. Just an illusion, never forget that, my love. I will be able to expound on that one of these days. About that life of delusion and suffering? That life is unveiled before me, I can see it…still a paradox in living. Neither is, nor can be in this world any permanent state of repose or happiness. All is vain, fleeting and perishable. In the twinkling of an eye we shall see the enchantress fate, which enslaves the world and its votaries, seizes the throat of another and another victim. And so exposed is man to be trodden down by the calamities of life, that one might almost be persuaded to affirm that he never had existence. This world, the end of which is destined to be miserable, can scarcely be worth the risk of so much useless violence." His expression was one of a lone dreamer.

"The hope is dying inside you, Your Majesty," Nur Jahan murmured with alarm. "Don't tell me, Your Majesty, that you don't find joy in hunting and feasting any more?" she asked, more so to jolt him out of his dream-state, than to seek answers.

"Those enjoyments too, my love, have been a source of pain and regret to me," Jahangir responded dreamily.

"Do you not see this jungle of deceit and treachery all around you, Your Majesty?" One desperate appeal escaped Nur Jahan's lips. "Are you not going to slay those evils with the rod of your justice, which has been your talisman since your accession?" Her heart was thundering ominously.

"The treachery and inconstancy of the world are to me as clear as the light of day," Jahangir murmured soothingly. His own heart was lurching in spasms of agony to comfort his beloved. "Tomorrow we journey to Jalalabad, and then to Kabul, as you know, my love. Kabul is the place where all treacheries must end, and they will! We will gain many adherents in Kabul, and by that time I will be done sealing the bond of trust and friendship with Mahabat to such a degree that he will be unable to entertain any doubt or insincerity on my part."

"And then that treacherous reptile should be sent to the gallows." Nur Jahan couldn't restrain her bitterness.

"The emperor is not so sure about the mode of punishment as yet, my love." Indecision and kindness were shining in Jahangir's eyes like the tender, little stars. "At times, I have dealt with treacheries with indiscriminate severity, now that severity too has been dispelled from my nature." His gaze was ruminative.

"It seems, Your Majesty, Mahabat Khan has become your friend, for real," Nur Jahan murmured, as if thinking to herself.

"Neither a foe nor a friend, my pearl." Jahangir elicited one snort of a laughter. "It's just that he fascinates me. I have never studied a human animal before. And he has provided me with the opportunity to study him and his madness, concealed within him, yet stark naked to my sight. The unbleeding sinews of vice and virtue, of cruelty and kindness, of fear and boldness, just to name a few. He is trusting like a child at times, and mistrusting, even his own shadow, at other times. He is both sane and mad, much like the turbulent sea with its surface-calm. Frequently, the angry waves corrupt the surface-calm with a maddening fury, but never leave the shore of sanity. Yes, I have studied the flora and the fauna in the beautiful valleys of Kashmir! I have studied the birds and the beasts, their behavior and anatomy, but never before in my whole life have I studied the throbbing idiosyncrasies inside the heart of a human animal." His eyes were revealing no profundities, but the stars of adoration.

"We should cage this animal, Your Majesty, for the pleasure of your intensive studies, gaining liberty at the same time." Nur Jahan's eyes were flashing.

"It might be interesting to study the caged animal, you are right, my love." Jahangir got to his feet, beginning to pace. "To study others, one learns to study one's own self." His voice was distant. "Are we all not the same, with similar appetites of lust, greed and ambition? Concealing our vices, and parading our virtues? God alone knows what evils breed and multiply within our hearts."

"If we could rectify the vices within us, Your Majesty, we would be capable of cultivating goodness, not ever breeding evil," Nur Jahan commented sadly.

"Not much time left for self-introspection, I guess," Jahangir murmured to himself. "I might die, even before I begin that quest."

"Your Majesty!" One agonized protest broke forth on Nur Jahan's lips.

"Not killed by the hands of Mahabat Khan, no, my love, no!" Jahangir's feet came to an abrupt halt in the middle of the tent. "Omens and dreams have visited me lately. Happy dreams though, where I sit laughing and talking with my father. My mother, uncles and aunts are there too, all those faces which have been erased from the memory-book of this world, for quite a while now. Even last night I was with my father, talking about hunting trips in Kashmir. He was reciting a poem which he had recited so often before the ulemas in Ibadat Khana when I was young. My memory is so clear now, that I can remember it word by word."

"Would you recite it, Your Majesty? It might dispel the gloom in your thoughts." Nur Jahan smiled.

"Remember the repose and safety which blessed my reign
The splendor and order which adorned my court, o remember
Remember the crisis of my repentance, of my oft-revolving beads
The canopy which I prepared for the sanctuary of the Kabah
Let the tears of affection shed rubies over my dust
In your morning orisons turn your thoughts to my soul
Let your evening invocations irradiate the gloom of night
Do not forget the anguish of the tear-flowing eyes
When the chill winds shall visit your courts like the autumnal blasts
Think on that cold hand which has so often scattered gold among you," Jahangir recited, as if reliving that dream.

"This verse is more chilling than the cold blasts one is sure to feel on the peaks of the Himalayas, Your Majesty." Nur Jahan shuddered visibly. "The daggers of ice are running down my spine, Your Majesty."

"Then you don't want to hear the quatrain my father recited after this verse?" Jahangir smiled dreamily.

"On the contrary, Your Majesty, this chill is refreshing. Chilling my pains and sorrows, and awakening within me the sense of void and vastness, to which my naked sight seems blind." Nur Jahan's wit was awakening, cold and razor-sharp. "If you didn't share that quatrain with me, I would be deprived of something very precious, which cannot be purchased, but with the wealth of wisdom."

"Didst thou see how the sky shed around its flowerlike fascinations
My soul is on the wing to escape this cage of darkness
This bosom, which the world was too narrow to contain
Has scarcely space enough to inspire but half a breath."

Jahangir stood gazing into the shimmering lakes of her eyes.

"The poetry of life, Your Majesty, is molded fresh in those words of your father." Nur Jahan's own eyes were kindling profundities. "If he was here, he would have pounded the Rajputs to dust with the power of his pen alone."

"Don't you know, love, he was illiterate?" Jahangir smiled.

"How could I not, Your Majesty? His virgin mind alone is witness before the seat of divine inspiration in him, as he himself would have said." Nur Jahan's eyes were speaking volumes. "The ink of knowledge in his mind didn't need the skills in reading or writing. It could have filled the oceans with wisdom, as far as I could imagine, if their liquid-depths could contain such wisdom-treasures."

"To test the wisdom of his father, my eloquent poetess, the emperor must return to his mock court before Mahabat Khan brings the wretched prisoners right here." Jahangir took one step with the intention of leaving, but then stood there thoughtfully.

"Your Majesty," appealed Nur Jahan with a sudden flash of fear and apprehension. "No matter how cowardly my brother has been, I don't wish his humiliation or any harsh punishments which may seem necessary."

"I hoard no ill will against him, my Nur. All men are cowards when it comes to saving their own lives, with the exception of the saints and the lovers, and of course the martyrs." Jahangir averted his gaze, torment smoldering in his eyes.

"Amongst the category of such men, Your Majesty, where do you stand, if I may be as bold as to ask?" Nur Jahan was donning the mask of cheerfulness.

"A saint and a sinner both, if I could be qualified as a true lover." Jahangir smiled, turning to leave.

"Be kind to Asaf Khan, Your Majesty…and to the others," Nur Jahan pleaded.

"Mahabat Khan alone is the arbiter in this mock court of the emperor, my Nur, remember." Jahangir drifted toward her. "But I will wage a mental war, and borrow some ink of knowledge from my father's mind, where wisdom still pulsates in the ocean of time." He snatched her hands to him, kissing them reverently. "On the other hand, here is one more opportunity to win Mahabat Khan's trust that the emperor spares neither kin nor friend." He fled, as if pressed by the agonies of his body and soul.

"Scarlet my wounds would pour red, hot coals under the very feet of Mahabat Khan," Nur Jahan murmured to herself.

As soon the emperor emerged out of his tent, the Rajputs lifted their horns to their lips to herald the emperor toward the open court. They were blowing on their horns with all the passion and ceremony of the royal subjects, as if the emperor was still the sole sovereign of power and command.

Jahangir seated himself on his throne most regally. In truth, he was the emblem of power and glory, his own courtiers ready to gratify the least of his whims or commands, if he could but command. Mahabat Khan had left no detail unfinished as to the dignity and solidarity of this open court. He had taken great pride in arranging and embellishing this open sea of silken splendor so that he could flaunt his royal prisoners in chains of misery and degradation.

The grassland itself was transformed into a tapestry of colors by the gold embroidered carpets so profusely unrolled from the foot of his throne to his royal encampment, as far as the eye could see. The courtiers in colorful turbans stood in attendance. Musicians were present too, evoking loveliest of tunes on their lutes and flutes. Their tunics of gold were splashed with so many gems, that they appeared to shoot rainbow of colors in rhythm to their music. The largest and the brightest of jewels was one octagonal amethyst in the emperor's turban, sparkling and shuddering.

Jahangir, seated on his gold throne, appeared to be suspended over them all like some remote deity. Even the small amethysts in his ears were absorbing color from the brocaded canopy overhead, and shooting beacons of fire and light. He was talking with his courtiers, and discussing the plans of his journeys ahead, as if all preparations were conducted solely by his own orders. The presence of the Rajput guards were dampening the spirits of all, but all were pretending not to notice their taut demeanor.

The Rajput guards were alert and vigilant, but Jahangir had learned to ignore them completely, rising above their scrutiny as if they didn't even exist. He was engaging his courtiers in conversations with a lively, carefree manner. The affairs of the state and the empire were discussed most intensely. The Rajputs and their horde of soldiers were not even mentioned, as if everyone was avoiding to acknowledge their presence which posed the threat of war and unrest. Many a covert glances were exchanged between the emperor and the courtiers in some bond of secrecy and friendship. Jahangir could not help but respect the silence of his courtiers concerning the Rajputs, and he had no wish to desecrate his own lips by voicing the intrusion of the traitors. It was enough for him to see the warmth and devotion into the eyes of his courtiers, and he was grateful for their silence and discretion.

Jahangir's attention was turning to Abul Hasan. Abul Hasan had escaped the inquisition of Mahabat Khan by the power of his own sheer genius and diplomacy. He too had won Mahabat Khan's trust, assuming the guise of a lowly servant who could be subservient to the ruler and rebel both, without instigating any malice on either side. Abul Hasan's fidelity was sworn to the emperor, Jahangir's honed perspicacity itself had asserted, and he had no room to cultivate any doubt concerning this matter. All his subjects were devoted to him, Jahangir could tell, and his thoughts were lulled to repose. Somehow, the serenity of the vast oceans was entering his soul and psyche. He was looking within, where the tempests raged and churned in abysmal depths, but they could not reach his surface-calm which he willed to hold and retain. Inside his mind and heart were all peace and silence, condoning doom and darkness, fearing neither death, nor misfortune. Jahangir was thinking, as he shot an abrupt inquiry at Abul Hasan.

"Any news from Agra or Lahore, Abul, which you might have neglected to report? Many could be charged with such a neglect these days on account of excitement during these pleasant journeys," Jahangir murmured with a stab at irony.

"All peace and prosperity, Your Majesty, I assure you." Abul Hasan bowed with the flourish of his arm. His eyes were shining with a gleam of devotion and conspiracy.

"How are my grandsons, Prince Dara Shikoh and Prince Aurangzeb? The emperor must reach Lahore soon before they grow up to be young kings, wedded to their own queens, retiring somewhere in our vast empire to rule over the little kingdoms of their own." Jahangir's gaze was intense and searching. He had caught the spool of conspiracy in Abul Hasan's eyes, and had tied a knot of understanding in his mind.

"Both are well, Your Majesty, and royally entertained by the courtiers. They have seen more of Lahore than any one of us could ever hope to explore amidst all these burdens of duties and uncertainties." Abul Hasan's expression was dauntless, and his look brimming with hints which he could not voice.

"The babes of suffered times," Jahangir murmured. His tone was loaded with innuendoes, which only Abul Hasan was sharp enough to catch. "How the emperor wishes to press them to his heart! Only Kabul stands in the way, then the emperor..." He stopped, noticing the fiery steeds of Mahabat Khan and his followers coming into view.

Mahabat Khan alighted from his horse at a respectable distance from the throne. He was ordering his soldiers to haul the chained prisoners forward without any delay, his look hard and merciless. He himself was taking charge of Asaf Khan and Abu Talib, and shepherding them both toward the throne. His eyes were shining with the light of power and victory, and a mad grin was carved over his face from cheek to cheek. Reaching closer to the throne, he had whacked the royal prisoners from behind, watching them with gloating, as they slumped at the foot of the throne in miserable heaps. Mahabat Khan himself was prostrating before the emperor in one lengthy curtsy.

"Your Majesty, here are the rebels, the cowards and the traitors, now groveling at your feet. These lying, cheating soldiers and courtiers disobeyed your orders, Your Majesty. These murderers, Your Majesty, are drunk with the blood of the noble Rajputs." Mahabat Khan began his tirade with the vehemence of a warlord. "I have brought them to you, Your Majesty, so that you could reward them with just punishments. I await your orders. If you command, Your Majesty, my own sword will wreak vengeance." His voice was choked by the flood of his own rage and madness.

"Cowards, not traitors, Mahabat," Jahangir intoned calmly. "And cowards need to be bound in the shackles of shame and ignominy, before death can release them from such tortures of the living." His look was aloof and wearied. "The emperor entrusts them into your custody, Mahabat. Keep them bound in chains and under strict guard. Their fates would be decided in Kabul."

"Yes, Your Majesty. They will be tortured with insults, till they receive just punishments in the very heart of Kabul," Mahabat Khan announced deliriously.

"Your Majesty," Asaf Khan pleaded, breaking the seal of his stunned silence. "Please allow us to serve this term of imprisonment under the custody of the imperialists. Mahabat Khan is quick to murder his prisoners without waiting for any orders from you, Your Majesty." Fear and hopelessness were shining in his eyes.

"Is this true, Mahabat, that you have already exacted punishment in the manner of death on some of the prisoners?" Jahangir's gaze was sad and piercing.

"Your Majesty." One flustered exclamation escaped Mahabat Khan's lips. "The ones who defied our authority to capture the fort had to be dealt with the blows of death…they were impeding our progress." He waved his arms imperiously, as he continued. "Abdul Khaliq and Mahammed Taqi were among the other few rebels who were put to the sword. Such disobedient lot, they deserved to die. Now the fort is occupied and garrisoned by the Rajputs. More will succumb to the same fate if they dare defy our orders…" He paused, laughing hysterically. "They were killed before we captured the fort, Your Majesty, not after we took the prisoners."

"How can one forget the most brutal and savage of murders…Muhammad Tathi…" Abu Talib murmured, as if awakening from the pools of his own chill.

An imperceptible shadow of pain crossed Jahangir's features, but his gaze was calm and intense. He was studying Mahabat Khan's eyes and moods with an intensity akin to awe and wonder. The rapt look in his own eyes was gathering commands, but none were escaping his lips.

"Yes, Muhammad Tathi, my spiritual preceptor. Chained and imprisoned and put to death. The innocent victim of violence and tyranny," Asaf Khan lamented aloud.

"He was a sorcerer, Your Majesty," Mahabat Khan sang deliriously. "An evil man possessed by the demons, that's what he was, Your Majesty. I had him chained, that's true. But the chains fell off by his magic and incantations, and he showered me with curses before his head was severed." His eyes were lit up with fear.

"He knew no magic, Your Majesty, but recited verses from the Quran for the salvation of his soul," was Asaf Khan's chilled lament. "The chains were not well secured, and when they fell off, he was accused of casting spells and raining curses."

"Have the chains slipped off the feet of the Prince Hoshang and Prince Tahmuras too, Mahabat?" Jahangir eased himself up, watching the dance of fear in Mahabat Khan's eyes with a great fascination. "Have they fled, or were they killed?"

"They are safe, Your Majesty. They are chained though, and imprisoned inside the fort," was Mahabat Khan's quick response.

"All these prisoners will journey with us to Kabul, Mahabat. Of course, in the custody of the Rajput guards. Keep them alive, Mahabat, till they receive just punishments from the emperor," Jahangir commanded, turning to leave.

"We halt at Jalalabad, Your Majesty. I have arranged special entertainments for you there." Mahabat Khan flung his own command at the back of the emperor.

Jahangir's pace dwindled at the mention of Jalalabad, but he neither turned back nor waved the Rajput guards away as was his wont when pressed by the sense of false amenity. Suddenly, he was overwhelmed by despair and weakness, as if his body and soul were sundering apart, and cleaving through the abyss of death and darkness.

The pine-valleys in Kabul were greeting Jahangir and Nur Jahan with welcoming scents. The seductive contours of the hills were an undulating profusion of verdure, cradling a tapestry of colors in wild flowers. Their gilded carriage, harnessed by white Arabian horses, was wending its way toward Shahara garden. A great multitude on either side of the road were greeting the royal entourage and waving colorful scarves. They were blissfully ignorant of the emperor's state of captivity and of his inner torment. The emperor was scattering gold and silver on the path of the well-wishers in his usual fashion of the Moghul custom which rewarded the spirit of welcome with its own spirit of generosity. The crowds were cheering, and Jahangir was acknowledging their joy with a cheerful wave of his arms, as if no power on earth could imprison him inside the castles of intrigue. He had, in fact, succeeded in winning Mahabat Khan's trust to such an extent that the Rajput guards around him were reduced to insignificant numbers, thus affording him the luxury of plotting, together with his empress, against this besotted traitor. Even now, they were alone in the carriage. A few Rajput guards were astride ahead of their carriage, or falling behind in a leisurely trot.

The shadows of death and darkness were left behind in Jehlum. Mahabat Khan had been quiet and respectful on the way from Jehlum to Jalalabad, heralding the emperor before the citizens of this town with exaggerated pomp and grandeur. At Jalalabad, he had arranged a sumptuous feast for the emperor with all sorts of strange ceremonies a little short of anointing him with sacred oils and holy chantings. By Mahabat Khan's own design and ingenuity, the emperor was hailed as a great Caesar, kaiser of the whole world, chosen by Allah to bless all people with the sunshine of his justice and kindness. With so much praise and pageantry, even the Rajput guards had begun to see a halo around the emperor's head, though they were obedient only to the commands of their demented leader, Mahabat Khan himself.

Jahangir was not affected by this aura of sanctity over his head, as more often alluded by his own courtiers than by Mahabat Khan. He was winning Mahabat Khan's trust with mental strategies, not with a godlike compassion brimming with love and mercy. He was keeping the nimbus of his own mercy and judgment subservient to the will of all knowing, all merciful, all omniscient God. That's what Jahangir was in the habit of telling Nur Jahan in rare moments of mirth and raillery.

Nur Jahan herself was the chief instigator in devising such plans of sanctity and holiness, though Mahabat Khan had thought this was his own original design entirely. She was the one who had bribed her followers in convincing Mahabat Khan to invest the emperor with the power of sanctity. Her faithful eunuchs and her much devoted courtiers, by her own commands, were quick to weave the tales of sanctity over the character of the emperor, consecrating him as the Lord of Love and Light. An ocean of awe billowed before the emperor wherever he went, and even Mahabat Khan could not help but think that he himself was being baptized by the waters of holiness. He was getting accustomed to prostrating before the emperor more often than ever, not knowing why he kneeled while he still commanded.

Nur Jahan had enough gold and jewels to bribe the lords and generals in Jalalabad to win secret alliances, thus strengthening the numbers of her imperial troops. The glitter of gold had also worked wonders over the hearts of the Rajputs, who had begun to doubt the authority of their subservient leader. Mahabat Khan too was affected by the glitter, not of real gold, but by the gold of trust and friendship with the emperor. He had become the emperor's confidant in matters great and small, convinced absolutely of the emperor's trust in him when the emperor had sought his advice and judgment concerning the governorship of Agra.

Jahangir had appointed Muzaffar Khan the governor of Agra before his journey to Kashmir, replacing Qasim Khan due to his covert alliance with Prince Shah Jahan. Qasim Khan, the brother-in-law of Nur Jahan's sister Manija, was sorely hurt, but couldn't seek Nur Jahan's attention at that time for his plea to regain the emperor's favor. Now, while in Jalalabad, Manija Begum had sent a request to Nur Jahan with a plea that her husband be reinstated to the favor of the emperor. The emperor, savoring this God-send opportunity to win Mahabat Khan's absolute trust, had presented the whole case to him, seeking his advice solely on his own judgment and discretion, pretending that the emperor didn't care for the empress or for her relatives, and that whatever Mahabat Khan's decision, the emperor would welcome it most gratefully. Mahabat Khan was so bloated with joy and pride in being the emperor's sole confidant that he had opted to reinstate Qasim Khan as the governor of Agra, disregarding even his hatred and mistrust for Nur Jahan and her family.

Mahabat Khan was now convinced beyond any doubt that the emperor was no more under the power and influence of the empress. And this knowledge alone was his joy and victory over all which he wished to seek or accomplish. What he wished to seek or accomplish, he himself was not sure. He had no fears though, and was feeling elated by his own sense of power and command over the emperor's emotions as well as over his decisions. No one could dare rise in insurrection against him, he had told himself, gloating over the fact that Asaf Khan, Abu Talib, Prince Hoshang and Prince Tahmuras were to remain in his captivity as long as he wished, since they were guarded heavily by a contingent of Rajput guards. He had already dismissed Prince Shahriyar as a craven and weak-willed prince who could never aspire to claim the legacy of the empire. Since he had absolved himself of the fear of insurrection on the part of Prince Shahriyar, his wish to accomplish something was becoming clear. He was paving the way clear for Prince Perwiz to the throne of Hind, Mahabat Khan had convinced his own self.

Prince Shahriyar was neither craven nor weak-willed as Mahabat Khan had presumed. This prince was much of a spy as to thwart the designs of the most skilled of generals, both in intrigue or warfare. He was working in alliance with Nur Jahan, the mistress of all intrigues and victories. Each succeeding minute of the day, he was becoming sure that he would accomplish the downfall of Mahabat Khan when the traitor could least suspect. Unsuspected by Mahabat Khan, he was free to roam the valleys of Kabul with no Rajput guards following at his heels. Much like the Roman Claudius, he had managed to deceive not only the Rajputs but also the imperialists, concealing his own designs and aspirations, and presenting himself as the most incompetent and unaspiring of all the princes. With this fortune of a deception as his talisman, he would trek the valleys of Kabul like a lone missionary, inciting the Kabulis against the Rajputs.

The Kabulis didn't need any coaxing and preaching, for their carefree spirits detested any intruders who could not share their sense of hospitality or camaraderie. The unfriendly and unsmiling faces of the Rajputs were enough to breed hatred and revulsion into the hearts of the Kabulis, and they were seething with rage to break the seals of these proud and presumptuous soldiers. Prince Shahriyar was there to hold flint to the maddening rage into the hearts of the Kabulis, and had succeeded quite adroitly. Though he himself might not ever be the Moghul Caesar. Prince Shahriyar had his own doubts.

The gilded carriage of the royal couple, with velvet awnings, was now dipping and rising like a thread of gold amidst the undulating hills of this tortuous valley. The slippery paths ahead appeared to be coiling and uncoiling with the languor of a serpent. The wind was hissing through the pines and the cedars, down below the ravines and the gorges sighing in their own abysmal deeps. There were no cheering crowds in this secluded part of the valley, and the ones who had cheered a long distance back, had retired to their wild abodes inside the very heart of Kabul. The royal entourage was to pass through a narrow, winding path concealed by the grand vistas all around, beyond which lay Shahara garden with sprawling lawns in all its glory of color and contour. Inside the carriage, Jahangir and Nur Jahan sat whispering, as if guarding their secrets from the very eyes of holiness in these glens and valleys.

"Did you pray at the tomb of your great-great grandfather, Your Majesty, asking for a boon of wisdom? We could use that, so that our courage and fortitude don't fail." Nur Jahan attempted a light-hearted query. She was letting her plans ferment on their own, into a sweet-scented wine of victory.

"Yes, love," Jahangir murmured, pressing her hand to his lips. "He advised the emperor to abandon his empress, and not ever trust her," he added, mischief dancing in his eyes like the wicked, little stars.

"Oh, the unfortunate empress! Now the whole world knows that the emperor hates her," Nur Jahan quipped.

"If they only knew how the emperor is smitten by her beauty. Eternally! And crippled by love." Jahangir smiled into her eyes. "Even your sister Manija knows not my pretense, which banishes you from my favor everlastingly. Her husband won the post of governorship through Mahabat's favor, not through any intercession on your part."

"How Mahabat Khan decided her husband's fate in favor of her is still beyond me, Your Majesty," Nur Jahan ruminated aloud. "Captive as we are, he is granting us the liberty to visit the tombs of our ancestors and the gardens, another great mystery still."

"And our visit to Shah Ismail, with only a handful of surly Rajputs! No great mystery though, the emperor retains his absolute trust," Jahangir murmured, an enigmatic gleam shining in his eyes.

"Regardless of that trust, Your Majesty, even if it unfurls the laurels of victory for us, the empress needs avenged," was Nur Jahan's anguished confession.

"Vengeance sits no nearer my heart, love, than the tragic memories long forgotten," Jahangir murmured soothingly. "How wistfully we spool and unspool the golden thread of our lives, knowing that in death it matters not whether we lie buried in mud with marble tombs over our heads, or blades of grass as our final shrouds." He paused. "The tombs of Mirza Hindal and Mohammed Hakim are sorely neglected, don't you think, love? Though the tomb of Great Babur sits there sculpted in marble, with open arms, to absorb the vast skies and the warmth in sunshine." His gaze was gathering profundities.

"No time for ideation, Your Majesty. We should be thinking of breaking the marble facade of Mahabat Khan's madness," Nur Jahan urged quickly.

"More dice, my Nur, and it could shatter like glass," Jahangir murmured.

"What dice, Your Majesty? You have kept me ignorant about something?" Nur Jahan's eyes were lit up with agog.

"When the time is ripe, my love, the emperor is going to tell Mahabat Khan that the empress is plotting to murder him. He will be advised not to parade his guards before the imperialists. That will be the time when our troops will rise against the Rajputs, and will imprison Mahabat Khan," Jahangir expounded.

"Your Majesty!" Nur Jahan could barely suppress her exclamation of joy. "The time is now, Your Majesty. Our plans need not be delayed to strike a final blow."

"What plans?" Jahangir contrived ignorance.

"Don't pretend, Your Majesty, that you don't know. Time doesn't allow us the luxury of levities." Nur Jahan was pretending shock and disbelief.

"I know, my love, but the emperor needs assurance from you, over and over again." Jahangir's smile was but a flicker of entreaty.

"You couldn't forget the royal hunting grounds, Your Majesty, where the Rajputs let their horses graze unattended?" Nur Jahan complied, as if rewriting plans in her head. "The Kabulis incited by Prince Shahriyar confronted the Rajputs, insulting and blaming these rude intruders for despoiling their pastures. This confrontation ended in a scuffle, and one Kabuli was killed. His friends came to Mahabat Khan for redress and vengeance. Mahabat Khan's evasive reply as to judge the guilty party with trials, has set the stage for rage and rebellion from the Kabulis. Mahabat Khan knows not how dangerous the rage of the Kabulis could be, or how savage their sense of pride. Prince Shahriyar has assured me that hordes upon hordes of Kabulis are staying in ambush at the very gates of the palace in Kabul to pounce on the Rajputs, waiting for an opportunity. When Mahabat Khan is away, they will strike. They will slaughter, or already are slaughtering the Rajputs, now that Mahabat Khan is with us, escorting us to this majestic site, Shahara garden."

"Maybe Mahabat Khan has an inkling of this tragedy? He has been quiet and distracted all morning." Jahangir's contemplations were being slashed by doubts.

THE MOGHUL HEDONIST

"No, Your Majesty," Nur Jahan affirmed quickly. "He has received some news from Agra, as you yourself guessed earlier. You should probe him further, Your Majesty. Tell him you hate the empress, and he would spill his guts out to claim you as his confidant."

"What hateful truths would come out of these hateful lies, my love, the emperor might never wish to know." Jahangir slipped his arm around her waist, grazing his lips against her cheeks.

The emperor was soon consumed by the bliss and magic of his beloved's nearness, kisses and endearments trembling on his lips. His passionate bliss was heaving sighs and shuddering, as the gateway to Shahara garden came into view with all its glory and splendor. The emperor and the empress were abandoning their velvety comforts to explore the velvety lawns and flowerbeds. Mahabat Khan was keeping his distance, his gaze averted and his expression inscrutable. The Rajput guards were scattered here and there, peering beyond the scenic splendor with absolute disinterest. They were wandering like the stray animals, oblivious to the scented air, which the goblets of roses were doling out to all, generously and indiscriminately.

With the hunger of an artist, Jahangir was feeding his sight with nuances sweet and colorful. He could not be denied the pleasure of inhaling this perfumed air, as if goblets upon goblets of wine from the hearts of the scented blooms were held out for his gratification alone. The lilacs in clusters of mauve and purple, matching his own silks, were absorbing sunshine and rustling in the wind. A dreamworld was unfolding before Jahangir's sight in the semblance of colorful tapestries, the amethyst in his turban blazing and following his own admiring gaze. Nur Jahan too was smitten by the beauty of this garden, her own embroidered silks the color of heliotropes in their oval flowerbeds. She was lured to the marble fountains, splashing and serenading the orange poppies as they swayed and swooned. The empress was attended by her eunuchs, her lady-in-waiting following her. But the emperor's only escorts were Mahabat Khan and a coterie of Rajput guards. They were not far behind, their expressions sullen, as if they were caught in the desert storm of their duties, rather than visiting the loveliest of the gardens.

The marble terraces gleaming under the sun were welcoming the emperor and the empress to their own polished hearths. They were walking on the carpet of silk in grass, edged with blooming wonders as far as the sight could reach and absorb. The narcissi, the anemones, the rununculuses, the dog-roses and forget-me-nots in abundant clusters were the nature's own portraits on the canvas of this garden. One narrow path spruced with red-brick dust could be seen shining like a ruby rivulet. It was meandering its way toward a double terrace, canopied with bridal ivy. The red Himalayan tulips in earthen pots were greeting the royal couple, as they mounted the marble steps to admire the bridal ivy. Mahabat Khan and his Rajput guards were suspended down below under the shade of the magnolia and wisteria trees in half bloom. Up on the terrace were hush and the white purity of silence. Both the emperor and the empress stood watching the spruce and camellia trees down below, their hearts filled with awe and fear. Mehr Harwi had ventured forth on the terrace, and Mahabat Khan was contemplating to do the same.

"Your Majesty, you should prod Mahabat Khan. He has not spoken a word since we got here," Nur Jahan murmured. She was aware of Mehr Harwi, and could also see her eunuchs mounting the marble steps under some spell of indecision. Without even meeting the emperor's gaze, she strolled away, her eunuchs and lady-in-waiting following her obediently.

Jahangir stood admiring the silken splendor of this garden, as if the urgency in Nur Jahan's tone had stirred not a single thought in his head. His gaze was following one hoopoe in its graceful flight. This sleek, slender bird, sailing in the wind with utmost freedom, was absorbing Jahangir's attention, and his heart had begun to throb with a sudden violence. His aesthetic senses were drugged with the wine of beauty from the nature's own benevolent cups, but they were hungering and thirsting for something more than wine and beauty. A sudden stab of pain was wrenching out the simmering violence from within, which was leaping to his eyes. His very gaze was tearing this veil of awe and hush with its own daggers of ice and fire.

The sea of color and the carpets of flowers were no more soothing Jahangir's senses, but cutting through the very fabric of his surface-calm. The wound of captivity, which he had bandaged so carefully, was ripped open and bleeding. It was foaming at the mouth with torments silenced, and spewing forth the bile of grief and despair. Jahangir was turning with the intention of joining Nur Jahan, when he noticed Mahabat Khan standing not too far away. The traitor was edging closer, reticent as before.

"You need not follow the emperor, Mahabat. He has no intention to escape this golden cage of captivity," Jahangir declared caustically.

"Your Majesty!" protested Mahabat Khan. "You know I am protecting your own interests, Your Majesty," he murmured. His gaze was wandering toward Nur Jahan where she stood leaning over the terrace with her back toward them.

"You look downcast, my friend. I have not failed to notice…still wearing that dejected expression which shone in your eyes early this morning." Jahangir donned a mask of concern.

"Your safety is my prime concern, Your Majesty," was Mahabat Khan's evasive response.

"My safety! The emperor is concerned about your safety." Jahangir let fall the seed of doubt, his gaze warm and intense.

"My safety, Your Majesty? Protected by a wall of Rajputs, I entertain no fears about myself," was Mahabat Khan's startled response.

"We will talk about it, Mahabat, when we are alone. When the empress is not with us," Jahangir murmured. His eyes were summoning the stars of secrecy.

"We will, Your Majesty, we will," Mahabat Khan murmured, his own look conspiratorial.

"What heavy burden is pressing you to gloom, Mahabat? Don't be afraid to share it with the emperor," Jahangir murmured, as if trying to placate the fears of a child.

"Not much, Your Majesty, not much," Mahabat Khan murmured to himself.

"There is something then." Jahangir's gaze was profound and searching. "You would share it with the emperor on our journey to Lahore, perhaps?"

"Our journey, Your Majesty." Mahabat Khan's eyes were gathering that demented look again, that look which had become his guide and master in all these days of tyranny and madness. "I meant to share some good news with you, Your Majesty." One feeble expression escaped his taut, unsmiling lips.

"Good news, Mahabat, and you have been keeping all that to yourself!" Jahangir elicited one snort of a mirth.

"So that I could keep the others to myself too, which are not so good, Your Majesty." An involuntary confession was wrenched free from his thoughts.

"The good news first, then?" Jahangir intoned calmly.

"Ambar Malik, Your Majesty, that Abyssinian dog finally died in his eightieth year." Mahabat Khan exploded with a sudden burst of vehemence.

"Now Deccan will be saved from the looming threat of terror!" Jahangir demurred aloud. "That Abyssinian slave, dead? One must forgive the dead, Mahabat, for the comfort of one's own soul, and for the salvation of that soul which is no more. Death demands a certain grain of respect from us all who tyrannize while living." He was trying to conceal his own sense of betrayal in innuendoes. "Though an Abyssinian slave, he rose to great power, and was a great warrior, the emperor must admit..." He paused, his gaze intense and smoldering. "And now, the not-too good news, Mahabat?"

"Prince Shah Jahan, Your Majesty, hearing of your captivity...though, you are not a captive, Your Majesty. I am your devoted slave, and working for your interests alone. Prince Shah Jahan has left Deccan, and is proceeding toward Ajmer, with the intention of rebellion, I am sure," Mahabat Khan expounded incoherently."

"Not so bad, Mahabat, not bad at all." Jahangir smiled. His heart was fluttering suddenly, but he was not heeding its warnings. "The emperor is not concerned about the rebellions any more. With you as his shield of devotion and friendship, you would crush all rebellions, intended or otherwise." He appeared to dismiss the subject as if it was insignificant. "Such news carries no more threat to me, since I have your absolute support," he added with an attempt at cheerfulness, but failed.

"That's not all, Your Majesty. More grievous news..." Mahabat Khan announced.

"The emperor is accustomed to griefs and tragedies," Jahangir assured him unconvincingly. "And there is nothing much too burdensome which the emperor can't carry on his shoulders with grace." Innuendoes were escaping his lips once again.

"Prince Perwiz in Burhanpur is very ill, Your Majesty," Mahabat Khan offered reluctantly.

"How ill? What cause?" A shadow of pain lingered over Jahangir's brow, but his gaze was cold and piercing.

"Overindulgence in drinking, Your Majesty." Mahabat Khan tackled the second inquiry first, not trusting his voice or thoughts. "The prince is languishing between coma and delirium."

"No reprimands will reach him, but mercy and compassion from God," Jahangir murmured. "Are the royal physicians with him?" Fatigue and weariness were silencing the storm of pain inside his thundering heart.

"He is attended by the most skillful of physicians, Your Majesty..." Mahabat Khan's quick response was swallowed by an abrupt crescendo of noise from the pounding of hoof beats.

The hush and beauty of Shahara garden were tarnished by this sudden sweep of a hurricane, where the horses could be seen flying with the speed of lightning. A large group of Rajputs with terror written all over their faces, had trampled the garden paths clear to the cascading fountains. They were leaving their panting steeds unattended, and racing toward the terrace, as if driven mad by the very whips of the demons. Their feet were coming to stumbling halts right below the terrace, where they were suspended chilled in some stupor of fear and hopelessness. The leader of these Rajputs was gasping for breath, and seeking Mahabat Khan's attention. He seemed to be blind to the presence of the emperor standing opposite Mahabat Khan. His sightless eyes were revealing the cold steel of forebodings, and he had begun to flail his arms.

"We must return to the palace, Mahabat Khan." This Rajput soldier appeared to be the master of his own commands. "The Kabulis are fighting with the Rajputs. One small skirmish is turned into a great battle…" He could say no more, for Mahabat Khan had begun to bark orders with the rage of a wounded tiger.

Chapter Nineteen

Another glorious day in Kabul was anticipating to glorify its lust for blood with another battle. The very eyes of the lusty sun could be gratified in its anticipation, if the Rajputs were to nurse their prides in attacking the Kabulis. Last night's fight with the Kabulis had proven disastrous to Mahabat Khan. All night long, the traitor general was heard raving and pacing incessantly. He could be seen wringing his hands in utter despair, and his loud imprecations could not fail to reach the shame and fatigue of the sleepless soldiers. Half of his soldiers were wounded and scattered amidst the heaps of the dying and the dead. Rajputs, the mightiest of his generals, had perished into the bloodbath of their own courage and recklessness. Half of his soldiers, who had escaped the swords of the Kabulis, were stunned by the swift tides of slaughter and savagery.

The ones who were dead could be applauded more than bereaved, for they had chosen the honor of death instead of the ignominy of defeat. The fortunate ones, not slain by the hands of the Kabulis, had held on to the banners of ascendancy till darkness itself had swallowed all melee and brutal encounters. The eyes of the Rajputs could be seen shining with hatred at the Kabulis, even after both the parties had retired to their posts at nightfall. The beasts and the soldiers, all were spent and exhausted by the sheer burden of doom and darkness in the valley. The sheet of silence itself had muffled the vows of vengeance on the lips of the warring foes, who could not even think of the morning, where cries of war could breathe once more. Mahabat Khan was in utter shock, mourning the great losses, and despairing of his own will to keep its sanity and power intact. He was mired deep into the marshland of his own ugly schemes, and his thoughts were struggling to swim to the shore of safety. But he was falling deeper and deeper into the abyss of grief and disconsolation.

While Mahabat Khan had paced in his room like a caged beast, Jahangir too had spent a night of extreme discomfort and restlessness. Now on the verge of victory and release, his pent up sufferings of the past few months were taking a toll on his health. No real asthma attack was imminent, but something inside him were constricting and expanding, as if the next laboring breath which he could take would be the last one for him. Inside the rose and ivory bedroom of his great-great grandfather, he had lain fighting this strange violence from within and without, attended only by Nur Jahan.

This palace, where he lay suffering now, had become Jahangir's only refuge from the painful present, as soon as he had come to Kabul. This palace was built by Babur with exquisite taste and passionate love, but now it was stripped bare of all its fineries with the exception of a few adornments which could not be removed. Jahangir had walked the empty halls against the shadow of his imagination, resurrecting well-recorded memories of the past with a yearning akin to love and nostalgia. He was always attended by the Rajput guards, but he had learned to efface them by the wand of his imagination, great and fantastic.

Nur Jahan never accompanied the emperor on such solitary tours of the palace, but she could follow his thoughts with the intuition of a keen beloved. And she could not miss reading his thoughts either, when he returned to the bedroom, and sat watching the ceiling in rapt silence and wonder. He would sit there quiet and brooding, while absorbing the faded colors in damask and tapestry, as if gleaning strength from the very walls and vacuums. This particular night, after the tumult of the war had subsided, Jahangir had entered this bedroom in some sort of swoon and exhilaration. His eyes were shining with the fire of hope and anticipation, but then he was absorbed in watching the faded splendor of this room with the same quiet and brooding intensity as before. While getting ready for bed, his breath had grown labored, and some stealthy pain in the pit of his stomach was carving its way down his back.

Nur Jahan was more of an angel to appease Jahangir's physical pains, than a skilled physician to offer remedies. She ministered to him with the love of a mother who could heal her child with faith and prayer alone. She had soothed his pain with watered wine, then had concocted her panacea for all ills, rosewater mixed with borage tea. The emperor was comforted more so by her endearments and encouragements, than by the potions she was so quick to brew and serve. Holding a prayer-book of love in her eyes, she had urged the emperor to will faith and strength, till the dawn of victory could bring them release from these briny waters of captivity. Jahangir would doze off, then awaken, finding Nur Jahan holding his hand, and lulling him to sleep with her eyes alone. Despite the restlessness in the night, he had awakened refreshed, his mental and physical pains dwindling, as willed by Nur Jahan.

The day had dawned, quite naturally and without the trumpets of fears. The coquetry of dawn had relinquished its hold to the lust of the sun. The white, crimson streaks of the early morning were washed by the molten gold in sunshine. Gold was everywhere, on the rooftops, over the valleys, inside the gorges, dancing in the glens and deep under the shimmering lakes. Kabul was awakened to a sense of peace, as if no blood was spilt in the night near the sacred grounds of the royal palace. Jahangir too had awakened with some astonishing sense of peace and silence. The damask curtains were swept aside, and the windows thrown open by Nur Jahan's explicit orders. She herself looked serene and rested, but her heart was burning in the fever of hope and fright. She was anticipating release, and dreading misfortunes.

Nur Jahan's wit and wisdom were at culmination this morning. She had spilled beads upon beads of ideas and possibilities, till the emperor himself was suffused with vigor and energy. He was ready to accomplish even the impossible. True, half of Mahabat Khan's soldiers were retired to the Hades, but the rest half were powerful enough to slay the imperialists, if covert measures were not taken to capture them off guard. Since the preparations for journey to Lahore were complete, Mahabat Khan would pose no objection to leaving this very day. Besides, he would wish to leave this hated city before another fight with the Kabulis could wipe off the entire contingent of his Rajput soldiers.

The morning hours were spent in a frenzied haste to bury the dead, and to burden the living with the tasks of yet another journey. Mahabat Khan was determined to guard his royal captives in the pomp and grandeur of a journey in conformity with the Moghul standards of wealth and opulence. The hour of the journey was nigh, when the emperor had summoned Mahabat Khan to his presence. Jahangir was pacing in the gilded parlor of his great-great grandfather, as if Babur himself had entered his spirit and psyche. He was attended by his own viziers, and of course by the Rajput guards. The emperor's viziers were composed and cheerful, while the Rajput guards, sullen and unfriendly. Mahabat Khan's breezy approach could not fail to attract everyone's attention, since his face was flushed with rage at being summoned by the emperor. Jahangir was dismissing all with an imperious wave of his arm, his very gaze indicating to the traitor that he wished to converse with him in utmost secrecy. The emperor's own viziers were leaving obediently, but the Rajput guards were not stirring, impudence and defiance shining in their dark eyes.

"You may say anything in their presence, Your Majesty. They are my trusted companions." Mahabat Khan waved his own arms, his tone wild and exigent.

"As you wish, Mahabat! This is of utmost secrecy, and concerns your safety more than mine," Jahangir murmured. He was holding the trump of victory inside his heart, but simulating fear in his eyes. "I have learned of this…a few moments ago. Should we postpone this journey?" he asked quickly without divulging anything.

"No, Your Majesty! I mean…what is it that you fear? My guards are brave and trustworthy. What have you learnt?" Mahabat Khan's gaze was feverish.

"The empress has designs against you, Mahabat…I thought I could trust her a little." Jahangir rubbed his hands as if in utter despair. "Remember, Abu Talib's wife, the grandmother of Khan Khanan? In league with her, the empress has construed an evil plot to assassinate you. Since she has succeeded in gathering covert alliances and gaining full support of the imperialists, considering that most of the Rajput soldiers are dead, we are exposed to great danger. It would be difficult to thwart the designs of the empress, even if the Rajputs fought till their last breath." He began to pace.

"What is to be done, Your Majesty, what…" Mahabat Khan stood there wringing his hands under some spell of stupefaction, stunned and bewildered..

"The only course left to us, Mahabat, is." Jahangir's feet came to an abrupt halt before this cowering traitor. His eyes were blazing with some inner fire of a revelation as he continued. "Yes, the only wise course! Stay concealed, surrounded by your own guards, Mahabat, while we journey. Don't let the Rajput soldiers come near the imperialists, lest they invent an excuse to provoke a fight. I will ride with the empress as if none of her secrets are disclosed to me. Once safe in Lahore, we will gain the support of more Rajputs, and then we will make our own plans." He pressed his temples, trying to dispel the inner violence inside him on the verge of a physical illness.

"A great plan, Your Majesty," Mahabat Khan breathed frantically. He was holding on to this plan like a drowning man, clutching at the reed of hope. "Let us not delay our journey any further, Your Majesty. I will be your obedient servant. Upon my life, no harm will ever come to you." He could not help noticing the emperor's pallor, his own heart thundering warnings.

"Come, my friends," Mahabat Khan beckoned to the Rajput guards. "The emperor doesn't need our protection! We will be the ones craving his wisdom and ingenuity to save our lives." He was commanding feverishly.

The sea of cavalcade with Rajputs still the bane of the imperialists, was sliding down toward Lahore via Jehlum. One more day's march from the Rhotas, and they would reach the same bank of the river Behat where the initial captivity of the emperor was staged, enacted and retained. During this entire journey, Mahabat Khan had effaced himself inside the chains of his own fears and doubts. He had stayed behind the shield of his own Rajput contingent, feeling quite safe in his own guarded sanctuary. His orders were hushed from behind the scene, urging his guards to keep strict vigilance over the emperor's gilded carriage.

Inside this gilded carriage, the plans of the emperor and the empress had been finalized, even before they had decided to encamp on the banks of the river Behat. This was the destination they had chosen to free themselves from the yolk of the Rajputs. The imperialists were to arrest Mahabat Khan, and to fight the Rajputs, if necessary. The long journeys and the burdens of anxieties, charged with silence and oppression from the traitor, were proving fatal to the emperor's health. But his will and fortitude were goading him to persevere, and he could feel the spurts of energy boosting his mental and physical vigor. Nur Jahan too was overwhelmed by fears and apprehensions, more so by the emperor's failing health than by the imminent threat of war between the Rajputs and the imperialists. A large contingent of the imperialists from Lahore were already encamped on the opposite side of the river Behat, and staying in ambush. They were ready to wage war if the Rajputs retaliated or resisted capture.

The blue turquoise waters of Behat were glittering under the sun, as Jahangir, attended by a few Rajput guards, stood watching the disciplined ranks of his own imperial soldiers. His pallor was accentuated by the citron robes hugging him closer at the waist under a jeweled cummerbund. The large diamonds in his turban appeared to radiate such aura of power around him this particular afternoon, that even the Rajput guards could not help noticing this subtle change in the emperor's demeanor. They were cowering behind him rather than guarding him, their hearts brimming with awe and dread. Despite the warmth from sunshine, the air was cool, gathering mist and haze in its frolicking gusts. Jahangir, sensitive to such weather, had felt chills even inside the warmth and luxury of his own tent, and had donned a velvet mantle lined with ermine, before venturing out.

The red velvet mantle of the emperor was flapping in the wind, and lending him the semblance of a royal magician who could dissolve all ranks into dust by the sheer intensity of his gaze, if he willed it so. The emperor's viziers and courtiers were keeping him company, their own fox-tail cloaks rippling and shuddering. Jahangir himself had ordered these cloaks for them, forever the master of Moghul etiquette and propriety, that if the emperor donned something special, his courtiers were bound to follow the custom. The emperor was the model of vogue and etiquette. He had not forgotten the time when he had holes bored in his ears, and had ordered all his courtiers to pierce their ears. Now the colorful jewels were glittering in the ears of all his courtiers, and he was transported back to the courts of Agra and Lahore. His gaze was returning to the soldiers who were wearing embroidered vests in the fashion of the cavaliers in peaceful times. Jahangir seemed fascinated by the colorful patterns on these vests, his gaze rapt and intense. Suddenly, he turned around, his gaze holding Buland Khan captive in its intensity.

"Buland Khan, go inform Mahabat Khan that the emperor forbids him to bring his troops on this side of the river for parade and rehearsal. The empress wishes to inspect the files of the imperialists, and he is advised to stay indoors," Jahangir commanded, his gaze shooting daggers at the Rajput guards, who stood there bewildered and speechless.

"Yes, Your Majesty," Buland Khan obeyed happily.

"Seize all these heathens and bound them in heavy chains." Jahangir issued another command with an imperious wave of his arm. His heart was dithering, lest the other Rajputs come trooping on to defend themselves and turn this peaceful takeover of power into a bloody fight.

The imperialists pounced upon the Rajput guards before they could unsheathe their swords. Their hands were clamped behind their backs and their hilts emptied of all weapons. This abrupt command for their arrest was such a shocking blow to the Rajput guards that they could not even move, their expressions chilled and stunned.

The air was charged with hush and forebodings, as Jahangir stood there towering over all like the mighty magician. His gaze was sailing over the colorful city of the traitor's encampment, where he lay concealed along with his followers. No Rajput soldiers were visible as the guardians of this low encampment, as if they were all hiding in their silken abodes to escape the wrath of the emperor. Jahangir's gaze was slowly returning to his own imperial captors with one flicker of a smile.

"No harm is to be done to these demented prisoners," Jahangir intoned rather kindly. "They will have time enough to repent and grovel into the mire of their own shame, till we reach Lahore. Then redress and punishment will follow." His look was enigmatic, rather compassionate.

"Should we send the signal to the imperialists on the other bank to join us, Your Majesty?" Abul Hasan asked, his eyes shining with relief and excitement.

"No, my faithful vizier, no." Jahangir's eyes were gathering a feverish glow. "No need, no need as yet. The Rajputs are sleeping, it seems. And they will prove to be the most humble of prisoners when they wake up, just like these unfortunate guards." He waved at his soldiers, his gaze alone commanding to haul these prisoners away.

"The imperialists are waiting for your orders, Your Majesty. Should I inform them of your decision?" Fadai Khan edged closer, seeking the emperor's attention as some reward for his secret efforts in spying and plotting.

"Muqarab Khan is assigned to carry the messages, but the emperor will wait till the traitor is delivered into his hands," Jahangir thought aloud, his breath heavy and labored. "Abul Hasan." He turned to his other vizier impatiently. "Go inform Buland Khan to fetch the traitor instead of forbidding him to come out of his evil lair."

Abul Hasan was too eager to obey the emperor's command, but no sooner had he reached half way that he espied Buland Khan racing toward him. Now both were racing toward the emperor, breathless and gasping.

"Your Majesty, Mahabat Khan has fled." Buland Khan was the first one to announce amidst throes of elation and disbelief. "He must have fled just after we pitched our tents, or during the night, we can't tell. All his tents are empty, all his soldiers gone."

"And Asaf Khan, and the other prisoners?" Jahangir asked weakly, holding his labored breath in abeyance.

"He took everyone with him, Your Majesty. Asaf Khan, Abu Talib, Prince Hoshang, Prince Tahmuras, Lashkar Khan and all," Buland Khan murmured with a trace of guilt, as if it were all his fault.

"The traitor couldn't be far. Send a contingent of the imperialists after him. He must be captured." Jahangir's voice rose and fell like the distant murmur of a thunder. He stood gasping for breath, unable to fend off the assault of asthma.

One hundred days of Mahabat Khan's demented reign had ended abruptly and peacefully as the emperor lay in his tent, attended by his physicians. Nur Jahan was beside him, pale and serene. Jahangir was recovering his breath, though issuing no orders, and entrusting all matters into the hands of the empress. All those past months of strain and suffering were now churning inside him like the angry waves, as if released by the very hands of relief which was courting rest and self-surrender. He was overwhelmed with fatigue, and all his strength was drained. His sight and senses were accosting reveries again. Anarkali, who was banished from his thoughts all those months of stealthy torment, could not be restrained from visiting him once more. He was seeking oblivion, welcoming the intrusion of long-cherished love and grief. A shining parade of illusions were drifting in his head, dreaming away dreams, slashed by the pincers of reality. Anarkali was pervading the serene, blue pools of Nur Jahan's eyes, smiling at him, offering him the bliss and comfort of eternity where there were no pains, no betrayals, no tragedies, no ailments, but the light of joy, love, peace. Absolute surcease!

Jahangir was waving the physicians away, gazing into the eyes of Nur Jahan. He could not see his empress, Anarkali, was there, donned in the pale blue gown of silk designed by Nur Jahan. She had borrowed the tiara of diamonds from the empress too. Her whole body was throbbing with the light of diamonds. A soft, radiant dream was lulling the emperor to a restful sleep. The paradise itself was his bed and pillow.

Nur Jahan was pacing softly, while the emperor rested in the mist-haze of his comforting dreams. Jahangir's breathing was even and unlabored, and there was a healthy glow on his pallid cheeks as he slept like a child cradled into the arms of relief. This fact alone was lending Nur Jahan's thoughts more strength and vitality to think about the matters at hand. She was concerned more about the emperor's health, and had changed her plans as to Mahabat Khan's arrest and retribution. Her prudence alone, garnished with the salt of intuition, had informed her that Mahabat Khan would resist captivity, and would surrender only after a decisive battle. So, she had made her decision. She could not afford the war of vengeance, since the emperor was ill. With the wisdom and resilience of a skilled general she had disciplined her thoughts, that she would rather let the traitor wander alone in self-exile, than command the imperialists to court danger and bloodshed.

The army of disciplined thoughts as her weapons, Nur Jahan had chosen Afzal Khan as her imperial messenger. She had personally dispatched Afzal Khan at the head of a large force, demanding from Mahabat Khan the safe release of the royal hostages. Her thoughts now, as she kept pacing, were following Afzal Khan, though her gaze now and then would turn to the emperor to make sure that his breathing was normal. The candle-lit warmth of the damascened tent was comforting her own thoughts. She could see the half lifted flap of the imperial tent, and her feet were carrying her toward this opening will-lessly. She could peer through the very fabric of dusk, it seemed, where the lengthening shadows of the evening were no more. The imperialists were celebrating their release with wine and song, and she was catching a few shreds of their revelry. Suddenly, she turned, with the intention of lighting more candles, and found the emperor awake. His gaze was bright and caressive, reaching out to her with all tenderness.

"Your Majesty." Nur Jahan floated toward him with the eagerness of a young girl. "How do you feel, Your Majesty?" She felt his brow, her eyes spilling joy.

"Alive and carefree." Jahangir snatched her hand to his lips, and showered it with kisses.

"Your Majesty!" Nur Jahan's low exclamation was caught in a limbo by the shuffling of feet outside the tent.

Hushiyar Khan's jubilant voice was heard bouncing off the tent, announcing the arrival of Prince Hoshang and Prince Tahmuras.

Nur Jahan was inviting the royal princes in a fever of hope and anticipation. Afzal Khan was lingering behind, and Hushiyar Khan was curtsying before retreating. The emperor was delighting in the company of his royal nephews, and shooting arrows of questions without even giving them the time to respond. Noticing the emperor's delight and absorption, Nur Jahan was quick to avail herself the opportunity of speaking with Afzal Khan.

"Where is Asaf Khan?" Nur Jahan demanded not too loud.

"Padishah Begum." Afzal Khan bowed his head. "Mahabat Khan is keeping Asaf Khan hostage till, he says, he is safe in Tattah."

"Then deliver this farman of the empress into the hands of this fleeing villain, Afzal Khan!" Nur Jahan's very eyes were flashing commands. "That the empress commands the release of her brother. And that if he disobeys, the imperialists have my orders to tear him and his Rajput soldiers to pieces." She waved an impatient dismissal.

"My Nur." Jahangir's attention was turned to her abruptly. "All the emperor wants is to reach Lahore, and to rest inside the comfort of his own palace." His gaze was bright and feverish.

"Yes, Your Majesty." Nur Jahan was drifting toward him with the smile of an angel. "The first thing next morning, Your Majesty, we journey to Lahore," she murmured, clasping his hands into her own, and closing her eyes.

Chapter Twenty

The red sandstone palace at Lahore, with its exquisite engravings of angels, nymphs and peacocks, had donned a mantle of mourning. The lions and elephants carved in stone at the gateways too were arrested in a haze of sepulchral silence, it seemed. They were absorbing the pale haze of the evening, splintered by the lengthening shadows of the pipals and poplars. Inside the palace, the emperor, seated in his own favorite room with walls displaying an array of stylized lotuses, was one pale ghost depicted on the canvas of time and place. Lonesome as ever, he was burdened by the weight of his own grief and suffering. Grief was no stranger to him, but the death of his son Prince Perwiz had landed upon him like a raging battle, countless daggers stabbing his heart without mercy, and reducing it to a bleeding sieve of eternal torment. Right now, he was in the company of his chosen royal household, and foundering inside the pools of his silent agony like a man with no will left to save himself from the valleys of despair and sorrow.

Nur Jahan, seated by the emperor, on the contrary, was courting no such silence and lonesomeness. She was engaging Ladli Begum and Prince Shahriyar into a lively ripple of conversation, more so to dispel the emperor's gloom than to evoke a sense of warmth and gaiety amongst the brood of this royal household. Prince Balaqi was reticent and contemplative as ever, more intent on watching the emperor than participating in any part of the conversation incited by Nur Jahan. Prince Hoshang and Prince Tahmuras were fascinated by the exotic tales narrated by Asaf Khan, who had the special gift of turning the mundane into a popular folklore. Karamasi Begum was pouring some court gossip into the ears of Sahiba Jamali Begum, but the latter was a statue of ice, oblivious to any sound or sight. Sahiba Jamali Begum was tasting only the salt of her own bitter, bitter grief. She was hugging the loss of her only son, her beloved Prince Perwiz, with a despair so chilled that nothing could melt her shock and disbelief to tears of grief and disconsolation. Prince Aurangzeb, barely nine, and Prince Dara Shikoh, a little over twelve, were trying to humor the emperor with their skills at mock sword fight. The emperor, though visibly attentive, was leagues apart from this scene of gallantry.

Immediately after his return to Lahore, the emperor was besieged by the grievous news of his son's death. Prince Perwiz in Burhanpur, the victim of his own excessive drinking, as the emperor had learned earlier, was further attacked by colic and fallen into a coma. He was cauterized five places on the head and the forehead. Though regaining consciousness for a few hours, the prince had relapsed into a coma from which he was never going to emerge to know the joys and pains in life. It was reported to the emperor that the prince could not voice the throes of his agony, but all were surfaced on his features tortured with pain. At the ripe age of thirty-eight, Prince Perwiz had succumbed to death, reducing the contenders for the throne to two, Prince Shah Jahan and Prince Shahriyar. His body was brought to Agra, and buried in his own garden by the command of the ailing and grieving emperor. After this tragedy, Jahangir's health had been on a constant decline, his moods changing from one of stoic resignation to maudlin depression. He had abandoned all affairs of the court and empire into the hands of Nur Jahan. The news of the various intrigues had a way to filter into his awareness, but he was not moving a finger to guard his wealth or empire. Nur Jahan was in absolute power in all matters of state and sovereignty, but powerless in the domains of her own fears and doubts. She was worried more about the emperor's health than concerned in checking the strings of intrigues.

The court gossip was blaming Prince Shah Jahan for the death of Prince Perwiz, alluding to some rumors that Prince Shah Jahan had poisoned his brother. Jahangir and Nur Jahan were aware of such rumors, but they had taken no action to refute or to validate such blame, which could tarnish further the already tarnished character of the rebel prince, Prince Shah Jahan. Jahangir's grief over the death of his son was so profound that he had grown insensible to all forms of gossip or rumor, so he was spared the need of punishing or acquitting his son based on the falsity or validity of the blame. Nur Jahan herself was so overwhelmed by the rapid decline of the emperor's health that she did not dare burden him with more tragedies, laced with blames or accusations.

Prince Shah Jahan, for the time being, was left alone to carve his own destiny of failure or success. Even before the imperial cavalcade had reached Lahore, Prince Shah Jahan was on the move to reach the sanctuary of Tattah. He had written a letter to Shah Abbas of Persia, hoping for alliance, but had received only reprimand and rejection. Shah Abbas had advised the rebel prince to be a dutiful son, and to cease being a vagrant. Unheeding any advice, Prince Shah Jahan had attempted to conquer Tattah, with the intention of making this city his own refuge and asylum! The governor of Tattah, Shariful Mulk, appointed by Prince Shahriyar, had fiercely opposed the rebel prince, and Prince Shah Jahan was left in the limbo once again. Destitute of soldiers and ammunition, Prince Shah Jahan had then abandoned the plan to subdue Tattah, and had marched toward Deccan via Gujrat and Bihar. While in Gujrat, he had learned about the death of Prince Perwiz, and had continued his march without even halting for a single day to mourn the death of his brother with due courtesy and propriety. Not very far from Gujrat, he himself had fallen ill, and was carried on a palki toward Deccan. He had chosen the route of Rajpipliya, arriving in Nasik Trimbak to retrieve his stores and equipage. His health was improving, and he had moved closer to Kashmir to regain more vigor of the body and mind. With his cavalry of two thousand, Prince Shah Jahan had decided to rest in the pine-valleys, hoping for favorable means to plan his next move.

Meanwhile, Mahabat Khan, after he had released Asaf Khan and the other prisoners, was reported to be seen on his way toward Tattah. He had changed his route though, and had marched straight toward the east. He was hoarding large sums of money under his name in the imperial treasury of Bengal, and was intent to retrieve it before the imperial farmans could rob him of such fortunes. Nur Jahan was informed of Mahabat Khan's each and every move, and had acted quickly to thwart his designs. She had appointed Rai Singh, Ali Quli, Safdar Khan, Sipandar Khan and Nurudin Quli to foil the treacherous designs of Mahabat Khan. They were supplied with a contingent of thousand men to intercept the traitor, and to fetch the entire treasury of Bengal to Lahore, before it could be pilfered. Abu Talib was to head this expedition, and transfer all the coins, gold and jewels into the treasury of Lahore.

A few months had elapsed since Nur Jahan had trusted all these men with such an imperative expedition, but so far she had heard no news concerning this matter. She was shadowed by her own fears, the emperor's ailing and grieving spirit entering her own and wreaking vengeance inside the quagmire of her own soul and spirit. She had had no time to inquire into this matter, not until recently, as the emperor was feeling a little reprieve from his illness so as to afford her the luxury of looking into the heart of the political matters, which needed the wands of justice and vengeance. She had sent orders to Abdur Rahim in Delhi to repair immediately to Bengal, and to furnish her with the news concerning Mahabat Khan's moves and treacheries. Abdur Rahim was aged, and in not too good a frame of health to venture such a long journey. But urged by the empress, he had consented to follow the fugitive with every last ounce of his will and strength.

Though a victim of his own lacerating spirit, Jahangir too had emerged forth to touch the anchor of action after feeling a little reprieve from his illness, which could permit him to think and act according to his own wishes. He had appointed Asaf Khan the governor of Punjab, with Mir Jumla as his assistant. Muqarab Khan, who had received the governorship of Bengal as soon as the emperor had reached Lahore, had met a tragic end. He was boating when a squall of wind had toppled his boat, and he was drowned. After this tragedy, Fadai Khan was transferred to Bengal to ensure its peace and safety.

Jahangir was still a prisoner to his grief, but the enormity of this grief itself was lending him an astonishing sense of peace and self-surrender. Prince Shahriyar alone had become his solace and his salvation. He, of course, was the protégé of Nur Jahan, and much beloved by her to gain and retain the emperor's favor. Last week, Prince Shahriyar, under the tutelage of Nur Jahan, had arranged a garden party to celebrate the first revival of the emperor's health, and his spirits had been greatly revived since the affable prince was the chief host himself. The emperor's grandees, too, as the guests of the royal prince, had been a source of great delight to the emperor by the virtue of their own light spirits unencumbered by the burdens of royal intrigues. Paradoxically, the emperor's griefs and tragedies had become a part of his self-surrender, his surreal peace as he named them, veiling his pains and torments against the mantle of illusion.

Illusion itself was the only reality which could hold open the portals of serenity inside the emperor's heart and mind. The same illusion was leading him closer to Anarkali. He could behold her standing in the window of his mind, eternally young in the eternal gardens of Kashmir, beckoning him to the paradise of perfume and surcease. He was longing to return to Kashmir with the impatience of a lover who could not wait to be united with his beloved. His paradise was calling him, his beloved, perfumed and bejeweled, wearing the crown of youth and beauty, and waiting! The light of his heart and soul could be no other than Nur Jahan, his beloved, this illusion. Yet this beloved was leading him to yet another beloved, Jahangir had begun to think in rare moments of half lucidity, half delirium.

Right now, the emperor was seemingly absorbed in watching his grandsons, but his mind had left its present abode into the realms of the subconscious. For some vague, astonishing whim of the subconscious itself, Jahangir was transported back into the times and trials of his captivity. He could see himself standing on the narrow bridge of his recent grief, yet looking down into the abyss of his past sufferings and trying not to jump into the waters of illusions. The waters of illusions were rising up to his knees, but before they could immerse him in complete oblivion, he was whirled back into the present by one loud boast from Asaf Khan.

"Asaf, what kind of promise did Mahabat Khan extract from you before you were released? I have heard he bound you to some sort of solemn oath," Jahangir asked abruptly. His look was dreamy, much in the semblance of a suffered monarch who really didn't wish to touch the rags of memories.

"An oath on the Quran, Your Majesty," Asaf Khan admitted reluctantly. "He made me take an oath, Your Majesty, somewhat of the context, that I would always be a brother to him since he was kind enough to grant me liberty."

"You should have fought him, Asaf, and gained release by your own strength." Nur Jahan flashed her brother an accusing look, before the emperor could collect his thoughts. "You should have made him like the dust on this earth, and punished him in a manner so as to make him an object-lesson for the whole world." Her hatred against Mahabat Khan was constricting her heart.

"A single man amongst the pack of tyrants, Padishah Begum?" Asaf Khan smiled ruefully. "He had me surrounded by the Rajput soldiers, and ordered them to kill me if I disobeyed. I am lucky to be alive as it stands." He made one hopeless gesture.

Jahangir was watching Nur Jahan. He appeared to be absorbing the sparkle in her eyes in some daze of memories, where his own query was lost and forgotten. The blue diamonds in her hair and around her throat were lending her oval features the fire and glow of marble. Her small, white hands were folded into her lap, sculpted and prayerlike. Jahangir was watching her hands now, gleaning the sense of vulnerability from that posture which he alone could feel and detect. The lines of suffering around his own eyes were relaxing into a tender smile. This smile was copied by the glittering diamond in his turban, and by the smooth, round pearls in his ears, it seemed.

"Let your brother live in peace, my Nur, and remind him not of the shameful past," Jahangir murmured tenderly. "A dead vizier is no use to the emperor, and while living he may yet assist the emperor in his own journey toward death." One wisp of a prophecy escaped his lips.

"Your Majesty!" exclaimed Nur Jahan.

"How unkind of you, Your Majesty, to stab me with another dagger of a tragedy while I am still chilled inside the pools of grief for my...our son. How could you even think...such terrible thoughts?" Sahiba Jamali murmured.

"Forgive the emperor, my mistress of beauty. My own grief has taken the liberty to voice such terrible thoughts. But we should cast away this veil of darkness...we would all wash our griefs in the scented valleys of Kashmir," Jahangir consoled, returning his gaze to Nur Jahan. "The preparations of our journey to Kashmir, my Nur, are they complete? The emperor regrets to burden you with everything, but your youth and courage are eternal as I often confess to myself, so you must take charge."

"Eternal as long as you are with me, Your Majesty." Nur Jahan elicited a brave smile. "I would be old and wrinkled in a flash, if you but mentioned death one more time." Her eyes were lit up with the fire of a challenge.

"You have not answered me, my Nur. Are we to journey early next morning?" Jahangir's eyes were gathering the stars of adorations.

"We are, Your Majesty, before the sun turns you to a statue of gold." Nur Jahan's wit was coming to her rescue to cheer the emperor.

"Why don't we stay in Kashmir forever and forever?" Karamasi Begum chanted aloud, to no one in particular.

"With your delicate constitution, you would be turned into a pillar of ice, my love, if we stayed in Kashmir forever." Jahangir flashed her a searching look.

"Mamma! Empires could not be ruled if we were to stay chilled in the paradise of comfort and luxury all the time." Prince Shahriyar began to laugh suddenly. He was aspiring to be an heir to the throne, and he could not suppress this feeling of power. *The only and the rightful heir to the throne*, he could not help but think!

"Your Majesty, look, I can beat Prince Dara in fencing. He doesn't know how to defend..." Prince Aurangzeb was seeking the emperor's attention.

Jahangir was falling prey to his own mute ruminations. The ebb and flow of royal parlance was barely grazing his awareness. His gaze was fixed to Prince Shahriyar with an unseeing intensity, and Prince Aurangzeb's intrusive tones were evoking no sense of reality for him. Now Prince Dara Shikoh was seeking the emperor's attention. His voice, though petulant, had the richness of song and music, and it had succeeded in breaking the chain of the emperor's mute ruminations.

"Prince Aurangzeb is a royal cheat, Your Majesty. Besides, he doesn't know the rules of fencing." Prince Dara Shikoh relinquished his sword at the emperor's feet, offering a gallant curtsy. "Your own jeweled sword, Your Majesty, I am unworthy." He was luring the emperor into his own aura of lighthearted gaiety.

"Your are worthy of all the jewels on this earth and in the skies, my gallant prince." Jahangir smiled, noticing Prince Aurangzeb standing in the background, sullen and downcast. "Learn to fence with humor, my prince," he chided the little prince, whose eyes were hoarding the ammunition of spite and hatred for his elder brother. "What misery shines on your little brow, my prince?" he thought aloud, startled by what he saw in the eyes of the young prince. "Prince Aurangzeb, my beloved grandson, you are too young to have that expression in your eyes...of misery and wretchedness. Smile for the emperor. I can't recall seeing you smile, ever."

Prince Aurangzeb forced a smile, his eyes still glinting inner rage, which he could not express. Prince Dara Shikoh's features were lit up with pleasure and amusement, as he stood watching the forced smile on his brother's face. His own expression was one of mischief, as if he was about to tickle his little brother to fits of laughter. Prince Balaqi's eyes were turning to Prince Aurangzeb, his look charged with the intensity of a revelation. Suddenly, he broke his silence.

"I have seen him smile, Your Majesty, when torturing one black ant in a bowl of water sprinkled with red pepper," Prince Balaqi offered tremulously.

"My own grandson with no better occupation but to tease the harmless ants." Jahangir's gaze was probing Prince Balaqi, as if he had seen him for the first time.

"Only when he is not practicing fencing or learning Persian, Your Majesty," Prince Balaqi murmured timidly, retreating back into his own shell of silence.

"To escape the rigors of learning, your Majesty, young princes have to find some means of diversion," Prince Tahmuras interceded for the young devil, with a dint of good humor.

"Our Prince Dara Shikoh, I am sure, entertains himself with no such diversions which may nurture the briars of cruelty," Jahangir ruminated aloud, his gaze sweeping over Prince Tahmuras and Prince Hoshang in one searching intensity.

"Prince Dara Shikoh is exceptionally loving and kindhearted, Your Majesty. He is a mystic and an avid reader, even at this tender age, as far as I can tell," Prince Hoshang opined aloud, his own expression light and carefree.

"Yes, my angelic prince." Jahangir's gaze appeared to hold Prince Dara Shikoh in a warm embrace. His gaze was wandering, and espying Ladli Begum. "And where is my lovely granddaughter?" he asked capriciously.

"She is taking her royal beauty rest with her royal ayah, Your Majesty." Ladli Begum smiled profusely.

"Ah, the beauty and innocence of childhood." Jahangir sighed, his gaze straying toward Prince Shahriyar. "Fetch the emperor a cool goblet of wine, my prince, to toast our journey to Kashmir," he commanded.

"Watered and scented with only a hint of wine, Prince Shahriyar." Nur Jahan was quick to issue her own command.

Prince Shahriyar was on his feet to obey both the emperor and the empress, his face wreathed in a winsome smile. On his way, he could hear Hushiyar Khan announcing the arrival of Abu Talib. Abu Talib's gallant entry was attracting the attention of all the ladies, and a sudden hush was pervading this vast chamber.

"What news, Abu Talib?" was Jahangir's laconic inquiry after Abu Talib had pulled himself up from his lengthy curtsy.

"Both good and bad, Your Majesty." Abu Talib lowered his eyes.

"If not evil or tragic, they carry no sting of pain," Jahangir murmured to himself. "Pour it out, Abu Talib, pour it all! The emperor has learned to mix both good and evil in a bittersweet concoction suitable to his taste!" His very eyes were issuing commands.

"Mahabat Khan, Your Majesty…he robbed the Bengal treasury of all its jewels," Abu Talib began cautiously. "But we caught up with him near Shahabad where he had concealed all the treasures. It was a rest house, and we were able to drive the guards away to retrieve the treasures. Unfortunately, Mahabat Khan himself escaped once again. He was pursued by the imperialists though, but he fled through the hills and the forests of Mewar, always dodging, always escaping. The imperial army has left the fugitive on his own now, bringing the treasures back to Lahore safely."

"The treasures of the world, vain and perishable," Jahangir murmured to himself. "And what evil abode is housing the wretched rebel now?" He made a feeble gesture, as if to stall further inquisition in his own thoughts.

"Passing through the territory of Rajpipliya and Bihara, he is in Junair now, Your Majesty," Abu Talib murmured back. "He has made alliance with Prince Shah Jahan. His own cavalry of two thousand is now joined with the dwindling troops of Prince Shah Jahan. It is also reported that Mahabat Khan has presented a large diamond of great value to Prince Shah Jahan. Prince

Shah Jahan, in return, rewarded him with war elephants, along with a horse and sword and a dagger inlaid with precious gems."

"The fleeting pleasures, and fleeting fortunes." Jahangir closed his eyes. "Not so bad, Abu Talib, not so bad. The emperor is spared the labor of mixing the good with the bad." He opened his eyes, his look wearied and distraught.

"Not bad, Your Majesty!" Nur Jahan could not help but exclaim, concealing her fears in one silken smile. "The alliance of the demented rebel with Prince Shah Jahan is quite alarming. We should send a large body of troops under the command of Khan Jahan to bury this evil serpent in dust forever." She was trying to control her anger.

"This world, the end of which is destined to be miserable, can scarcely be worth the risk of so much violence." Jahangir's look was wearied, gathering profundities. "I said that before, another time, another place, didn't I? Why does the emperor have to repeat his own thoughts?" His next feeble gesture was arrested in the air, as Mutamid Khan trundled into the room unannounced.

"Your Majesty." Mutamid Khan swept his arm in one impeccable curtsy. "Abdur Rahim died in his sleep suddenly, Your Majesty. He died in his own palace in Delhi."

"And he was supposed to…" Nur Jahan closed her eyes, as if to shut out the vision of fear and death from her sight and psyche.

"A blessed death envied by the saints and the sinners alike," was Jahangir's wearied response. "Now leave us, Mutamid Khan. The emperor needs to rest before his coveted journey to Kashmir."

Mutamid Khan scrambled himself to his feet, retracing his steps obediently. Jahangir watched him, waving his arms to dismiss the rest of the royal brood. His gaze was holding Nur Jahan captive in some urgency of need and desire.

"Come, Nur. Lull the emperor to sleep with your sweet voice. The scented pine-valleys in Kashmir await us. The reek of death and tragedies, we leave behind in this land infested with greed and malefic designs." Jahangir's look was enigmatic.

Chapter Twenty-one

Kashmir was the loveliest this spring in beauty and splendor, enhanced by the profusion of scents and flowers. Crowned in golden-red, the wreaths of sunset were adorning Baghi-Bahar in the most exquisite of shades and nuances. Jahangir and Nur Jahan were seated on one marble bench splashed with velvets and damasks. Below the terrace, they could see the beautiful arena of garden with all its glory in silk and tapestry. This garden was Jahangir's favorite, and visiting it was like paying homage to a shrine. He had already made three pilgrimages to this favorite shrine of his, and still was not sated with the quiet deeps within it. Each time, he was tempted to return to this garden with the longings of a lover, and each time gleaning some mysterious powers from its silence and pulchritude. The last two times he had visited Baghi-Bahar in the company of his entire household, but this time he wished to be alone with his beloved Nur Jahan.

Jahangir was holding on to the empty goblets of silence within him and without, as he sat admiring the loveliness of Baghi-Bahar. Inside him were joy and peace, and some mute rivulets of sorrows too. His very eyes were brimming with the wine of nature's beauty, and this glorious hush was filling his heart with awe and bliss. All his past sufferings seemed dulled, rather drugged by the sweetness of hush and solitude. The rivulets of sorrows were surfacing in his thoughts, creating bubbles of prophetic visions which he had seen and arrested so often lately, but with the self-surrender of a pious devotee. These prophetic visions were his sweet companions, urging him to quaff the wine of beauty to his fill, for never again would he be able to taste such pleasures. Death was looming over his shoulders, he could feel its breath and shadow. And yet this shadow was not hovering like some evil tyrant, but like a messenger of joy and peace. This strange, yet familiar messenger was clothed in darkness, revealing light! The scent of beloved, Anarkali herself?

Jahangir was consumed by this shadow, as if his eyes could behold Anarkali in each bloom, in every blade of grass, and inside the heart of each valley, scented and glorious. Glory was arrested, even inside the intricate pattern of each leaf, polished by the gold of dusk, he was thinking. He was keenly aware of Nur Jahan beside him too, and humbled by her love and nearness. Anarkali was no other than his beloved Nur Jahan. Jahangir's thoughts were courting the sad beloved in solitary contemplations.

Nur Jahan, my soul and my sadness, her wit and gaiety are abandoning her under the weight of my own illnesses prolonged and prolonging, Jahangir's thoughts were murmuring, quiet and unobtrusive. *Illnesses, I have lost my appetite. Asthma has become my bane and torment. I don't even crave for wine anymore. Ah, but the wine of love! Nur Jahan, my beloved...can't endure to be parted from her, not ever. Am I dying? I am not afraid of death, rather welcoming this mantle of surcease...longing to be with my beloved....* His thoughts were coming to a stalemate, a paradox in themselves!

Paradoxically, he could not think of himself as an entity, apart from Nur Jahan. She would always be with him, as was Anarkali. Both were one, his one and only eternal beloved. They would stay with him in all the living, pulsating cycles of illusions. They would follow him on the path of darkness, in his afterlife, where the lovers were united without the threat of ever being parted. Jahangir's thoughts were comforted, inhaling the scent of mysteries, along with the perfume of life and beauty.

Baghi-Bahar was cradled against one verdant hill, woven in the colors of silk and tapestry in flowers, and serenaded by the fountains and terraces. A profusion of bluebells and narcissi were a filigree of color around the flowerbeds of roses. Down below the tapestry of colors, Dal Lake gleamed and shuddered, its turquoise blue waters a fantastic mixture of gold and emerald. Beyond the voluptuous contours of Dal Lake could be seen fields upon fields of poppy and mustard, all molten-gold and flaming-red. Jahangir's gaze was bouncing down from terrace to terrace, reaching closer to the marble inclines gouged with scallops, where the waterfalls choked and spluttered. He was fascinated by the pink and white almond blossoms which appeared suspended in the air like the mists pure and gossamer. An island of white clouds was sliding over the elegant pavilions from nowhere, and Jahangir held his breath, his gaze rapt and wistful. This white island was bleeding, lacerated by the naked streaks of red-gold from the dusk, and still pouring cottony-haze over the chenars.

Nur Jahan, appareled in blue and mauve silks, seemed to be a part of this lovely nature. The color of her dress was blending with the half-parted blooms of saffron in the background. The pallor and transparency of her oval features were heightened by the rivers of sadness from within. She seemed oblivious to the hush and beauty all around her. Her gaze was fixed to the domed pavilions over the distant pool, where the blue Kashmiri irises stood admiring their own silken reflections.

Nur Jahan's thoughts were not in Kashmir, wandering aimlessly in some continents remote, where there were no intrigues but peace and harmony. Yet intrigues had become a part of her, she could not slough off their assault or impudence. Her thoughts were returning to Bengal, where Mahabat Khan, in league with Prince Shah Jahan, sat concocting more evil plots than ever before. Yet again, her thoughts were wooing the valleys of Kashmir. They were getting feverish and restless, following Prince Shahriyar who was on his way toward Lahore, fraught with despair and tortures of the damned. Prince Shahriyar had suddenly fallen ill, a victim of fox's disease as diagnosed by the physicians. He had lost all his hair, becoming bald within a span of few days. His eyelashes were the first ones to go, then eyebrows and mustache, and finally there was no beard left to shave. The physicians could do nothing to cure him, and had suggested a change of climate from the cold in Kashmir to the warmth in Lahore.

One alien and deformed portrait of Prince Shahriyar was emerging in Nur Jahan's head like a throbbing canker. Inside that canker was one marble grave. She dared not look into its white purity, but a pair of eyes were watching her from the shadow of death; they were the beloved eyes of the emperor himself! She was shuddering inwardly, averting her gaze from the octagonal marble pavilions, which alone seemed to be the demons of her sightless ruminations. These demons had been chasing her since she had arrived in Kashmir. Some sort of nameless grief had settled inside her, which could be felt churning and expanding the most, when the emperor suffered the assaults of asthma or feverish delirium. Her heart was literally breaking, each passing hour of the day or night, it seemed. Though, she was forever striving toward hope, gluing those broken pieces together with utmost skill and precision, more so to keep the emperor happy than to mend her own wounds which could not cease their pain and clamor.

This heliotrope spring with its heart-warming colors had drugged the emperor to repose and silence. He was vaguely aware of his beloved seated close to him, yet his thoughts could witness that they were continents apart. The pashmina shawl over his legs was warm and comforting, and so was his saffron silk robe, even more comforting in its smooth, luxuriant texture. There was an airy sensation in his limbs and thoughts, as if he could soar high into the clouds, along with the finches and the kingfishers. His purple turban, studded with diamonds, had some ethereal quality too, matching the violet vistas and the sparkling dusk. The little diamonds in his ears were twinkling to meet the invisible stars, it seemed. His pale, sunken cheeks were borrowing more pallor from his saffron robes, and his eyes were feverish.

The hush, the stark naked lust of the garden, and the vivid, pulsating colors, all were magic and enchantment before Jahangir's eyes, calm and reverent. His aesthetic senses were drinking the soma of life from the very cups of this paradise. *Loving surcease, and abandoning existence*, he was thinking. He could hear the whisper of death close behind him, on the very lips of his shadow. The air itself was holding its breath, releasing a sweet sigh, a gentle murmur, suspended over there somewhere, welcoming the realms divine. He was listening to those sounds, they were getting loud and louder still, rustling through the leaves, and reaching him in a shower of bliss. This blissful, gentle murmuring in the wind was so awesome that even Nur Jahan could not help but be affected by its presence. She was abandoning the journeys in her head, and returning to the valley of awareness. So abrupt was this sense of awareness that she was jolted out of her oblivion. This pulsating throb of life in nature with all its fecundity could not even catch her exclamation, which escaped her lips involuntarily.

"How life tosses and turns in this bliss of a paradise, if one could hear the silence, Your Majesty." Nur Jahan turned to the emperor, gazing into his eyes.

"The emperor hears only the drums of death, my love." One splinter of a prophecy escaped Jahangir's lips.

"Your Majesty. Now you have touched the hem of the inevitable. You will be surely living with a hag from now on. Didn't I warn you before? One more time, if you mention…" Nur Jahan wrinkled her dainty nose, trying her best to make the emperor laugh, and condoning the bolts of thunder inside her own heart.

"In this paradise, love, the emperor can live with any creature, no matter how hideous or loathsome!" Jahangir snatched her hand, kissing it laughingly.

"Then you have no need of me, Your Majesty." Nur Jahan joined him in his mirth. The ominous thunder in her heart was fading and dissolving.

"Need, love!" Jahangir murmured tenderly. "Without you, there is no need, no love, no passion, no life. You are my need, my soul, the light of my eyes."

"And my own love has no claim on your whimsical moods, Your Majesty.

Your moods, which divorce me from your life, if you even but think of death." Nur Jahan's eyes were flashing challenges.

"Claim the light of my soul? You possess the emperor, body and soul, whatever is left of him." Jahangir smiled, gleaning sadness from her eyes, not challenges.

"And yet we seem continents apart, Your Majesty, sitting in this paradise, so near, so close. What gulfs, Your Majesty, I do not know. I have this feeling of late, that is, that you are being drawn farther and farther away from me," Nur Jahan murmured.

"Because you love not the emperor enough, not as much as he does." Jahangir slipped his arm around her waist and pressed her closer. "Like Adam, I am destined to love you till... well, my Eve." His lips met hers in one tender kiss. "You have fed me the apple of knowledge, and I can't help but love you till eternity. No gulfs separate us, my pearl, none, but the drifting clouds in memories."

"Eve, not Adam, is the true love, Your Majesty, if the sacred texts are to be believed," Nur Jahan murmured. She was choking back her tears, which were forcing their way into her eyes for some indescribable reason.

"The texts contaminated with lies, if the emperor dare say." Jahangir smiled. "Strange, this concoction of tales is coming to my mind. I read those stories when I was a young prince, the stories told by charlatans, pretending to be scholars."

"Stories of love, in paradise, are they, Your Majesty?" Nur Jahan urged softly, at once the mistress of poise and serenity.

"Of Creation, where sin and fall have nothing to do with love," Jahangir ruminated aloud. "Azrail is the angel of death, one historian wrote, though connected with the creation of Adam, having been sent by God to bring various kind of clay from the earth for the formation of his body, and having fulfilled the mission in which Gabriel and Michael had previously failed, is not mentioned as sharing his sin or punishment. Satan is the one who was cast out of paradise. He penetrated into paradise not withstanding the vigilance of its porter, by entering the mouth of a serpent that had on one occasion strayed outside. The latter at that time was a quadruped, but being cursed at the fall, was deprived of its feet and condemned to the form of a reptile. The peacock is said to have conducted Eve to the forbidden tree. So the peacock, at its expulsion, was deprived of its voice."

"I would rather study the flowers of Kashmir, Your Majesty, than the birds of paradise, not to mention the demons and the reptiles," Nur Jahan intoned dreamily. Her senses were being lulled into bliss, partly by Jahangir's tender tones, and partly by the hush and beauty of this garden.

"And what have you studied so far, my love?" Jahangir asked wistfully.

"The swallow-worts, Your Majesty, the flowers of the Asclepcas," Nur Jahan began with an abrupt animation. "The rare varieties, the white ones are more rare than the ones tinged with rose and purple. The Hindus lay those flowers upon the idol of Mahadeva as sacred offerings. They have sacred qualities too. An acrid, milky juice is extracted from their wounds through the shrub. That juice is then used for medicinal purposes. It is supposed to cure all kinds of ailments, epilepsy, hysterics, convulsions, offering relief even from pain caused by poisonous bites. Its beauty alone is the panacea for all ills," she concluded passionately.

"For all, my love?" murmured Jahangir, his look distant and poignant, that far-off look which Nur Jahan dreaded the most, that look brimming with soft, tender warmth, meaning that he was with Anarkali.

Nur Jahan shuddered, feeling the presence of her rival inside the very torments of her suffered heart. She was watching him, and discovering something new and strange. Jahangir's eyes had the mysterious gleam of some inner fire, as if some heartrending sorrow inside him was lit to a conflagration. She was holding her breath, as if she had divined the cause of this fire. This fire was the very epitome of the emperor's fear for pain and death; one lone revelation was slithering in her mind.

"If this flower could cure your asthma, Your Majesty, I myself would go searching for it from continent to continent, from the jungles of Sahara to the snowy peaks of Kashmir," Nur Jahan sang prayerlike.

"The emperor was not thinking about..." Jahangir divined her thoughts as soon as he met her gaze. But he was stricken mute by the blue flames of pain and purity in her pleading eyes. They were reaching out to comfort him with their own warmth of love and understanding.

"That flower would do no good to Prince Shahriyar either, Your Majesty." Nur Jahan too had read the emperor's thoughts. "With all his hair gone, the unfortunate prince, he thinks he has contracted leprosy, fleeing like a leper too, or forced to flee by the orders of the physicians. Shamed and disgraced, he confided to me!" She appeared to drain out her own fears, her look still pleading.

"There is no disgrace in being the victim of a violent disease, no matter what the ailment, my Nur," Jahangir began profoundly. "Illness of the soul, that should be the cause for disgrace. The soul, concealing its deformity and corruption from the eyes of all, grows more hideous in its own sight than any naked sight could judge or perceive."

"As long as the eyes behold not the cankerous souls, Your Majesty, they strive to cure the flesh only, attaching no disgrace to the soul which is always left to fester everlastingly." Nur Jahan sighed to herself.

"With bodies clean and souls stinking, mankind has learnt to stifle the reek of ignorance which follows them at their heels," Jahangir reminisced aloud, as if looking into the eyes of the past horrors with a sense of detachment. "The animals of this earth, Nur, and the demons expelled from Paradise! And yet what has this to do with our own Paradise?" He smiled, his gaze arresting the colors in this garden. "We have to leave this paradise again, to journey back on the familiar, yet unknown paths. Prince Shahriyar, yes, my unfortunate son. We must be with him; he needs our love and support. Soon, tomorrow, much too soon." He looked into her eyes. "Should we say farewell to our children with pearls and gold rings in their noses, before we journey to Lahore?" He got to his feet. The pashmina shawl fell to his feet in one gentle rustle.

"Their liquid-gold bodies we might carry in our hearts forever, Your Majesty." Nur Jahan sprang to her feet with the alacrity of a young girl.

The fields upon fields of silken blooms were welcoming the royal couple as they strode away to see their gold children. The scented air was drugging their senses to a wild surrender. The blue pool with goldfish was still a few paces away, but Jahangir's feet were coming to a sudden halt by the clusters of pansies bedewed by the waters of the fountains. He was crushing Nur Jahan into one eager embrace, his voice hoarse with desire and yearning.

"On second thought, my pearl, the emperor wishes to roll down on these lawns, and cover you with flowers, along with his kisses." Jahangir's very heart was gathering colors from the clusters of pansies in mauve and vermilion.

"Your Majesty!" Nur Jahan squirmed and giggled in the emperor's arms on the verge of swooning. "The men guarding your palki will be scandalized if they happen to see us…" Her protests were smothered by the shower of kisses from the emperor's lips.

"If the emperor was fit to ride, he would rather go hunting than lovemaking in the open. And as for the intruders, he would break their legs if they dared straggle into this paradise of ours." He was laughing and murmuring endearments.

The silken pansies with innocent groans were being ravished under the weight of the emperor, and so was the empress. The jewels in flowers were bruised, and the jewels on Nur Jahan's royal person were twinkling with glee.

"Love, tell me, would we come to this paradise again?" Jahangir could feel the impending violence of another asthma attack, but was trying to ward off all fears, mental and physical. His need and urgency for consummation was lifting him to the heights of absurdity and delirium.

"Again and forever, Your Majesty." Nur Jahan could barely murmur amidst the rapture of her passionate swoon.

"Forever and forever," Jahangir kept murmuring, and stabbing deeper and deeper into the lotus of her desire, again and again. The rapier of unsurfeit in him had to be withdrawn by the sudden assault of asthma.

Chapter Twenty-two

The hunting grounds in Baramagala were charged with excitement of the royal hunt, as Jahangir sat waiting for the beaters to drive the deer to a close range. The imperial entourage had journeyed from Kashmir rather somberly, the ailing emperor attended by the empress and the physicians. He was carried on a palki, and was immersed in his own world of peace and oblivion, eating sparsely, and demanding wine only when hurled back into the arms of his own feeble and unhealthy consciousness. Reaching close to the picturesque spot of Baramagala, Jahangir had felt a sudden burst of energy due to the little reprieve from his pain and shortness of breath. There and then, he had decided to hunt. He was pressed by his own whimsical mood, as if challenging the fates, if not putting his depleted vigor to test and challenge. All his aesthetic senses were alive and throbbing though, and he had promised Nur Jahan an opulent tour of the lovely sites after this great hunt.

This hunting ground was one tortuous terrain of a pleasure-haven, concealed quite seductively at the bottom of a high mountain. The elms and the cedars were a collage of undergrowth, their trunks dipping down into the mouths of the declivities, and their limbs rising above the precipices, as if spurred by the wand of magic and mystery. The emperor, in his riding habit of citron and turquoise, was leaning slightly over the parapet built exclusively for his own hunting pleasures. His matchlock lay abandoned on the wall, as he adjusted his gun over his shoulders for an unerring aim. The large diamond in his turban, catching a shaft of sunlight, was blazing suddenly. This blaze was lending his pale, emaciated features a subtle flush. But actually this flush was coming from within; his heart had begun to throb with a strange violence he had not ever encountered before.

Nur Jahan, not seated far from the emperor, was hunting down her own wild beasts, in fears and doubts. She was seated under a red canopy with a white parasol, both matching and complimenting her silks and rubies and diamonds. She too had lost much of her color and vivacity, though her health suffered no major setbacks. A luminescent pallor had settled upon her cheeks permanently, and the dark circles under her eyes were witness to the measure of her inner torment and suffering. Right now, most humbly and most earnestly, she was praying for the health of the emperor, summoning hope and courage as the most devoted of her guardians. She was anticipating the boons of health from her merciful God, and praying and praying.

The mute prayers in Nur Jahan's heart were dying, stabbed by one lone fear, alien and nameless. Her gaze was turning will-lessly toward the Pir Panjal range, where the white streams gurgled and churned down the rocky banks. She was fascinated by the wildness of these streams, foaming at the mouth, and rising in a fantastic uproar of glee and violence. Her eyes were riveted to those streams, which could be seen raging like the tempests, and disappearing somewhere into the deepest of gorges and ravines. A great storm or some seething fury were in those waters, the waves glittering and dashing themselves to pieces in jets of glassy foams against the giant rocks. She was sitting there rapt, watching, listening, her own eyes shining with mute agonies of the heart and soul. That savage beauty of the waters was entering her own spirit, dancing the dance of death and destruction, and chilling her thoughts. Only her eyes were sparkling, and courting their own dance of fire and ice. Something inside her were wild and screaming, on fire and numbing, yet neither chilling nor scorching. So profoundly absorbed was she into the waters of chill-violence from within and without, that she knew not whether she lived or dreamed life.

The emperor was not dreaming, but exhilarated by the prospect of hunting. His heart was climbing the rungs of elation, as if all his ailments had left him, and no more would he suffer any torments of the body and soul. He was feeling giddy and weightless, as if he could conquer the kingdoms in heaven and on this earth with the sheer power of his psyche, and could float into eternity forever. He could see the beaters driving the deer closer and closer, and he raised his gun with the precision of a skilled hunter.

The shot boomed through the woods, and hit the intended victim on its hind calf. The stricken deer bounded off, causing panic and flight amongst the rest of the hunting doe and dear. One foot-soldier, in his attempt to urge the frightened deer back into a close circle, strayed and stumbled closer to a precipice, and was seen falling with a dizzying speed. His head was dashed against one rock, his body whirling down the valley, splattered with blood.

Jahangir flung his gun away, his eyes bulging out of their sockets, as if he had witnessed the most awful of horrors ever encountered before! He was suspended there inert, all his senses numb and stunned under the stupor of this sudden shock. Slowly at first, and then swiftly, a tide of fear was rising inside him like one billowing omen.

This is a sign of my own death. I am going to die...soon. Jahangir's heart was drumming an ominous beat.

Jahangir was still standing there inert, suspended alive in the aura of doom and darkness. He thought he heard the angels sing, or was it the laughter of Anarkali, trilling down the hills and sailing over the mountains? Then the fury of a pandemonium was in the air, as if all the demons in the hell were let loose and were cutting their way out of the leaping flames. No, the hell was still invisible; all he could see were his own soldiers carrying the bleeding lump of a body out of the hunting grounds. The deer too was scattered in fright or relief; Jahangir's own burning gaze was tearing the veil of life and confronting death. Death was looking him in the eyes! Death was standing before him mighty and inviolate! Death appareled in all its fineries of horror and ugliness was grinning and mocking.

The emperor is going to die.... One flame of a fear was licking Jahangir's thoughts to awareness. *Why I am afraid? The emperor does not fear death. He longs for it, to be united with his...* His thoughts were hissing and challenging. The ominous throbs inside his heart were searching the rags of his longings.

Nur Jahan had heard one shot, but the raging streams inside the whirlwind of a dance in her head, had obscured all other sounds. Her dream-oblivion inside her mental framework was so intense that this fatal fall would have gone unnoticed by her even if the man landed at her feet that particular moment. The mute, stunned soldiers scurrying down there could never enter her dream-oblivion, and she would have remained thus, immersed in her own silence, had not the echo of the shot fired by the emperor returned to her with the impudence of a warning. She was straining her ears to catch this warning, but she could hear nothing. There was a complete hush, and the silence so stark that one could hear a reed whispering. The bubbling waters in her head were retreating, and her senses were gathering only the chill of silence.

Something like a yawning abyss was uncurling its lips inside the very recesses of her soul and psyche. A cold shudder was tracing its way in her spine down to her very toes, but she had leaped to her feet without even being aware of her impulse and restlessness. Her eyes were fixed to the statue of an emperor, and she was sleepwalking toward this fresh dream. Jahangir had not moved, his own gaze acknowledging her approach in utmost silence. His pallor was heightened and his eyes shining with the mysterious light of peace and knowledge. Both stood facing each other, both gazing and speechless. Nur Jahan was a bit discomfited, cursing her wits gone mad which could not elicit one sane expression. Besides, she was puzzled by that mysterious light in the emperor's eyes. *The statue of ice, my husband and the emperor,* she was thinking, *not melted by the flashing intensity in my own eyes.* By the sheer will of her own practiced calm, she heard herself toss one thoughtless plea.

"May I hunt, Your Majesty?" Nur Jahan took a step closer, her thoughts now racing downhill to explore some heaps of the imponderables.

"No, my Nur, you are not to tempt the tragic fates which challenge the emperor," Jahangir murmured with the somnambulance of a dreamer.

"Your Majesty!" One feeble exclamation was chilled on Nur Jahan's lips.

"The emperor's wish to hunt has sentenced one man to a horrible death... He fell down the precipice." Jahangir made one hopeless gesture, his breathing heavy and labored. "This is an omen, Nur, an ill omen. The emperor is going to die."

"No, Your Majesty, no." One violent protest trembled on Nur Jahan's lips. "This doesn't mean anything. You are getting well. You will live to rule till eternity. You cannot die. You cannot leave me. I will fight the fates..." She paused, becoming aware of her own raving.

"The emperor has not found the water of immortality as yet, my love," Jahangir murmured tenderly. "No, love, he will not die, not until he reaches Lahore and proclaims you the empress of the world." He reached out and claimed her hand.

"Your Majesty, why do you torment me so?" Nur Jahan murmured in response. Her heart was thundering with the violence of a presage.

"To make you love me more than any man ever being loved before by an earth-goddess like you, my pearl." Jahangir stood caressing her hand, as if holding the fortunes of the worlds into the very palms of his hands. "But, love, before the emperor forgets, make sure that you bestow grants and stipends on the family of this deceased man. He was not included in my hunting plans, my Nur, and yet he died a wretched death. Compensating his family might assuage the emperor's heart a little. Our journey to Lahore should suffer no more delays, unless the emperor takes the road to nonexistence." One sliver of a prophecy escaped his thoughts involuntarily. He stood there forlorn and ponderous, smiling to himself. His smile was fading, a pale and withered smile to begin with!

"Your Majesty." Tears of pain and hopelessness were stinging Nur Jahan's eyes.

"Love! The light of my soul." Jahangir gathered her into his arms in one eager embrace. "No more of this, love, no more, I promise. Pardon the emperor." His heart was thundering in unison with his beloved's.

Both the emperor and the empress stood there locked into each other's arms, both listening to the rhythmic thunders inside the hearts of one another. The fear of death was constricting the emperor's heart, but he was divorcing all fears, burying all fears inside the chilled tombs of his own past sufferings. His thoughts were running wild, and groping for some anchor in sustenance. They were stumbling in the dankness, and wrenching themselves free from doom and death. A few reeds of old tales were waving their arms, urging him to comfort his beloved with words and ideation. One long forgotten reed of a tale was swaying and swooning. The winds of time itself were surfacing in his memory, and words were pouring out of his lips, urgently and desperately.

"Have you ever read about the incarnations of Krishna, love?" Jahangir's tone was a mingling of elation and tenderness. "He lived one hundred and twenty-five years in one incarnation alone. He had sixteen thousand one hundred and eight wives, each of whom gave birth to ten sons and one daughter. And each wife thought that she alone shared her husband's bed." He was gasping for breath, his beloved sobbing softly in his arms.

The royal encampment, halted at Rajauri, was gathering sepulchral hush from the night studded with a myriad of stars. Below the encampment, the river Ravi glinted dreamlike, its waves calm and silvery under the moonlit sky. The guards, keeping watch and pacing aimlessly, seemed to be drugged by the beauty of this night. The incessant roaring from the mouth of the confluence was lulling their senses to peace and camaraderie. And yet the cool, night air with the gentle whip of a command, was keeping them awake and vigilant. Down the river, where the rough and slippery banks could be seen meandering, was also revealing the forms of a few men, those of the imperial guards. They had strayed there without even noticing the span of their own wanderings, but now stood listening to the whispering cataracts and night shadows. The full moon was etching them in pale silhouettes, who could be seen feasting their eyes on hues russet and emerald from the thickets further down the cataracts. More guards were seen straggling toward this scenic splendor of the night. They were conversing in low, solemn tones, probably discussing the fate of the ailing emperor and of the distraught empress.

The emperor had fallen ill a little after the tragic experience during his hunt, precisely so, after his delirious profusion in relating the tale of Krishna.

The ghost of that foot soldier who had fallen from the precipice was never to leave him. He was to haunt him during the nights in the most horrible of nightmares. Jahangir had lost all appetite, eating nothing and growing weak in body and mind. He would sleep most of the time, and only a few sips of cold water were his daily portion of meals. He was losing consciousness, and could only be revived in brief intervals when coaxed by Nur Jahan's pleas to drink at least a little of watered wine. The physicians were in absolute despair, striving to discover some magic potion which could cure the emperor and their own hopelessness. Their devotions and ministrations had proved unsuccessful, and they themselves were growing weak in body and spirit. Nur Jahan was succumbed to shock and disbelief. She had a feverish look in her eyes, which could be seen shining in all the sleeping, waking hours of the day or night.

The emperor was carried in a palanquin from Baramagala to the village of Thanah. After a few days of rest there, the empress had commanded the encampment to proceed toward Rajauri. Their next stop was intended to be in Chingiz Halti, near the city of Bhimbar. But while passing through Rajauri, the emperor's condition had grown worse, and he had fallen into a coma. The empress, still in a state of shock, had ordered a quick halt. The emperor was transported to his old summer house in the precincts of Rajauri, attended by Nur Jahan and a team of royal physicians. He was installed in his favorite chamber, that's where he lay now, completely oblivious to the world around him. At times, he could break through the fetters of his unconsciousness, murmuring feebly and opening his eyes briefly. But those times were rare and numbered few, lending no solace to the suffering empress. Besides Nur Jahan and the physicians, the ailing emperor was attended by Asaf Khan, Mutamid Khan and a few younger princes.

Nur Jahan, in white silks with only a string of pearls as her royal adornment, was seated by the emperor's bed in a prayerlike silence. Her hands were clasped into her lap, and her eyes were closed. She seemed oblivious of all, even to her own mute sufferings. Pure and Madonna-like, she was immersed deeply in the purity of her own white dreams. Her pallor had a glow of peace and tranquility, as if all her energies were directed toward the emperor in bringing him back to life. The large bed, upon which the emperor lay unconscious in coverlets of satin and velvet, was splashed with haze from the candles burning low in a silver candelabrum. The physicians had pushed back the crimson canopy dripping with laces, and were now leaning to check his pulse and breathing. One of the physicians was trying to feed the emperor with a sweet concoction which he had just prepared. Suddenly, the emperor's eyes were shot open, his look still opiate and drugged. His gaze was sweeping over all slowly and swiftly, kindling the ripples of confusion and incredulity. It was arrested on Nur Jahan, murmuring her name even before his lips could utter it.

Nur Jahan felt the warmth of that gaze and stirred. The blue blaze of agony in her feverish eyes was reaching out to the emperor.

"Isn't this exactly one year since Prince Perwiz died, Nur?" Jahangir murmured feebly. His voice was clear though, and his eyes flashing.

"Yes, Your Majesty." Nur Jahan sought his hand and clasped it to her breast.

"Wine," Jahangir murmured.

Hakim Rukna raced past the jade chiffonier toward the chest where the gold flagon lay abandoned. He was the first and the only one to obey the emperor's command to fetch him a goblet of wine.

"Nur, promise…you will never leave me…forever…in Kashmir…" Jahangir was murmuring, his eyes closing shut.

Hakim Rukna, with his hands trembling, was holding the goblet of wine to the emperor's lips. With one convulsion of a shudder, Jahangir's head was thrown back on the pillow, his body limp and listless. The wine spilled on his white robe was tracing a rivulet, ruby red as the blood freshly spilt.

"The emperor is…" Hakim Rukna's voice was choked, but all present understood the stifled verdict.

Nur Jahan's head drooped on the emperor's breast, soundlessly and hopelessly. Her cries of agony were silenced inside her, along with her unvoiced grief she could not ever express. Her own white sleeves were stained with ruby red blood in wine, as if she was wearing her heart on one of her sleeves.

Mutamid Khan, stricken with grief, was reciting one delirious hemistich. *The World-Seizer has left the world.*